CW00486818

MY LITTLE RAMADAN

SEQUEL TO THE LIFE IS YOURS TRILOGY
BOOK 4

ABIGAIL YARDIMCI

Copyright © 2023 by Abigail Yardımcı

All rights reserved.

Published in 2023 by:

Soft Rebel Publishing Ltd

20-22 Wenlock Road, London, N1 7GU

The moral right of Abigail Yardımcı to be identified as the author of this work has been asserted by her in accordance with the Copyright, Designs and Patents Act 1988.

Except as permitted under current legislation, no part of this work may be reproduced in any form or by any electronic or mechanical means, including information storage and retrieval systems, published, performed in public, adapted, broadcast or recorded without written permission from the copyright owners, except for the use of brief quotations in a book review. All enquiries should be addressed to: Soft Rebel Publishing Ltd.

Cover design by Bailey McGinn

ISBN: 978-1-9168986-7-7

For Mam . . .

. . . and the Motherhood Massive

CONTENTS

HOW THIS BOOK WORKS

In 2010, I was living in the Highlands of Scotland with my Turkish husband and our two year old son.

I'm originally from the North East of England but we'd met in Turkey, had a long-distance romance and decided we just had to be together. A wedding, a pregnancy and a childbirth later and the Turkish Army was threatening to pull us apart with demands that my husband sign up.

To avoid this, we settled in the Highlands and started a new life. I had a few family ties there and he reckoned he could handle the dialect. Our son would have been happy anywhere as long as he had access to Bob The Builder DVDs and Jammie Dodgers.

Things didn't run smoothly - when do they ever? And I decided to shake things up a little by fasting for the holy month of Ramadan, to show some support to my poor husband who was missing his family and his culture.

To this day, I really don't know what I was thinking. I was struggling with postnatal depression and anxiety, so why did I think this was a good idea? Rather naively, I hoped I'd be rewarded with some kind of spiritual enlightenment that would make the whole motherhood thing easier.

I started writing a blog to record my experiences. And now, years later, I have turned those blog posts into a novel. As with my other books (the Life Is Yours Trilogy), I've exercised a lot of artistic license. Names are changed, events are mixed-up and drama has been heightened to a delectable level.

I hope you enjoy My Little Ramadan - it contains themes very close to my heart. So get your thermals on, we're off to Scotland. But first stop, Turkey . . .

PROLOGUE

Manevitaş, South Eastern Turkey
December 2007

My eyes are burning as he tells me, once again, that he loves me.

My nostrils sting, my cheeks are slick with sweat and a fire rages in my throat, refusing to be drenched by his soft tone. The plastic cup in my hand is full of vomit. He takes it from me as the coach rolls over a nasty bump and some of it spills over his fingers. He doesn't flinch.

Why, oh why, little baby, did you make me throw up now? I thread my fingers through my hair to check for lumps of the stuff. The last thing I need is to meet my fiancé's family with puke dripping off me.

His mam was furious when she first heard about our engagement. "Has she got *any* spiritual beliefs? At all?" Those were the words he translated to me after the epic phone call. And who could blame her? As far as she was concerned, I was just some English tart on holiday. Hardly good enough for her son.

Once she realised we were serious enough to keep a long distance thing going, to arrange for me to move to Turkey, to get engaged, she said, "Okay. Fine. Bring her to me. If she has a good soul, I will be able to tell."

We meet Mesut's older sister as we get off the coach in Manevitaş. I'm struck by her eyes. Huge, generous pools of liquid brown, framed by her hijab, a smile residing softly beneath. I feel she's absorbing me as she watches me climb quietly into the car. So this is the one who stole her brother's heart.

I try to steady my breath during the short car journey, using the trundle of the tyres against cobbled streets to find a soothing rhythm. Mesut holds my hand tightly, making it even more clammy. At least the sickness has passed. I use my free hand to cradle my belly, making sure nobody except Mesut could possibly notice. *It's okay, little baby, they're going to love us.*

At the heavy, iron door of the flat, we take off our shoes and step into a quiet corridor. Mesut smiles at me and somehow it melts *and* empowers me. "Now you meet my mum."

The silence froths. He leads me into a central room decked out with overlapping beige carpets and long, flat cushions on the floor woven with intricate, floral patterns. There's a huge window to my right, the winter sun filtering through floor length net curtains. There's a small TV in one corner and a copper coloured stove spreading fierce heat from the other. And there she is, leaning against the back wall, sitting on the floor.

She's smiling, so that's something. Her round face tilts towards us and I can see the smile extends to her eyes, as they land on me with surprising grace. She wears a white headscarf, tucked in closely around her ample cheeks, and it flows generously over her shoulders. She's wrapped in a gown dotted with tiny, golden flowers that merge together to radiate a light that seems unique to her.

White-socked toes poke out playfully at the end of her outstretched legs. I'm sure Mesut said something about how women are supposed to sit with their legs tucked in so this gives me a slight jolt. I've worked so hard to remember all of the customs, but I guess that his mam is another matter. She is, after all, lady of the house.

Mesut whispers quiet, silken words in Turkish. I don't know what he's saying but by the glisten in his mam's eyes, they must be words of love, of devotion. He finally drops my still shaking hand and now takes up hers, kissing it and then pressing it to his forehead with a purposeful reverence. It lasts a good few seconds, as if he's soaking up the very presence of her. I might be imagining it, but I think she lights up even more from this brief moment with her son.

Now it's my turn. I copy Mesut's tone and keep my whisper soft. It just feels right. "Anne, Nasılsın? Tanıstığıma çok memnun oldum."

Mother. How are you? I'm so pleased to meet you.

I've practiced it so many times.

And when I kiss her hand, trying also to press it to my forehead, she firmly takes both of our hands and presses them to my ever-so-slightly rounded belly. I look back at Mesut.

She knows.

She removes her warm palm from my tummy and there's a slight shuffle of her legs. Maybe she has a pain or needs to move. But as I glance down what I see is the last thing I expect.

It's a baby.

Lying there, with her outstretched legs working as a kind of cradle, is a sleeping baby wrapped in a blanket. I can't believe I've walked into this room, had some sort of mystical exchange with my new mother-in-law, and not even noticed she's holding a baby.

I've never seen anybody hold a baby on their legs like this but, by the way Mesut is crouching down and cooing over the little one, he's obviously seen this a thousand times before.

"This is your nephew. Is my sister's new baby, Gökhan."

The baby begins to wriggle and fuss, so Mesut's mam leans forward and places a hand on his belly, just as she had on mine only seconds ago. She rocks her legs from side to side and the baby immediately drifts back off to sleep.

Mesut's mam sighs in rhythm with baby Gökhan then pats the space on the cushion next to her, looking directly at me.

"She is wanting you sit with her," Mesut says.

So I do. I sit down on a cushion next to her. We look at each other for an instant that feels like it speaks a million words – words of trust, love, understanding and acceptance – and then I do the only thing that feels right. I drop my head so that it's resting on her shoulder and she kisses me on the top of my head.

I think she already knows I'm a good soul.

1

DAY 1 – INCONVENIENT LOVE

Muirdrith, Highlands of Scotland, UK
Weds 11th Aug 2010
Sunrise / Suhoor: 5.29am
Sunset / Iftar: 9.11pm

Question:

Do you think it's possible for a bone-tired mother of a Beast-Child to write a daily blog for a whole month?

Further Question:

Do you think it's possible for a bone-tired mother of a Beast-Child to write a daily blog for a whole month whilst also supporting the deep-rooted beliefs and pursuits of her incredibly hot, Turkish husband?

Last Question, I Promise:

Do you think it's possible for a bone-tired mother of a Beast-Child to write a daily blog for a whole month whilst supporting said hot, Turkish husband even if it means starving herself during daylight hours. Yes, you heard that right. I said *starving.*

I know.

Why am I already filling this blog with such madness? Well,

it might interest you to know that today is the first day of Ramadan for Muslims everywhere. As in, all over the world.

So worldwide, today, millions of people have been fasting. Not just resisting the staple three meals a day, mind you, but resisting anything at all passing the lips during daylight hours. This is regardless of lifestyle, occupation, responsibilities, or anything else you can think of. Muslims, if they're worth their salt, should not be eating, drinking, kissing, gossiping, sipping, swearing or swallowing.

Why do I care?

Hot, Turkish husband is a Muslim.

Hence the launch of this blog!

At least I hope I can make it into a blog. I managed to set this all up today – in between approximately five billion tantrums from my toddler – as a distraction for my frazzled brain. I figure I've done the hard bit and (just about) done all the technical stuff. Surely I can whack a few words out on a daily basis and entertain you all a bit.

How hard can it be?

Okay, so where to start? Right. My name is Jess and the very fact that I am not a Muslim might lead you to assume that my husband, Mesut, is a Muslim of the modern variety. And you'd be right. After inspecting him closely for the first three years of our marriage (and believe me, I have. He's kind of a younger, darker, sexier version of Gandalf from Lord of the Rings, if that's your thing), the way I see it is that he has his God and cherishes the relationship they have, but doesn't push that on anyone else.

Mesut smokes like a chimney, doesn't own a prayer mat or seem to have any idea which direction Mecca is in (which is good, considering there is no room for a prayer mat on the floor of this god-awful flat on account of all the baby-changing equipment and cat hair-covered charity shop toys). He is a Muslim in a subtle, innocent and generally not-bothering-anyone-else type of way.

But this year, for the first time since I've known him, he has decided to be a very good Muslim and take part in Ramadan. He's not new to this. He's obviously done it plenty of times before I rocked up and changed his life with my wicked Western ways.

Mesut is from South Eastern Turkey, a part of the world that proudly embraces its historical and cultural roots. His mam and dad have recently returned from their once-in-a-lifetime pilgrimage to Mecca, he has approximately fifty-seven nieces and nephews with a variety of Quran-inspired names, and every member of his family undoubtedly and continuously knows which way Mecca is because I've seen them, with my very eyes, bow down towards it five times a day, every day.

Unfortunately, we haven't seen his family in about a year and a half. We had been living in Turkey, in the South Western holiday resort of İpeklikum where we first met four years ago, and where I was actually brave enough (or stupid enough, depending on which way you look at it) to give birth to our baby boy. But we moved to the UK when the fear of god ran through us (or it could have been Allah, I'm not fussy) that the Turkish National Service might split us up.

Mesut has, funnily enough, always struggled to see the merits of signing up to be part of a dangerous operation such as the Turkish Armed Forces. But, pretty much as soon as we met and dragged each other kicking and screaming into the most inappropriate of holiday romances, we knew it would catch up with us one day. I guess we just thought, *fuck that*, and went ahead and fell hard, got married and made a bambino anyway, gleefully hoping the authoritarian demands made by the Turkish government might bloody well back off.

They didn't.

So as a pay-off for our inconvenient love, we found ourselves in the middle of a highly complex, expensive and intrusive visa application process.

Fun.

After a gruelling few months of submitting evidence that we weren't just another cautionary tale, and having our bank balance bled dry, the visa application was, all credit to Allah, successful. And, just because we never do things the easy way, we decided to move not to my native North East of England where I have a multitude of friends and family who can support us with pretty much EVERYTHING, oh no, but to the Highlands of freakin' Scotland.

Want a quick and easy way to traumatise a Muslim? Stick him on a snowy Scottish hill in the middle of the worst winter the UK has seen for thirty years. Gets them every time.

Seriously though, we were lucky enough for my auntie to offer Mesut a job in her pub in the seaside town of Muirdrith (he was basically head-hunted across a couple of thousand miles which is a bold claim for any barman. His cocktails are totally worth it), so that's why we're here.

We've started off living above said pub which is the absolute epitome of a Scottish alcohol facility and is likely the main reason Mesut now knows more swear words than I do. Our two-year-old son, Baki, has learned to be rocked to sleep to the eternal thud of the Black Eyed Peas and I have learned to stay out of the way of the bar manager we are forced to live in close quarters with.

She's weird. And likes cats a little too much if you ask me. They're everywhere. Slinking, skulking, snooping and lurking . . . there's no possible way to count how many she has. It's unnerving. I'm similarly unnerved by the passive aggressive notes I find all over the place on a daily basis. They can be about anything from the way I fold the towels or how I'm slamming the microwave door too hard, and they always start with a condescending: *'Jess, could you please consider . . .'*

Anyway, back to us. Yes, our first winter here was dreadful. Yes, Mesut now pronounces 'fuck-a-duck' with alarming venom AND a Scottish accent. Yes, we have struggled financially, emotionally and physically to adapt to this remote, freezing and barren environment. But, we are together. And that is what we always wanted. We spent the best part of two years dicking about with a long-distance romance so we really can't complain about being together now, even if it is in two pathetic box rooms with cat hair clinging to everything.

So that's it in a nutshell. Holiday romance, love, marriage, baby, meeting the in-laws, army panic, visa hysteria, moving to Scotland, winter from hell, financial mess, dodgy flat above even dodgier pub, trying to pull our shit together and now . . . Ramadan.

It was a few weeks ago when Mesut and I were chatting late into the night, snuggled on our patchy sofa which is just a pebble's throw from our actual bed. We were keeping our voices low and trying not to wake Baki in the next room, although I'm not sure why as the sickening thud of shitty house music downstairs in the pub was shaking the walls of the flat as usual.

Mesut was telling me about Ramadan and all of the reasons why Muslims fast at this time. "I know is very hard, Gulazer . . ."

He calls me 'Gulazer' all the time. It means 'Yellow Rose' in Kurdish and it's just kind of stuck. His whole family in Turkey use that name, I don't think they know the name 'Jess' even exists. Anyway, I digress.

"I know is very hard, Gulazer. But I really wanting do whole thirty days this time. I so far from Turkey and family and customs . . . is making more important to have time with Allah. I do this month for him and for me." Oh god, he was doing that thing where he gives me the big brown eyes flashing through the long, black, dripping strands of his hair that famously hang over his face.

"It's really important to you, isn't it?" I said, downing the last of the cheap white wine he'd 'acquired' from the pub for me the other night, because it was, after all, Fuck-it Friday.

"Yes. Of course," he said, simply. "I knows Baki not old enough yet, but one day he will see me doing Ramadan every year and he will wanting it too. I needing do it for him. Our baby."

I nodded sagely, trying not to let on that there was a strange surge of emotions rippling through me. Maybe it was the wine, the late-night chatting, the indisputable handsomeness and the Gandalf-like wisdom of the man, but somehow I uttered the next words, "Do you want me to do Ramadan with you?" A credible pulse of terror blipped through my body before he bowed his head, took in a sharp breath and then looked at me tenderly . . .

"That would be good."

The terror melted away as quickly as it had arrived. I could see by the look on Mesut's face and by the way his whole body had softened, that I had offered to do something completely unexpected but very, very much appreciated. In that moment, I knew that he never would have actually asked me to do this. He wanted *me* to want it.

"Fuck-a-duck!" he shouted, with total glee and a Scottish slur. "You doing Ramadan!" And he squeezed me really hard with those big old hands of his.

"Shush!" I half whined / half laughed. "You'll wake the Beast-Child."

"You're kidding, isn't it?" Mesut beamed. "Baki is not even waking to the Black Eyes of the Peas."

"Yes, yes. I suppose we've trained him well." I let him pull me over to our bed, knowing exactly how he was going to show me his gratitude. And as long as he didn't mind Asda's entire stock of muslin cloths and babygros chucked across the bed, the sorting of which having been abandoned hours earlier for the obvious merits of Fuck-it Friday, then I was as game as he was.

What now though? What now that I'm bereft of cheap white wine and the reality of fasting is setting in? I mean, come on, can I really go without food and drink from sunrise to sunset every day for a month?

But don't worry, there are a few exceptions, according to the Quran, you can bow out of fasting if:

- **You are pregnant** (*Not me. A two-year-old is quite enough at the moment, thank you very much*)
- **You are ill** (*Does a rash from all the cat hair count?*)
- **You are a child** (*Put it this way, I haven't been asked for ID in a lonnnng while*)
- **You are travelling on a long journey** (*I guess this was originally intended for people on camel-back, crossing arid landscapes. Anyway, I'm staying put in Muirdrith. The least arid place on earth*)
- **You are menstruating**

Yes! Success! I have my period right now!

Thank you Mother Nature for sorting me for Es and whizz. I've never been so grateful for my monthly agonies as I am right now, slap bang at the start of Ramadan. Who says it's not a girl's best friend?

Having said that, the weight of my commitment is looming because Mesut informs me that after the painters have gone (his words, not mine. He's worked in a Scottish pub for far too long) I will have to have a thorough scrub in the shower and begin the very next day.

So, although this is the first day of Ramadan, there's not much to report I'm afraid. There will be more, I promise. I've got to fill this blog out somehow, haven't I?

Maybe it'll be nice to look back on, especially for Baki as he gets older. I'm actually rocking him now, as I type this with one hand. The other hand, the one that's cradling him, went dead hours ago. We're snuggled up on the famous patchy sofa where the deal was done (actually, must go back and edit bit about bedroom antics on top of his baby stuff. Not big and not clever). Baki looks so sweet and innocent with his long, dark lashes almost touching his sticky, pink cheeks. His little barrel-shaped belly swelling with breaths that are finally calm and content. You'd never know he's had me run ragged all day.

You can tell by one quick glance at the shit-show of debris surrounding us right now that today has been a stay-at-home day of epic proportions (why do I always think it will be easier to stay at home?). Baki's numerous changes of clothing are flopped in bright fabric puddles all over the place. How can one toddler go through seven outfits in one day? There are several nappy sacks that need my attention, empty yoghurt pots, splattered plastic bibs and a kaleidoscope of DVDs that have been tossed from their cases and left in prime position for me to slip on when I eventually get up. I can hear the army of cats purring like a line of revving motorbikes outside my door and I feel nerves bubble in my chest. One more glance across the room shows me three crumpled-up notes written by the owner of those bloody cats just today. Three! Apparently my shoes were muddy last Wednesday, I'm using the wrong coat hooks and a two-year-old doesn't need the telly on that loud.

Allah, give me strength.

It's eleven thirty at night, the Black Eyed Peas will be

providing the pub-goers with their cue to vacate the building any minute now, and I'm wondering how in holy hell I'll have the energy to clear all this up before Mesut gets back. Even though it's August, it's so cold in this flat, and having Baki's warm, chubby body crushed against mine is far more enjoyable than the thought of moving even an inch towards ending the evening with a bout of cleaning.

I'd promised myself a good two hours ago that I'd only rock him until I'd finished my Twix that I'd stashed in a hole in the sofa cushion (life hack for knackered mothers. You're welcome) then I'd pop him in his travel cot next door, leaving time to write this blog post and tidy up. But then one Twix turned into three (okay, maybe four) and the music from downstairs cast me into a hypnotic state of inertia. Then I realised my laptop was within grasping distance, just under one of Baki's discarded, drool-soaked vests. One swift swipe with my furry-socked foot and it was on my knee, and now I'm tapping out this blog post to you. That's multi-tasking, right? I'm #winningasamummy. Or something.

I'll be honest, it's very hard to feel any kind of winning as a mummy. That's what I'm finding anyway. Maybe you can (please) tell me in the comments that I'm not alone? I love Baki as ferociously as I've ever loved anything but I think maybe some of the love I had for myself has been absorbed into him. I don't know.

What I do know is that I'm ready for Ramadan. As soon as Mother Nature has done her thing and my period has left me alone, I will be on it like a bonnet. I think a good detox is exactly what I need. A chance to realign my health, my body, my mind and my spirit. Don't worry about me, Dear Reader, because Muslims have been doing this since forever. There has to be something in it. By the end of the month I'll be like a whole new person – strong, capable, sure and upright.

Maybe a smidge skinnier too. Ramadan is going to change everything.

This is my chance to really shine as a mam, a wife and good old Jess. I used to be shiny, after all.

I've got a feeling. That this month's going to be a good month.

Watch this space . . .

GILLIE_LASS77
Woah – Jess, this is amazing! Are you sure about this though, honey? You know what you get like with food sometimes. Just keeping an eye out for you.
Jess.AKYOL
Ah, best friend of old. I KNEW you'd be the first one to comment. I'll be fine, Gillie. Don't worry about me.
GILLIE_LASS77
Okay, if you say so. When you told me about this Ramadan malarkey on the phone the other day I didn't actually think you meant it. You're mad, do you know that? That man doesn't know how lucky he is. There's no way you could part me from my Ginsters for a whole thirty days. #justsaying
Jess.AKYOL
Nobody would dare part you from the Ginsters. #alsojustsaying

Not-A-Granny-Flora
My thoughts exactly, Gillie! Jess, we need to talk about this. How are you going to look after Baki on an empty stomach? Being a mum takes sustenance. I'm sending you a food parcel.
Jess.AKYOL
Mother, please, there is absolutely no need. How is Dad? I can't

believe that's your username. YOU ARE A GRANNY NOW! When will you accept it?

Fab4CoolDad
Well, I think this is going to be a real experience, Jess. And I know my son-in-law will be chuffed to bits you're supporting him. Your mam's worried but I'll tell her about the Muslims I met on my travels back in the day – they all practiced Ramadan and were perfectly fine. I'm listening to a particular Beatles song tonight, in your honour and to celebrate the occasion. Because I think this is going to be a month-long 'Magical Mystery Tour' for you!
Jess.AKYOL
Thanks, Dad. Mesut says, 'Merhaba'. I remember you playing that track in the car on those long road trips up to Inverness to see family when I was little. Now I'm up here and you're down there – weird eh?!

Angnonymous
What a braw way to support your husband. I'm sure he's very pleased.
Jess.AKYOL
Thank you. He totally is. Thanks for reading!
Angnonymous
It's a pleasure. I'll be back tomorrow. 😉

funmum
I can assure you, you're not alone, Jessica. We can't always be winning as mummies and I bet you're doing great with little Baki. x
Jess.AKYOL
How sweet of you to say – thank you! x

2

DAY 2 - TRICKY LITTLE SYNAPSES

Muirdrith, Highlands of Scotland, UK
Thurs 12th Aug 2010
Sunrise / Suhoor: 5.31am
Sunset / Iftar: 9.09pm

Hello, Dear Reader. And welcome to the second day of my non-fasting, fasting challenge.

Yet again, thanks to my monthly 'curse', I have spent the day eating and drinking to my little heart's content. This was despite valiant efforts to cut down in preparation for when the Ramadan fasting begins proper, on account of advice from my already-fasting husband.

Okay, so the efforts might not have been all that valiant. Well, actually, maybe there wasn't much of an effort going on at all. For I have decided that the best way forward is to eat like a queen. Why should I start by denying myself the oh-so-delicious things when I will be going without them for a whole month anyway?

PLUS I did a big shop today. Considering Beast-Child can't speak yet, he does a crazy-good job of screaming his extreme distaste for supermarkets, refusing to be subdued even by a giant bag of cheesy Wotsits.

And come on, everybody knows it's impossible to keep your stomach empty when you've just got home from a big shop and you're enduring the aftershocks of stress imposed upon you by a two-year old's ever-increasing paroxysms of rage. That is common knowledge.

Other than that, my day has been fairly non-eventful. Baki has been at nursery since the supermarket episode (aren't nurseries *amazing*?) so I've had the sanctuary of our two piddly rooms in this shit hole flat to knock about in.

Before I became a mam two years ago, I can hold my hands up and say I was a bit of an arty-farty type. I used to have a business called Firebelly which I ran with my best friend, Gillie and my ex-fiancé, Jack (therein lies a whole other story). We used to work with all kinds of people to bring out their creativity through projects in painting, drama, dance and all sorts of other art forms. I bloody loved it. Well, for a very long time I loved it, anyway.

One day, the fiancé made a sharp exit and the short version is that my whole life got thrown up in the air, whirled around a bit, then came crashing back to earth with alarming velocity. I'm not going to lie. It left me in a bewildering place of sadness, as is often the case when a person of great significance makes a run for it out of your life. Bloody inconsiderate if you ask me.

Thank god for him though, really.

Because if he hadn't had the guts to leave then I wouldn't have gone on to realise that the business was also no longer for me . . . that I needed and wanted a whole lot more for my life than catering to other people's creative needs. I actually had an Oscar-worthy moment on a mountainside in Central Turkey about four years ago, where I went up a mountain feeling lost, confused, on the cusp of something terrifying . . . and came down a mountain feeling enlightened, powerful, motivated and full of intention.

I shit you not.

I knew then that what I needed to do was drop the self-imposed responsibility of convincing everybody else they needed to be creative, and actually get on with doing it myself.

So that is how I spent my Baki-less afternoon today. I'll admit I procrastinated like a pro, picking up notes from Cat-Crazy Flatmate (must not leave the butter out where cats can be tempted to lick it) and by trying to organise all of our stuff so there isn't an avalanche every time I open a door. Eventually I stopped, threw a few blankets over my shivering shoulders, and parked my bum in the Jess-shaped divot on the patchy sofa of fame. I whacked out a Snickers from the hole in the sofa cushion (will have to re-stock the Twixes), fired up my laptop and started work on my novel.

That's right – a novel!

I started writing this novel about four years ago. And yes, I'm aware that four years is a ridiculously long time to be working on a single novel but for your information . . .

- It has now morphed into three novels anyway
- I'm Mam to previously confirmed Beast-Child who will not even be mollified by overly salted and puffed up savoury snacks which is, my friends, a full-time job
- I have lived in three different countries and navigated three different lifestyles / cultures in the time since I first put pen to paper
- My dad was diagnosed with cancer a couple of years ago and had to have invasive surgery which took up a whole lot of my head and my heart

- I had to battle my way out of a mental fog which shrouded my every move for the best part of a year

I don't want to dwell on that last one here, on this blog, because you're here to find out what high jinks I get up to during Ramadan really, aren't you? I'm guessing you don't need to be weighed down by insights into my fragile psyche.

Or maybe it is important, actually, to give you the proper picture of what happened. It's nothing complicated. It was all just a bit of a shock.

Basically, when we moved here to Muirdrith a bit more than a year ago, I did the sensible thing and made an appointment at the docs to register myself and the Akyol family. Baki and I have been virtually one single entity since he was born, but on this particular day, Mesut had an apparent personality change and offered to look after him while I went to my 'Well Woman' appointment. Looking back, I'm wondering if he knew more than I did about how well of a woman I actually was.

I remember feeling very strange as I walked along the path to the doctor's surgery without my little fella in tow. And then in the same breath, guilty as hell that it also felt quite nice to be on my own for once. The day was bright and nippy. I pulled my coat tightly around me and felt the edges of the collar brush my cheeks. I stuffed my hands into the pockets and looked down at the ground, mentally calculating how I'd navigate all these bumps and dips in the pavement if I ever had to push the buggy along here. Which I was bound to, at some point. I mean, babies get sick, right? It's just a matter of time.

When I walked into the doctor's office I got a pleasant surprise. There was a flowery fragrance in the air and the doctor sitting there, going through the pleasantries, was a young woman with a soft, kind face and long, brown hair that nearly touched her knees. She explained the fragrance was called 'Vitality' and contained notes of ginger, black pepper and cedarwood which would help flagging energy levels and aid in healing. I thought I may have stepped into some kind of parallel world where the NHS actually values holistic therapies but no, this was just one person I'd been lucky enough to find.

I went through the formalities of having my height, weight and blood pressure taken. All the while, feeling my defences (and I didn't even know I'd had any) soften and relax around this woman. She asked me about my family's health history, how I was settling in to Muirdrith and what it was like being a first-time mam. Aside from Mesut, this might have been the first adult conversation I'd had in a while so, to be honest, it was refreshing.

Then she hit me with a question:

"Do you feel healthy?"

It was such a simple, direct question, that the answer rose up in me before any of my tricky little synapses had a chance to fathom something different.

"No."

And then the tears. Oh god, the tears.

I cried and cried in that doctor's office and shocked myself with the magnitude of feeling that question had triggered. I didn't feel healthy. At all. Not on any level or in any form did I feel healthy. Not in my body. Not in my mind. And certainly not in my soul.

How long had I been ignoring *that*?

I remember the doctor mentioning the words 'Postnatal Depression' and I didn't understand how they could possibly apply to me. Didn't I have everything I ever wanted? I was finally together with the man who'd stolen my heart four years ago, we had a beautiful baby boy together, Mesut had a job, we lived in a picturesque seaside town, regardless of the shitty flat above the shitty pub. And wasn't it too late for postnatal depression anyway? I thought that hit women like a truck just a few days after the birth, not eight months afterwards? I mean, I was functioning for god's sake. I was looking after my boy and doing big food shops and making doctor's appointments and all sorts. How could this feeling be depression?

"Depression is a very complex and personal thing," the doc explained, pushing a mammoth box of tissues towards me. "You might have been living with it for quite some time. From what you've told me, it sounds like you've had a string of huge life-changes in a very short space of time, and even if a lot of them were of your choosing, they can still have an impact on your mental health. It's very common for mums to have a delayed depression – especially when you factor in that we tend to get through challenging events on adrenalin which must, at some point, run out."

Made sense I supposed. Especially when I looked back on a few key moments since Baki had arrived.

- The searing pain of breastfeeding and the further torture of whisking my tiny baby, who had malnutrition, to a strange, echoing hospital where I didn't understand the language or anything that was happening
- Trying to cope, understand and keep faith in the first few weeks when Mesut told me he didn't know how he would ever bond with our new baby
- Sitting on a rock overlooking a sun-drenched İpeklikum, tiny Baki at my side, wailing in his pram, and hot, mechanical tears tracking my own cheeks too, seemingly for no reason
- All the women in Mesut's family knowing how to stop Baki's tears far better than I ever could and

their whispered dialogue under scarved heads that shook to and fro in quiet disbelief
- Their shocked, confused and disgusted faces when they saw me bottle-feeding him and the repeated explanations Mesut had to give to defend me
- The heavy, grey veil that weighed me down in bed each morning and the gargantuan effort it took to cast it aside and put my feet on the ground. And how it always found a way to slip back over my shoulders and weigh down on my head, a sinister filter that allowed me to see my baby's beauty but absolutely, categorically, nothing else

I asked the doctor, "Isn't that just what being a mam is like? It's meant to be hard, isn't it? Maybe I just haven't adapted as quickly as everyone else?"

"No, you don't need to feel like this all the time. We can get you some help."

I sat in that office with those fragrant strands of essential oils softly stroking my consciousness, I felt that heavy, grey, stifling veil as I shifted in my seat. What would life be like if it lifted? If I could dare to imagine such a thing.

I walked back to our flat in a bit of a daze, with leaflets about counselling and medication in hand. Again, my eyes dropped downwards as I mentally assessed the uneven surface of the path and found that it brought me some comfort. Groove with jagged edges – will have to tip buggy's front wheels. Bump with dark splotches – will need to swerve buggy around. Mound with grass growing out of it – might have to cross road.

After that day, I threw myself into getting better. I had several appointments with my lovely health visitor, Nicky, who is totally great but has cultivated in me a growing distaste for mental health questionnaires. I had three CBT counselling sessions and despite their tendency to plunge me into a deep state of psycho-analysis which lasted for days at a time and thus free Baki up to watch as many episodes of Bob the Builder as he damn well pleased, they did do me some good.

I started Zumba, on account of all the endorphins that it's supposed to give you – it certainly does nothing for my dignity, that's for sure. I now go to the local Parent & Toddler group, which I actually quite like and have made a couple of friends. I breathe in sea air, I talk to people, I wear bright colours, I drink water, take vitamins and sleep as well as I can. I'm ticking all the boxes, right?

It was pretty hard talking to Mesut about it all because he's obviously from another culture and I suppose they do mental health differently in Turkey. When I started bleating on about Zumba classes that would boost my mood he looked at me like I was from another planet, not just another country. I guess in his world, there are so many women supporting each other in a continual carousel-type motion that none of this gets discussed with husbands. Yet another culture shock for him.

And me.

Anyway, I guess what I'm trying to tell you is that being a mam, so far, has not been a smooth journey. I feel loads better than I did that day in the doctor's office, and that heavy, grey veil makes fewer appearances. Having a baby in a foreign land is a strange thing indeed and I guess it would be enough to kickstart some kind of mental happening in anyone – add that to droves of disorderly hormones and you've got a recipe for . . . well, whatever I was living.

So do you see, Dear Reader, why I may be dragging my heels a bit with the writing of these novels? The mountainside in Central Turkey wasn't wrong . . . I definitely need to claim creativity as my own and being a mam won't stop me. Ramadan will help with that, I'm sure of it.

I know the novels will be good when they're finished. The words are straight from the heart you see, as that's the only way I know how to write. Have you noticed?

(*Chuckles at laptop and feels sorry for plight of poor reader*)

As you might imagine, I have a love-hate relationship with this epic task I have set myself. But do you know what age-old writer's strategy keeps me going?

Biscuits.

Tea and biscuits.

Tea and coffee and biscuits.

And perhaps a slice of cake.

When I'm writing, the trips to the cat-ridden kitchen are almost as frequent as the terrible metaphors I come up with, but that doesn't stop me from doing either of those things.

What the holy heck-fire am I going to do when my period ends and I find myself fasting for Ramadan and the novel-writing pit-stops are no more? Will the progression of my story come to yet another halt? Will this be the time I give up on it entirely? Will it be stuffed into a drawer, ripe for gathering dust and forgotten about forever, thus denying the world of the transformative impact it could have had on potentially millions of readers had I just had access to regular caffeine and sweet pastries?

Fuck it.

I'm starting to feel woozy.

Maybe a biscuit would help.

GILLIE_LASS77

Sweetie – are you okay? I didn't know things had been that hard for you. Ring me! We need to speak more often.

Jess.AKYOL

I'm fine, Gillie. Just needed to be honest here on the blog – you know me. Yes. Let's talk. My phone is always on.

Anonymous
Thank you for talking about your mental health. Not easy. Will keep reading.
Jess.AKYOL
Thank you for reading!

desire96!#
Just desired to let you realize I enjoy browsing on your world-wide-web internet site joyous occasion.
Jess.AKYOL
Wow. I'm so pleased for you, desire96!#. It truly is a joyous occasion.

ask_yo_girl_about_me
Great blog site! I actually really like just how it is truly swift in my personal eyes as well as the information that is written. You are great. The site is very great. This post is very very great. This comments is very great. The resulting is very great to. I will look further too more stuff from you. Possess a good time!
Jess.AKYOL
Great!

NO_Just_DON'T(1)
I don't see how you can be a good mum and starving yourself at the same time? I'd urge you to re-think this. For the sake of your little boy.
Jess.AKYOL
Baki will always be my first priority so if the fasting is too hard I will stop. Thanks for reading.

funmum
Jessica, don't listen to that last comment – you'll do fine. I read something once that really helped me . . . "There's no way to be a perfect mother and a million ways to be a good one." Jill Churchill, I think?
Jess.AKYOL
You're so sweet. Always wanted to be the perfect mam though. I think Ramadan will help. 🤞

Fab4CoolDad
Still waiting for your novels, love. I know you've really been through the mill but you'll get there. The Beatles would be proud because one day you'll be a 'Paperback Writer'.
Jess.AKYOL
Always loved that song. And yes, indeed I will get there. Thanks, Dad.

Angnonymous
I'd read your novels. Especially if they're as good as your blog.
Jess.AKYOL
Thank you. Hopefully I will finish them one day. Thanks for coming back to read my blog.
Angnonymous
I'm a man of my word. Plus I felt a pull. Can't wait to see what happens next!
Jess.AKYOL
God, I hope I can deliver.

3

DAY 3 - EQUIPPED

Muirdrith, Highlands of Scotland, UK
Fri 13th Aug 2010
Sunrise / Suhoor: 5.34am
Sunset / Iftar: 9.06pm

It's day three of Ramadan and Mesut is inexplicably cheerful.

He bounds upstairs from work at night, as if he's a not-so-distant relative of Mr Motivator. He leaves Cat-Crazy Flatmate downstairs in the empty pub, doing the stock-taking and writing passive-aggressive notes for her co-workers to her little heart's content. Then he practically skips into the kitchen, where the cat army parts like the red sea for Moses and he begins preparing a feast. He's tossing green salad, frying slices of spicy meat, splitting eggs into hot, crackling oil and tearing up chunks of Muirdrith's finest white stotty. He brings it all through to our room on a solid, bamboo chopping board, sits cross-legged on the patchy sofa of fame and eats it with all the enthusiasm of a toddler being left alone with a huge bowl of ice cream.

Now this is not the typical behaviour of my husband, Dear Reader. I usually have to stealthily trick him into making a cup of tea. Hunger must be the determining factor in this new-found passion for culinary activity.

Is it just the hunger though? Really? I suspect the man is in his bloody element. I suspect it is all down to the fact that he is (and forgive me for the intensity of the phrase) serving his God.

He is performing a ritual that not only bags him a few brownie points when his mother calls, but evidently also opens up a communication channel with the divine one. At least, that's my best guess.

Through his actions (i.e. not eating, drinking, swearing, kissing or smoking) during the day, Mesut is opening himself up. He is showing his God his commitment, his ability to be disciplined, his gratitude for a healthy, happy existence. He's saying, "Hey, Almighty One, look at me! I bloody love you, I do!" The man is more relaxed. He's more at ease. I'd actually even say he seems empowered.

Disclaimer: I must remind myself that this is merely day three and Mesut's nicotine withdrawal possibly has not yet kicked in. Will he really be so empowered when he's gagging for a fag?

But no matter which way I look at it, and no matter what happens from now, I am mightily impressed by my husband. He was recently deployed at work to start producing 'Haggis Kebabs' in the pub's humble little kitchen. Disgusting, I know. And I'm still not sure if this is a case of racism or positive discrimination, but it came with a slight pay rise so we both thought, *what the heck*?

He can sometimes be doling out food for a strong twelve hours a day. Apparently there is no accounting for the insatiable appetite of the Scottish pub-goer, even if that means haggis kebabs in the morning along with their whisky-laced coffee. During all of that food preparation, how can at least one tiny little chip or a sneaky onion ring not tempt him? Would Allah really have a massive problem if a snack of the deep-fried variety made it past his ever-so-lovely lips?

The point is though, that my awe is irrelevant. Mesut is happy with his efforts and is positively basking in the glory of Ramadan. Good for him.

Will I be able to do the same?

I have a weekend coming up with absolutely fuck-all to do except entertain a two-year old. No out-of-the-ordinary activities planned to distract me. No appointments to break up the day. Unless, of course, you count stamping in endless muddy puddles, wiping inexplicably snotty noses and changing outstandingly dirty nappies. A typical weekend for me then: mud, snot and poo.

Actually, maybe that is enough to curb my appetite.

In other news . . . I have finally reached the last day of my period. To mark the occasion, I invited my friend Bernie over tonight, so we could share a giant takeaway from the pub. Plus many, many delicious chocolates and cups of tea. One thing I do like about the Scots is that they do not shy away from a decent meal.

Not that Bernie is a Scot. She certainly looks the part with her thick, auburn hair and smattering of freckles on plump, rose-white cheeks, but at best, she's an honorary one. Her hubby is about as Scottish as they get and she's lived here in Muirdrith since she 'felt it calling' to her a number of years ago. She's an incredible woman, really. She has three grown-up children (one of whom babysits Baki once a week so I can go to Zumba). She had her first children very young to an abusive partner who she eventually fled on account of her incredible bravery and emotional resilience.

She is now remarried to a lovely bloke called Logan, and has a cheeky little girl called Frida as well as another bambino on the way. She is one of the most down-to-earth and delightful people I have ever met and her personality is only enhanced by the fact that she receives regular visits from angels.

Yes, angels.

We can be in the middle of a chat about the snarky mam at toddler group, or the state of sticky buns from Asda these days when she'll suddenly blow into the air (*"It's just orbs in my way, poppet"*), or shiver all the way up and down her body (*"Oh Jess, they do like to waft their wings to get my attention"*), or whisper something incomprehensible over her shoulder (*"Sometimes they just need to be bloody well told to back off. Now is not the time!"*).

Only Bernie could scold a messenger of God.

It takes a bit of getting used to. But I eventually realised she wasn't pushing all this angel stuff on anybody else. She is definitely not the type to suddenly give you a cryptic message you never asked for and then wander off into the distance, leaving you to deal with all your shit. And aside from the celestial congregations, she really is the most practical and level-headed person you could meet. She got me involved in the Parent & Toddler group, helped me sort a nursery place for Baki and managed to source some of that 'Vitality' oil when I eventually told her about my distressing trip to the doctor's surgery. "Don't worry, Jess," she'd said, "having children is all at once a miraculous and terrifying thing. Us women are built to withstand it, but that doesn't mean we won't buckle a bit in the process."

It was lovely chomping delicious food with Bernie tonight. And she has sworn to support me during Ramadan, even offering to help me out with Baki when things get rough.

Having cleared all the chip bags and kebab wrappings away, and ensured the chocolate foils are thrown out and away from the prying eyes of my sugar-addicted two-year-old before he demands a breakfast of a similar nature, I am now wondering what tomorrow will bring. I'm rubbing my full belly as I write this. Should I wake up before sunrise so I can have a bit of brekkie? What about brushing my teeth? I'm not sure that's even allowed during daylight hours.

Hmmm. Not liking the early start concept so far. I can see how, as a whole family, it might be lovely to rise and gather for a starlit morning meal. Squinted eyes, whispered banter and hungry hands grabbing precious food, the sun starting to chase the stars with the beginnings of its delicate, fruitful rays.

I can't quite see how that's going to work for me. Rising alone (Mesut is dead to the world because of working so late), blurred vision, stubbed toes, tripping over prowling cats in the hallway and pouring Vimto on my Weetabix. Nope. I think I'm best going to bed armed with a jug of water and a couple of custard creams.

Okay. It's done. I'm equipped for the night ahead. Let's hope the morning brings me strength, courage and abnormally high levels of hydration.

Night.

Not-A-Granny-Flora
Has my food parcel arrived yet? You could put that by your bedside. I remembered custard creams.
Jess.AKYOL
Thank you, Mother. I'll let you know when it does.

AngelBernie
I can't believe you had the energy to write this after I left. I still feel like I'm in a food coma on your squishy sofa! Love the angel chat. Glad you don't think I'm a total screwball (although there's still time).
Jess.AKYOL

I'm more of a screwball than you. Look who's starving herself for a month.
AngelBernie
Point. Made.

LifeIsYoursLindy
OMG, Jess – is that really you? It must be! There are too many coincidences for it to be anyone else. And you're still writing your novels???? Well, at least you'll have time to make me sound like the most amazing confidante. Guess what? I live in Madrid now! 😀😀😀
Jess.AKYOL
Wow, Lindy! Madrid? Sounds like you've got your own story to tell. I think about that night on the beach four years ago, so often. And you *were* the most amazing confidante. I'd never have even started my novels if it wasn't for you! How did you find me? Not that I'm not DELIGHTED that you did!
LifeIsYoursLindy
Good old stalking I'm afraid. Found you on the evil Facebook then there was a link to here. I'm going to follow you with this Ramadan thing. It's good to see you're still mental / keen on doing things in the name of love. Count me in! 👍👍👍

Desire96!#
I am feeling desire to get onto the internet comments that you bring with your eventual blog site. It is not a hoax. I am desirous.
Jess.AKYOL
My eventual blog site is very pleased about that.

NO_Just_DON'T(1)
All of that junk food? No wonder your little boy has a sugar addiction with a mother like you.
Jess.AKYOL

Why are you so interested in what I eat? Jeez.
NO_Just_DON'T(1)
Jeez is derived from the word, Jesus. Wondering what your husband would think of that. You know, being a Muslim and all.
Jess.AKYOL
Keep wondering.

Fab4CoolDad
Well, love, you know I'm not a religious man, but George Harrison was. And he wrote a song all about his relationship with God. Might help? It's called 'Long, Long, Long'.
Jess.AKYOL
Wow Dad – this is impressive so far. Are you going to recommend a Beatles song for me every day of Ramadan?
Fab4CoolDad
Game on. 😉

Angnonymous
AngelBernie sounds like a braw friend. You'll need people like her this month.
Jess.AKYOL
I will. She's awesome. Thanks so much for reading! Tiny thing though. I'm cool with you being anonymous, obvs, but I think you've made a little typo with your username?
Angnonymous
Have I though?

4

DAY 4 – THE ENVELOPE

Muirdrith, Highlands of Scotland, UK
Sat 14th Aug 2010
Sunrise / Suhoor: 5.36am
Sunset / Iftar: 9.04pm

Today is the fourth day of Ramadan and, as you know, my own first day of fasting. And I'm sorry to say, Dear Reader, that this early on in the game, I nearly jacked it all in.

I'm not even sure how I'm here now, typing this out to you. But it seems that after just three blog posts, I feel compelled to come good on my promise of writing every day. Even though I am having trouble stringing an actual sentence together.

I really don't know where to start with telling you about this day. Okay. *Deep breaths, Jess. Explain . . . slowly.*

Lists. Lists always make me feel better. So here's one to show you that it was all going so well at first:

1. I served my son a delicious, nutritious breakfast without pilfering a single Choco-Pillow from him

2. I visited a friend for coffee and refused the coffee inevitably offered to me
3. I got over the usual eleven o'clock hump without any refreshments whatsoever
4. I made a point of NOT licking my fingers when clearing up Beast-Child's mid-morning snack (yoghurt) which was routinely spilled / hurled at the wall

It wasn't until Mesut and Cat-Crazy Flatmate were on their way out of the door to start their afternoon shifts that all hell broke loose.

Well, an internal hell anyway.

I was just marvelling at the fact that I had no fresh notes today, documenting my downfalls as a flatmate, when I had a stack of letters thrown at me by the Cat-Crazy woman herself. "Sorry." She grunted, behind her signature cat hair-covered fleece, and avoiding eye contact with me as per usual. "These got mixed up with my post and I meant to give them to you. Hope it's nothing urgent." And then, in a whirl of clinking keys, slamming doors and my husband's long, luscious hair whipping behind them, they were both gone.

The stack of post was, it turned out, from about a week ago. A few bills I was happy to keep ignoring, some newsletters from local estate agents I'd dreamily signed up for in a moment of madness where I believed Mesut's wage might actually pay for a decent flat. And then one more envelope, that looked a bit crinkled and possibly stained by a bit of cat pee, if I'm honest, but I ripped it open anyway and scanned the official-looking text.

My heart fell into my belly with a definitive thud.

After the initial cry, I couldn't find my breath.

Baki crawled onto my knee, grunted and pummelled his

palms against my cheeks. I guess he was trying to animate my frozen face. Or pound some colour into it.

It was from Children's Services.

Even through my tears I got the basic gist.

Somebody has reported me, anonymously, for neglect.

NEGLECT.

And now Children's Services has a duty to ensure Baki is not at risk and that I'm looking after him properly.

They will be following up this report by making a visit to check on Baki. Here. At the flat.

In two days' time.

Two days! Cat-Crazy Flatmate is so caught up in writing me her own toxic letters of accusation that she didn't give me this, infinitely more important one, that has fucked my life right up in a matter of seconds.

What am I going to do, Dear Reader? How am I going to prove I'm not a risk to Baki? I don't even know if I should be writing about this here, in the public domain, but I've got to get some advice. I knew I wasn't #winningsasa-mummy but even I didn't know things were this bad. Okay, so we live in a shitty flat above a pub, which isn't ideal and we haven't got two pennies to rub together, but surely not everybody has their lives completely sorted when they bring a baby into the world? Is this because I had postnatal depression? Was it wrong of me to feel the way I felt? Is it because Baki can't speak yet? Am I doing something wrong?

I was in such a state of shock after I read the letter that my poor, starving brain went into denial mode. I stuffed that fucking letter back into the envelope and tried to seal it back up. I don't know what I thought I was going to do with it, but having it there, in my grasp, even in my vicinity, just didn't seem like an option.

And to top it all off, do you know what I did next? In an effort to seal it and get it out of my life?

I licked the envelope.

What the actual fuck?

Besides the fact that I'd potentially just ingested dried cat piss, I'd also failed at the first hurdle of Ramadan.

Can I do *nothing* right?

I collapsed into a beanbag in Baki's tiny room and waited, solemnly, to be struck down. I cowered under what I imagined to be the dark storm clouds of Allah's fury, waiting for a lightning bolt, an earthquake, or perhaps a monsoon. But then I remembered I don't really believe in a god, at least not in that sense . . . and if there is one, would he / she / they have better things to do than smite me for licking an envelope?

The smiting is probably reserved for neglectful parents, so either way I'm done for.

All day I've been dealing with a.) the disgusting, bitter taste of the gluey / pissy edges of the envelope, unable to neutralize it with a nice, cool glass of water and b.) the reluctant and dawning comprehension that somebody doubts my parenting abilities enough to report me to Children's Services.

Who?

I don't even know that many people up here in the Highlands yet. I can't bear the thought of even trying to work out who would do this. Were they really acting in Baki's best interests? Or have they got it in for me?

How the holy heck-fire am I going to get through this visit with Children's Services? The letter says that as well as a social worker, it'll be my health visitor who comes so at least I'll have a friendly face in Nicky, who surely knows I'd never do anything to harm Baki. She's always been so nice and helpful and even laughed at the nickname, Beast-Child when I was recounting his many and varied tantrum methods.

Maybe I'll just conveniently go on holiday. Pop back down to the North East of England and hide under the protective wing of friends and family. I mean, for all they know, Cat-Crazy Flatmate might never have even given me that stack of post at all, meaning that in a parallel world somewhere, I'm the most perfect and brilliant mother of all time and *I* should be visiting Children's Services to offer *them* training opportunities in Parenting 101.

Dear Reader, what am I going to do?

I've moved through most of this day in a daze, to be honest. Baki, much to his excitement, was allowed to stay up an hour and a half later than usual, just to give me something to do other than fantasise about ways I can avoid this visit. I think we've exhausted his entire collection of Bob The Builder DVDs, scribbled over every single page in his 'Animal Farts' colouring book (thank you, Auntie Ella) AND we invented a fantastic new game called count-the-tassles-on-the-hallway-rug-and-make-them-dance-to-a-variety-of-songs-by-Eminem. I suggest you go out and get a rug with tassels immediately. It really is a pleasant way to spend an evening.

And when the Golden Hour finally came (9.04pm to be precise), I surprised myself by being far more interested in a huge glass of orange squash then any food you could have put my way. I guess my hunger was crushed by the Letter of Doom. So, if you're at all interested in starving yourself I can recommend getting Children's Services involved. Classic appetite-killer.

And you'll be glad to know that Mam's food parcel finally arrived today. Jeez, she wasn't joking when she said she'd remembered the custard creams. I've never seen so many in my life. Not to mention the cherry bakewells, apple turnovers, French fancies and battenburg cake. Basically, the cuisine of my youth. Plus a giant tin of beans which must have cost a *fortune* to post but apparently worth it on my mother's part because she enjoys flogging an age-old joke about me wafting around our chintzy home as a spotty thirteen-year-old lamenting loudly that, "there's no food anywhere in this house – not even a tin of BEANS!!!"

Maybe I'm not the only neglectful parent.

The parcel included a note, barely decipherable on account of Mam's journalist shorthand which was, I imagine, useful during her newspaper career of the eighties, but not so much these days. In my distinguished role as her eldest child, I'm making my best guess that this is what the note said:

Jessie,
Remember you've got Scottish blood which means you need sustenance more than most. More than Mesut, even. Give some of this stuff to Baki too. Has he had battenburg before? Oh, and there are beans, in case you haven't noticed. Just in case you find yourself in the predicament of having no food left in the house, "Not even a tin of BEANS!!!" (You have to say that in a whiny, spoiled-teenager voice – what a wee darling you were!)
Love,
Mam x

I'm not going to lie – it was much appreciated after the day I've had. Will just need to hide the contents of the parcel during daylight hours so their very presence doesn't throw me into a shit-storm of binge-eating / self-loathing. Because that, I'm afraid to say, also sounds a little like the cuisine of my youth.

And in case you're wondering, Mesut was alarmingly chill about the Letter of Doom and the envelope-licking fiasco. He put it like this:

"Allah is knowing we good, good parents to Baki and these official people will see it too. And Gulazer, you not worry about licking envelope. If you licking your fingers or anything else like that and is just you forgetting, is okay. Allah not gonna care if you just slipping in your mind, Gulazer."

Oh, I'm slipping in my mind, alright.

I just don't want to slip alone.

———

Not-A-Granny-Flora
We'll talk about the letter and sort it. Now eat some cake!
Jess.AKYOL
Done.

LifeIsYoursLindy
Oh poor you, Jess. What a shitty day! I wish I was there. I would give you Spanish Rosquillas. Have you ever tried them? Like donuts but even better. My Spanish lady (yes – lady!) says you must come here one day and she'll take you to the best Rosquilla shop in Madrid!
Jess.AKYOL
Yes to all of the above.

Night-sun-ella
Oh noooooo! Are Children's Services actually *on* something? You deserve a freaking trophy for all that you've been through since becoming a mummy! I'm glad the farting animals gave you a bit of comfort. Isn't it the most brilliant colouring book you've ever seen? How many two-year-olds can say they got one of them for their birthday? On that, is Baki talking yet? My Dotty can say 'Boobies are mine'. #veryproud. Keep up the blog posts, gorgeous one – loving it because it helps me picture you all the way up there in the Highlands, tapping away at your computer with a tartan scarf casually thrown about your shoulders and a

whisky on ice by your side. I expect there's an open fire too – please say there is!

Jess.AKYOL

Ella, the farting animals have provided so much comfort, you wouldn't believe. Baki's not talking yet at all, except for screaming to the high heavens as many times as you like per day. And I'm not really that far away from you, am I? Turkey was further! Note to self: must wear more tartan. And get flat with open fire.

Night-sun-ella

Yes! Please do. Tartan is the new black! Here's a crazy idea. Next week I have a window where things quiet down at work. Shall I bring Dotty up to see you? I can chase Children's Services away. We could wear tartan together and beat them off with a bunch of heather or something! And don't worry because I can eat for both of us during the day – it's a special skill.

Jess.AKYOL

OMG, would you? I haven't seen Dotty since she was permanently fastened to your boob.

Night-sun-ella

Well, don't expect much of a change there. My extensive collection of dungarees is finally coming into its own. Let's make this happen! I'll text you, sweetie. Can't wait!

Anonymous

Really? You are doing Ramadan when you are not even Muslim? Is sinful I think. You not even proper mother.

NO_Just_DON'T(1)

I rest my case. It seems Children's Services are already ahead of me. I wonder if they know you're also putting starving yourself ahead of caring for your child?

Anonymous
Your husband is not true Muslim if he married you. Allah will not forgive it. I feel sorry for you both.

AngelBernie
Poppet, don't listen to those stupid, anonymous comments above. And don't freak out about the Letter of Doom. The angels are telling me it's just another challenge you'll rise above and they are, after all, messengers from the man himself. Save me some battenburg. Baby needs it.
Jess.AKYOL
Thank you, Bernie. Battenburg saved.

Angnonymous
Letter of Doom = overcomeable. Envelope = easy mistake! Don't worry, Jess. You've got this.
Jess.AKYOL
Thank you lovely person who I don't know but am starting to like quite a lot.

Fab4CoolDad
Your mam is going to ring you about the letter. I'm sure it's just a misunderstanding so try not to lose sleep over it. Instead of focusing on that, I'm going to respond to the battenburg element of your day. The Beatles, I believe, wrote a song for every occasion, every mood, every feeling. So today . . . I remember the first time you tasted battenburg cake as a little girl. It went something like this: 'Got To get You Into My Life'.
Jess.AKYOL
Thanks Dad. You always know how to cheer me up.

MesutAk1

You not worry about Doom Letter, Gulazer. Seni seviyorum. Her zaman.

Jess.AKYOL

So you're finally reading my blog posts? Love you always too, Gandalf.

5

DAY 5 - PERFECT-MAM STAKES

Muirdrith, Highlands of Scotland, UK
Sun 15th Aug 2010
Sunrise / Suhoor: 5.38am
Sunset / Iftar: 9.01pm

And so the mood swings begin.

It is an absolute mystery to me how the husband flounces around the kitchen of an evening, in apparent delight that his stomach has been empty all day when I can't even muster a smile.

"Come on, Gulazer!" he beams. "The emptiness is good feeling, isn't it? Is clearing us for something better."

I honestly don't know how I didn't clock him one.

I'm telling you, Dear Reader, that all day long – but especially at sundown – I have been a Very Serious Person Indeed. I could rival Baki's frighteningly thunderous frowns which I had, until now, assumed were a direct gift from his Turkish forefathers. Now, I'm not so sure.

At sundown, my meal-preparing path must not be crossed by anyone. I need orange squash and I need it now. I need pasta and I need it now. I need chocolate and I need it, like, ten hours ago. It is a Very Serious Matter Indeed.

Maybe Mesut is right. I am so far missing the divine element of Ramadan. To be fair, I have been somewhat sidetracked by the Letter of Doom and find it hard to believe that Allah would want me to go through this shit-storm without any sustenance in my belly. But even so, I'm not exactly doing this for my entry ticket at the pearly gates, am I?

I would like to know, if anyone fancies giving me some insight, how Mesut seems completely unmoved by the fact that Children's Services has been called upon to question our parenting abilities. Yet again, that man's self-esteem is as rock hard as one of Baki's day-old discarded Weetabix bowls.

On a positive note (and it's at times like this I have to scavenge for such things), I will say that I have managed to get through my second day of Ramadan with no envelope-licking incidents. But is that sliver of pride enough to keep me going for another couple of days, never mind the rest of the month?

To make matters worse, I am exhausted. And I can't stress enough that those words, coming from the mouth of a mother, are *potently* rich with meaning. When I say 'exhausted', what I really mean is 'depleted to within an inch of my life'.

It's to be expected I suppose. What with the not eating and all. But for some unfathomable reason, I hadn't expected it. Before the Letter of Doom, I had imagined dashing about my motherly duties as usual, just with a barely-there, rumbly belly kind of feeling that, if anything, would make me feel more *alive.* More *present.* I didn't think for a second that my daily activities, basic responsibilities and actual will to live might be compromised.

(*Disclaimer: that last line was built in for comedic effect, please do not add to the already hefty load of Children's Services or make them rock up on my doorstep any earlier than need be*).

Sunday is the only day of the week that Mesut usually manages to get off, so today we made use of the freakishly high temperatures in Muirdrith and took Baki to the beach just down the road from our flat. Now, I'm a big fan of the beach. It is on beaches that I have had some of my most soulful, exciting, peaceful and awakening moments, but all I found there today was my inability to access ice cream. As you can imagine, this led to a dramatic lie down on the sand.

For quite a while.

Well, I say it was quite a while, but it wasn't long before I felt the raking grip of mam-guilt, swiftly followed by the soul-draining fear that somebody might be watching and further confirming to themselves that I am, indeed a shitty mother. I could almost hear their thoughts screaming inside their tiny, prying minds: *Look at her, lying there whilst her toddler flings himself into the waves all alone. Where are his arm bands? Where is his sun hat? Where is the love?*

So I flipped myself up with the vigour of an Olympian gymnast (not really) and dashed over to Baki's side to make oohing and aahing noises at floating crisp packets, wipe his snot surreptitiously into the sea foam, and shield him from the white Scottish sun on account of the fact that I had, indeed, forgotten to pack his sun hat.

This went on for several million hours before Mesut found himself at the wrong end of a phone call stating he was needed to go into work. Apparently Auld Fergus required a haggis kebab to accompany his Sunday dram and the absence of it was not acceptable. We packed up the beach things and dragged a kicking, screaming Baki home for yet more lying down, somewhere away from prying eyes, and I felt relief that I might be able to lose conscious awareness of my empty tummy for an hour or two.

Will I ever learn? Toddlers *never* sleep when you want them to. It wasn't long before I gave in with the shushing and the stroking of Baki's chubby cheeks and resorted to a hella lotta CBeebies instead. Thank god for Mr Tumble, that's what I say.

But please don't worry. As much as I love a pre-school telly-fest, I didn't allow Baki's eyes to turn square today. In fact, after the harrowing task of serving up veggie sausages, rice and peas for his dinner, I decided I would make a real effort in the perfect-mam stakes and venture outside for a short, early evening stroll to the park with my beloved child. It would be civilised. Or something.

Short evening stroll? Nope.

Civilized? Nope again.

Let me get this straight. I love my son. He is the apple of my eye, the light of my life, the jewel in my crown, (ALL of the things) and I'd do anything for him. But bloody hell, could a person – two years old or not – ever walk slower than him? I know toddlers are curious little beings, but he really does take curiosity to an uber level.

Apparently, we live in a town where every single crevice in every single wall, every single petal on every single flower, every single letterbox on every single door, and every single fag end in every single gutter, is astonishingly, grippingly fascinating.

Beast-Child's endless enchantment with these things was seriously threatening my enduring efforts in this perfect-mam activity. Honestly, how am I supposed to at least appear to be a mam of the first class kind, when he is screaming to climb into a drain?

It's just not possible.

Anyway, by the time we got to the deserted park, my body took over my brain and before I knew it I was lying down. On the ground. Hopefully nobody noticed the alarmingly unkempt woman collapsed on the tarmac, dead to the world whilst her young son played unsupervised on the park equipment.

Evidently, that was enough of doing perfect-mam things for one day.

I eventually managed to peel myself off the ground and I'm sad to say that the slow walk back was almost as painful – until inspiration hit me.

Bribery.

"Come on, gorgeous boy. If you walk very quickly and very nicely for Mammy, you can have a snack at the shop on the way home."

For somebody who can't yet even say the word 'snack', he sure lit up as soon as he heard it. Which, to be honest, pissed me right off because it meant he knew exactly what he was doing all along and wasn't actually exercising his natural curiosities as an ever-evolving toddler after all. And at the end of the walk, he was the one chowing down on a Thomas The Tank Engine chocolate lolly, not me.

Unfair.

I made up for it later though, because the hole in the patchy sofa of fame is pretty well stocked on account of me not diving into it on a daily basis anymore. So I'm typing this with a chocolate-lined tummy and a final burst of energy to a.) bring you my news of the day and b.) consider that the perfect-mam thing might seem more achievable after a good night's sleep.

Oh and c.) contemplate what the fuckery-fuck I am going to do about the imminent visit from Children's Services.

Answers on a postcard please . . .

Not-A-Granny-Flora

If you're that tired, you need to just stop fasting and get this meeting over and done with on Tuesday. You'll feel much better after it. Mesut will understand.

Jess.AKYOL
If only life was that simple, Mam.

Fab4CoolDad
I disagree with your mother. It was always going to be hard but I think you can keep going. Get an early night tonight and maybe this Beatles classic will help you drift off? 'I'm So Tired'.
Jess.AKYOL
Aw, thanks Dad.

GILLIE_LASS77
Fasting must be soooo hard, Jess! Will miss the blog posts if you decide to jack it all in though. I don't know what to say about the visit thing. Totally outside of my sphere of experience. I will say that I've seen you get through worse. And with style too. 😉
Jess.AKYOL
I don't know. Maybe I have been through worse. But this is about my baby, Gillie, my BABY!

Angnonymous
Don't give up! I'm on the edge of my seat here.

AngelBernie
Remember the angels have got your back, Jess. And me too. Baki can have an afternoon at ours playing with Frida if you need yet more lying down?! And just for future reference, 'perfect mams' need to lie down too.
Jess.AKYOL
Thanks, Bern. Filed for future reference.

NO_Just_DON'T(1)
Lying down in the park? Lying down on the beach? Your poor

son. No wonder he can't speak yet if you never interact with him.

Anonymous
Fasting won't work because you're not a Muslim. You can't reap the benefits of somebody else's religion. It's selfish.
MesutAk1
She not selfish, Anonymous Person, she just good wife. Read different blog if you not like this one.
Jess.AKYOL
Seni seviyorum, beautiful man.
MesutAk1
Love you too, Gulazer.

6

DAY 6 - COSTA DEL CAT HAIR

Muirdrith, Highlands of Scotland, UK
Mon 16th Aug 2010
Sunrise / Suhoor: 5.40am
Sunset / Iftar: 8.59pm

Right, today is the day before I have to face this whole, neglectful parent thing, and I'd like to start by saying that Ramadan has torn apart any hope I might have had of dealing with that.

Let's see . . . aside from my entire day collapsing in on itself for the lack of punctuated meal times, I have also been dealing with a dry mouth, a short temper and yet more mood swings.

Yes, I'm aware, it's my own stupid fault for having a husband of the intense holiday romance variety who I am continually smitten with and therefore likely to join in such spiritual shenanigans. Nobody actually *invited* me to fast for Ramadan. Not even him. But how was I to know my world would be turned upside down?

Imagine this: you get up almost illegally early in the morning to tend to an outrageously cute but equally demanding

Beast-Child. You do all the mammy-type things expected of you: preparing meals, offering snacks, trips to the park, building tower blocks, calming temper tantrums, trying to encourage basic speech, nappy-changing . . . you get the general gist.

And then you have to face up to the terrifying fact that in less than twenty-four hours, professional, child-stealing people will be waltzing through your door, ready to assess your aptitude as a parent. You decide there simply cannot be this much cat hair covering ALL of the surfaces when this happens and you take it upon yourself to scrub, clean, de-fuzz and scour until it is all gone, despite the fact that said cats are watching your every move as you go.

You then realise that there are an abnormally high number of stinky cat litter trays within your pathetic excuse of a home and you decide to do a cull, even at risk of irate notes being stuck to your bedroom door later. Surely the cats can choose between five rooms to crap in rather than fifty-seven. It seems reasonable.

Cat litter trays discarded, and the remaining ones re-lined, re-filled and cleaned with supermarket bleach, you turn your attention to the fact that there is not one damn biscuit in the house that you can offer to the child-stealing professionals tomorrow (Mesut has already consumed the entire food parcel sent by Mam. Except the beans. They're mine). *No matter!* You think, feeling a slithery glimmer of glee as the next thought forms in your head. *I can bake something myself!*

That's right Dear Reader! Once Beast-Child was in bed (grasping his favourite silicone whisk rather than the Bob the Builder plushie I spent half of my life savings on), I abandoned any cerebral clarity I might have ever possessed and started baking.

Cat-Crazy Flatmate was still working down in the pub with Mesut, so I had the kitchen to myself. Well, that's if you don't count the many pairs of feline eyes of judgement raining down upon me from their favourite spot on top of the fridge. I didn't care what they thought though, suddenly caramel shortbread seemed like the answer to everything.

So at the time I would usually be mentally thanking the inventors of dummies for their miraculous sleep-inducing powers, curling up with a decent book or a bit of Gok Wan on the tellybox, I was actually storming around the kitchen like a tornado, preparing a multitude of sweet treats.

Once sundown came and went (around nine o'clock tonight) I started downing glasses of Vimto as if I was a Scottish Laird chugging the finest, age-old whisky, scoffing raw cookie dough and spooning dollops of melted chocolate into my gob. As I went, I was manically washing ALL the dishes, high on the prospect that my culinary efforts were going to make everything alright and feeling rather like a fifties housewife caught in a five o'clock flurry.

Only it wasn't five o'clock. It was midnight. And there was still a blog to write.

By the time Mesut trailed his weary bones into the kitchen, I was crouching on the cracked linoleum, head in my floury hands and bewailing the loss of the quality of my next batch of scones on account of Baki not releasing his death grip on the silicone whisk. Even in his sleep he is a stubborn little so and so.

"Gulazer, what you doing? Is late."

"Yes, I know, but tomorrow is happening and I need to bake."

"Why? Why you need to bake?"

"Because if I can distract Nicky and the social worker with lovely sweet treats, then they won't think so hard about whether or not I'm a good mam."

Then he sighed. Normally I love it when he sighs. His sighs always seem so full of meaning, complexity, longing even. They make me want to burrow into his arms and become part of them.

And tonight, more than most nights, the idea of being whipped wistfully into the swirl of a sigh was so inviting.

But it wasn't one of those kinds of sighs.

"Gulazer, you coming with me. Now." I knew that tone. Mesut pulled me up off the floor and led me out of the kitchen, past the bench laden with perfectly packed Tupperware tubs of treats, and down the hallway. I noticed how blooms of icing sugar and flour fell to the floor with each of my weary steps and I tried not to cry about the fact that I'd only just vacuumed those carpets.

We arrived outside the door to Baki's room and he pushed it gently open. A soft wash of golden light settled across our little boy's cot, and his forehead, cheeks, lips, caught it with surprising luminousity. "You see?" Mesut whispered. "He perfect. He is like that because of you."

My body collapsed a little bit against Mesut's. "But he's cuddling a whisk. What the hell is that about?"

"He perfect." Mesut repeated, and closed the door.

Next thing I knew, I'd been deposited on the bed, with a hot cup of tea by my side, my laptop fired up and waiting, and a roll of toilet paper to wipe away a few stray tears. The last word I heard from Mesut was, "Blog." before he slipped off to the kitchen to tidy up my mess.

He's a keeper, that one.

Before I started recounting all of this to you, Dear Reader, I noticed I had an email from an address I didn't recognise. And opening that email was the best thing that happened today.

I have a friend called Lindy. Well, I say friend but I guess I don't actually know her that well. I met Lindy on a Turkish beach a few years ago, when Mesut and I hadn't been together long. Actually, it was New Year's Eve. 2006 was turning into 2007 and Lindy found me warming myself with a halfway decent little fire I'd built on the beach. I was on my own because

I'd shooed Mesut away in favour of a bit of me-time with the fire and the stars and the waves before the clock chimed midnight. It had, after all, been a hell of a year.

Lindy and I spent a blissful night chatting and eating and drinking and you'd never have known we'd only just met. She listened to me talking shit all night, which was extremely generous of her, considering she was clearly going through her own stuff.

Anyway, we really enjoyed each other's company but haven't seen or heard from each other since. Until she found me on here! Who would have thought that My Little Ramadan could bring about such a joyous reunion?

So the email I got from Lindy today went like this:

"Jess, I have to tell you how thoughtful and loving your Ramadan gesture is. Love is about sharing, respecting each other, doing things as a couple and showing how much you care for one another in a deeply respectful way – even if it's something that challenges your own beliefs. Jess, you taught me that. Please keep going."

Okay, so it's hard not to be all British and bashful and bat every kind word Lindy said back at her in an aptly self-deprecating way. But Mesut has taught me well so first thing in the morning I am printing that beauty of an email out and pinning it on the fridge. I want to see that message every damn day.

For now, I'm off to bed and hoping to replace the nightmare that awaits me tomorrow with delicious dreams of lumpy scones and gloopy caramel shortbread. And one particular toddler's beautiful, luminous face.

Night.

LifeIsYoursLindy

Glad you liked your email, Jess. Can't believe I've found you again. And remember, it's ALL TRUE!
Jess.AKYOL
You're just too lovely.

Angnonymous
I'd try your lumpy scones, Jess and I'm pretty sure your mate Bernie would too. If I remember rightly, she's partial to a scone? Good luck tomorrow!
Jess.AKYOL
You're right. Never known Bernie to turn down a scone. But how do you KNOW that Angnonymous?
Angnonymous
Just a hunch . . .

AngelBernie
My scone addiction is widely known, but even I'm a bit freaked out by the message above. Who is Angnonymous? I'm going to have to call in Archangel Uriel on this one . . .
Jess. AKYOL
Well, let me know when Uriel figures it out. I could do with the distraction right now . . .
AngelBernie
Will do. He's usually pretty accurate. And don't worry about tomorrow, poppet. Come along to toddler group in the morning and we'll calm your poor nerves. Even without the standard tea and biscuits.

OliverChen1!
Jessica Akyol! Matey! Loving your photos of the glorious Highlands on Facebook. I hope life up there is treating you well? Sounds like you've got a whole lot of stuff going on right now but knowing you, you'll come out of it smelling like roses.

Yellow roses, obviously. And Ramadan? Wow, what a challenge. I know you said in one of your earlier posts you were worried you hadn't finished writing your novels yet but, to be fair, these blog posts are a new writing project if ever I saw one.
Jess.AKYOL
Flipping heck. How do you always know the right time to chime into my life, Oliver? Is it a skill you were born with? Did you life-coach the midwives as they swaddled you and handed you to your mother? Anyway, I'm so glad you're reading my blog!
OliverChen1!
A gorgeous little birdie may or may not have told me about it.
Jess.AKYOL
Is this gorgeous little birdie impossibly glamorous, a huge fan of Ginsters and is her number in your little black book?
OliverChen1!
I couldn't possibly say . . .

GILLIE_LASS77
Well maybe he couldn't possibly say, but I could. 😉
Jess.AKYOL
Waahhh? You guys, don't tease me! My nerves can't take it at the moment!
GILLIE_LASS77
Fine. No more clues until tomorrow . . .

ask_yo_girl_about_me
Greatness in magnitude. Lucrative is great and simply your article is a stonishing. Your clearness is great and with your permission is is grab your RSS feed to keep up with great posts that are expert on this subject.
Jess.AKYOL
You're back! A stonishing. 😀

Fab4CoolDad
Ah, love, we know you'll be okay tomorrow. I remember you baking when you were little, with your babysitter, Sandra. Remember? Even then your caramel shortbread was always delicious, so these people from Children's Services will be bowled over. Whatever is around the corner, I'm sure Mesut wants to say this (in the words of The Beatles): 'Thank You Girl'.
Jess.AKYOL
I'll play it to him Dad, that's a lovely one.

Night-sun-ella
Hello my lovely! Have only skim-read today as I'm so busy packing everything into Keith-the-Van for our imminent trip. Shall I bring a potty for Dotty? Or do you have one? Although, she does rather like peeing in the wild.
Jess.AKYOL
Ella, I have a plethora of potties. Sorted for wild peeing too – you are visiting the Highlands, after all. Can you bring something for you and Dotty to sleep on? I reckon we could squeeze an air mattress into Baki's room and he can come in with us. Can't wait to welcome you to Costa Del Cat Hair. Lord knows I need you here right now.
Night-sun-ella
Air mattress: tick. Keep some tick-boxes for hugs, hugs and more hugs. One more day of work and then I will be zipping up the A9 to squeeze the living daylights out of you.

7

DAY 7 - THE VISIT FROM HELL

Muirdrith, Highlands of Scotland, UK
Tues 17th Aug 2010
Sunrise / Suhoor: 5.42am
Sunset / Iftar: 8.56pm

This morning I discovered that sugar hangovers are a thing.

It all started when I couldn't, at six in the morning, find Baki's Bob The Builder and The Legend of the Golden Hammer DVD. This is usually a skill so impressive it could get me into the final rounds for admittance to the territorial army. But not today.

Today Baki's mangled, mournful cries, which only I know means he wants to watch said DVD, weren't even enough to cut through the fog that was hugging my brain. I had just enough consciousness to dole out a bowl of Choco-Pillows and placate him with a three-month old Bob The Builder comic, before I collapsed onto the beanbag in his room and wondered why last night I had thought consuming only sugared goods had been a good idea.

Suddenly chocolate, cookies, cake and scones seemed like the devil's work.

Never mind. At least I had plenty of the devil's work left over, stored in Tupperware tubs in the kitchen, that would wow the professional child-stealers later on.

But first, Parents & Toddlers Group.

Now that Baki was happy enough with his lot, I shuffled out to the hallway, in search of painkillers that might bring me into the land of the living. Getting through a morning at Parents & Toddlers requires the strength of an ox on a good day, so I knew ibuprofen was essential.

Before I even got as far as the bathroom, I noticed a note stuck to the outside of my bedroom door. Cat-Crazy Flatmate.

Jess, could you please consider returning all of the cat litter trays to where they were before? I'm worried this will put the cats out of their daily rhythms. Thank you.

I'd been expecting this. There was no way I could have got through an entire day of cleaning yesterday AND the removal of said litter trays without a written rebuke of some kind. I shrugged and pulled the note down. It would be okay. Cats were adaptable and surely clever enough to find their own toilets. She was underestimating her own feline army. One of the cats, a great, hulking ginger one with white splodges shimmering all the way along its crooked tail, curled around my ankles just as I thought this. A sure sign I was right.

After this came the crushing realisation that the ibuprofen I'd been hankering after was obviously, completely banned. What had I been thinking? Flashbacks of licking the pissy, gummy envelope from Children's Services haunted me as I slowly got myself and Baki dressed and ready for Toddlers. Honestly, only a few days into Ramadan and I am already regularly teetering on the brink of failure. The heavy, groaning ache inside my head was a firm reminder of that, as well as all the ways I would have to prove myself today.

Anyway, Dear Reader, I did okay somehow. I successfully avoided the holy trinity of Parents & Toddlers which everybody knows is tea drinking, biscuit dunking and gossip. I suspect there was the occasional mam who got some kind of sick satisfaction out of chomping their Kit Kat in my general vicinity, but for the most part, people were very considerate and actually wildly interested.

"Well there's no way I could go without chocolate," one lady said as she wiped an alarming amount of snot off her son's nose and his accompanying lump of play dough.

Loud rumbles of agreement. "For me it would be Crunchy Nut Cornflakes," said another mam. "They are the most convenient form of sustenance I have ever known. I carry them with me everywhere. Does anybody want some?" She produced a battered box from her baby's changing bag, with nappy sacks mysteriously stuck to its edges. "They're clean, I promise!"

Nobody took her up on her offer but, a surprising amount of people then rooted around in their own bags to produce their snack of choice. Dried apple slices. Chewy muesli bars. Small tubs of Pringles. Mini haggis portions (well, if you can't carry haggis in your handbag in the Highlands, where the bloody hell can you?).

Bernie, god love her, produced a pouch of cherry chocolate liqueurs. "These are to die for," she sighed. "I can't eat them now because, you know, the great unborn would protest, but I carry them around with me everywhere. Just having them near makes me feel better. Jess poppet, do you want some to keep in your bag?"

"Thanks Bernie," I said, as Frida flung herself on her mother's knee and eyed up the highly inappropriate chocolates. "I'm sorted for out-of-bounds snacks. Watch out or your daughter's going to be high on cherry-flavoured toxins."

"Oh, it's just like Calpol, really!" Bernie laughed, waved off my comment and in the same graceful swoop of the hand, she popped a liqueur in Frida's mouth. "She loves them." Baki suddenly dropped a handful of building blocks and made a bee-line for us, his sugar radar operating on the highest level evidenced by his chubby, flexing fingers and little red patches on his cheeks spreading with every obstinate step. I had to do something to abort his mission. I was guessing Ramadan wasn't the best time to tell Mesut that his son has dabbled in alcoholic stimulants. And, let's face it, the last thing the Beast-Child needs is further stimulation.

I scooped him up and tickled him silly, hitting that secret spot above his knee that drives him crazy, whilst Bernie hid away the offending items. He was still a bit squirmy and cross when I put him down so thank the lord for snack time just happening to be in that very moment. He could fill his boots with toast and jam instead, even if I couldn't.

It was while all the little ones were snacking, and the mams were hovering like dancing bees around the table, that I noticed the nerves about this afternoon's visit really kick in.

Then inspiration struck me.

"Who fancies a playdate? At mine?"

A lot of heads popped up and looked my way. Crunchy Nut Mam stuttered, "But d-d-don't you live above *that pub*?"

"Erm, yes – but there's plenty of space upstairs. Come over. After this. I've baked and everything."

"But you're fasting," somebody else said. "You don't want us lot in your home, eating your food."

"Yes I do!" I nearly shrieked. "I really do. Baki will love it and I have a job-lot of caramel shortbread that needs eating. Say you'll come? Just for an hour?" There were quite a few mumbles about work or nap times but those without instant excuses found themselves nodding in my direction. It seems my powers of persuasion are only enhanced by this Ramadan lark.

My enthusiasm wasn't even dampened by Bernie's urgent whisper in my ear. "Poppet, haven't you got your visit this afternoon? You know. From Children's Services?"

"Yeah. But it'll be okay. They won't mind if I have some friends over. It'll look good, don't you think? Like Beast-Child actually does have some friends? And that I'm, you know, *liked* or something?"

Bernie, being the awesome friend that she is, gave me a soft but scathing lecture that of course Baki has friends and of course I am liked, but I don't need to prove that to Children's Services. And as much as I love her and her angelic wisdom, I knew, in that moment that she was wrong.

I *totally* needed to prove it.

And I would have been able to prove it too. I really would. If things hadn't gone so horribly tits-up.

NB: Honestly, Dear Reader, if you've had enough of my moaning for one day, I suggest you skip ahead. Or close your browser entirely. I wouldn't blame you. Nobody would.

Remember when I called my baking the devil's work earlier? Well I was wrong. The devil's work is cats. Only cats.

After Toddlers, four mams and their kiddos came back to the flat with me. Yes, the time of the Visit from Hell was nearing, but I was determined that if I couldn't avoid it, I would at least enter into it with a flawless sense of initiative.

Nicky and the social worker would be admitted to my spotless, fragrant flat, be bestowed with delicious baked goods on china plates and then happen upon a scene of exuberant mothers bouncing pink-faced toddlers on their knees and exchanging recipes for organic nappy rash cream or traditional Highland methods for potty training. Baki would be at the centre of it all, making everybody laugh with his adorable efforts to dance and then he'd rush into my arms, suddenly realising he can speak after all, and shrieking, "Mama my best friend!", showering me with kisses of indisputable love.

So powerful was this mirage of possibility that I wasn't even put off by Bernie grabbing me by the arm as we all tumbled into the hallway and hissing, "Where the flipping heck is everybody going to even sit? Did you think about that?"

No, evidently I had not thought about that. But no matter, because I am resourceful and adaptable and it only took thirty seconds to crash into my bedroom, artfully throw kiddies' toys over the unmade bed that Mesut had left in his wake and plump up the cushions of the patchy sofa of fame. Bernie joined in with my bright and perky tones, encouraging everybody to come through, find a spot to sit and wait whilst I went to put the kettle on and retrieve the tonnes of baked goods from the kitchen. This was all going to be okay. Cramped, but okay.

Nothing could have prepared me for what I saw next.

My baking . . . my lovely, sweet, delicious baking, was lying all over the kitchen floor, boxes upturned, lids flung in all directions, cakes demolished, scones torn apart, cookies well and truly crumbled.

It was ALL ruined.

I was vaguely aware that Bernie was by my side, gasping the air that I couldn't even find. "What the f . . . Jess. What happened?"

"I – I don't know . . . I . . . It was fine when I left this morning. All stacked up on the counter. It was fine." Then something cold, wet and sharp dug into my leg and I looked down. Baki. Biting my calf in lieu of the sweet delights he might have had. I scooped him up and he started to wail. Like my soul.

"Jess, what's this?" Bernie had spotted a piece of paper, folded up in the middle of the crumbly, sugary explosion on the floor. I knew instantly what it was but couldn't even guess what it would say.

Bernie picked it up and read above Baki's wails, "Jess, could you please consider putting lids on when storing your food? I'm afraid the cats have attacked it and I have to go to work now." Bernie stared at the letter and then at me. "Really? She just left this shit after *her* cats attacked it? What the hell, Jess?"

I knew there was more extreme lamenting to be done but I am so used to Cat-Crazy Flatmate's ridiculous notes that I just nodded slowly and felt a distinct wedge of dread lodge in my tummy. "Now we have nothing," I murmured.

"It doesn't matter. Let's just make tea and clear this up." Bernie started busying herself as I stood there with Baki clinging to my torso, tears being gulped back with insane amounts of devastated resolution, puddles of sad caramel and mounds of crushed cake all around me.

Before I knew it I was in the Co-op.

Yes, yes, I know I should have told Bernie where I was going. I should have stayed there and helped her with the epic clear-up that was apparently a result of *my* lack of lid-closing efforts. But all I could think about was the fact that I now had nothing to offer the professional child-stealers and that seemed like the worst crime in the world. Worse, even, than the parental neglect I was accused of.

Baki was still clinging onto me for dear life as I gate-crashed the Co-op in my fit of tenacious determination to buy sweet foodstuffs. Granted, I'd usually have him securely locked into a buggy during retail situations, but there had been no time for that.

I grabbed boxes upon boxes of shortbread and piled them high in one hand whilst allowing Baki to stretch and reach a fuck-lot of Crunch Corners with the other. That's okay. He could eat them later, that is, if I was deemed fit as a parent and he wasn't snatched away.

I took my now over-tired, squirmy little boy to the queue at the cashpoint and set him down on the ground. I checked my watch. Three minutes until the Visit from Hell. If this queue hurried the heck up, I could do this.

(*Just wondering. Have you ever tried to stand in a queue in a shop with a toddler? If you haven't I can lend you mine any time just so you can try it out.*)

Unfortunately, the quite frankly elderly-as-hell cashier in the Co-op seemed to be competing for the 'Slowest Sales Assistant on Earth' title and Baki saw no reason whatsoever to stand in place next to his mother for that length of time. He wanted to touch the shiny, wrapped objects on ALL of the shelves, fling them off and stamp on them repeatedly. He saw endless merit in dashing out of the automatic doors every time they opened, not giving the tiniest little shit that there was a main road outside and that we lost our place in the queue every time I had to run out there and effectively save his life.

During the absurdly long wait in said queue, he climbed on fridges, knocked over displays, did body-rolls under shelves, tore not one but *four* magazine covers and nicked things out of other people's baskets only to chuck them across the floor.

When, after a million years, we finally got to the till, the decrepit cashier leaned forward before scanning my things, winked a twinkling green eye and bounced her grey, wiry curls at me. "Aw, don't worry m'eudail. He's nought but a wee lad. You're doing a grand job, so you are." She patted my hand and then grabbed a Kit Kat off the counter. "This one's on me." She smiled and popped it in a plastic bag along with the shortbread.

Great. So I was now a bitch as well as a failing mother.

How could I have mind-cursed the nice old lady?

There was no time to indulge in my inadequacies, or the

tears that were threatening to burst into the open. I had to get home.

As Baki and I rounded the corner of the pub and started our climb up the steps to the door of the flat, we heard voices and looked up. There was Nicky and the social worker right at the top, about to knock on the door. The social worker's clutch of a battered clipboard and Nicky's curve of a frown was enough to push me into yet more of a head spin. My voice went all high and tinny. Fuck knows why.

"Nicky! I'm here! No need to knock. Me and Beast-Ch . . . me and Baki were just getting provisions from the shop. Here. I'll let you in. My keys are here somewhere."

Baki and I wriggled past them on the top step whilst Nicky did her best to smile and exchange pleasantries and tell me the social worker was called Aja. I kept going with my stupid, jangling voice and ushered them through to the hallway and into my room. At least they'd be impressed by all of my friends having a casual playdate together. Surely the room would be filled with motherly joy and childlike frolics by now – a scene that would have formed effortlessly in my absence. This was exciting. Before they'd even sat down, these child-stealing professionals would know there was nothing to worry about here.

As soon as I opened the door, the stench hit us.

And then the screams.

Nicky took in the scene before her and then swapped looks with Aja. "Jessica . . . are those . . . liqueurs?"

I worked hard to train my gaze on what the hell was going on, but Bernie put the picture together for me before I could figure it out. She jumped up in the tiny space available, left a flurry of baby wipes and cherry liqueur wrappers, and expertly took Nicky and Aja's coats. "Och, just a few little chocolates to calm some frayed tempers. Hardly an ounce of alcohol in them, really. We needed a distraction after the cat had his little accident and Jess here was out shopping so it was all we had . . ."

"Accident?" I squeaked.

Crunchy Nut Mam squawked up at me. "The cat shat in my handbag, Jess. Then Frida stepped in it. It set off World War Three with this lot. You know how kids are partial to a bit of shit."

I laughed. Because, I honestly didn't know what else to do. Then I was vaguely aware that Nicky was speaking.

"I'm sorry if you're busy with friends, Jessica. But we can't put this visit off I'm afraid. Is there somewhere, erm, a bit quieter we could go?"

"No need!" Crunchy Nut stood up and so did the other mams, grabbing their kids and steering them around the mountain of alcohol-filled sweets in the centre of the floor. "We'll go, Jess. Thanks for having us. It's been . . . well . . . we'll see you at Toddlers next time, eh? Good luck with the fasting."

As the women filed out of the door, leaving my shattered dreams of commune-like camaraderie in their wake, I stared at Bernie's wide open face. "Don't worry. It's all cleaned up now. Honest." She spoke in a kind of plea directed at Nicky and Aja. "No harm done to anyone. Do you want me to stay and plate up the food you bought?"

"No, it's okay. You go." I whispered, and knew it was time to face the music alone.

I'm not going to give you a blow-by-blow account of how the Visit from Hell actually went, Dear Reader. I expect you've had enough of my dramas for now. All I can do is thank you for sticking with me for this long, really.

In summary, Nicky and Aja sat facing me, perched on the

edge of the patchy sofa of fame with a lingering tang of cat shit in the air, appropriately understated revulsion twisting at the corners of their mouths. I couldn't even bring myself to apologise for what had happened, to tell them about the hidden litter trays or the home baking that would have replaced the liqueurs. I just threw boxes of Co-op shortbread at them. It all seemed ridiculous. And it was, Dear Reader, it was.

Baki is still here though. He's not been stolen from me. So at least I know I'm not an actual danger to my child. However, there were a few things said that may not have directly stabbed me in the heart, but at least pierced it a little.

1. The report of neglect has come in to Children's Services more than once over a period of the last few weeks, and from multiple anonymous sources
2. They are aware of my fasting for Ramadan and whilst they can't tell me not to do it (out of respect for Mesut's religion), they had a few words of 'advice' about looking after myself adequately so the same can be done for Baki
3. It has been reported that I have been seen stealing bottles of wine from the pub. Stealing! I hardly think my husband occasionally giving me an abandoned bottle of wine *that has already been paid for,* is stealing. And they were for Fuck-it Fridays anyway, so surely that's fine?
4. Nicky has my mental health questionnaires on file and she and Aja were asking about my postnatal depression. I told them that the therapeutic effects of Zumba, CBT counselling, making friends and going to Toddlers twice a week was ample evidence that I was better now. The occasional 'stolen' bottle of wine might have helped too

5. Eyes were cast dubiously around my living space and I felt I had to give every single thread of a reason why we are still living in this shit hole. Not helped by the repellent thump of inexplicably hard trance music literally shaking the room we were sitting in (and on a Tuesday afternoon. *Why?*)
6. They have taken down an itinerary of my typical week as well as my daily routine with Baki. They seem satisfied that I'm doing okay but Aja explained that the situation will have to be monitored, mainly due to the multiple reports and the cat shit incident today. Something to do with the dangers of Toxoplasmo-something which leads to weakened immune systems and breathing problems in infants

How the fuckery-fuck did we get from Co-op shortbread to kids not being able to breathe?

Due to some wonder of the universe that I simply cannot comprehend, Baki mercifully went down for a nap as soon as Nicky and Aja left. The poor lad was knackered. This gave me a chance to trudge to the bottom of the steps outside my front door and sit in a shaft of glittering sunlight that seemed to be there just for me.

I swept my eyes across the grey car park at the back of the pub, the line of ugly, half-melted wheelie bins overflowing with pub debris and the flash of pavement directly opposite, which led to the High Street. For such a dull scene, I wondered why everything sparkled and glowed. And then, after a few more seconds, I realised it was from a glorious combination of the dipping, late-afternoon sun and the onset of hot, unstoppable tears.

Now.

Now I could cry.

And I did. A lot.

It was inevitable, really.

"Wheesht, lassie. What's all this about?"

You'll never guess who it was.

Only the flipping Co-op lady.

"Wheesht now. You're having a bad day, are you so? Well, we all have those from time to time, eh? Where's that lovely wee boy of yours?" She stood in front of me, a Co-op bag in each hand, a mossy-coloured, quilted jacket hung over her shoulders and a vivid yellow cardigan peeping out from underneath it. She wore a pin badge of bright purple thistles on her coat collar that glinted in the same sun I'd been basking in and the grey of her tightly curled hair took a bit of a shine from it too. Her face wore the look of somebody on a mission, but happy to stop for unexpected pleasures, and she suddenly seemed a whole lot less decrepit and elderly than she had earlier on.

I sniffed. "He's . . . he's sleeping. And yeah, it's been a bad day. Thank you for stopping, but I'm okay."

"Of course you are, my darling. Even champions lose some rounds. Next time you're in the shop and you're feeling like this, just give me the nod. I'll make sure there's a Kit Kat for you. Lord knows us mothers have got to look out for each other."

I didn't have the heart to tell her that it would be several hours before I could even sniff the Kit Kat she'd given me earlier, so I just nodded and smiled. That seemed to do the trick and she marched away, her shopping and incredible kindness in tow.

It was thanks to the Co-op lady that I was able to find the energy to climb up the stairs and go back into the flat. It was thanks to her that I took out all the cat litter trays I'd hidden away yesterday, lined them again and placed them back in their rightful places. Without her I might not have had the presence of mind to finally remember where I'd left the DVD of Bob the

Builder and the Legend of the Golden Hammer (under Baki's travel cot) and entertain him with it for the remainder of the day.

Even though he probably needs an update from me, rather than this blog, I've been too exhausted to wait up for Mesut tonight. Since sundown, I've eaten a glorious Super Noodle and baked beans combo, climbed into bed with a practical bucket of tea and my long-awaited Kit Kat from the Co-op lady. It is from here I have been writing to you, Dear Reader, and reflecting on one hell of a day.

And maybe, just maybe, if I squint my eyes, my outlook and my psyche, I can see there are some positives shining in there somewhere. Could it be that Ramadan is working some kind of magic on me after all? Tomorrow might tell . . .

Night.

AngelBernie
What a day, poppet! You deserve more credit than you're giving yourself. Plus I feel all defensive of my cherry liqueurs now. They really are harmless. Honest. Oooh – just got a little kick off the babe to tell me you're amazing. There are a few angels fluttering for you too.
Jess.AKYOL
Bernie, I nibbled on one of your liqueurs before my Super Noodles and I can report that they are rank (Geordie word – look it up). But thank you for today. What would I do without you?

CrunchyNut_Mummy
Bernie told me all about your blog, Jess. Why did you not tell everyone at Toddlers? We'll all be reading it. My handbag is

done for, by the way. Might pester your flatmate for a new one.

Jess.AKYOL

Oh god, this is embarrassing! Thank you so much for reading and I'm sorry for today. I just needed moral support, I guess. Sorry about your bag. I'll see if I've got a spare one you can have.

please_do_not_ignore_it

Thank you for your nice post I really enjoy to visit this type of post. I feel very happy while I'm entering your post. Thank you for your nice post..

Jess.AKYOL

Thank you for your nice comment.

Angnonymous

Co-op lady is ace. It's those unexpected moments of kindness that really break / fix us at times, isn't it?

Jess.AKYOL

Oh my god, totally. I'm glad you get it.

Angnonymous

I think I do.

OliverChen1!

Jess, I love your honesty. That's a day that would have anybody running for the hills, matey. What postnatal depression though? Do I need to read back on these posts?

Jess.AKYOL

Maybe. If you want to know what's gone down since I saw you last. I'm cool though – don't worry.

Not-A-Granny-Flora

Don't worry – the social workers are just doing their job and they'll see soon enough they have more urgent matters to attend to. Our cats pooed everywhere when you were little and you turned out alright! Do you want me to send you some Kit Kats? Because I can do that. The Co-op lady sounds nice. I knew the Scots would look after you.

Jess.AKYOL

No, I don't need Kit Kats, Mam. The beans have only just come into their own.

Fab4CoolDad

Tell the Co-op lady you have much more expensive tastes than Kit Kats. See if she's got any of these (George Harrison liked them) . . . 'Savoy Truffle'.

Jess.AKYOL

Will do, Dad. Though I think the poshest the Co-op stretches to is Bernie's cherry liqueurs.

NO_Just_DON'T(1)

Is it any wonder the social workers are coming back? Cat faeces is toxic to babies, everybody knows that. Except, it would seem, you.

Night-sun-ella

Noooo! This has been the shittiest of shitty days for you, sweetie. But never fear because after an epic journey in Keith the Van, Dotty and I will be in your general vicinity! I can hardly believe that I get to squeeze you tomorrow . . . the cats had better make way . . . 🐱🐱🐱🐱🐱

MesutAk1

Always I tell you living with cats is not good idea. One day, Gulazer, we have own flat and not cats anywhere. You sleeping now, I even take laptop off top of your belly and then I read your post. You looking so sweet and beautiful. I sorry I working today.

And I knows visit not from hell like you says. Nicky sees you a good mum like you are. Is all okay. Seni seviyorum.

Jess.AKYOL

God, did I fall asleep with the actual laptop on me? That's not good. What if it had fallen off and broken? Or decapitated a random cat on the way down? It's morning now and I can't even contemplate these things without coffee. Plus you're snoring and Beast-Child's going to start wailing from his room any minute. Must go and get him before Cat-Crazy Flatmate wakes up and beats me into submission with passive-aggressive notes about the volume of his screams! Love you too, Gandalf. Always.

8

DAY 8 - REFRESHMENT-BASED FRIENDSHIP

Muirdrith, Highlands of Scotland, UK
Weds 18th Aug 2010
Sunrise / Suhoor: 5.44am
Sunset / Iftar: 8.53pm

Dear Reader – you're back! I'm so happy because a wonderful thing happened today.

And an awful thing, I guess.

Wonderful Thing = Ella arrived! She rocked up in Keith the Flower Power Van with her daughter, Dotty, rapping on my door and bearing a huge bouquet of wild flowers, heather and spiky branches that she had "gathered from the bounties of the Scottish roadside". Apparently we are to use it to beat off Children's Services.

Awful Thing = Ella is mortified that I have not factored in how Ramadan might affect her visit. Especially when she arrived positively bedraggled and starving after an ELEVEN HOUR road trip with a toddler which is enough to finish off the best of us.

"Where are your biscuits?" Ella wailed, slamming and crashing her way around my kitchen as I tried to wrestle her 'bouquet' into a pint glass. "Surely you have some Hobnobs lurking in here somewhere?"

The two toddlers raced into the room on hearing the word 'Hobnobs', jaws stretched open and eyes wide with the flawless anticipation that sweet, oaty goods were about to be hurled their way.

"Oh buggar. Sorry. No Hobnobs in the establishment. There's some shortbread left over from yesterday's Visit from Hell? Or there's a Co-op just around the corner. We can go and get whatever you want."

"Well, yes, we are going to have to do something about this . . . situation," Ella said, flinging her hands towards my very empty kitchen cupboards. "Ooooh, hang on. Can I eat these?" Ella pulled a bumper pack of Muirdrith Oatcakes out of a cupboard and scrutinised the label. "'*The spirit of Muirdrith baked into pure, humble oats.*' If I chuck some sugar over them, they might come up to Hobnob standards. What do you think?"

"That might work, but do you see how you got these out of the cupboard with a Scottish flag sticker on the door? That means it's not ours. That's Cat-Crazy Flatmate's cupboard. So no oatcakes for us."

"Ah," Ella nodded and looked around the tiny, grease-brown kitchen. "She's got a fair amount of cupboard space, hasn't she? All those flags! You should put Turkish flag stickers on yours."

"Not something I have the time or inclination for, Ella. And hopefully we will have our own actual kitchen one of these days and there will be no need for stupid stickers on stupid doors."

"Quite." Ella put the oatcakes back and gave me her most winning, piercing-studded smile. "Well, put the kettle on then. A cuppa will do for now."

Poor Ella. I should have thought this through. I know, better than most people, that due to her constantly high levels of energy she needs food like the rest of us need air. And I know fine well that her early evening pick-me-up involves a pint of cider and black and a sharing bag (not to be shared) of Flaming Hot Doritos – even more so since Dotty was born. Why didn't I think to chuck those particular items in my basket yesterday when I was freaking out at the Co-op?

Just so you know, Ella is one of the best people in my life. I met her years ago when I worked in community arts and was at some boring seminar-type-thing. I was there with Gillie (also in the Best People League), who I ran my business with at the time. We both clocked Ella in seconds as being somebody who looked 'interesting' (i.e. vastly younger than the majority of the community arts crowd and partial to an impromptu puppet show using buffet implements). A hop, skip and a leap of faith later and the three of us were as inseparable as a coven bound by blood magic.

And Dorito magic. And that of Cider / Chardonnay, depending on how we were feeling.

It was another kind of fortuitous magic that Ella and I had our first babies at around the same time. Not long after Mesut appeared in my life, Ella had her wicked way with a dating app and bagged a decent, bespectacled bloke called Miles. He is the absolute opposite of anybody you could imagine her ending up with. He's as serious as she is playful. As reserved as she is flamboyant. He's a professor at Cambridge University – a professor of Musical Theory, no less.

It's strange to see one of your best mates with a man who appears, to all intents and purposes, to be in a different universe. Especially when she uproots her whole life and goes to live with him in said universe. Although, having said that, I doubt Miles was going to give up his Cambridge professorship to go and watch Ella make puppet shows in a sleepy town in the North

East of England. To be fair, Ella could storm any place with her awesome puppets. Even Cambridge.

Anyway, it's all turned out beautifully because now they have Dotty and she is just a beauty to behold. She wears glasses, like her dad and has the sassy sparkle of her mam, minus the legendary facial piercings. It gives me a special kind of motherly thrill to see Dotty and Baki in a room together. Even if they are wailing loudly about Hobnobs. I plan for them to have the closeness of cousins because Ella has definitely earned her status as sister to me over the years.

After Ella rampaged the Co-op (I stayed at home to divert the babes with all sorts of buzzing, flashing, plastic shit), we got those kitchen cupboards stocked up. I gave her a briefing. "Ella, please know that just because I'm fasting, there's nothing stopping you from raiding the biscuit tin or the fridge whenever you like. Just avoid the Scottish flag stickers. I'm not going to let you go hungry. Honest."

"Too bloody right!" Ella's face surfaced from my open biscuit tin. "Jess, our friendship is more or less built on biscuits. And cakes. And pastries. And, well, *mutual* alcohol consumption. But it's cool. Dotty and I will sort ourselves out during the day and by night we can cement and honour those years of refreshment-based friendship."

"Err, yeah. Sounds good. Except I agreed with Mesut no alcohol. Not til the end of the month. You can knock yourself out though. Obviously."

She looked a little deflated. "Ah. Okay. But hang on, I'm here for a few days and that includes Saturday so what, my fabulous nutcase of a friend, are we going to do about . . ."

It suddenly hit me. "Oh shit . . . of course . . . what about . . ."

"X Factor!"

I ask you, Dear Reader, is it even possible to get through the active viewing of X Factor without chips and dips and WINE???

Should we call Simon Cowell and make sure we aren't breaking some universal code of practice? Will it affect the phone polls if we aren't consuming snacks and wine by the bucket load? And if so, would he consider changing the start time to after sunset on account of all the Muslims who could, by their very own religious efforts, knock off the cosmic algorithms of the entire thing?

Ella was mortified.

Me too.

Yet another precious routine of mine torn apart by Ramadan.

A routine I really need after the events of yesterday.

Never mind. We softened the blow tonight by getting the little ones in bed early. Ella helped me drag Baki's travel cot into mine and Mesut's room and find the only workable space to put it (at the foot of our bed, wedged next to the drawers which now won't open). This has left only just enough space in Baki's room for Ella to pump up her air mattress, upon which she and Dotty will be sleeping together. "No worries – we've been co-sleeping since I popped her out, Jess. Miles gets conjugal visits once in a while but mostly he sleeps in the farty, stinky spare room."

After a fairly epic bath and bed routine, Ella and I worked together in the kitchen to make a feast for sundown. God, it was *so* nice to have company. As you know, Mesut is usually pouring pints or doling out kebabs at the second the sun goes down, so I'm generally alone for the big moment. Having Ella there, telling her about the nightmare that was yesterday and how impossibly hard it's been fasting whilst also undergoing a personal crisis, was cathartic beyond belief.

She thought it was hilarious that as soon as 8.53pm came and went, I was nibbling on a date and taking careful sips of water before anything else. "Don't you just want to attack a tower of steaks? Or down a pint of cider?"

"Well, yeah, at first. But you quickly realise that just makes you feel sick, which obviously has knock-on effects for the next day. So now, I try to remember what Mesut told me and have the dates. Apparently they're full of magnesium and potassium. Fibre and carbohydrates. Basically, they're a quick fix to replace any lost energy."

Ella nodded thoughtfully, and twiddled the ruby-red stud embedded in her bottom lip. "And you've needed a fuck-load of energy lately, sweetie, what with the Children's Services shenanigans and cat's shitting everywhere and writing that flipping blog every day. I honestly don't know how you do it."

"I know, right? But you know me and writing. I always find a way."

"Indeed you do." Ella eyed up the steaming garlic baguettes we'd just drawn from the oven, and the veggie spag bol waiting for us on a tablecloth on the floor. "Anyway, speaking of energy. Can we?"

"Let's do it!"

And we tucked in good and proper, sealing that refreshment-based friendship of ours in lovely, oozy, garlicky style.

Whilst we ate together tonight, I realised that as much as this month is about me learning how to fast, about denying myself certain things at certain times to make way for the hollow delight of cleansing, it's about something else too.

I think it's also about joy.

I've always been a fan of garlic bread. But tonight it took on a whole new meaning. The golden crust was radiant and inviting, the crunch of it between my teeth sweetly gratifying and contrasting perfectly with the soft, whipped cloud of hot, baked dough. It seemed nothing could improve on this winning combination . . . that was until the garlic butter, stealthy and smooth, trickled onto my tongue with the salty kindness of a mellow kiss.

Has garlic bread always tasted this good?

Or is Ramadan helping me find the joy in food?

I'm thinking that tomorrow the Co-op needs to be relieved of its entire stock of the stuff. Baguettes, flatbreads, pizzas, dough balls – I don't care, as long as it's oozing with that incredible, garlicky, elixir of life.

Probably a good idea to get up at four in the morning though, and ensure floss, Listerine and toothpaste has reached every possible crevice in my mouth. Then, hopefully, Ella and Dotty will not jet back to Cambridge to escape the horror that is my breath.

And I need them in my life right now. Because Ramadan is helping me find the joy in them too.

Night.

Night-sun-ella
Noooooo! They can't cancel X Factor. It's okay – I'll eat and drink the equivalent of what all the Muslims would have been consuming to make up for it. Phone Cowell and let him know.

Jess.AKYOL
On it. Why didn't you just come into my room and tell me that? How are you even still awake after all that driving?!

Night-sun-ella
I'm not. I'm in a state of hypnagogia (Miles taught me that word when I was postnatal. I'm surprised I remember it). I have a toddler fixed to my boob. Told you those days weren't over. Good thing I have my trusty dungaree-pjs.

Jess.AKYOL
Trusty they are. And a sight to behold.

GILLIE_LASS77
That's it! I'm dropping everything and coming up there. Tell those babes that their favourite Auntie Gillie is on her way, with an abundance of Hobnobs. Anything else you want me to bring, Jess?
Jess.AKYOL
Really? Ah, no. Just your beautiful self. Mesut will be outnumbered!

LifeIsYoursLindy
Is this the Gillie and Ella I remember hearing so much about that night on the beach, Jess? How lovely – a reunion!
Jess.AKYOL
Yes! Tis them! Hopefully I only said nice things about them. I can't remember. We drank quite a lot of Turkish wine that night, didn't we?
LifeIsYoursLindy
We did, and it was delicious. And don't worry, you're safe. I just remember you talking about how close you all were and how Gillie and Ella got you through the break-up with your ex. Is Gillie still seeing that dodgy Turkish gangster-type?
Jess.AKYOL
I bloody hope not. Hopefully I'll get an update when she gets here. She lives back in her homeland down south now so lord knows how she'll get here. She'll have even further to travel than Ella. I do have a habit of moving to far-flung places.

Angnonymous
Maybe a fast from X Factor as well as food and drink is in order? Dare I say it, it might be worth exploring?
Jess.AKYOL
Angnonymous, I love you for reading but I cannot accept this kind of blasphemy on my blog.

Angnonymous
Okay, I get it! Will not blaspheme again. Keep going – you're doing amazing.

AngelBernie
Ah, the Angel, Isdra is with you tonight I reckon, poppet. Maybe Ella is Isdra in disguise! She sounds completely fab and I can't wait to meet her.
Jess.AKYOL
Isdra? Okay, spill.
AngelBernie
She's the angel of spiritual, physical and emotional nourishment. I can tell you're feeling it in that there garlic bread. She acts as the Den Mother for the garrison – making sure they are fulfilled and happy. Basically, the Angel of Food.
Jess.AKYOL
You are completely bonkers, and I love you.

Fab4CoolDad
If I know you and Ella (and I think I do) you'll solve the X Factor conundrum. The Beatles can help you, of course . . . 'We Can Work It Out'.
Jess.AKYOL
Of course! This makes me feel much better. Thanks Dad! 

Combustable.Apocalips
X Factor not permitted in Islam. Singing not permitted. I am not permitting you to watch the X Factor if you say you doing Ramadan. Music can be diversionary and therefore not permitted.
MesutAk1
I think you knows, brother (or sister?) that music is okay if not interrupting prayer time.

Combustable.Apocalips
You are loathsome person if you permit this. You disgusting and shocking to me and all other Muslims.

MesutAk1
And you calling me names definitely not permitted. May Allah bless you.

9

DAY 9 - ICE CREAM INJURY

Muirdrith, Highlands of Scotland, UK
Thurs 19th Aug 2010
Sunrise / Suhoor: 5.46am
Sunset / Iftar: 8.51pm

I'm six days into my fasting challenge and today I got my first proper dizzy spell.

It's fine if you want to take a moment to congratulate me.

It's hard to understand how one can feel at all light on the feet when one has consumed all the garlic bread in the world the night previous. But that's the way Ramadan showed up for me today.

The spell hit me as I sauntered down Muirdrith high street, in a *my-child-is-at-nursery-for-the-entire-morning* type of way, so it serves me bloody right really. That'll teach me to be so happy to be rid of my beautiful boy.

Considering the garlic bread, I'm not sure what caused the dizziness. So let's look at the facts:

1. My body had not been fed for at least 12 hours

2. It was hot (well, hot for the Highlands of Scotland, anyway)
3. Last night's sleep pattern was constantly interrupted by Mesut nudging me awake to drink pints upon pints of water
4. I continue to be in the nightmarish reality that actual, formal people in an actual, formal department of the council think I am a mother worthy of investigation
5. I am possibly allergic to garlic bread (nooooooooo!)
6. All of the above?

Regardless of the cause, feeling dizzy was shit. Given my already pale, northerly complexion (I fit right into the Highlands as much as my husband sticks out), it does not become me.

I just about managed to ward off a blackout on the high street and returned home to the capable and tattooed arms of Ella. "Come on, my favourite little waif. Get yourself in bed and have one of your famous lying down sessions. You know, just to liven things up a bit."

Poor Ella. She's such an on-the-go type of gal. Back in Cambridge she'd probably be spending her time off teaching Dotty how to make puppets out of Miles's old socks or something. I wonder if Mesut would miss a few of his . . ?

As it happens, Ella spent the morning cooking and enjoying a brunchathon with Dotty in the kitchen whilst I pretty much melted back into bed. Thank god Cat-Crazy Flatmate was downstairs stock-taking with Mesut so she couldn't monitor Ella's kitchen cupboard usage which I'm assuming was questionable, at best. Thankfully, by the time I had to go and pick up Baki, I felt marginally less woozy and actually quite excited to see his chubby little chops again.

Ella, Dotty and I went to meet him at the colourful gates of

'Wee Bairns World' only to be told he'd been "An absolute angel sent from god" (must remember to tell Bernie she has a potential protégé) and that I must be doing something right to be mam to a child such as him.

Nearly cried.

Obviously.

All power to the Co-op lady but it seems it's not just her kindness that can transform me into a gibbering wreck.

"Right, enough of this, Jessica Akyol – show me some of magical Muirdrith!" Ella used her thumbs to wipe some warm tears off my cheeks and gave me one of her glinty, winning grins. She and Dotty were fuelled up on eggs and hash browns and I had some snacks I could give to Baki, so off we went.

I'm not kidding when I say that sometimes it feels like Muirdrith has everything you could want from a town. A beautiful beach landscape that stretches out forever. A thriving high street. And a river that is so fresh and vivacious, you can't help but smile as you walk along its banks.

As we strolled along there today, I noticed there were the most intense, jewel-like greens everywhere. If there's one thing that Scotland does well, it's green. After having lived in Turkey for a while, it's quite a refreshing change from the golden gleam of dry sand, the starched-white shocks of apartment blocks and the silver rush of solar panels winking down onto sun-cracked, cement-grey streets.

You might think the Highlands would always be stealing your eyes to the sky. It is, after all, pretty impressive. I can't argue that the stereoptypical thunder-grey clouds swollen with rain don't impress against such startling expanses of violet. Or that spectral, snow-brushed planes of diamond white don't hover over us with alarming regularity. And granted, I do adore the way those skies print their stubborn image onto the river's surface, however warped or buckled they might become. But it's the greens that get me.

It's the soaked, shimmering leaves that hang over the river, the long, writhing grasses that steal into it, the mossy rocks that soak under it like hidden gems. On more than one occasion in the months since we moved here, these greens – in their whole, sacred spectrum – have saved me from disappearing entirely under the grey veil of depression.

Walking there then, with Ella, Dotty and Baki, I smiled and let my gratitude warm me. How good it was to feel like that with some of my favourite people by my side.

We neared the harbour and I heard the friendly, musical clang of bobbing boat masts. This is one of my favourite sounds but was unfortunately short-lived, because Baki suddenly realised where we were and decided he wanted an ice cream from the imminently close seaside parlour place, meaning he started his high-pitched and frankly ungentlemanly screeching, reserved especially for frozen dessert situations.

Of course, you know and I know that one day, with the proper training and tuition, he will be able to say, "I'll have an Ice Cream please, Mammy, if you'd be so kind." Sadly, we are nowhere near that yet, so his desperate gibberish rose in volume and tenacity as we got closer to the parlour.

"Oh how lush!" Ella cried. "He really is the cutest, isn't he?"

I thought it best not to answer.

Especially as Dotty was tugging at her mam's stripey dungarees and whispering for an ice cream. *Whispering*! How the effing hell did Ella get her daughter to *whisper* when she wants something?

Anyway, once we got to the offending ice cream establishment and Baki had slammed his fist at the picture of the ice cream he wanted (triple chocolate bomb explosion, obviously), we were met with the dreaded and trembling statement by a seemingly terrified twelve-year-old girl, "Sorry, we don't have any of that one left."

Even before I knelt down to the buggy, all set to use my most practiced, calming and soothing maternal tones, Baki knew what was going down. The kid ain't stupid. Especially when ice cream is the primary motivator.

I'll spare you the details, but you perhaps need to know the basics . . . Baki suddenly declared it:

National Tantrums Day.

Or, more accurately:

National Tantrums in Public Day.

Or, if you're really going for the proper title: *National Ice Cream Related Tantrums In Public Resulting in Intense Humiliation / Minor Injuries to Mother Day.*

I was today years old when I learned that waffle cones can actually sustain injuries to soft tissue i.e. I now have a sexy cut-lip situation going on thanks to the tenacity of said cone being thrust in my face.

I swear to fuck knows who, if Allah doesn't beam me down a medal or a sticker or something for not licking my goddamn lips when banana-chunky-choc-nut ice cream was plastered *all over them*, I am FINISHED.

All the while, Dotty had her whispered request met with a vanilla cone that sat beautifully in her happy little hands, her eyes wide with fascination at the scene unfolding before her. She'd never seen her Auntie Jess in such a state before. And hopefully never will again.

When we finally got back to the flat, Ella and I over-ruled Baki and declared it, *National Whatever Toddlers Bloody Well Like Day*, and grasped for a DVD, any DVD, that might bring us a few moments peace. It turned out Shrek hit the mark.

And it was today, day nine, that I really bewailed the loss of a cup of tea. Surely, days like these are the reason the British are so famous for bestowing a humble cuppa with truly transformative powers. Ella flicked on the kettle with a sorry glance my way. "I'm sorry, sweet cheeks, but I'm gonna die if I don't have a cuppa right now." I hung my head and nodded.

Anyway, it seems Ella was wrong. Because at that moment, Mesut magically swooped in with a frosty bottle of Chardonnay that had been abandoned in the pub and lo and behold, Ella did not die!

When the Beast-Child was finally tucked up in bed, this time right next to his perfect, whispering, bespectacled friend, and the sun had set on yet another day, I had to use my last scrap of willpower not to reach for the bottle too. Mesut never would have known. He spent ten minutes with us when delivering the stolen-not-stolen wine for Ella, but then had to go back to work . . . but I just couldn't do it. I haven't come this far to buckle to the evils of alcohol now. And besides, it was sweet, cold water that my body really wanted. So that's what it got.

And dough balls. ALL the dough balls.

Not-A-Granny-Flora

For goodness sake, Jessie, you're having dizzy spells now so I do wish you'd stop. At least Ella is there to look after you. And your husband is bringing you wine! Maybe show some appreciation?

Jess.AKYOL

Mother, I'm very grateful but Mesut brought the wine for Ella, not me. And it was just one teensy dizzy spell. I am FINE.

Night-sun-ella

It's all good, mumsy. I'm keeping an eye on her and she really is doing a fandabydozy job. I'm ultra-proud of her. Baki really

tested her patience today but she was AMAZING how she dealt with it, regardless of the cut lip and ice-creamy face.
Jess.AKYOL
Oh god, I do love you. Will you marry me? Ooops! Already married.
Night-sun-ella
I would SO marry you though. When am I going to properly see that long-haired lover of yours? Today's wine-delivering effort was simply not enough! Does he sleep or work, like, all the time?
Jess.AKYOL
Let's wake him up tomorrow morning! Ramadan or not, he needs to see you!

Fab4CoolDad
As long as the dizzy spells are few and far between I reckon you'll be alright, love. Anyway, The Beatles quite liked feeling dizzy. Try listening to . . . 'Dizzy Miss Lizzy'.
Jess.AKYOL
Good choice, Dad! Hopefully there will be no more dizzy spells though.

Angnonymous
I LOVE that part of the river in Muirdrith. So serene. Lap it all up, Jess. You're very lucky to live there.
Jess.AKYOL
So you know Muirdrith then? You live round here?
Angnonymous
Kinda.

GILLIE_LASS77
Brace yourselves girls . . . I will be in your jewel-green midst tomorrow! And I have a surprise for you.
Jess.AKYOL

Yey! Careful with the surprises though . . . I'm a bit of a waif these days, apparently. Don't know if my nerves can take it.
Night-sun-ella
Really, Gillie? Tomorrow? Oh I can't WAIT to squeeze your cheeks! (and yes, ALL of them 😉)

OliverChen1!
Sounds like a tough day, matey. Keep going! I'm thinking my camera would like those greens by the river.
Jess.AKYOL
Thanks Oliver. It would! You should get yourself up here, it's a photographer's dream.

ShelleyMadMum
Hi Jess. I go to the same Toddler group as you at the Community Centre. We've bonded over the custard creams a couple of times. CrunchyNut_Mummy told me about your blog! It made me laugh when u talked about Baki raging over ice cream – I'm glad it's not just my twins who act like devils when we go out!
Jess.AKYOL
Really? Oh, that makes me feel better. Hopefully we will bond over custard creams again one day! Thanks so much for reading.

CrunchyNut_Mummy
Don't worry, Jess. Ice cream always gets them going!
Jess.AKYOL
Doesn't it? If only I'd had your box of Crunchy Nut to chuck at him. Might have saved myself an injury.
CrunchyNut_Mummy
Told you they were lifesavers!

MesutAk1
I am thinking you and Ella maybe should getting married. You

in same bed together now, sleeping like lambs. And Baki and Dotty on weird air mattress thing. Only place for me to sleep is patchy sofa, Gulazer, and for long time I not getting comfy. Finally I realising it because of your strange storage space for chocolate and biscuits in hole of sofa cushion. I take all out now and we find new place in morning. Sofa not proper place for family-sized Galaxy chocolate. And please, you not let Ella near me in morning. It very late night in pub with fighting and things breaking everywhere. So glad you sleeping and not hearing it. I kissed your bad lip and it will getting better. Baki not mean it. İkinizide çok seviyorum.

10

DAY 10 – A GIFT

Muirdrith, Highlands of Scotland, UK
Fri 20th Aug 2010
Sunrise / Suhoor: 5.48am
Sunset / Iftar: 8.48pm

This morning, Ella potentially crossed the ancient and moral boundaries of Ramadan.

It wasn't entirely her fault.

All she did was greet Mesut in her customary way. The way she's always done it.

She stuck her tongue in his ear.

Okay, so she burst into the bedroom, where he was still sleeping on the patchy sofa of fame, and stuck her tongue in his ear.

Okay, so she burst into the bedroom, while he was sleeping on the patchy sofa of fame, climbed on top of him, bounced around a bit and *then* stuck her tongue in his ear.

She was just being friendly.

"Eurgh!! Nightsun! Really I not wanting swear at you but for love of Allah, please get OFF!!" There aren't many whose tone of voice could cause Ella to stagger back like that, but Mesut is definitely in the running.

However, when he stumbled into Baki's room in his dressing gown ten minutes later, to find us all watching Shrek for the bazillionth time, he'd softened quite a bit. "Nightsun!" he beamed. "You knows you can't do ear thing when I fasting. Is shameful. But I can hug you. Come here!"

She threw every ounce of herself at him and squeezed hard. "Oooh, you naughty man! Where have you been? I've been in your humble abode for the last two days and have hardly even seen you! You do have a wife and a child you know."

"I knows, I knows," he said, sheepishly, as she finally released him. "Is Ramadan, you knows? Sleeping is best way to getting through, Nightsun."

Let me just step in here and explain the 'Nightsun' thing.

Okay, so it was 2007, and I'd been having a long-distance relationship with Mesut for about a year. I invited Ella to come on holiday to Turkey with me to meet him properly (she'd met him before during a whirlwind girlie week away before he basically shook my world right up, but all she really remembered were his outstanding Pinacoladas, and he certainly didn't remember her on account of the millions of tourists he dealt with every season).

Anyway, we were very excited to be spending a fortnight together in Mesut's apartment and even more excited to be picked up by him and a friend at the airport in the dead of night. I'd jokily stated on the phone a few nights before: "We want to be picked up from the airport, whisked to the nearest beach, and we want to drink Turkish lager under the stars." This was my knee-jerk reaction to having worked like a dog in the weeks leading up to the holiday. I was desperate for some escapism.

Mesut totally delivered. One hour after stepping off the plane, there we all were, sitting on the smoothest of sands, drinking the coolest of lagers and enjoying the gentle, ghostly ripple of moonlit waves at our feet.

Ella was so completely chilled, which was very unusual for her. She'd just finished a mammoth puppet program touring juvenile detention centres, of all places, and she was overdue a holiday.

"Ah, isn't the moon beautiful? It's so bright," she exclaimed as she tipped her head up to the sky with a long, contented sigh.

"I am not understand," Mesut said. "Moon? Bright?"

"Yes, the moon, in the sky," Ella said, gesturing to the huge great silver disc that was our only light here on this remote stretch of sand. "It's so gorgeous, don't you think?"

Mesut flashed a glance my way. Even in the darkness I could sense the mischief. "I not knowing this . . . moon." He looked up at the sky, searching for what Ella could possibly mean.

Ella looked at me and I just stared back blankly. Should I dig her out of this or not? "You know," she half-pleaded, "the moon, the big bright thing in the sky at night. It's above us right now. It's almost full. It goes away during the day . . ?" I could sense her getting a sweat on. She'd been so intent on getting along with Mesut, so nervous about meeting him because she knew how much he meant to me. She'd already fretted profusely about the language barrier and how it might affect their connection. Oops, come to think of it, I may have mentioned that to Mesut on the phone.

Now Mesut's mate was in on it too, as they both shrugged, with very convincing looks of confusion plastering their faces. Ella stepped it up a notch. "Okay, it's a bit like this." She still had her arm outstretched, so blatantly pointing at the bloody moon, she must have thought Mesut a complete fool. "It's like the sun, but during the night. You understand?" She slowed her pace of speech. "They swap places. So, the, moon, is, almost, like, a night sun . . ? A sun that shines at night. Does that make sense? A Night Sun?"

The poor lass was sweating.

"Mesut, you idiot!" I shouted. "Ella, he knows perfectly well what the moon is. Look at him!" Mesut was rolling about laughing, holding onto his friend's shoulder and biting his knuckles to curb the laughter.

That was all Ella needed. She sprang up from her spot on the sand, launched herself at him, pounding him all over with her fists. "You total shithead! Do you know what that means? I bet you bloody do, because you are one!"

"I tell you what I knows!" Mesut said, as he tried and failed to seize her flying fists, "You not Ella anymore. You now called Nightsun. Your new name!"

Now she was laughing too, and sticking her tongue in his ear until he cried out in surprise and they both fell back on the sand, giggling. Bloody hell. An hour into our holiday and my fiancé and my bestie already needed supervising.

And so, Nightsun stuck.

And it's still sticking three years later.

After the excitement of getting Ella and Mesut in the same room together, 'Nightsun' and I went on to have a jam-packed day with the kiddos. And during the events that unfolded, I have happily and unexpectedly concluded that whoever invented Ramadan totally knew what they were doing. Despite what us uneducated Brits may think, I have identified three enormous benefits to participating in this seemingly nonsensical ritual.

Shall I share them with you? Oh, go on then . . .

1. Genius Money Saving Strategy: I was scratting about in my purse today, to find money for an admission fee to the Black Isle Wildlife Park (I knew Beast-Child would be right at home there). A very strange phenomenon had taken place. The money I'd put in there at the start of the week was still there! Can you imagine such a thing? That means that I've gone a whole five days with hardly spending *anything*. That means no superfluous 'topping-up'. No silly purchasing of 'essentials' inexplicably omitted from the shopping list. The emptiness of my belly is, in turn, facilitating the fullness of my purse. Maybe the current coalition government should consider passing a Ramadan law in order to solve the British economic crisis. Let's face it, stranger laws have been passed (did *you* know it's illegal to handle salmon in suspicious circumstances?)
2. Genius Time Saving Strategy: When you're denying yourself in such a way as I am right now, there is a tendency to wish the day away. Anyone who has ever had a shitty little job and watched the clock will tell you that this approach will, guaranteed, make time go even slower. So today, when I asked Ella what time it was, I assumed the volume of wildlife-related activity we had undergone with the kiddos would have brought us magically to bedtime. But no. "Two pm" came the reply. How the effing heck do these magical hours keep appearing? Is Paul McKenna in on all of this? And why can't I find these extra hours when I do actually want them? It's so fucking sinister

3. Genius Exercise Avoidance Strategy: You are most likely, by now, familiar with my special penchant for napping. And as part of this totally justified inertia, I have also managed to avoid any and all forms of exercise since Ramadan began. As I've mentioned before, Zumba really helps me in the endorphin stakes, and therefore warded off the grey veil of depression when it was at its heaviest. However, on account of the sweat I am likely to produce during all that hip-shimmying, I think it is only safe to avoid it at all costs. And probably for a while afterwards too, just until my body adjusts. And then, of course, I'll ease myself in gently because, you know, I don't want to pull something. Maybe it's better I avoid exercise properly until after Christmas. You see? Perfectly legitimate exercise avoidance strategy

In conclusion, I think the entire Muslim population might be onto something here. Either that, or I'm just pissed off that yet again I did not get an ice cream while we were out and about and I am hopelessly looking for justification for my actions.

I think I'll sleep on it.

BLOG POST / UPDATE:

Well, Dear Reader, I did, indeed, go to sleep to allow the apparent benefits of Ramadan to sink in. However, I was rudely awakened by a loud knocking at the door around midnight.

Ella scuttled to the door before me, her Dotty being a bit of a light sleeper. "Is that the mental cat woman or your bloody husband without a key or something?"

"I doubt it. I can still hear the Black Eyed Peas doing their usual round-up. They won't be back for a bit." Then there was a distinct giggle behind the door. And the possible clinking of a glass. "Fuck, Ella. Do you think we've got winos on the doorstep?"

"Come on Jess, I'm fucking FREEZING out here!"

Shitting hell. It was a wino that knew my name.

I tentatively opened the door a couple of inches, only to have it flung forcefully into my face by a flurry of maroon hair and fur coat. "Really, Gillie?" I heard Ella exclaim as I extricated myself from behind the door. "Midnight?"

"Yes! It took us that long to drive up here, you loons!" True to her word, Gillie had landed.

Hang on a minute. 'Us'?

Gillie strode into the porch, shivering in her floor-length fur coat. I could barely see past it on account of its rainbow fluffiness and occasional cluster of sparkly threads clearly meant to beguile the eyes. I wanted to ask her why on earth she was wearing a fur coat in August but I could see she had somebody with her . . . somebody trying to climb the steps below and emerge behind the distracting spectacle of her fashion choices.

Fuck me.

It was Oliver Chen.

"Alright, matey? I do believe this is not the first time you've been surprised to see me." Oliver came at me with open arms and warm smiles, fondly alluding to the time Gillie had arranged for him to land slap-bang in the middle of our life-changing trip to Istanbul four years earlier.

They had a bit of a 'thing' back then.

I have no idea about now.

"Here you go. Something to help you celebrate when you get to the end of Ramadan." He pushed two bottles of red wine into my hands. "And Ella! How long has it been, matey?" Ella beamed, already under the awesome spell that is Oliver. No tongues in the ear at least, we can all be grateful for that.

After I bundled the new arrivals into the flat and dumped their luggage in the hallway amid swarming streams of curious cats, we delicately extricated Baki out of his cot, popped him in with Dotty, and got all cosy on the patchy sofa of fame. Gillie cracked open the red wine and she and Oliver furnished us with the details about how they've miraculously landed in Muirdrith together – all spoken in a tone I had to keep hushing on account of Cat-Crazy Flatmate inundating me with notes tomorrow about unwelcome house guests and / or inappropriately reverberating voices.

As it would seem, Gillie and Oliver noticed each other commenting on my blog and not having seen each other for many, many moons (Nightsuns?), suddenly looked each other up on Facebook. They chose exactly the same moment to do friend requests, reportedly sending the social media platform into a digital meltdown which they both found highly amusing. "Facebook flipped out as much as we did when we found each other," Gillie said. "It froze and unfroze my account I don't know how many times until we were finally able to message each other. Kind of an apt metaphor, don't you think?"

Fuck me, I don't know what to think. And I'm not going to think it here, on my blog, anyway.

Oliver continued. "I was down in Brighton doing a photo shoot for a catalogue and I didn't realise Gillie lived so close. It meant total sense to hook up." Ella raised an eyebrow at me. A conversation for later. "When she said she was planning on driving up to Scotland to see you, well you know me, Jess. Carpe diem and all that. Plus it meant we could share the driving and get it all done in one day. AND we could come and make sure you're not a.) falling apart with all this fasting and b.) surviving this whole Children's Services nastiness. We're so chuffed to be here. Aren't we, Gillie?"

Gillie yawned, big style. "Yes, yes of course. And Jess – can you put us up for just one night? We'll get a hotel tomorrow."

Flashbacks of the last time Gillie and Oliver shared a hotel room in Istanbul. Did not go well. Gillie might be one of my oldest friends but even she surprised me with the way she broke poor Oliver's heart. "Um, ordinarily I'd say yes, you know that, but we're a bit pushed for space. My Cat-Crazy Flatmate has all the extra rooms for her cats and she'd probably have a meltdown if I stuck you in with them. Ella and Dotty are in Baki's room with the air mattress. Shit. I suppose you could sleep on the sofa in here? I've got some spare duvets somewhere."

"What about Keith the Van?" Ella beamed. "He's comfier than you'd think."

"You've still got that battered old thing? I suppose we could. As long as there was something to sleep on, and some blankets to keep warm. It's only one night. What do you think, Oliver?"

"Carpe diem!" Came Oliver's reply.

And that's it. That's how two of my favourite people in the world have been sent out into the Scottish night air, to find their way across the bottle-strewn car park to Ella's rusty old flower power van, and wrap up tight in cat-hair adorned duvets I found under our bed. They'll be fine. They've got red wine, they've got some Co-op shortbread, and they've got each other.

Or something.

I'm back in bed, Baki is back in his cot, and I think I've fully updated you, Dear Reader. Mesut got in a little while ago and tumbled into bed next to me, without even removing his work apron. Bless him, he is exhausted. I can tell by the snores. He only ever snores when he's bone-tired.

I'm bone-tired too, but my heart is warm and heavy at the delightful proximity of so many awesome people. There is an obvious contrast to the isolation I've felt to date and I only seem able to name it now, now that my friends are here.

It's strange to finally admit that I may have felt pretty lonely since we started our life in Muirdrith. Especially in the first few months. Mesut has been working all the hours, because he wants so much to better our situation, and I've been left alone with Baki. My auntie, who gave Mesut the job, is so busy with her other pubs dotted across the Highlands that I've hardly seen her since we moved here. The CBT Counsellor was fab but hardly what you'd call a friend and if it wasn't for Bernie, I might have gone round the actual bend. On my worse days, I've even been known to get excited at the very sight of one of Cat-Crazy Flatmate's notes.

As amazing as our little boy is, the mourning I have felt for that phase of my life where I got to talk to whoever I wanted, whenever I wanted has been fierce. Is that yet another reason to believe I'm an awful mother, Dear Reader? I feel like that's a thought for another day. Right now, I'm so unbelievably happy that my good old friends are in such close proximity. It feels like a gift.

My belly might be growling but my heart is not.

Iyi geceler.

LifeIsYoursLindy

Ah, how lovely! You're all together again! And I remember you telling me about Oliver – isn't he the one who basically life-coached you into oblivion? He was one cool character, Jess. Fingers crossed there's hope for him and Gillie.

Jess.AKYOL

Yes, he's so lush. Hasn't changed a bit either. I must ask him how he spikes his hair like that. Baki would rock that look.

just-a-mum
Hi. I'm new to your blog but all caught up and loving it! You're so lucky that your friends are visiting you. I know what you mean about motherhood – it can be really lonely sometimes. Have you found any online parenting forums? There are a few that are quite good. They help me a lot.
Jess.AKYOL
Thanks so much for reading and welcome! Do you know, I've never even thought of looking. When the droves of people have left and it's just me and Baki again, I'll have a look.

Fab4CoolDad
It makes me and your mother feel better that you've got your friends with you now, love. So the only song to recommend today is . . . 'With A Little Help from My Friends'.
Jess.AKYOL
This is getting more and more impressive, Dad. I'll introduce Baki to this beauty of a tune in the morning. x

Angnonymous
Love your list of positives. Maybe we could make lists like that about life in general anyway?
Jess.AKYOL
Oooh, Angnonymous, you've just reminded me about the journal I used to write in. It got me through some tough times. I used to write lists of positive things that had happened every day – and no matter how shitty the day, I could always find at least one good thing. Thanks for the reminder.
Angnonymous
I aim to please. 🙂

AngelBernie

Well this is all very exciting. When will I get to meet all these friends of yours, poppet?
Jess.AKYOL
Might bring them to Toddlers, but for you, any time you want! Let's sort it. Gotta sleep now. Have drunk all the water in the world. Night, Bernie.
AngelBernie
Night, beautiful one.

NO_Just_DON'T(1)
I'd love to know how on earth you think having all of these people around your boy will help matters with Children's Services. They won't have forgotten about you, you know. Those kinds of allegations don't just disappear. Next thing you know, you'll be making *him* sleep in the van.
Jess.AKYOL
Thank you and goodnight. 

11

DAY 11 – THE WALL

Muirdrith, Highlands of Scotland, UK
Sat 21st Aug 2010
Sunrise / Suhoor: 5.51am
Sunset / Iftar: 8.46pm

Things in the world of Ramadan took an interesting turn today. And I'm not just talking about the overabundance of striking personalities now in my household.

This interesting turn has been nagging away at me – or should I say *burning* away – for the last couple of days, but I chose to ignore it in fear of sounding even more whiney on this blog than I already do.

Today, during morning ablutions that were shoehorned in between Ella soaking her breast-milk-stained dungaree-pjs in the bathroom sink and Gillie more or less transforming the shower cubicle into an actual Turkish bath, I had to face facts: I have a lady problem.

The sympathetic among you will piece the evidence together (lack of hydration + possible post-sundown nooky on a few sneaky occasions) and work out exactly what I mean.

The socially-awkward among you will flit across these paragraphs, work out roughly what I mean, and avoid asking supplementary questions.

And if you want the sordid details – well, you're not going to get them. All you need to know is that I sent Gillie and Ella to the chemist and directed Oliver and Mesut to supervise the toddlers while I cowered in the bathroom, wishing my lady parts would bloody well cool it, all the while reading the latest note taped to the mirror. *Jess, could you please consider warning me next time you invite this many of your friends to stay? The toilet clogs so easily.*

Always the rebel, Mesut left Oliver to supervise Mr Tumble viewing, while he came to check on me. "Gulazer, can I come in?"

I let him in and he gave me one of those hugs that exudes the longing for more but is hampered sweetly by genuine concern. "I'm okay, really," I told him. "I've had this loads of times before. I just need some medicine and some rest and maybe a hotty botty and I'll be fine."

He looked down at my bum, confused. "Hotty botty?"

"I mean hot water bottle," I laughed. "Mam used to say it when I was little. It stuck."

He grinned. "You do have 'hotty botty' though."

"I'll take your word for it. But right now that's not the part of me that's hot."

"Oh no, Gulazer. You not well. You knows if you poorly you not needing do Ramadan. Is rules. You have days off if poorly."

I mulled this over as he gazed at me, his molten brown eyes lapping gently at my mood so that I felt better already.

Maybe this was an opportunity. An opportunity to be relieved of all the Ramadan duties that have held me back for the last week or so. This meant I could gorge myself silly on Ben and Jerry's, devour Doritos watching X Factor and guzzle wine with my beautiful friends who had travelled oh so far to see me.

This. Could. Be. Wonderful.

But just hold on a cotton-picking second. Is this challenge not all about perseverance? Is it not about agreeing to support my husband and coming good on my promise? Is it not about commitment and stamina and hitting the wall and climbing the wall and fucking the wall right off?

Well, I think we all know the answer to that.

And there's another twenty blogs posts in me yet.

So that's how I reached my decision. My compromise.

I am allowing myself to drink water for the rest of the month. And maybe cranberry juice for the next couple of days to help remedy this unfortunate situation. But that's all. That's it.

Mesut huffed and puffed a bit when I told him. "Gulazer, you not do this. Just stop Ramadan if you want it. I not think bad of you. You tried and that means a lot. What is point, Gulazer? Drinking water during Ramadan is not Muslim way."

He's right about that. Obviously. But what we have to remember here is that I am *not* Muslim. Which means I have a pretty cool advantage. I can call the shots. I can choose how much of this to undertake and exactly how much qualifies me to have a meaningful experience AND helps me sleep at night, knowing that I am learning and growing and demonstrating to Mesut that I have a solid investment in honouring and respecting what makes him, well, him.

And I cannot tell you how much easier this day has been as a result.

Yes, granted, there have been constant hunger pangs but honestly, my energy levels could have rivalled those of Mr Tumble himself. And not only that, but I think I have reached the heady heights of super-mam status again. If only Nicky and Aja had been around to see it.

Baki has totally simmered down with the tantrums. He has graciously accepted and eaten all of the meals I've given him today, we have played together without anybody sustaining an injury and every single dish is done. No, not just done, gleaming. Even Gillie said (on the rare occasion she could tear her eyes off Oliver), "Steady on, Jess. You'll have someone's eye out with that dishcloth."

And thanks to my freakish energy reserve, I suggested we all go to the local fun fair. Not something I would have dared embark on with the Beast-Child ordinarily, but as I had my trusty entourage to back me up, the sky was the limit. And it nearly was, for poor Baki when he went sliding down that mammoth inflatable slide. I have never seen a child flee so high into the air by natural forces before my lack of better judgement allowed him to go anywhere near it again.

Lesson. Learned.

Other than that, the fun fair was, well, fun. I can't remember being this happy for a long while. As if the merriment of the flashing lights, the ravishing scent of spun candy and the cheerfully clashing pop tunes weren't enough to warm the heart, I had my friends, my son AND my husband all in one place.

Well, kind of in one place. It was interesting just to watch all these people who owned a little piece of my heart as they meandered through the fair, finding their own attractions and distractions.

Gillie and Oliver are more or less a unit now. Or as Ella has fondly labelled them, 'Goliver'. Prior to this, the last time I saw them together was a very awkward goodbye hug in the spookily beautiful region of Cappadocia in Turkey. Oliver's heart steeped in disappointment as heavy as the mountainous landscape that threatened to swallow us up there. Fast forward a few years and they are here, in the Highlands of Scotland, this afternoon their open-mouthed smiles flooded with fairy lit wonder as they sat, legs dangling on the ferris wheel. They have booked a little B&B to return to of an evening which is probably a wise move. Best to let whatever this new joy is grow outside of my shitty little flat.

"Nice to see Goliver letting their hair down!" Ella yelped as she raced past me after Dotty, who was making a beeline for some looming great structure involving chains and spikes called The Tower of Terror. "Dotster, there's no bloody way you're going on that!" And she scooped her daughter up in a swirl of genius distraction which worked beautifully because Dotty started pointing at a quivering mountain of candy floss instead. Ella grinned at her and off they went to indulge. Lucky buggers.

Then I heard a squeal. Baki. I twirled round to see him with Mesut, both of them stuffed into a bright yellow, acrylic aeroplane that stuck out precariously on a metal arm, chased by an equally garish whirl of boats, motorbikes, unicorns, racing cars and seahorses. Baki's words may not be fully-formed yet, but hearing him yell random sounds with all the heartfelt glee he could fit into his little body was enough to make my heart throb, big style.

I stood there, soaking up the warmth of having my people nearby and marvelled at what proper hydration can do for the body. I mean, I was feeling AMAZING. Okay, so it's no secret that us humans need water as much as we need oxygen, but isn't it incredible, that we dick about day to day, going from one thing to the next, completely and absolutely taking for granted the miracle that is the human body? Give us air and we breathe. Give us light and we flourish. Give us water and we thrive. Give us love and we . . . randomly undertake ridiculous challenges that inflict horrible peeing issues . . .

Ironically, right then, my little moment of bliss was interrupted by the fact that I had been downing water and cranberry juice like it was going out of fashion. Oh, I hated this. Knowing that the peeing was an act of detoxing and just what my body needed, but also knowing it was going to hurt like hell.

(*You never know, if I start typing the word 'Cystitis' over and over again, I might get a lucrative sponsorship deal with some foul-tasting but miraculous lady powder. Is that how algorithms work? Keep your fingers crossed for me. Cystitis. Cystitis. Cystitis. Cystitis. Cystitis. Cystitis. Oooh, what if I put as hashtag on it? What then? #Cystitis. #Cystitis. #Cystitis. #Cystitis. #Cystitis. #Cystitis. #Cystitis.*)

Unfortunately, the only options available for relieving yourself at a Scottish fun fair in the middle of a far-flung field involve the words 'Porta' and 'Loo'. I know you'll understand when I say it was with a heavy heart that I signalled to Mesut where I was going.

Having found the offending structures hidden behind The Tower of Terror, of all places, and somehow gotten through a crookedly crouched and hovering burning sesh yet again, I stood up to find my head spinning a little bit. I washed my hands in a daze and stepped outside to breathe any air at all that wasn't PortaLoo air. This #cystitis was perhaps worse than I'd given it credit for because I felt sick to the stomach.

I stumbled to a spot where The Tower of Terror cast a hulking, dark shadow on the grass, and I breathed deep. I looked up at the vast and menacing edifice, saw its long, black lines, grey grooves and rusted fixings. A white light from another fairground ride blazed repeatedly off its metallic panels in ghostly shapes that were as hypnotic as they were confusing. It reminded me of something.

Sudden white flecks. White blobs of light with slow and speckled patterns moving within them. Curved, hopeful shapes emerging from the blackness, masses of light and dark competing with each other for softness, roundness, longing. The rhythmical, mechanical whir as a soundtrack to the stuttering shapes, clicking, sticking, tricking. A full bladder screaming . . . a heart thudding heavily but not in the right body . . . the cold press on my belly . . . the voices soft and whispered but drawing out a sickness, a weakness, a fear . . . *it's not what we'd hope to see . . . it ended days ago . . . it's not your fault.*

Next thing I knew I'd hit the damp grass. My body dropped. Like lead.

"Shit! Jess! What's happened?"

I knew that voice.

"Come on, poppet. Easy now, but try to sit up." When I opened my eyes the first thing I saw was the familiar swell of a large stomach encased in stretchy red fabric. I wanted to close my eyes again. Let the damp grass take me as its captive. The sight of the stomach was too much.

But it was okay. Because it was Bernie.

"That's it, poppet. Just like that. Put your head on my lap. Are you here with Mesut?"

I nodded. I think.

"Logan, honey? Go find Mesut. You can't miss him. Long, black hair. Skinny. He'll be with little Baki. Just look for the only wizard-looking bloke in Muirdrith and that'll be him. And take Frida with you please!" She turned her head down to look at me after barking instructions at her husband. "Jess, what happened? Is it the fasting? Did you keel over because of how hungry you are? Do you want a cherry liqueur?"

'I don't know," I gasped. "Cystitis, PortaLoo, sick with the pain . . . but . . ." I pointed at The Tower of Terror, not knowing how to explain to Bernie what on earth had just happened. "Can I just have Mesut please?"

"Of course, poppet – he won't be long." Bernie helped me to sit up on my own and gave me a drink of her Fanta. The sweet, fizzy stuff washed down my throat and I could almost sense the sugar reaching my veins, igniting my spirit a little. I'm sure Allah would give me that.

When Mesut arrived, he had everybody else with him. Ella held onto Dotty and Baki with eyes that screamed worry, Gillie and Oliver stood frozen to the spot, hands clasped tightly together and Mesut swooped over to me in that soft, silent way he has, the smooth motion that expels trouble and invites peace. "Gulazer. What is happen?"

I let myself be folded into his arms with a heavy sob. The sickness, the dizziness, the confusion was gone and they left behind the glittering clarity of what I needed to do next. I needed to go home with Mesut. Now.

Dear Reader, I hope you aren't worried about me after what went down at the fun fair today. Maybe you've pieced it all together and are reading this in the cold, harsh light of recognition. Or maybe you're mystified by the drama of me collapsing in the epicentre of carnival frivolity for no apparent reason other than the chilling phenomenon that is a PortaLoo.

Funny that the whole collapsing thing happened slap bang in the middle of Ramadan too. But honestly, I really don't think it had anything to do with that. Here's what it had to do with:

When Mesut and I got home, we allowed our army of caregivers to bathe Baki and Dotty whilst we headed to our bedroom to talk. After shooing about a million cats off our bed, we climbed in and Mesut wrapped me up tight first in our duvet and second, in his arms.

I tried my best to tell him what had happened when I'd seen those white lights on the back of the fairground ride. The quickened heartbeat. The overwhelming sickness. The trembling in my bones. The sadness in my soul.

"But why, Gulazer? Is just lights at the fun fair. Maybe you see doctor now."

"No, that's not it, Mesut. Those lights, and the sounds, the mechanics of the ride, it just took me back. Do you remember how dark and quiet it was in the doctor's room earlier this year? Do you remember those white shapes we saw on the screen and thought they were going to be . . . we were going to have . . ."

"Our next baby." He finished for me.

"Yes."

"But, we talk about this at the time, remember?" He stroked my hair back from my cheeks. "You was seeming okay. Just few days of sad and after operation at hospital, you say you feel okay and you knows it just Allah's way."

And yes, he's right – that's more or less what I said. Once I'd done a lot of crying and the bleeding had stopped and the hospital had looked after me, I'd let logic take over.

It's okay.

It happens to lots of women.

It was so early anyway.

I have Baki.

I'm very lucky.

I'm through this.

I'm over this.

I'd hardly told a soul. Mam and Dad, of course, and my brother, Max – they all knew. They'd offered to come up to the Highlands to look after me, to help out with Baki, but I'd point blank refused. And after that I didn't really want to tell anyone else, which was most unlike me. I'm usually so connected to matters of the heart that anyone and everyone around me gets a piece of the action, whether they want it or not. But not this time. This time I was cradled in the reassuring arms of logic.

Millions of women had coped with this before me, which meant I would cope too.

But now, after today, I'm wondering if logic is no match for the wisdom of the body. Something as seemingly unrelated as a urine infection had bloated my bladder up until it actually remembered the last time it had been that swollen. Then all it took were the sadly reminiscent white lights, the tragically rhythmical mechanical sounds and an unexpected moment alone to whip up a storm of trauma.

Because I can call it what it is now. A trauma.

A miscarriage *is* a trauma.

And do you know something? When I had those CBT sessions for my postnatal depression, I never brought this up once. Even as it was happening, I'd just called in sick, said I had a bug or something, and rearranged my session. I saw the depression as a separate thing. Something I needed to sort for Baki. The removal of that heavy, grey veil would not be disturbed by something as menial as a miscarriage. It would not inhibit my progress. I had to get on with life.

I even remember my probably-wise-to-it counsellor, Sue, saying at our last session, "Jess, if you need me again, you know where I am. You've made a lot of effort to get better but it's not a linear thing. You'll only be human if you need to come back."

After talking everything through with Mesut, and him insisting he take the evening off work to stay with me, we went to see what the tribe was up to. We emerged into the hallway from the bedroom in a quiet haze, my eyes streaked red but my bones hugged tight. The only sound I could make out was the incessant purr of ever-present cats. Where was everybody?

We looked in the kitchen and found Ella and Oliver arranging some sausage rolls on a tray. Apparently, Dotty and Baki had been fed and watered and packaged off to bed in Keith the Van where Gillie was with them now. "They're like little angels sleeping," Ella smiled. "I made a hammock-type-thing out of a sleeping bag and they're swinging like baby apes above the front seats. Gillie's crooning over them as we speak. I think she's even put fairy lights up."

"But what the hell are they doing out there? Children's Services will have a bloody field day if this gets out . . ."

"Chill your boots, Jess. Don't be a nutcase. We've got a plan." Ella nudged Oliver and he grinned back at me too.

"Ella's right. You need a break from this . . ." He looked around him at the desperately brown and aged kitchen, the oil-edged notes stuck to most of the cupboards, and the litter-trays in every corner of the room. " . . . place. Come with us. We've got a surprise for you."

Ella chucked a coat at me as we traipsed through the corridor. Oliver led the way with his mega tray of sausage rolls and his chin tipped in a gleeful way. Ella danced a little as she walked. Mesut squeezed my hand but glanced at me with questions unspoken. Why were we walking across the car park? Why were the kids in Keith the Van?

As we got closer, I saw Gillie's back end hanging out of the opened front passenger door. I could just about make out her voice humming a little tune that sounded vaguely familiar and soothing in a way that was quite surprising. Her bum swayed along to the tune and I realised she must have been singing to the kiddos.

"Is that the X Factor theme tune? Questionable choice of lullaby." I laughed.

"They bloody loved it!" Gillie jumped down from the van and closed the door softly. Then she hugged me. "It got them to sleep in ten minutes flat. Blimey, you look better, sweetie. You're a much better colour. You feeling okay?"

"I am. But why are the children living the gypsy lifestyle? Is our flat really that bad?" I peered in at them and Ella was right.

They did look like angels. Dotty and Baki were snuggled into an orange sleeping bag cocoon that was tied with rope from one side of the van to the other. Their soft little limbs pressed beautifully together, their cheeks were rounded, rosy and facing each other, and their fingers were twitching in a sleep that seemed as deep as it was carefree. The battery-operated fairy lights strung above them cast a golden sheen that heightened their slumber to fairy tale proportions. Dear Reader, I don't think I'll ever forget that image as long as I live.

Next thing I knew, Mesut had been torn from my side and Gillie and Ella each linked an arm through mine. They pulled me round to the back of the van, where I could see the back doors were flung open, inviting in the dark shiver of the night that was fast approaching. Soon it would be time for sundown.

"It's nearly X Factor time," Ella practically shrieked. "And during which the sun will nick off. Now, Oliver's figured out the teccie stuff so that we can stream the show and watch it together, and Gillie and I did the rest . . ." There was a broad ribbon of light pouring from the van doors onto the tarmac, and I thought I could smell something delicious too. "Welcome to *Chez Keith* – the ultimate in van dining!"

What I saw, Dear Reader, was an arrangement of objects so pleasing to my heart it nearly did a somersault then and there.

The back of the van had been transformed into what can only be described as a plush den of tranquility. Everywhere I looked I saw cushions, duvets, blankets and pillows, plumped and ready for bodies to sink into them. Yet more fairy lights criss-crossed above us, woven into the hooks and holes of Keith the Van's ceiling, making it come alive like a piece of gleaming honeycomb. Make that Highland honeycomb actually, because somebody had taken apart Ella's bouquet of heather and thistles and added them to the mix too. It looked totally beautiful in a mis-matched, wildlife-chic kind of way.

My attention was caught by my laptop, which sat raised on an upturned wine box, quite clearly pilfered from the pub, at the corner near the doors. Its screen was already flashing with promises of X Factor madness and the sounds of the legendary voiceover booming out against the metallic cave. "We can sort the volume however you want it," grinned Oliver. "We'll have to see how loud the pub gets."

Then my stomach growled and I saw an oasis of colour at the back of the van. A generous spread of food was laid out across a mis-match of trays taken from our kitchen and elevated on Ella's boxes of puppet stuff. I could see chilli-speckled sweet potato wedges. Hummus dotted with sun-dried tomatoes. Glistening cubes of white cheese and dishes of glossy green olives. Sticks of veg splayed out in artful rainbow circles. ALL the Doritos. Not to mention a thoughtfully placed deep dish overflowing with bright pink candy floss. "That was my idea," said Gillie, noticing that I'd clocked it. "A girl can never have too much spun sugar."

"True." I agreed, then used my last ounce of energy to heave Gillie and Ella into the van and onto the abundance of soft furnishings. I lay there and hugged them tight, needing the warmth and press of their bodies as much as I needed their food. "Thank you so much you beautiful people, you. I still can't believe you're all here."

"Well, you'd better believe it, matey," Oliver chimed in. He and Mesut had plonked themselves on cushions by now, awkwardly opting out of the human bundle that lay before them. "And we're ready to talk if and when you want to, okay?"

"I know. And this sounds a bit weird, but I think I'm all out of words now. Maybe, after X Factor, I'll go and write my blog post and then, well, you'll know more about what happened. For now, can we just concentrate on a bit of Cowell action?"

"You sound like a cat in a vacuum cleaner," Oliver returned.

"You have the personality of a door handle!" Ella howled.

"You made it your own," Gillie giggled.

"Gillie!" said Mesut, slapping his own forehead. "Even I knows that Louis, not Simon!"

And just like that I realised how westernised my poor husband has become.

Not too westernised though, to point out that it might be time for X Factor but it wasn't quite time to break the fast. One more hour to go.

So do you know what my incredible tribe did? They turned the volume on that laptop right up, got comfy with their hunger and waited for that cheeky sun to slip behind the seascape of beautiful Muirdrith. Once it did, and the most incredible ruby reds and soothing strands of saffron flooded the back of the van like comforting flames of hope, we feasted.

I'm telling you, that was the best food I have tasted in a long while.

Who knows what made it taste better? The recognition and acceptance of trauma? Friendship? Hunger? Exhaustion? Love? Keith the Van?

Love. Let's go with love.

Anonymous
Is not right drinking water in Ramadan. What do you think you are doing?
Jess.AKYOL
Not dying.

AngelBernie
Hope you're feeling better now? How brave are you to share all of this on your blog! I wish you'd talked to me, poppet, I've been

through something very similar so I do understand. I should have known really because the angels have been nudging me about you for a while now. Nudge me back if you want to know what they've been saying.

Jess.AKYOL

Thanks for rescuing me today, Bernie. And consider yourself nudged.

AngelBernie

Cool. So the strongest voice is Archangel Raphael who is supporting your healing. You might have noticed he's sorting you out for emerald greens and green light to absorb the physical and spiritual ailments.

Jess.AKYOL

No way? I'm always walking down by the river and thinking how amazing all of the greens are. I was there just the other day with Ella and basking in the light of the leaves, the mosses, the grass and the reeds. Weird.

AngelBernie

Not weird at all. And there's Serephina. Who tells me she's blessing all the changes that happen in your family. She's helping you with all the upset.

Jess.AKYOL

I think you're the angel, actually. 😇

AngelBernie

Maybe one day, poppet. 🤞

Angnonymous

So lucky AngelBernie was there for you at the fun fair. She does seem to have a way of appearing at the most crucial moments, doesn't she?

Jess.AKYOL

You're right. She totally has that way. Is it just me, or do you seem really quite interested in her?

Angnonymous
I have no idea what you're talking about.
Jess.AKYOL
Oh, but I think you do.

Not-A-Granny-Flora
Jessie, please call me. I'm worried sick. Glad you watched X Factor though. Did you see the green-faced witch lady? She must have made you laugh, at least.
Jess.AKYOL
We'll chat tomorrow, I promise. Yes, saw the green witch. I want to BE her!

Fab4CoolDad
Oh Jess. My Little Darling. This one's for you. 'Here Comes The Sun'.
Jess.AKYOL
Not fair. You made me cry, Dad. 😘

GILLIE_LASS77
Beautiful, brave lady! Can't believe how much fun we had in Keith the Van tonight! And what a bloody rigmarole it was getting the kiddies out of the hammock and back to bed. We did it though . . . are they all tucked up and still fast asleep now? I could always come back and sing X Factor melodies at them if need be. In other news . . . the B&B we're staying in is hilarious! There's a lovely old dear who speaks mostly in Gaelic and there are thistles everywhere. We even had to move some off the bed before we could get in! Hope I don't have thorns in my bum in the morning.
Jess.AKYOL
Well if you do, I love you so much I'd even pick them out for you. Sleep well and thank you millions for today.

OliverChen1!
Just checking in as well, Jess, to say thank you for letting me into your little fold. I felt honoured to be part of your story today, even if it was tinged with a lot of sadness. And by the way, did I mention? Mesut is an absolute gent. He lives up to your descriptions. You did good, matey.
Jess.AKYOL
You've been part of my story for a good while now, Oliver. Beware when the books come out!

ShelleyMadMum
Yes, u r very brave Jess. Why don't people talk about this more often? It's so v common. I went thru it twice before I got the twins. Devastating, it was. And u r right to listen to ur body if ur triggered. Sometimes they know more than we do.
Jess.AKYOL
Wise words, Shelley. Thank you so much.

CombustableApocalips
No wonder Allah took your baby. You not deserving.

NO_Just_DON'T(1)
So now you really have put your toddler in the van? You should be disgusted with yourself and your friends. No religious endeavour can excuse this kind of behaviour. Wake up and be a proper mum before you lose everything.

Night-sun-ella
Jessica, Jessica, can't you seeeee?
You mean the absolute world to meeeee!
Dotty adores you and so do IIIII!
We know you love us so you need not replyyyyyy.
Your awesomeness stands out loud and proooouuuud.

And makes me feel I'm floating on a clooouuud!
I'm so glad we came to visit yoooooooou!
Even if we can't eat Scottish steeeeewww.
This fasting for Ramadan is really touggghhhh
But we know you're doing it in the name of looovvvve!

Jess.AKYOL

I've said it before and I'll say it again. You are MADE for X Factor.

just-a-mum

What a full-on post, Jess! Well done for being so brave and sharing what you've been through with the miscarriage. I have a few friends who have suffered too and I will let them know about your blog – it might resonate. Love the angel speak from your friend, AngelBernie.

Jess.AKYOL

How lovely of you to keep reading! And thanks so much for the kind words.

DoUKeepGetting#Cystitis?

Total + dependable relief frm chronic #UTi is here 4 u! Visit doukeepgettingcystitis.com 4 all your #interstitial emergencies – u never be sorry again and #cystitis will be banished!!!

Jess.AKYOL

Wow. The power of hashtags.

stella-mumsy

This means a lot that you wrote about this. Thank you.

Jess.AKYOL

You're welcome. It was good to write it down. x

FatimaNazar

Hello! I just found your blog recommended on a Ramadan

support group. I can see how brave you are being during all of this. I think it's lovely that you're doing Ramadan to support your husband. I wish my partner showed as much interest in my faith. And if you need to drink water – do it. It is still a good effort and I'm sure he will appreciate it.

Jess.AKYOL

Wow! I can't believe my little blog is reaching new people! That means so much – thank you! So lovely that you read my post.

FatimaNazar

It's great. I will be back.

12

DAY 12 - SNOWBALL

Muirdrith, Highlands of Scotland, UK
Sun 22nd Aug 2010
Sunrise / Suhoor: 5.53am
Sunset / Iftar: 8.43pm

Never, since I started this Ramadan tomfoolery, have I written my daily blog post before sundown.

I'm not sure why. I suppose that all of my energy has been poured into distracting myself from the task right up until the crucial time when I can indulge in basic nutrition again. So usually, as I'm writing, my belly is nice and full and my mood has significantly improved.

But, because variety is the spice of life (or because my friends have deserted me and I am booooorrrrred), I'm writing this post during my countdown to feeding time.

Brave, I know.

Disclaimer: My huge apologies in advance if my cavernous belly causes me to inflict insult or injury upon the readership. I cannot be held responsible for my actions in such an intense state of malnourishment.

I woke quite late this morning. Yesterday's occurrences must have wiped me out because Baki's shouty demands for a sunrise fix of Bob The Builder usually drag me out of bed before I'm even properly awake.

This morning, however, Ella must have tip-toed into our room to scoop him out of his travel cot before I stirred. When I finally hauled my sorry ass out of bed and into the other room, I found the three of them – Ella, Dotty and Baki – wearing their *swimsuits*, of all things, with the air mattress propped on its side against the wall, newspaper spread over the entire floor and an apparent tribute to Jackson Pollock in full swing.

"How . . . how the flip have you got him to paint, Ella?"

"Good morning, Ella. Good morning, children. How wonderful to see you all tapping into your creativity!" Ella chirped back at me, her cheeks rising in a full, playful grin.

"No, yes. Sorry – it's amazing to see you all, erm, tapping in. And totally – good morning one and all. But . . ." I looked at Baki and all I saw was a paint-smeared, toothy smile that could have inspired many an artist. "He never, ever wants to paint with me. If I even get a palette out he starts screaming and doing that freakish archy back thing."

"Well, maybe that's your first mistake," Ella said. "Don't bother with a palette, or even a brush, just go straight for the paint pot and, well, hands!" On that note, all three of them stuck their arms in the air, laughed wildly and wiggled their fingers to show me just how utterly paint-soaked they were.

Coming from that artistic background of mine, I've always wanted Baki to enjoy creative activities. When he was tiny, I was practically gagging for him to be old enough for paints and crayons and I had to hold myself back. Especially after Mesut caught me painting his feet for footprints when he was only two weeks old. Yet another culture clash we had to figure out.

So you can imagine my deep, deep disappointment when

the toddler version of Baki revealed his intense dislike for any such arty pursuits. Apparently . . . paint + mother's enthusiasm = god almighty tantrums

It's basic maths.

This morning though, as I stood at the door, watching Baki smear and smooth and stroke and swirl the paints into broad arcs of pure expression, his little eyes wide and his lovely, chubby body spattered and kissed in colour, I marvelled at him. It's not often I'm gifted the role of observer, as I'm usually so intensely entangled in Baki's ventures, but Ella was giving me that opportunity right now.

I tried to concentrate on him, Dear Reader, and not the automatically toxic thoughts that were trying their level best to squeeze in. But I have to admit, they are very persistent . . .

Why can't I get him to do that?
Why can't I be as good a mum as Ella?
Why doesn't my child do what I suggest?
How do I always get everything wrong?
Why does he hate me?
What's the point?
This is why I'll never have any more children.

I know I've moved to the Highlands, but I think I've learned how to snowball things a little too well.

There must be at least a little bit of wisdom in me, however, because I did catch the thoughts before they could send me into a crumpled heap on the floor. I caught them and I thanked them and I sent them on their merry way. *Go and bother someone else,* I thought. *I've given you enough of my time.*

I settled back into watching Baki and took some slow, deep breaths. Then I had a go at rearranging those thoughts so that they'd resemble something a little more helpful.

Look how much fun he's having.
How brilliant that he can do that without me.
I'm so glad he has his Auntie Ella.
He must feel really safe and happy.
I'm doing a good job.

I WILL get the hang of this positive thinking lark eventually. I think Ramadan might already be helping. Who's to say if I would have even noticed that snowball of misery if I'd simply reacted by dashing to the patchy sofa of fame and pulling a family pack of Twixes out of the secret cubby hole? Who's to say the snowball wouldn't have upgraded to an avalanche?

Just something to notice.

When Goliver arrived, The Pollock re-enactment was more or less cleared up and the toddlers were in the bath, now experimenting with seven bottles of bubble bath and Auntie Ella's natural tendency towards flamboyance. A recipe for success if ever I heard one.

Gillie was most disappointed to find she'd missed out on the arty stuff. "Aw, but Jess – we haven't painted together since the Firebelly days!" She was referring, Dear Reader, to the arts business we used to run together in another life. It had been our absolute passion for about ten years but we walked away from it with our heads held high a few years ago, ready for new adventures, which we got in abundance. "Anyway, it doesn't matter. Oliver's got something exciting to tell you."

Oliver sat on the edge of the air mattress, which had been reinstated to its spot on the floor of Baki's little box room, leaned forward and propped his elbows up on his sharply-angled knees. I recognised this as Oliver's very reserved way of showing he was incredibly, mind-blowingly thrilled about something.

"Jess, we had a very interesting evening after we left you last night, didn't we, Gillie?" Gillie nodded at him, practically busting a gut, but I could tell they had previously arranged for Oliver to do the news-telling. "We got chatting to the lady who runs the B & B we're in. Thistledown Lodge."

"Oh, the place where you're worried about getting thorns in your bum?" I asked, remembering what Gillie had said about thistles in her comments last night.

"Exactly." Oliver smiled. "And anyway, she asked what brought us to Muirdrith and we told her we knew you and that you were doing this Ramadan thing with Mesut."

"She was so interested!" Gillie chimed in.

"Yeah, she really was. And then she worked out that she knows who you are because she also works at the Co-op and has seen you in and out of there a few times with Baki."

Aha! The kindly old lady who almost reduced me to floods of tears with the humble buying of a Kit Kat and well-intended endearments on the steps outside the flat – she is also the Thistle-Dispenser Lady of Thistledown Lodge!

Oliver seemed a little baffled by my explanation. He shook his head, filtering out the excess that was keeping him from revealing his news. "Anyway, believe it or not, she wants to talk to you about something incredibly exciting. And she's coming round . . ." He flicked his wrist towards his face, peering at his watch, ". . . now! She's coming round now. Before her shift starts at the Co-op."

"Wah? I'm still in my pyjamas!"

"No matter!" Gillie chimed in. "She honestly won't care. Just hear her out, sweetie. I honestly think you're going to love this. Where's Mesut? Still in bed?"

I nodded. Of course he was still in bed. It was still way before midday. And he had a late shift at the pub tonight. I'd have to get Ella and her ear-tonguing magic in action if we had a hope of getting him up now.

And then somebody knocked at the door.

"That'll be Mona!" Goliver cheered in unison and they both bounded off to greet her, leaving me in a quite frankly stinky, fuzzy pyjama fug that I wouldn't have subjected my worst enemy to.

There was no time to change myself, so I hastily flung some cushions around the room and arranged things so they were a little less Tracy Emin and a tad more Laurence Llewelyn-Bowen. Then I spied a can of air freshener I'd previously stowed away from Baki on a high shelf and spritzed it quickly round the room, dashing through its miraculous mists myself. That would have to do.

"Jess, this is Mona." Oliver showed our guest in and I was suddenly reminded of her lovely, warm smile. She brought an air of the Scottish outdoors with her, and a sense of purpose practically tripping off her stout and spirited limbs. Despite this, her movements were slow and languid as she moved towards me. I remembered how frustrated I'd been with her that day in the Co-op when the queue had been so long. Now though, her slowness helped the buzz of the room calm right down.

She reached out and took my hand in hers, not even flinching at my unruly appearance. "Jessica. How fabby to meet you properly. Can you believe your friends here are staying with me at Thistledown? What a wee stroke of luck, eh?"

"Luck? Erm, Mona – would you like to sit down?" I gestured at the wide range of sitting choices in Baki's room which included cushions and / or cushions.

"Wheesht, lassie. I'm fine standing. My knees would never forgive me if I tried to venture all the way down there. This is just a quick visit, to ask you a little something, really. Ollie here thought you might be interested."

"I did. Tell her, Mona. Go on, tell her." Oliver was holding onto Gillie for dear life, his teeth set in a smile not unlike the one Baki uses to get an extra biscuit.

"Okay then. Jessica, I think that fasting for Ramadan with your husband is nothing short of, well, brilliant. And I know I won't be alone. You might have noticed that Muirdrith isn't the most culturally diverse part of the world . . ."

"Understatement," Gillie coughed.

"So as luck would have it, my daughter, Ailsa, is a reporter for the Highland News – that's the regional rag, you know. And she's always on the look-out for stories of personal interest. And if they're multicultural, well, all the better really. So . . ."

"So . . ." I repeated, still not getting it.

Gillie couldn't help herself. "That's you, sweetie! You're the multicultural story of personal interest! Well, you and Mesut."

"That's right," Mona added. "I offered these two a wee night cap when they came rolling in last night – only the best drams at Thistledown Lodge I'll have you know – and well, we stayed up rather late if truth be known, and we got talking about your blog thingie and your fasting efforts and how your other half is as far away from his homeland as he possibly could be, bless him. And, well, I might have sent Ailsa a bit of a jolly text under the influence if you know what I mean. But anyway, m'eudail, she replied this morning and she thinks your story is . . ." Mona reached into her quilted jacket pocket and pulled out a mobile phone in a sparkling, purple case shaped like a thistle. She pushed her glasses to the end of her nose and squinted at the screen, ". . . 'of outstanding appeal'. So she'd like to meet you. To talk about an interview, if you would?"

"An interview?"

"Yep." Oliver clapped his hands together loudly then rubbed his palms. He was in full scheming mode. "Isn't that great, matey? A newspaper article might help your blog get more noticed. More attention on your writing can't be a bad thing, can it?"

"I suppose not . . ."

"Definitely not," Gillie squealed. "So, Mona. What's next?"

Thistle-Dispenser Lady went on to say she'd take my number and give it to her daughter and then I'd probably get a phone call in the next few days. Thistle-Dispenser Lady gave me a whole bag of Kit-Kats but, regrettably, no thistles. Thistle-Dispenser Lady left to go start her shift at the Co-op and suddenly the whole flat seemed lighter, brighter and more hopeful for having had her in it.

"She's a bit magic, is she not?" Gillie said. "There's something about her."

"Something about who?" Ella emerged from the bathroom with two squeaky clean children, wanting an update on what she'd missed. Gillie told her to hold that thought whilst she dashed to the kitchen to make cups of tea and plate up the Kit-Kats.

When we finally all sat together in Baki's room, telling Ella about the whole newspaper idea, I felt exhaustion creeping in. I'm thinking now that yesterday must have done me in more than I realised, and this nasty bout of #cystitis still hasn't fully left me alone.

So it didn't matter how many times Ella jumped up and down on the spot at the thought of my face being on the cover of the Highland News, or how many times Beast-Child and Dotty copied her to hilarious effect, I was undeniably knackered. And please consider that by this point, everybody else had been furnished with Gillie's cups of tea and Kit-Kats to amplify their enjoyment. Not me. Not a crumb.

And that's how I'm sitting here now, writing to you. Mesut has finally rolled out of bed and gone to work, my wise and wonderful tribe have whisked the children away for outdoor adventures along the river, and I am supposed to be getting some shut-eye before they return.

Alas, the shut-eye is not happening. Even though the decision to drink water again has undoubtedly been a good one for the sake of my urinary tract, it may have put me at a bit of a disadvantage with my belly. Since yesterday morning, when I began to allow myself fluids again, it has been making an almighty ruckus about its unmistakable emptiness.

Before this, I had been beginning to – dare I say – *master* the daytime ritual of a foodless existence. But now it's breaking me.

I am tempted to Google 'does drinking water kick-start your metabolism?' Does it make your tummy expect that food is the next thing on the agenda? Am I ruthlessly messing my tummy about? Will it ever forgive me and can we ever rebuild our previously solid relationship? Is there a future for us? Please, for the love of chocolate-related foodstuffs, say that there is.

Maybe couple counselling would help.

Shit. My mother is calling. Forgot to ring and tell her I was fine after incident at the fun fair yesterday. Better answer. Goodbye, Dear Reader. Let's speak again tomorrow.

LifeIsYoursLindy
Jess, I've just read back over the last couple of days. I'm so sorry to hear you went through all of that with the miscarriage. It's brutal. Glad you've got lots of support there though. My lady says 'Mucho ánimo'. Basically, she sends you all the love.
Jess.AKYOL
Tell her 'muchas gracias'. Does this lady have a name?
LifeIsYoursLindy
She does. Estrella. It means star.
Jess.AKYOL
Oh good lord. I think I just melted.

Not-A-Granny-Flora

I feel miles better now I've spoken to you AND that you're drinking water again. Go for it with the celebrity interview and remember us when you're famous. Your dad hopes you're enjoying the songs he keeps sending. I keep telling him he should send you 'Feed The World' but apparently a.) that's bad taste and b.) it's not the blessed, bloody Beatles.

Jess.AKYOL

Not a celebrity, Mother.

Fab4CoolDad

Ignore your mother. She has zero musical taste (but you should let her proof-read your interview – she's very good at that). Next thing we know, the Beatles who are left will be writing a song about you! For now, try listening to: 'A Day In The Life'.

Jess.AKYOL

Clever! I wonder what John Lennon had to say about Ramadan?

Angnonymous

Aha! Co-op Lady is also Thistle-Dispenser Lady. I could have told you that if only you'd asked. She'll make sure your story is heard, make no mistake.

Jess.AKYOL

Angnonymous, who ARE you?!

Angnonymous

Och, now that would be telling.

Jess.AKYOL

Yes it would! 'Och' though? Right, you're Scottish. I'm off the starting blocks . . .

FatimaNazar

Glad you're feeling better today. And see? Even if you drink water the press still want to speak to you. I think an article would be great – it would raise awareness of Ramadan and why

Muslims do it every year. Be sure to include the link once it's published!
Jess.AKYOL
Lovely to have you back again! I will, thank you. Not sure if it'll come to anything, but we'll see.

CrunchyNut_Mummy
Jess, I'm back! Sorry I missed the last few days. Just got caught up. I'm SO sorry to hear about the miscarriage. You should have told us at Toddlers, we would have looked after you! Highland News though, eh? Everybody would see that. Exciting!
Jess.AKYOL
Nice to have you back! I'll keep you posted.

Publicity_4_U_2
Need fast and professional public relations? Join our mailing list now for unending professionalism in your very best businesses. We are in all the papers! www.publicity4U2.org
Jess.AKYOL
What, all the papers in the WORLD?

stella-mumsy
Yes, I've heard drinking water can make you hungry. Might make things harder, not easier!
Jess.AKYOL
I think you might be right.

MaxAttax
May as well get in on this. Mam keeps going on about it so should do brotherly thing and read said blog. Looks like just in time too cos soon you'll be famous and forget all us mere mortals. Tell Baki he can always come live with his cool Uncle Max if his mother gets too up herself. Peace out.

Jess.AKYOL
Brother! Welcome! And what are you talking about? You're the one who has performed in the flippin' WEST END!!!
MaxAttax
Maybe so. But never again. They're all fucking luvvies. Peace out.
Jess.AKYOL
Nothing like you then.
MaxAttax
Nothing like me. Peace out.

funmum
Lovely blog posts, Jess – loved your earlier one about the ice cream tantrum! You'll have to read that to Beast-Child when he's older!
Jess.AKYOL
He'll be getting the whole blog printed and wrapped in a bow for his 18th. 😂 😉 Thanks for reading!

Night-sun-ella
I can't believe I'm going tomorrow! Haven't properly met your pal Bernie yet – only when you had your brief period of oblivion at the fun fair yesterday where she was basically Wonder Woman. Can we meet her tomorrow before Dotty and I embark on the epic road trip to end all road trips? I know I could pop next door and just ask you this but I'm training myself up for when I can't reach out and squeeze you whenever I like. Oh how I love to squeeze you!
Jess.AKYOL
Yes, I'm sure we can meet Bernie tomorrow. I'll find out if she's free. We'll have to do virtual squeezes! I'm always up for a virtual squeeze. #BlogSqueeze
Night-sun-ella

And what about ear-tonguing? I need to ear-tongue your husband! Tell him we're going to invent the virtual way.
Jess.AKYOL
#BlogEarTonguing – god, I'm going to miss you

AngelBernie
Would love to see Ella and everyone else tomorrow, poppet. Why don't you all come over? I'll sort some Scottish scran that you obviously won't be able to eat but you can bask in the joy of me catering for your friends. Plus you can have a doggy bag for sundown.
Jess.AKYOL
Sounds absolutely amazeballs, Bernie (This is Ella now – couldn't resist urge to run into next room and squeeze Jess – she is currently laughing her head off because I had my dungaree pjs on wrong way round and was flashing my wares. Hysterics currently thwarting her attempts to type. She will be in fine fettle for tomorrow so don't fret. We'll be there)!
AngelBernie
Hah! Ella – what an image! I'm so glad she's had you there these past few days. We worry about her, you know. And by 'we' I mean me and these angels of mine. Never alone and all that.

13

DAY 13 - BLESSINGS

Muirdrith, Highlands of Scotland, UK
Mon 23rd Aug 2010
Sunrise / Suhoor: 5.55am
Sunset / Iftar: 8.40pm

This morning, Dear Reader, was a time for getting things *done*. I filed bank statements, paid bills, made calls, swept floors, washed dishes AND went to the doctors. On reflection, I think this may have been a complex avoidance technique because I knew Ella and Dotty were leaving today. Ticking boxes seemed like the best distraction.

The trip to the doctors was something Gillie and Ella insisted I do, no matter how many times I pled the case for wasting a health professional's time. The #cystitis would sort itself out eventually and there was nothing to be done now about the sad loss of my baby.

Bollocks to all of that (Gillie wrote in a text this morning). *You're not yourself. We made you an appointment for 10.15. Put your big girl pants on and get yourself over to that clinic. G.*

Gillie and Ella didn't know about the long-haired hippy

doctor of essential oil fame, but they did well to get me an appointment at all. So, I walked into the consulting room to find a rotund, ruddy-cheeked bearded bloke who promptly confirmed that a.) I have, indeed had a water infection most likely brought on by dehydration, b.) I should be referred to a counsellor again to help deal with miscarriage trauma and c.) no, he'd never heard of an essential oil called 'Vitality' and why would he want to have an oil burner – which is essentially a fire risk – cluttering up his desk anyway?

That was me told.

After I picked up my prescription for antibiotics, I trudged through town and back towards the pub. I stepped over and around pavement cracks, gulping back a lump of something hard and heavy in my throat, and wished the doctor hadn't referred me for yet more counselling sessions.

It won't exactly look very good to Children's Services now, will it? I'm supposed to be over my little bout of depression and be a fully-functioning mother now. I am making beds and changing nappies and washing clothes and doing ALL of the motherly things without crumpling on a regular basis these days. The recent fun fair incident being the one and only exception. Surely there's somebody in more need than me? Isn't it selfish to take somebody else's place?

The shadow of the pub stretched out across the ground and met the edges of my footsteps as I crossed the high street. I took a deep breath as my whole self was plunged into the swamp of it. Suddenly, in the heavy soak of that shadow, the palms of my hands throbbed to hold Baki. It's so lovely that Ella has been helping me with him while she's here - lord knows I don't usually have that kind of offer - but why does my body actually ache for him whenever he's not with me? And then when we're together, all I want is a break. God, this parenting game is paradoxical as hell.

When I got back, I found Ella sitting on the bottom step outside the flat watching Baki and Dotty 'take turns' on a plastic trike in the paltry square of wasteland at the edge of the car park. She had an envelope in one hand and a steaming mug of coffee in the other. "I'd ask you to take your pick, doll, but I'm going to give you the only non-consumable." She gave me the envelope and a kiss on the cheek as I sat down next to her. "That cat-crazy friend of yours chucked it at me before she left for work. Said it got mixed up in her post or something."

"What, again? This is getting ridiculous. And she's not my friend. I think I know her cats better than I know her. Especially that one." I nodded towards the beast of a ginger feline who stared back at us from the top of the steps, with an alarming combination of contempt and curiosity. His scrappy ears twitched and his gnarly tail curled possessively around the wrought iron railings.

"Holy shit cookies, that is one mean looking moggy. Is he like, the leader of the mob or something?"

"I have no clue, Ella. But he always seems to be about. I wouldn't be surprised if it was him and him alone who knocked over all my baking that day Nicky and Aja came to visit."

"Well, he's certainly burly enough to have done it himself. Who knows what she's trained them to do. Anyways, what's in the letter?"

Oh, Dear Reader, the letter. I knew it was coming. You knew it was coming. But that didn't make it any easier to read those words this morning. At least this time I didn't lick the envelope in a frenzied panic then quiver under a storm-cloud of pious judgement.

"It says Children's Services are coming back, Ella. On Wednesday. For a review."

"You'll be fine, beautiful girl, you'll be more than fine. It's probably just procedure. Dotting some js and crossing some fs.

It's all gravy, baby. Anyhoo . . . more important matters. How did it go at the doc's?"

I told Ella about the #cystitis medicine and the possibility of more counselling sessions. Wow, it wasn't even midday yet and already I was managing a shitstorm of my own questionable mental health and the imminent storming of professional child-stealers. Plus the ominous stares of a ginger cat. "Jeez, Ella. Shall I call Bernie and sort out our visit to her house? I need a break from all this."

"I've already sorted it. Goliver are arriving in a bit to pick you and Baki up. I'll follow with Dotster in Keith the Van and leave straight from Bernie's later on. After I've filled my boots with Scottish fare, naturally. Oops! Sorry, sweetie. That's if you don't mind?"

"Of course I don't mind, you loon. Fill your boots right up. You've got a long journey ahead of you. I'm getting used to this hunger lark now, anyway. Even if I don't have a god to guide me all the way through it."

"It's barmy, isn't it?" Ella went a bit misty-eyed and chimed her lip stud against her coffee mug with a surprisingly soothing tone. "You know, that someone can believe in a god so completely that they'd go to such physical and mental extremes?"

"I'm kind of envious though," I sighed as I watched Baki whack Dotty over the head yet again because she was enjoying the trike for longer than he deemed acceptable. "To wake up each morning and feel alive because of a deeper purpose. To live for a means bigger than yourself."

"But we've both pretty much got that now though, haven't we?" Ella gestured towards our offspring. "I wake up for her. I feel alive because of her. Dotster really is my deeper purpose. Corny, but entirely true."

"Yeah, it all changes once you pop a sprog." Baki plodded

over to me, cheeks red with trike-related rage. He was so mad he was silent, and slumped his chunky body against my legs, speaking without words about the kind of comfort he wanted. I felt our bodies press together, the pulsing warmth of blood, flesh, love. Tears and snot smeared across my right knee and his cheek rested there, in the warm spill of it. "I'm just about there, I think. I adore Baki . . ."

"Obviously." Ella gestured at the snot situation.

"Obviously. And I could burst when I even try to contemplate how much I love him. But sometimes . . . I lose *myself*. It's like the love I have for him has the power to overshadow any love I have for myself. They don't tell you that about motherhood. The bastards."

"Bastards." Ella nodded. "It is hard, doll. And you've had it especially hard because you did a crazy amount of work to fall back in love with yourself after your split with Jack. You were practically on cloud nine when you moved to Turkey all huge and pregnant. Can you remember?"

Of course I can remember. I'll never forget what it felt like standing there at the departure gate of Newcastle Airport with Dad (Mam didn't come to wave me off – she won't admit it, but it was all a bit overwhelming for her. She'd stayed at home, insisting the wheelie bin needed hosing down. Of course. What else would you do when your heavily pregnant daughter is about to emigrate to distant shores?). Dad's hand rested heavy and warm on my shoulder. His eyes burned brightly as he gave me all the advice he could think of regarding moving to a foreign country, having a baby, living in a different culture and finally getting to know the man you've married. In the end, he got lost for words and even a little choked up. "If in doubt, just listen to The Beatles, Jess. They'll always make you feel better." I remember Baki had kicked me in the ribs at that very moment. A sure sign that we had another Beatles fan on the way.

"You've been through tonnes, sweetie." Ella continued. "First you tried to get Mesut a visa to be in the UK for the birth but it was just too fucking hard and unpredictable and *expensive*. So that didn't happen. Then you spent the majority of your pregnancy working like a dog so you could earn the money to pay for healthcare out in Turkey, just so you and Mesut could be together for the birth. And I remember those luscious letters you sent me about everything you were learning. The new culture, how tricky Turkish was to master, and what it was like when you had Baki and he didn't thrive and your boobs were in agony and all the hospital visits that went with that. That would be enough to drive the toughest of us away from joy, away from self-love."

Ella is right. Of course she is. And it *was* good to go through it all on the front step today, the August sunshine kind enough to give us a little coaxing to speak from the heart. At that moment, Baki snapped up his soppy head from my knee and trundled back off to Dotty who had now turned the trike upside down and was making the wheels spin round and round. Ella handed me a baby wipe from the secret stash that ALL mothers have about their person and I rectified the snot-fest on my knee.

"Yeah. And I remember that letter you sent me after you had Dotty. About breastfeeding. Do you remember?"

"Oh Christ, I hardly remember writing that thing to be honest. I was in a right daze after Dotty came along. I just remember having this powerful urge to warn you about how fucking hard breastfeeding is. Nobody bloody tells you! I felt it was my duty because I was the first one out of the two of us to go through it."

"Ella, it was the best letter ever. Only you could write in such exquisite detail about squirty milk and crusty nipples and enclose a shopping list entitled 'Titty Survival List'."

"Twas my duty," Ella guffawed. I love it when she does that.

All her facial piercings kind of knit together and sparkle as much as her words. It feels like a blessing.

Which means it probably is one.

Once Goliver arrived, we tore Baki and Dotty away from the trike (that's parent-speak for '*we took the trike with us, it wasn't worth the drama*') and made our merry way to Bernie's house. When we arrived and were ushered into the conservatory, Gillie and Ella did a little yelp when they saw the tartan tablecloth, the vases of (yet more) thistles and a veritable Scottish banquet. Bernie had outdone herself.

"I hope there's something for everyone," she practically sang. "I did some chunky vegetable soup, and some Muirdrith oatcakes and cheese to dip in. Then there's a wee bit of smoked salmon, and Frida's absolute favourite: haggis bon-bons with peppercorn and whisky sauce." Bernie was joyfully oblivious to the inappropriate concept of feeding one's child whisky *anything*. Flashbacks of cherry liqueurs, once again. "Then for afters there's a bit of strawberry shortbread and Scottish tablet."

Fuck it. Scottish tablet. Potentially my nemesis. Dear Reader, have you ever tried the stuff? It's a bit like fudge but more crumbly, more melt-in-the-mouthy, more just plain deliciousy. See? Even the thought of it makes me lose my grasp on the English language.

So, I crept in a way that I hoped nobody else noticed, to the opposite side of the conservatory. No way was I jeopardising my Ramadan efforts for a bowl of what was essentially crystallised condensed milk. I hid behind Frida's doll's house, nursing my little glass of water. Hopefully the siren call of the tablet would not be heard from here.

This afternoon at Bernie's was just the tonic I needed after such an eventful morning. Just warm and friendly and cheery. I loved watching how Goliver and Ella connected so effortlessly with Bernie, not something you can ever guarantee when you introduce friends you've made over the years and in entirely different circumstances. Who's to say there wouldn't be a clash between Ella's exuberance, Gillie's tenacity, Oliver's acuity and Bernie's fearlessness? But there wasn't. If anything, it all came together in the most wonderful cocktail of friendship I could have hoped for.

Everybody raved about the food, which didn't surprise me because it looked (and smelled) amazing. Bernie is one of those people who seems to glide around the kitchen so effortlessly and simply 'throws' these things together. Nigella wouldn't get a look-in.

I remember when I came to her house for the first time. Mesut and I had not long moved into the flat, and were wide-eyed and frantic whilst we got used to the millions of cats and the Black Eyed Peas thumping mercilessly through our floors. To me, Bernie's house had completely personified the colour orange – warm, cosy, welcoming, full of promise and friendship and protection. Photos of her three older kids everywhere, sticks of incense slotted into little nooks, Frida's toys scattered about the place, books about angels stacked haphazardly and always, always the rattle and boil of the kettle, the quiet, cheering chatter of the radio.

I left Bernie's house after that first visit, smiling up at the dramatic northern skies, thanking the universe for throwing us together, and vowing that I'd find a way to get us out of the flat with that prolific-note-writing-woman. Already I'd had it with being reprimanded for wrongful towel-folding or the excessive number of noise-making toys Baki owned. I didn't know then just how hard a task that would turn out to be.

So you can imagine how blessed I felt today then, to have my little tribe thrown together under Bernie's roof. Baki, Dotty and Frida went to town on the strawberry shortbread and were now in a food coma of sorts, slowly rolling on the grass of

Bernie's back garden, alternately playing on the trike of doom. The rest of us were sitting in a generous ray of sunshine, while Bernie made up a doggy bag for me for later. "No haggis bon bons for me, remember Bern. Ramadan is not the time to break the vegetarian habit of a lifetime."

"Ah. Bless you, poppet. The angels are proud," Bernie called from the open door of the conservatory, whilst none of us batted an eyelid. Even Goliver and Ella were used to the angel-talk by now. I'd even go so far as to say we liked it. I mean, who doesn't like an angel?

"Speaking of angels," Bernie trilled as she came back outside to join us, tossing a doggy bag in my lap before she lay down on a sun lounger. "They've been bothering me to chat to you, dear Oliver."

"They have?" Oliver tweaked an eyebrow upwards.

"Yep. You're a photographer, aren't you?"

"That I am."

"Right, well, I think we need your skills here in Muirdrith. At least, before you go back home, anyway."

Oliver's other eyebrow tweaked. She really had him now. "Tell me more."

"Gladly." Bernie melted backwards in her lounger and wiggled her toes in excitement. She went on to explain to Oliver that sometimes the angels move her to organise things and she's not always informed why, but she knows she can trust them and that there will be some deeper purpose.

Dear Reader, I have personally, seen this in action. Like the time she anonymously left second-hand books all over town for a whole month, which prompted the local council to establish a new literary festival. Or the time she paint-bombed the side of a derelict building and some local millionaire noticed it, bought it and turned it into an alternative education centre for disadvantaged young people.

More recently, Bernie published some seemingly random numbers in the ads section of the local paper, and next thing we knew, the steering group of a local hippy commune won the lottery and put all the money into doing the place up. They chatted on the local news about how one of their members had seen these numbers printed in the paper, felt strangely drawn to them and bought a ticket on behalf of the group. Now it looks like the people of Muirdrith will have access to classes and courses in yoga, meditation, eco-living and more all in state of the art, eco-friendly facilities, basically because of Bernie and her weird orders from the angels.

Honestly, it's like magic in action.

"I've got no idea why the angels keep going on at me about this. It could be of huge benefit or it could be small, poppets, but I'm being told that Oliver HAS to do a photo sesh for our toddler group. And I like the idea, anyway. Don't you think that would be fun, Jess? Let's get all the parents and kiddywinks together, and offer them to have their photo taken. By the lovely Oliver."

Gillie smiled up at Oliver from her spot snuggled close to him. "Wouldn't you usually charge for that kind of thing?"

"Yeah. But this is different, Gillie. This is from the *angels*." Oliver flashed a grin at Bernie and she knew he was genuine. "I'm totally up for that, Bernie. Let's do it."

"Wonderful! This is going to be magic." Bernie clapped her hands together several times and beamed a smile of champions out at all of us. Then she flittered her fingertips around her head and shoulders in a way that I'd seen her do a hundred times or more. It was as if she was brushing something pesky away. "Yes, yes, I get it. You can have your little party now. But I've done what you wanted, leave me to mine now please."

We went on, in our excitement, to talk about the logistics of it all. Ella is gutted she's going to miss it, but helpfully suggested we stage the photo shoot at the beach, which is easily the most picturesque part of Muirdrith (Google it. You won't believe the magnificence).

Gillie has said she'll help parents with the babies and Bernie is bringing Scottish tablet for sustenance. It's all arranged for the day before Goliver has to go home, which is Wednesday, the same day as my next visit from Children's Services. Well, at least I'll have some distraction from my crappy parenting, I guess. And Bernie insists there's plenty of time to get the word out, reminding us all we are not alone. "The angels have their ways of making this kind of news known, my loves. People will be there. You just wait."

Ever the gentleman, Oliver quickly brushed the attention off himself and turned to me. "Jess! You'll soon be getting a call off Mona's daughter, won't you? What are you going to tell her for this newspaper interview?" His spiky quiff cast a comical shadow over his face that made him all the more loveable. "She'll probably ask you what you've learned or something."

Ella chimed in. "She's learned that garlic bread is the food of gods and to avoid your toddler stuffing an ice cream in your face at all costs."

"Yes, I still have the scars." I said, brushing my fingertips over my mouth which is now less 'sexy cut lip' and more 'has she got a cold sore?' I shot Baki a disapproving look that bounced off his chubby little body and straight back at me. How do toddlers *do* that? And I did have something to share, actually. Something I haven't even really told you, Dear Reader. "Well, erm, I have been keeping a bit of a record."

"Yes, yes. The My Little Ramadan blog. Don't worry, we're all die-hard readers now." Gillie looked up at Oliver for a supporting nod. She got it.

"It's not just that though. I really love writing the blog, but well, I found my old notebook from, you know, a few years ago when everything . . . happened." I am referring, of course to the year 2006 when my fiancé Jack up and left and sent me spiralling into a whole year of not just heartbreak and grief, but also wonder, adventure, self-discovery and love. I kept a journal back then, more or less coached by Oliver, and it inexplicably helped me to process everything that had been going on. "I just need a bit more than typing at a laptop. I need to feel a pen or pencil in my hand. The roughness of the paper under my palm. It feels more immediate. More raw."

"Totally!" Oliver grinned. "Glad to hear the game is back on."

"It is! There are quite a few blank pages left so I started writing the things I'm learning during Ramadan. Just to look back on one day. Maybe help Beast-Child when he decides he wants to do it."

"Fabulous!" Ella stuck her hand out for the book. "Have you got it with you? I know you have. You used to carry it around everywhere." She was right. As usual. Her eyes widened as I took the notebook out of my bag. "I forgot how pretty this little thing is with all its beads and bells. Can I look?" Ella flipped way past all the notes from 2006 and to the back pages where I've started writing new stuff. She found the words scrawled across a double page spread:

Ramadan Learning Curve

And began to read . . .

1. *Food is amazing*
2. *Dehydration causes a million horrible things to happen to the body (and mind) so we could all be a lot more grateful for the clean water that flows from our taps*
3. *Food is amazing*

4. *Being a mam is hard enough as it is, but without the proper sustenance it is next to impossible. I cannot believe Baki still wants to be around me. It's a miracle*
5. *Food is amazing*
6. *I <u>am</u> able to discipline myself! If I can fast for Ramadan, who knows what else I can do?*
7. *Food is amazing*
8. *Mesut, although prone to epic sleeping bouts, is a wonderful, warm and devoted husband. Love him so much*
9. *Food is amazing*
10. *I am a bloody excellent wife*

"You are a bloody excellent wife." Ella launched herself at me, potentially compromising the stability of the plastic garden chair I was sitting on. "And a bloody excellent friend too! Now let me squeeze you before Dotty and I jet off into the much-awaited sunset!"

Therein followed all the merriment and chair-tumbling you can imagine whilst we busied ourselves appearing as if Ella's departure was totally fine. I mean it is, of course. We don't live in a fairy tale and people have to get back to their lives. But as I waved Keith the Van off, standing outside Bernie's house this afternoon, clinging to Gillie a little more than I'd care to admit, I got a rush of total love that told me something. It told me, *this has been an important chapter, Jess. This is friendship in its element. Instead of gripping it, try letting it go . . . the space you create will be divine.*

I glanced at Bernie, because this sounded distinctly angel-like. She was crouching on her doorstep, hugging Frida close. She must have felt my eyes land on her because she looked up, and smiled so broadly I could feel the warmth from the other side of the street, pulsing in sincere invisible circles that fell gloriously and softly around me. She shrugged and turned her smile heavenwards, the direction she knew best. And that, Dear Reader, felt like the most important conversation I've had during the whole of Ramadan.

Aside from this one, that we're having now.

Of course.

Not-A-Granny-Flora
Well done for getting yourself to the doctor's. Hope you had a nice time with Ella. Is your brother reading these posts now? I think he should be showing you his support, even if we all know Ramadan is ridiculous.
Jess.AKYOL
Mam, Ramadan is not ridiculous – you can't say stuff like that. It's people's beliefs! Your son-in-law's beliefs, to be precise. Anyway, yes, Max read yesterday as I recall. Don't know if he'll be back. Had a brilliant time with Ella. Sad she's gone but hopefully I'll see her again soon.

MaxAttax
Yes, I'm here. Reading like a devoted brother. Keep going, Jess. I am showing you my support (might join in myself just to send Mam over the edge). Peace out.
Jess.AKYOL
If you did, I'd read your blog from the start.
MaxAttax
Shoulda. Woulda. Coulda. Peace out.

AngelBernie
Jess, you silly soul, you've made my eyes leak.

Jess.AKYOL
Well I'm just glad my silly soul found your silly soul, leaking eyes or not.

Angnonymous
Scottish tablet – my nemesis too. I bet AngelBernie makes blasta tablet.
Jess.AKYOL
She does. I am eating it now and may well stash some in the patchy sofa of fame for a later date. Yet again, you mentioned Bernie.
Angnonymous
Did I? Hadn't noticed. 😉

HaggisBonBonWonders!!!
Traditional haggis bon-bons made by the ancient and reverant McCampbelkenziedonald family in the Scottish Highlands encased in golden breadcrumbs for extra wonder. Perfect with peppercorn sauce and a wee dram! Follow us on social media for the perfect Scottish experience. We love your post – now you can love ours!
Jess.AKYOL
I would but . . . Can you check your ancient family name? McCampbelkenziedonald? Not sure it exists therefore have qualms about your balls of encrusted meat.

OliverChen1!
Loved hearing gems from your notebook today, Jess. Takes me back to old times. Remember that meditation we did by the lake in Durham? That was awesome. Maybe we can do one on the beach after our photo shoot on Wednesday. Can't wait!
Jess.AKYOL
Of course I remember. Thought you'd landed from a distant

planet asking me to do stuff like that in broad daylight. It was the start of something beautiful though . . . and yes, I would be up for more on the beach.

OliverChen1!

This is at risk of being called a soppy git, but I'm glad I met you, Jess Akyol. Not least because I got to meet Gillie too. That business course when I first saw her feels like a lifetime ago. Can't believe we're being pummelled by thistles in the Scottish Highlands now when last time I looked we were drifting in a hot air balloon above the mountains of central Turkey!

Jess.AKYOL

You're being *pummelled* by thistles now? What has happened to Thistle-Dispenser Lady? Is she on speed?

OliverChen1!

She's certainly raised the bar. Pummelling was maybe a slight exaggeration. But there are thistles in the soap now. And hanging from the shower curtain. Gillie says it's the final straw / thorn.

Jess.AKYOL

Well I'm afraid you're going to have to put up with it. Thistle-Dispenser Lady is, after all, the key to my imminent fame and fortune.

GILLIE_LASS77

Jess, there aren't many people I would endure thorns for but you, my dearest friend, are one of them. Nice post today, by the way.

Jess.AKYOL

Thanks gorge. I will tend to your wounds and then when I'm famous, I will pay somebody to do it, I promise.

GILLIE_LASS77

I should think so. George Clooney will do. Oh, and keep your

eyes peeled on the comments. If I have my way, you might have a new reader tonight. xxx
Jess.AKYOL
Oooh. Who?
GILLIE_LASS77
Nope. Not telling.

CrunchyNut_Mummy
Oooh, I love the sound of the photo shoot, Jess. Count me in. I'll spread the word too. What time on Wednesday?
Jess.AKYOL
Great! Glad you can be there. I'm thinking afternoon. I'm sure the angels will get a message to you somehow. 😂

Fab4CoolDad
It won't be long until you see Ella again. It never is with you two. Maybe Ella can listen to this while she's driving down south in Keith the Van . . . 'Hello Goodbye'.
Jess.AKYOL
Ella will love this, Dad. Thanks. xxx

ask_yo_girl_about_me
It's great to read your post and your great words in my eyes. I would love to connect sometime eventually because it would be great. Hit the link to have great times with me and eventually others too. www.greattimesaheadeventually.cn
Jess.AKYOL
You're back! Eventually. 😉

Combustable.Apocalips
I don't know how your husband can stay with you. You mocking Islam with all of this.
MesutAk1

She not. She learning. You not helping. Go away. Gulazer, please start deleting these posts.
Jess.AKYOL
Gladly.

NO_Just_DON'T(1)
If you delete the comments you're basically restricting freedom of speech. You can't expect to write a blog like this and not have comments on it that you find challenging. You bring it on yourself, just like yet another visit from Children's Services. Your poor kid.

stella-mumsy
I've never had haggis bon bons but they sound delicious!
Jess.AKYOL
According to everyone else, they are. Managed to keep Baki off the whisky sauce, thank god! Thanks so much for coming back and reading.

MesutAk1
I loving you as always, Gulazer but we need talking about this reporter. Is not in Muslim way. And I will miss Ella too (don't telling her).
Jess.AKYOL
Okay, beautiful. Whatever you need. Ella might see your comment and your secret will be out, but probably not until tomorrow as she'll be driving all night. Hope Dotty sleeps through it.

KadafiDancingKing
Mrs Jessssssssss! Remember me? I am not believing it! Mrs Gillie found me on Facebook and tells me you are doing Ramadan with Mesut. And you are both in İskoçya now? No!

How will I ever show you my new dance moves? You will be very impressed. And I am impressed with you, Mrs Jess. Always following your goodness and your heart. Remember our talks about destiny in İpeklikum? And you have a baby boy now too! His name is Baki? Did you know 'Baki' is meaning 'eternal'? Eternal like your loving Mesut. This is making me very happy to be here on your blog site.

Jess.AKYOL

Flipping heck, Kadafi? Gillie said I might have a new reader but I never, in a million years, imagined it would be you! How the heck are you? How is life? You're still dancing and wowing all the girls in the bars then? I could NEVER forget our talks about destiny in İpeklikum – your appearance was timing of the most divine kind! Oh how I miss your cheeky (and incredibly handsome) face. Please send me videos of you dancing, I want to see what your hips are up to these days. Are you still working at MegaTour? Wait til I tell Mesut I've heard from you. He'll be so pleased! And yes, we have Baki – he is beautiful and wild and stubborn and strong. You'd love him.

KadafiDancingKing

I not working at MegaTour anymore. Now I studying to be English language teacher. I knows I can do it because you remember my English is very good. Dancing just for fun but I will send you videos of other night in Beerbelly Bar. Is still there but very change now. Mesut sometimes text me. He not tell you? He still very private person then. Hope you are both happy in the freezy hills of İskoçya. Will be hard for Mesut coming from hot, hot Manevitaş. Keep following the goodness, Mrs Jess!

Jess.AKYOL

I'll try, lovely boy. I'll try. Xxx

14

DAY 14 – THE MUSLIM WAY

Muirdrith, Highlands of Scotland, UK
Tues 24th Aug 2010
Sunrise / Suhoor: 5.57am
Sunset / Iftar: 8.38pm

It's happened folks. Ramadan has finally shown itself to be the massive, gaping chasm of culture and religion between myself and my husband, that it actually is.

This particular gaping chasm has not quite warranted plate-throwing or sofa-sleeping, but we are on the money for frequent, disappointed glances and long, mournful silences.

Mesut asked last night, in the comments of yesterday's blog, if he could talk to me about this interview idea for the newspaper. I thought he wanted to be in on the action. You know, to make sure they get all the details right and so that his religion is depicted in the correct way.

How wrong could I be?

What he actually wanted to say was: "Please don't do it."

This is not the first time I have felt crushing disappointment from one simple but intensely-meant statement from Mesut.

And I'm sure to the heavens it won't be the last. But it knocked me sideways.

"What do you mean, don't do it?" I asked in the middle of wiping Baki's yogurt-covered cheeks as he sat in his highchair in the middle of the kitchen. Cat-Crazy Flatmate was just next door in her bedroom / cat sanctuary, sleeping off the nightshift from yesterday, so we had to keep our voices low.

"I meaning . . . Please. Don't do it."

"It's okay. I'm not going to reveal anything too personal. I know you're a very private person. All they need to know is that I have a husband who is Muslim and that's why I'm fasting."

"But you not fasting. You drinking water now. Is not proper and you knows I don't care but you cannot speak of it in newspaper. Is not Muslim way."

Deep breaths, Jess. Deep breaths. Now is not the time to fly into woman-on-a-soap-box-mode (my default mode thanks to past relationship scars. Anyone else? No? Just me? Okay then). "So what is it, exactly, that is not the Muslim way? How would me talking to a newspaper worry you, exactly?"

These are the times our relationship comes under scrutiny. Not only do we have to explain to each other the deep-rooted, entrenched details of our opposing cultures so that the other person might be able to find a tiny ounce of understanding, but we also need to find the words in a language that only one of us speaks natively. So if you ever contemplate a holiday romance turning into something more, just take a moment to ask yourself if you're also ready for THAT.

I could see Mesut mentally calculating both things right here, right now, in our kitchen. He took Baki out of his highchair, sat on a stool by the door and propped him on his jiggling knee, which Baki absolutely adores. He whispered Turkish endearments into his son's ear as he hung his head low, his hair now clouding any chance I had of figuring out what he was feeling. But I could hear, "Oğlum. Benim küçük maymunum. Seni seviyorum. Değerli oğlum."

Then he looked up.

"Gulazer . . . First of all, you have to understand. This Ramadan new and different for you. But for me, and all the other Muslims, is just normal. This my life. Is not special. Is not different."

"But it's interesting to so many people, Mesut! And besides, don't you want to spread the word of Ramadan?" I did my best dazzling smile showing all my teeth and everything. Within seconds I could see that tactic would get me nowhere because he matched my manic grin with a frown that took over his whole face.

"Gulazer. You even knows *why* Ramadan is holy month?"

"Erm, something about Allah talking to Muhammed?"

"No. Allah chose Muhammed, peace be upon him, specially, but he sending Angel Jibreel to communicate. To give his exact word and revealing everything in Quran. Between Jibreel and Muhammed."

"Okay. So Muhammed and Jibreel had a month-long chat?"

"Is not just chat, Gulazer. Is exact word of Allah. Through Jibreel, directly to Muhammed, who told everybody else word by word and didn't change anything. No newspapers, no blogs, nothing like that. Is so long ago times. He saying direct words from Allah and is first time everyone hearing. And why Allah choosing Muhammed? Because he knows he can be trusted with Word of God. If not Muhammed, then whole of Quran could be, how you say, mis-interped?"

"Misinterpreted?"

"Yes, it could be *mis-in-ter-pre-ted*. In Islam we try not doing gossip and false words. Is only Allah's truth. And you knows, in Ramadan, fasting not just about food and drink . . ."

"Yeah, I remember. You told me you're also not supposed to

swear or shout or lose your patience or gossip about others. Is that right?" (*Inward cringe. Have been swearing rather a lot on this blog*)

"Is right," Mesut nodded, now setting Baki down and pinching his ample cheeks before patting him on the bum and sending him off to play in his favourite kitchen cupboard of plastic bowls and plates. "We thinking fasting is like shield against wrong actions, against saying and doing wrong things. A way to be clearer and closer to Allah."

"Okay, but I don't understand what any of this has to do with me doing a teensy little interview for a newspaper?"

"Because is not word of Allah, is word of you. And reporter might getting things wrong. Might twist and turn words into something else. We not have control over that. Is just not right."

"But I'll try to get everything right, I promise! And it's only a little regional paper – probably not that many people will read it. And how is it any different from my blog? You've been alright with me writing that every day, haven't you?"

Mesut turned a gaze upon me that has honestly taken me years to get used to. It's a gaze that has power in it, and stubbornness in jumping, frightening sparks. But it also has softness and a heavy wash of love. God help me, I'm a sucker for that gaze because I know it brings his truth even if it's a truth I don't want to hear.

"I not liking you writing that blog."

It felt like I'd been punched in the stomach. "But you've been reading. You've been commenting! You've been seeing off those arseholes who say nasty things about me!"

"Tabi. Of course I have. But honestly, Gulazer, that is exactly problem." Raised voices now. Baki pulled out of his cupboard of delight, peering around the door with curious blue eyes. "I not liking where it taking you. Too much misunderstanding. You want to be good but really I am thinking is not good. You doing Ramadan."

I spun round to the sink, rolled up my sleeves and started washing the dishes. Aggressively. Because everyone knows that's the universal signifier for wives that are pissed off with husbands but don't want to have a screaming match. Yet.

Mesut took some deep breaths and lowered his voice to a barely audible murmur. "I fasting. I not shouting at you. Just think about my meaning. Please."

And he walked out.

That's what I've been left with. A potent resentment towards the man I love, hopelessly entangled with a grudging kind of respect. I'm so pissed off that he could let me get this far through Ramadan, have me believing he was happy I was supporting him and broadcasting the news to the world . . . but I'm also in awe that he has such deeply held beliefs he would ask me to reign myself in.

Fuck, this is hard.

I know it won't have been easy for him to say that about my blog. He knows that writing is my thing. He knows that I need it to keep grounded in myself, to notice and make and celebrate my connections with the world. Writing is *my* Islam. Just because my religion isn't a world-wide-recognised thing, doesn't mean it's not absolutely crucial to who I am and how I exist.

I have to be honest, I was SO tempted to raid Baki's Milky Bar stash that I stomped to the fridge once Mesut dicked off. But something stopped me in my tracks. Lindy's note that she emailed me just a few days into this whole thing:

"I have to tell you how thoughtful and loving your Ramadan gesture is. Love is about sharing, respecting each other, doing things as a couple and showing how much you care for one another in a deeply respectful way – even if it's something that

challenges your own beliefs. Jess, you taught me that. Please keep going."

Instead of powering on through and completing my livid swoop into the dark delights of the fridge, I paused.

Love is about sharing.

Deeply respectful.

Challenges your own beliefs.

My tummy growled but my heart growled louder.

The game was still on.

I tore Baki away from his cupboard and took him through to his bedroom, which is now sadly devoid of Ella and Dotty and their air mattress. There he sat scarily close to the little portable TV screen, plastic hammer in hand, bashing his changing bag repeatedly, whilst waiting for me to get my act together and bloody well put Bob The Builder on.

The flat fizzed with silence. A silence that told me Mesut was long gone. Maybe he'd gone to work, or maybe he'd gone walking or something. I knew I needed to just let that be as it was and pay attention to my own feelings now. I mean, if there's something I've learned from my previous CBT counselling, it's to not automatically wrestle with difficult stuff. Those feelings, they're already there, so why would I make them worse by wrestling? It's so hard but these days I try my best to just feel it. Absorb it. Move through it.

And I grab my notebook for it . . .

Mesut is unhappy because:

1. *Ramadan is not anything out of the ordinary for him and he doesn't see why it should be shouted about in a newspaper article*

2. *He is worried that the reporter may twist and warp my words thereby creating a vehicle of gossip about the very discipline that should deter such a thing*
3. *He has stopped seeing the value in me doing Ramadan now that I am drinking water*
4. *He doesn't really want me to continue writing my blog*
5. *He feels misunderstood by his wife*

I am unhappy because:

1. *I have had the wind taken out of my sails regarding my commitment to Ramadan*
2. *I thought the interview might help get some attention for my writing (selfish?)*
3. *My husband is putting his religion before my own deep-rooted values and beliefs*
4. *I want to keep writing my blog but feel it has now been thwarted*
5. *I feel misunderstood by my husband*

After four years together, Mesut and I have certainly been here before.

It reminds me of the time we were visiting Mesut's family in Manevitaş in South Eastern Turkey. It was winter and it was time for Bayram, the Turkish word for Eid. Eid is an Islamic celebration held twice a year (the first one is at the end of Ramadan) and this was the second one, better known as Kurban Bayram. This particular celebration involves sacrificing a sheep, cooking it, eating it and offering parts of it to poorer families. A real party for vegetarians like me, as you can imagine.

Mesut and I had been together for two years by this point,

but were still making discoveries about each other on the cultural front. However, I did think he knew me well enough to guess that I might not have wanted to be an active part of sacrificing the poor sheep that had just been brought up and through the family house and onto the roof where everyone was now standing. I was downstairs, with his pregnant younger sister, who had been excused from witnessing the event due to being with-child and therefore over-sensitive to such things as blood and guts and gore. For some inexplicable reason, Mesut had not even clocked that my vegetarian status should / could earn me the same discretion.

He stared at me in open-mouthed horror when I absolutely refused to come up and watch such a thing. He'd clearly told his family I would be there and, for them, it was a momentous occasion that they wanted to show me. But nothing was shifting me. We all have our boundaries and mine was right there, on the side of the sheep's life.

(*Personally, I think they're lucky I didn't stage a very loud protest / dramatic freeing of the sheep involving banners and loud speakers and bolt cutters. Instead, they got the quiet protest of my distinct absence. All I felt I could do, given the circumstances.*)

This fasting may not have cleared my path to Allah, but I have to make it good for something. I have to let it clear things for *me*. So Mesut can have his opinion, but I can also have mine. And I'll let those words from Lindy's note sit in my consciousness softly. Because if love is about sharing, then I need to speak up too.

Night-sun-ella
Flippin' heck I'm gone for one day and it's all gone to pot! Only

kidding. Jess, you fabulous nutcase, you and Mesut will work it out together. Don't lose the faith.

Jess.AKYOL

I'll try not to, Ella. And I'll keep on keeping on with Ramadan. Still want to reap the apparent benefits. Hope the drive of doom wasn't too bad? Did Dotty behave herself? Miss you so much! #BlogSqueeze

Night-sun-ella

Ooooooh I miss you more than I miss those delicious haggis balls that Bernie kept filling my plate with. #BlogSqueeze and #Blog-YourHeadInMyLapAsISingYouSongsThatYouSecretlyLove-LikeJudyGarlandAndTheSpiceGirls – Yes Dotty was amazing. But I nearly knocked over a sheep. Could have brought it back up for Mesut to sacrifice on the roof. Fun.

Compustable.Apocalips

THIS COMMENT HAS BEEN DELETED

stella-mumsy

Wow – your husband's culture sounds so interesting! Very different though, so must be hard.

Jess.AKYOL

Hard sometimes. Lovely sometimes.

GILLIE_LASS77

Jess, I'm so sorry we weren't there today to talk to! Oliver and I had a fab day out at Loch Ness though. Thought I saw Nessie but Oliver says it was just a branch. Disappointing. Don't worry – tomorrow's photo shoot will keep your mind off it all. Remember to get Oliver to take some pics of you and Baki. Bet nobody else ever does that.

Jess.AKYOL

That does sound nice, actually. Glad you had a good day and

that you nearly made a discovery of global importance at Loch Ness. #BetterLuckNextTime

OliverChen1!
Yes, we will have a fantastic photo shoot tomorrow, matey. Meanwhile, wish us luck with the thistles.
Jess.AKYOL
Lovely! See you tomorrow. So glad you're both here – remember to check the toilet for thistles too.

Angnonymous
Sounds like your spirit is being tested Jess. Ramadan suddenly got real.
Jess.AKYOL
Indeed it did. So, you're a.) Scottish ✓ b.) somehow connected to Bernie ✓ and c.) a bit spiritual ✓. Am I getting close?
Angnonymous
Scarily.
Jess.AKYOL
#airpunch

NO_Just_DON'T(1)
THIS COMMENT HAS BEEN DELETED

FatimaNazar
How lovely that you are honest about your cultural clashes with your husband on this blog. I read so many posts that are either complaining heavily about partners from another culture OR posts that are too sugar-laced. This is real. Thank you, Jess (and I hope you sort it out).
Jess.AKYOL
Aw, that means a lot. For obvious reasons, I didn't know whether to post today or not. You're right! In the Turkish-English forums

I've been on there is so much dross. I've never been one to buy into stereotypes and I'm not about to start now. Are you Turkish? I'm guessing you're Muslim but not sure where you're from?

FatimaNazar

I am from Iran but live in America with my husband. We've been together twelve years but still sometimes we learn new challenges with each other! He is not Muslim like me but we manage to get along somehow.

Jess.AKYOL

Yeah, it's ongoing, isn't it? I think it makes us stronger couples in the end, though. Thank you again for reading my posts. I'm glad you found them.

KadafiDancingKing

Follow the Goodness, Mrs Jess. Follow the Goodness.

Fab4CoolDad

Blimey. Relationships are hard. Give it a bit of time and it'll come good. So, in other words: 'Let it Be'.

Jess.AKYOL

I hope you're right, Dad.

15

DAY 15 - FOLLOW THE GOODNESS

Muirdrith, Highlands of Scotland, UK
Weds 25th Aug 2010
Sunrise / Suhoor: 5.59am
Sunset / Iftar: 8.35pm

Flip, I'm hungry.

Can't say the other 'f' word on account of it being pre-sundown.

I'm sitting quietly and alone on the patchy sofa of fame, now that Baki has been bathed, fed, watered and put to bed. I am filling in the last thirty-four minutes and twenty-seven seconds before feast time. That's if you can call Doritos and hummus a feast when it is not even accompanied by the standard mug of wine.

Today has been awesome. And I mean that in the true sense of the word. I'm not ashamed to admit I may have been caught with my gob hanging open and my eyes full and wide on more than one occasion. And that's why these last few silent minutes spent alone before sundown feel somehow fitting.

I need to let all the good stuff settle.

Nicky and Aja came back to see me today. This time Mesut was there too and the occasion was thankfully bereft of cat poo, cherry liqueurs and the Muirdrith motherhood collective. I did not throw boxes of shortbread at the poor women this time, despite the potential child-stealing powers they had that were rattling my nerves.

Aja explained that the person / people making the reports of neglect had been in touch again, but that they'd noticed a pattern that gave them cause to suspect the reports could be malicious. They were far too professional to give me any really sordid details but there was mention of me supposedly being on drugs at the local fun fair, leaving Baki on his own in a van all night and apparently I'm now starving him for Ramadan too. "These kinds of reports have all the markings of somebody trying to do you right down, Jess. We can see how much you love and care for Baki and we have confirmation from the community centre and Wee Bairns World that, although his speech is delayed, he's always clean, happy and engages well. Apart from the cat faeces and the alcoholic confectionery that featured in our first visit, which we understand were one-off events, we're not seeing any huge cause for concern. We want to support you and Mesut to be the best parents you can be and make sure little Baki is safe and happy."

"That's all I want too," I mumbled.

Nicky nodded. "We get that, Jessica, we really do. There are procedures we have to follow in light of the initial reports, but we don't need to escalate this. Rather, we need to find out where you need support and make sure you get it. Baki's too precious not to."

The fact that somebody else saw the sublimity of my boy (who was currently wiping his snots onto Bob The Builder's face) made me crumple then and there. A singular sob caved my body inwards and Mesut caught me almost before I knew what was happening. "I'm sorry," I sniffed, speaking directly towards my own folded navel. "I'm just so relieved you don't think I'm an awful mam."

"It's never as black and white as that," Aja explained, handing me a tissue out of her bag. "We just want to do our best to understand your situation as a family. Nicky and I can see that you're doing all you can, despite some pretty challenging circumstances."

"Challenging circumstances?" Mesut asked.

"Well, yeah." Nicky gestured to the very room we were sitting in. "We know you'd rather live somewhere else and have a bit more space, independence and, erm, well, privacy?" She said this as not less than three cats were winding their way around her shins, rubbing their gunky eyes on her trousers and purring in a fashion that was less adorable and more menacing.

"Yes. We want it." Mesut squeezed me further in towards him. The first real physical contact we've had in days.

"We can understand that," continued Nicky. "So Aja here is going to put you in touch with the right people to advise you on housing. And finances too, if you like. We can get an adviser to make sure you're getting all the correct benefits."

"Oh, we can't get benefits. Because Mesut isn't a British citizen, we're not entitled to anything." I know this to be true after some desperate Google-searching in the early days of stepping foot in the Highlands. We have to rely on his pint-pulling / haggis-kebab-making skills to keep us afloat. There isn't exactly any disposable income left over to splurge on luxuries like our own flat.

"I wouldn't be too sure about that," Aja smiled, all warm and hopeful. "I've worked with lots of multi-cultural families and you'd be surprised what you're entitled to. After all, Jess, you're a British citizen, and a tax payer to boot. We'll get you sorted, don't worry."

After that little gem of very-much-appreciated wisdom, the four of us talked about other things that will help keep our little family unit strong. Apparently I've been doing all the right things by going to the Parent & Toddler group, enrolling Baki in nursery, and getting out and about with him on a daily basis. Rather than carting me off to the local loony bin on hearing I'd been referred for more counselling, they were actually really pleased I was open to such a thing, and relieved to hear the doctor had heard me out.

Mesut, who is still finding it hard to look me in the eye, was amazing. He sang my praises like his life depended on it and if Nicky and Aja weren't my biggest fans by the time they walked out of the door, it wasn't thanks to him. I know we've got unresolved issues, but the way he spoke about me today reminded me that it'll take more than a cultural conundrum to rock the foundations of what we've got together.

Just as Nicky and Aja were shrugging their bags back onto their shoulders and heading out into the sunny splendour of Muirdrith, Nicky turned to me and smiled. "You probably won't hear from me until Baki's next health check, Jessica, so I'm just going to take this chance to say . . . Oh my god, I bloody love your blog!"

"Me too!" Aja gasped. "My Little Ramadan is just brilliant! Please keep going with it and, well . . ." She glanced at Mesut, whose awkward smile was frozen on his face. "I'm sure you'll figure it all out between you. Sounds like you've weathered much tougher storms."

And she's right.

Sadly, the mention of the blog brought a certain darkness back to Mesut's eyes, and it was with a quiet, sombre voice he told me he was leaving for work. I didn't even have time to give myself a pep talk about the metaphorical gold stars he'd just given me in front of Nicky and Aja, before I received a practically pulsing text from Bernie:

Get yourself to the beach NOW!

It was time for the photo shoot.

Ah, Dear Reader, what a sight it was to behold. By the time I'd packed Baki into his buggy, fists and legs flailing in order to counteract any lift in mood I might have been feeling, and trudged down to the beach repeating to myself over and over like a mantra, '*I am not a prisoner to my toddler's tempers*', the photo shoot was in full swing.

I stood at the edge of the dunes, scanning the landscape for my friends amongst this amazing swarm of people. Oliver was easy to spot, his huge and impressive camera winking in the sunlight, swinging down low at his hip whenever he dropped it on its strap, to direct his subjects. Clusters of people hovered around him, waiting their turn to be photographed on the sun-sliced beach. There was many a jean leg artfully turned up around bronzed ankles, jaunty sun hats set on nodding heads, an alarming number of bright white, just-laundered shirts giving the whole crowd an androgynous, glamorous edge.

Children ran everywhere, threatening to spontaneously ruin their crisp, coiffed looks with one singular stumble into a rock pool. And there was Gillie, running amongst them with just as much energy, her curls streaming behind her like ribbons of red wine, a laugh pealing out of her that warmed me down to my toes in the sand.

I stepped forwards and turned Baki's buggy backwards. It's a trick I've learned through many unnecessary struggles, that when on a beach, dragging a buggy backwards on its back two wheels is infinitely easier than trying to push it forwards.

You can have that one for free.

I heard Bernie shout, "Poppet!" and my eyes landed on her

sitting on a glittering plane of sand, with Frida playing with a bucket and spade nearby. She had thistles (of all things) in her hair and her cheeks were as rosy as I've ever seen them. She was scoffing her own Scottish tablet (this time dotted with glacé cherries) like there was no tomorrow, but the best thing about this scene, Dear Reader, is that she had her T-shirt rolled under her boobs and tucked into her bra so that her bold and brazen baby bump was out and proud.

"Isn't it beautiful?" she practically shrieked. "It's not finished yet. We're just having a little break." I had no idea what she meant but Baki was arching his back to be sprung free from the buggy so I did the deed then managed to catch Gillie's eye who instantly blew me a kiss from her throng of children, and mouthed the words, *I'll keep an eye on him.*

"What's not finished yet? The photo shoot? Why have you got thistles in your hair? You look like a huge, Scottish, preggers Messiah."

"Nooooo, poppet. The photo shoot has just begun. Isn't it a massive success already? How did you get on with the child-stealers?"

"All good. They no longer want to steal Beast-Child. Never mind that. Thistles? And what's not finished?"

Bernie laughed from the depths of her belly so that I'm sure her baby must have felt it in his tiny soul. "This. This isn't finished yet." She raised a hand and pointed at the side of her belly that I couldn't see, so I moved around to take a look.

"Oh my god, that's amazing!" Bernie had the most exquisite beginnings of a wreath of thistles painted onto her tummy. The purples of the blooms glowed with a luminosity that came second only to Bernie's rosy cheeks and the greens and silvers of stems, leaves, thorns and roots looked like they were actually growing and stretching across the surface of her skin. I've seen bump-painting before but never anything like this. It was better than the most intricate tattoo. "Who *did* that?"

"Only your mate, Gillie. She's an amazing painter! Why didn't you tell me?"

"Wow! Yeah, she's always been good but I've never seen her do anything like this. The Scottish air must have inspired her."

"Either that or the famous Thistle-Dispenser Lady."

"What do you mean the Thistle-Dispenser Lady? What's Mona up to now? Is she here?"

Bernie pointed way down the beach to where I'd just seen Oliver, and there was Mona, lugging something huge and wiry across the sand, in much the same way I'd just dragged Baki's buggy. Oliver ran over to meet her, and they started lugging it together. "What the hell is that? It looks like a willow frame or something."

"Very perceptive. While Gillie was painting my bump, she told me that Mona has the most incredible willow archway thingie in the gardens at Thisteldown Lodge. She was raving about the way Mona has decorated it with different breeds of thistles and vines and crap like that. Gillie was totally into it, so that's basically the inspiration for my bump painting."

"Beautiful. But why are Mona and Oliver now knee-deep in waves with that weird structure. Isn't Thistle-Dispenser Lady a bit old for those kinds of shenanigans?" I pointed across the beach to where the two of them now stood, waves splashing at their legs, whilst they were heaving together two halves of something spiky and wiry.

"I'd say she's stronger than you think, poppet. Apparently Mona was so touched that Gillie liked the thistle archway, which, incidentally is in memory of her late husband, and she knew that Goliver had the photo shoot on the beach today, so . . ."

"So . . ."

"So she brought along a new one she's been working on. She decided it would be the perfect addition to Oliver's photo shoot so she took it apart, loaded it into her car, and somehow, with her seventy-year-old bones, dragged it all the way here from the car park.

"No way! She felt that strongly about the photoshoot that she did that?"

"Indeed she did. But I've told you once and I'll tell you again, the angels know what they're doing with this shit."

"Evidently." I flopped down on the sand, just as Gillie returned with Baki on her shoulders, both of them breathless and giggling. She set him down and he lunged at me, whinging for snacks, as Gillie flopped to the ground.

"That's it! I'm bloody exhausted. I'm off childminding duty and indulging in some art therapy. Bernie? May I?"

"Do it!" Bernie laughed, and Gillie picked up the paints at Bernie's side, ready to work a little more magic on that glorious bump. I chucked some cucumber sandwiches at Beast-Child, who predictably whined for Wotsits instead. He got them because a.) my will power is shot to shit and b.) I needed to watch the spectacle that was Oliver and Mona in peace.

It took them around twenty minutes to get that thistle-wrapped archway in place. By which time, the sun had dipped a miniscule but magnificent fraction in the sky so that it gleamed with golden glamour on the shivering crease of the rolling waters. Mona was right. The archway looked amazing.

I watched the families line up into a queue that nobody had organised but materialised anyway thanks to good old British manners. Oliver moved around with his own jeans turned up but still soaked to the knee, his bare feet trudging through wet sand, his spiky hair threatening to flop in the salty air and his smile as wide as could be. He directed mams and babies, whole families and sibling groups with a professionalism that seemed almost out of place here on the beach. I say almost, because Oliver has an uncanny knack of applying his talents anywhere and everywhere. Why should Muirdrith beach be any different?

"Isn't the young man marvellous?" By this time, Mona had strode over to join us away from the photographic hordes, treating herself to a proper sit down on a folding stool she'd had slung across her back like a bow and arrow. "You've got a good one there, Gillie. If you didn't have him snared, I'd have him in my sights for our Ailsa. More's the pity. Anyway, how's it all going, wee Jessie? Still in the throes of Ramadan, are we?"

"We are. We are drinking water now and we are pissing off one's husband by essentially making popular dross out of what is, to him, the most sacred and untouchable thing. But we endeavour."

"Endeavouring is what marriage is all about, m'eudail. You've got to keep that love strong and determined. But sometimes things get prickly." She let out a little squeak of laughter. "Like a thistle. Do you still want to meet with our Ailsa for an interview, luvvie? If it's going to rock the boat I can ask her to call the whole idea off, you know. It's nay too late."

"Let me think on it, Mona." I suddenly felt myself sink a little deeper into the sand. I still wanted to do the interview, but was it really worth risking my marriage and did I have anything interesting to say anyway? Who would want to read what an exhausted mam of a Beast-Child had to say?

About then, Gillie finished painting Bernie's bump and I can hands-on-heart say I have never seen an artwork so gorgeous. "There." Gillie smiled, and blew a kiss at the tummy. "Thank you, little baby, for not protesting too much."

Once Oliver was done with all the other families, we all helped pull Bernie's significant mass out of the sand and she hobbled over to the archway. Frida skipped over to join her mam and Bernie took one of the thistles out of her own hair, only to pop it into Frida's. The sun slid generously over the canvas of

Bernie's tummy and Frida lay her head, instinctively, against the cave where her future sibling lay. I saw how Oliver's shoulders dropped, presumably knowing he wouldn't have to direct this one in the slightest . . . just angle that camera and catch what he could.

"It'll be your turn in a minute. Then I'm taking him back to Thistledown Lodge to ravish him. Oops. Sorry, Mona." Gillie put her paints away and gave me a cheeky nudge.

"Don't mind me, m'eudail. Use your youth while you can. Do all the ravishing you want."

"Do you want to ravish him sooner rather than later?" I asked. "I'm not sure I'm up for a photoshoot. You know how I get when I'm in front of a camera and I really don't want to spoil today. It's been too nice."

"No, Jess. You've got to do it! Come on, Bernie said the angels want it this way. You can't argue with the angels."

"I reckon I could take them on," I grumbled, already imagining what it would be like to stand in front of Oliver's lens. I don't know about you, Dear Reader, but I have never felt that having a zoomable, mechanical implement pointed at me makes for heightened self-esteem. I doubted even the magnificence of the now glimmering ambers and silvers of the beach could enliven my pale skin, my sagging body. "Maybe Oliver could just photograph Baki. Or you? I'm sure Baki would like some pictures with his favourite auntie."

"No fucking way, Jess. You're doing this. And you're a beautiful momma. Right, Mona?"

"Och, she knows that, so she does." Mona tipped her sun hat and smiled beneath it. Who was I to argue with an old woman who'd just dragged half her garden across town?

Just then my phone pinged and I reached for it out of my bag, glad of the distraction. There was a video message with the caption, 'Follow The Goodness'. "Gillie. I think Kadafi's sent me a video."

"What? Oh quick, let's have a look before Oliver shouts you over. I bloody love this boy!"

You might have noticed from my blog comments a couple of days ago, that Kadafi was a surprise visitor to the blog. Only a surprise because I hadn't heard from him in so long. Since I first met Mesut, to be precise.

I'll give you a quick yet vital summary:

Kadafi is the much younger cousin of a dodgy Turkish gangster-type bloke who Gillie had a fling with way back when. We first beheld the spectacle that was Kadafi in the bar Mesut used to work in, where he entranced young and old alike with his dance moves. Imagine, if you will, the energy of Jim Carey, the charisma of Antonio Banderas and the spiritual kudos of Oprah. Meet: Kadafi.

"I did ask him to send me his new dance moves. Oh please, please, please let that be what this is."

All three of us bent over my little phone. Crappy Turkish pop music blared out and we were immediately entranced by the screen and its contents. Suddenly we were no longer sitting on Muirdrith Beach, but lounging on sofas in a sun-soaked bar, sweet cocktails in hand and our breath stopped by the dance phenomenon that was before us. The swerving hips . . . my god. The flipping, dipping torso . . . oh jeez. The thighs that defied gravity . . . what next? The broad, bronzed shoulders that rolled and swayed of their own accord in effortless time to the beat. But what really topped it off, what made this whole performance absolute electric, was the corners of a heartfelt smile raised to the sky, the smirking eyes drawing anybody who watched into his bliss. This was Kadafi.

Unapologetically, beautifully, and authentically . . . Kadafi.

"He's gone and done it again," I said, as the image snapped to black and the music faded out.

"What, defined the words 'hot and 'bothered'?" Gillie fanned herself with Baki's sun hat, abandoned hours ago.

"Nope. He's shown me what I need to do." Summoned by a new energy, I practically jumped to my feet, stretched my arms towards Baki until he jumped into them and I stood up straight and strong.

"Time to be more Kadafi."

"What?" Gillie wailed, looking up at me. "Are you going to go and dance for the camera or something?"

"No, you fool! I'm going to bloody well have my photo taken with my baby boy. And I'm going to . . . Follow. The. Goodness."

"Right, well before you do that . . . allow me." I thought she was going to whip out her paints again but no, Gillie's talents extend far and wide. She gathered my hair up into a messy knot, tied my baggy t-shirt in a bow at my waist, hitched one side of my long skirt so that it showed off a flash of thigh, rubbed my cheeks until they glowed, then took a thistle from an enthusiastic Mona and tucked it behind my ear. "There. Now you can follow the goodness."

"I will," I grinned as Baki and I started walking across the sand. "Oh, and Mona?"

Mona beamed at me, potentially knowing what was coming. "Aye, m'eudail?"

"You can tell Ailsa I'll do that interview."

And do you know what, Dear Reader? From that point on, I think the goodness was following me.

<u>Not-A-Granny-Flora</u>

Good news about Children's Services. Knew they'd see sense in

the end. I wonder who made the reports in the first place? And really, Jessica. Do you need somebody else's dance video to show you how to be confident? You're just fine how you are and you always have been. I'm sure the photos will be lovely.
Jess.AKYOL
Thanks, Mam. I think.

Fab4CoolDad
Your mother and I always counted ourselves lucky we created something so gorgeous. But until you believe it, 'I Want To Hold Your Hand' to help show you the way.
Jess.AKYOL

Angnonymous
I did hear there was something going on at Muirdrith beach today. Apparently the photoshoot caused quite the stir. Well done Jess and co – Scottish tablet all round!
Jess.AKYOL
Are you actually watching me? I'm eating Bernie's cherry tablet as we speak. Cos that's what tablet needs. Cherries.

LifeIsYoursLindy
Great post as always, Jess. I remember you talking about Kadafi. Tell him to post his videos on here please so we can all see the dancing phenomenon for ourselves! P.S. I bet the photos will be gorgeous.
Jess.AKYOL
KadafiDancingKing, can you do that? Lindy, he really is a sight to behold. Consider this fair warning, no matter which way you're inclined.

NO_Just_DON'T(1)

THIS COMMENT HAS BEEN DELETED

Compustable.Apocalips
THIS COMMENT HAS BEEN DELETED

Anonymous
THIS COMMENT HAS BEEN DELETED

OliverChen1!
I'm so glad you followed the goodness and joined the photo-shoot, matey. The pics are looking good so far – I'll send them to you and all the other parents soon. Looks like Kadafi's video saved the day – I'd hate you to have missed out just because of a little confidence wobble.
Jess.AKYOL
The boy is a god / Allah send. As are you. X
OliverChen1!
I tell you who's a godsend – Mona! That thistle archway made all the difference to the shoot, even if it did take an army of us to pull it apart and carry it back to her car. Gillie and I gave her a bottle of whisky tonight, to say thanks. Hoping she's eased off on the thistles for our final night's stay.
Jess.AKYOL
It would kind of be a shame if she did. I want to know where else she is capable of stuffing them.
OliverChen1!
That's fighting talk.

AngelBernie
Loving the vibes of this post, poppet. It has ALL the things. Currently cannot bring myself to wash off Gillie's masterpiece. Babe has been kicking lots too, so I think he's loving it as much

as I am. Hope you've eaten your own body weight in cherry tablet tonight, like I did on the beach today?
Jess.AKYOL
Obviously I have. My teeth may have dissolved by the morning.

MaxAttax
Not gonna say much on this other than, is EVERYBODY in Muirdrith a hippy? If so, I'm staying away. Peace out.
Jess.AKYOL
My brother: never one to stereotype. #soproud

funmum
I think I need to follow the goodness too. And perhaps visit Muirdrith. Is it always that exciting?
Jess.AKYOL
Nope. But today was a good day.

CrunchyNut_Mummy
OMG Jess, today was amazing! Oliver is the most kind and patient photographer and I think he might have got some really nice shots of me and the kids for once! Please don't let him leave Muirdrith!
Jess.AKYOL
Sorry, but I think he'd follow Gillie anywhere and she's off tomorrow. Glad you could come and that you got some nice pics. It really was a lush afternoon.

GILLIE_LASS77
I BLOODY LOVE YOU!
Jess.AKYOL
Duly noted. 😂

16

DAY 16 – ANGEL ON OUR SIDE

Muirdrith, Highlands of Scotland, UK
Thurs 26th Aug 2010
Sunrise / Suhoor: 6.01am
Sunset / Iftar: 8.32pm

Happy middle-of-Ramadan to you, Dear Reader.

It's officially the sixteenth day of Ramadan, which means I should be happy as the proverbial pig in crap. And crap is where we are, Dear Reader, but I'm afraid to report I am far from happy.

Mesut and I had some bad news last night, in the form of a long-distance phone call. His mam is in hospital after suffering a heart attack.

I know.

This is her fourth attack and apparently it's a touch and go situation. She had a rough night but is stable for now, according to Mesut's older brother, who was the one to call us in the middle of the night. Her doctors want to transport her to a specialist heart hospital on the other side of Turkey, so now the family has to decide if she's strong enough for a journey like that.

"How can I help them make right decision, Gulazer? If I not even see her?"

Poor Mesut. He's in bits.

I get it. I really do. When my dad had an operation on his pancreatic cancer the weeks after Baki was born, I flew over to England the soonest opportunity I got. Thankfully he's all better now. And I have a British passport, which for some unfathomable reason, gives me the power to skip about the globe as I wish. I don't understand how where you are born can affect how much of the world you are allowed to access.

Even though Mesut and I went through some type of existential visa hell to finally get him here to the UK, if he goes back to Turkey to see his mam now, there's no guarantee that the British Government will even let him back in.

Then there's the matter of the Turkish army. There's every possibility that if they clock him moving through a Turkish airport, they'll snap him up to carry out the National Service he never got round to doing (I'm not exaggerating – I know people who have been snatched – it actually happens).

It's hard for me to even imagine the position he is in. Torn between his ailing mother and his baby boy and wife? And there was me worrying about having my photo taken on the beach yesterday.

Anyway, we booked the ticket. It tore a bit of me out to do it, but I think that bit of me might be with his mam, so that's okay. I dusted off a credit card I vowed I'd never touch again and we gulped back the fear of how we'll pay it back. Gulping back the fear about if / when I'll see him again took an extra special effort.

He has to go. I know he does.

Strangely, this development – on account of its sheer gravity

– has gently drawn us towards each other again. The subject of the newspaper article and my blog are now tiny little pinhead-type things, whilst Mesut's mam hovering between life and death is everything.

Although, he is worried about leaving me at a time when we know somebody around here must have it in for us. I mean, who would go to the bother of reporting me to Children's Services unless they really wanted to do some harm? I just can't understand it. And it must be somebody close by because all that crap about me doing drugs at the fun fair and supposedly leaving Baki in the van all night . . . those things are lies built around real events. How did that person know? Why do they care?

I don't know what Mesut thinks he can do about all of that if he's here, but getting on a plane right now is shredding him to bits.

Sometimes I look back on the days when I first met Mesut on holiday in İpeklikum. It took me ages to figure out that I was romantically interested in him but I knew, more or less from the start, that he was going to be important. I knew he already had a piece of my soul and probably always had. And because of that, I knew we had the capacity to change each other's worlds.

We once spent a blissful night together in the hotel I was staying at (dubbed 'Shit Class Hotel' but that's another story) and when I woke in the morning I watched him sleep all twisted up in bright white sheets, the morning sun streaming in golden pools through the window and sliding over his long, dark limbs.

Instead of feeling the holiday romance glow that you might expect, the satisfied, serene buzz I would have hoped for . . . I felt absolutely shit scared.

I looked at that man lying there on my bed, a sleepy smile just detectable through the splayed-out, black strands of his hair, the shoulders gently shuddering with every sleep-drenched breath he took, his legs, heavy and still, and my fear was unmistakable.

But it wasn't a cold fear. It wasn't the kind of fear you sprint away from. If anything, I wanted to get closer to it. It was a sense of beautiful foreboding, whose inevitability had already claimed my heart. By meeting in this little holiday town, we had changed each other's paths forever, and I knew, down to my absolute core, that those paths were now strewn with difficulty.

They would also be strewn with love like I couldn't even imagine, passion that would fire me up and companionship that I'd never tire of. But the difficulty would be there too, I knew it.

I wasn't wrong.

Sometimes it feels like every life hurdle for us is a million times more challenging than it would be for a 'typical' couple. It's no wonder holiday romances get a bad rap and I know we're in the minority in making this one work. I don't know what forces were in play the day Mesut and I met, but thank god we were brave and curious enough to accept this 'other-worldly' love for what it is.

A bloody big mystery.

As Baki was napping this afternoon, I watched Mesut pack a small suitcase and asked him, "Will you keep fasting? Now that all of this is happening?"

He blinked at me in surprise. "Why I stop?"

"Well, I didn't think you had to keep doing it if you were travelling. And what about the fact that you must be feeling completely emotionally unstable? Wouldn't you be excused at a time like this?"

"You right, I don't have to keep doing if I travel but . . . is my choice really. Sadness not make big difference. I think I will keep doing. Ramadan will help me. You not get it yet, Gulazer? You closer with Allah when you fasting. You really not feel it?"

I took a breath and let his question settle. Did I feel it? A oneness with god? Not really. As you know, Dear Reader, I have been as introspective as the best of them so far – thinking about my identity, where I am in the world and a lot of my crap seems to be surfacing. Not least my miscarriage and how to be a better mam. But how to put into words for him. "I think I'm closer . . . closer to something."

"Is good . . . is good you getting that closeness." He popped the last couple of t-shirts into his bag, zipped it up and pulled me over to him to sit on the edge of our bed. The warmth of his hands on my body was welcome. "You might need it when I gone. Tell me something, Gulazer, you remember what my mum saying to you first time you meet together?"

My mind plunged back into a fog of pre-Baki memories and I waded through them to find the moment he spoke of.

It had been pretty special meeting his mam. I remembered the almost unbearable nerves that twisted in my throat. The tenacious grip of morning sickness after an eleven-hour coach journey from İpeklikum. The criss-crossed carpets she'd sat on at the back of the living room and her legs outstretched with her baby grandson cradled against them. The heartening press of her palm against my belly, already nurturing a tiny baby Baki that we hadn't even told her about. I'd sat with her then, moved by a force that came from the spirited depths of instinct, and laid my head against her shoulder. Thanks to my connection with Mesut, it looked like I was already connected to her.

"I think she said something about love being the mother? You had to translate it for me at the time, but I remember she spoke with such a determination, even though it was just a whisper."

"We are born out of love. Love is our mother."

"Wow. What do you think she meant?"

"I not know but I can tell you she known for this, my mum. She gives people messages."

"Oh! A bit like Bernie?"

"Yes, just like Bernie. And also, what she saying to you – is from her favourite poet, Rumi. You knows him?"

"I don't. But it's really beautiful. *We are born out of love. Love is our mother*."

"Yes. And she is knowing that day, without us saying anything, that you pregnant. I think she give you message. Especially for you."

"Oh, I really wish I knew what the message meant!"

"Is not matter now. You will find it. Did you know, in my religion, being mother is . . . most important job ever. Mother is most worthy of a person's companionship and respect and love - above all others."

"Woah."

"Yes. We expect children to feel like this about their mums. They can never disrespect her or swear at her or hurt her. They must always, always be good to their mums. Even more than towards their dads. First is Allah. Then is mum."

It was that first moment, with my head on Mesut's mam's shoulder when I probably first got a glimpse of this deeply-rooted belief. Those precious moments with her had been so unexpectedly ethereal that they had enough loving energy to brush the edges of everything that came afterwards. I remember thinking, despite the fear of where our relationship might take us, we at least had an angel on our side.

And now we're on her side.

I took Mesut to the airport not long after Baki woke up, and we said goodbye in an inexplicably cold snap that blew in from the mossy, indigo planes of nearby Culloden Battlefield. Baki practically ripped his dad's hair out in chunks before I pulled him away. Poor kid. What kind of mam will I be with Mesut away? I drove back to Muirdrith trying to avoid the entertainment of that very question, slipping into a trance that kept my feelings at bay.

The rest of today was spent under the watchful eyes of Goliver as Bernie, yet again, put on some Scottish treats before they hammered it back down the A9 to England. Now they're gone and I'm back, sitting alone on the patchy sofa of fame, wondering how in the holy heckfire I managed to keep it together enough to feed and bath Baki and get through a trillionth rendition of Room on the Broom.

I don't even want to break my fast tonight. There's no room in my belly for food when it's packed full of fear. Maybe there will be room tomorrow.

Tomorrow. We'll see.

Not-A-Granny-Flora
I'm so sorry to hear about Mesut's mum. Can you send love from me and your dad? Please eat something. I'll call you later.

Fab4CoolDad
Tell Mesut to play this for his mam when he gets there. Because it's what I hope happens to her . . . 'Getting Better'.

AngelBernie
I'm so glad we could be there for you today, poppet. Mesut's mum sounds absolutely amazing and I loved seeing the photos of her that you showed us this afternoon. I reckon she's an angel too so whatever happens she'll be okay. 🥰🥰🥰

Angnonymous
Well if everyone reading this blog is anything to go by, Mesut's

mum has a whole lot of love beaming her way. I'm sure she'll be feeling it.

OliverChen1!
Jess I'm so sorry for the heavy day you've had. Wish we could have done more and we both feel awful that we had to leave you today of all days. Sorry we didn't get to say goodbye to Mesut but please tell him Gillie and I send our love. On another note . . . I may or may not have left you a little gift somewhere in your flat. Happy hunting!

KadafiDancingKing
Please tell Mesut 'geçmiş olsun' for his mum. I in Turkey and not too far from Manevitaş so please telling him anything I can do I will do. And, Jess, I very proud of you for following the goodness. x

NO_Just_DON'T(1)
THIS COMMENT HAS BEEN DELETED

MaxAttax
Love to all of you, especially Mesut's mam. Hope he dodges the Turkish army. Peace out.

Compustable.Apocalips
THIS COMMENT HAS BEEN DELETED

Anonymous
THIS COMMENT HAS BEEN DELETED

17

DAY 17 – DUMMY STATUS

Muirdrith, Highlands of Scotland, UK
Fri 27th Aug 2010
Sunrise / Suhoor: 6.03am
Sunset / Iftar: 8.30pm

As Mesut isn't here for me to share this with, I thought you might like a little update on the latest passive-aggressive note in my life. Here goes . . .

Jess, could you please consider NOT leaving religious propaganda in places such as the coat cupboard? Nearly tripped on it as I was getting my fleece. Thank you.

There are two main reasons, Dear Reader, that I have a problem with this note:

1. It's not a coat cupboard, it is an EVERYTHING cupboard (as demonstrated by the sacks and sacks of cat litter, five thousand fleece jackets and twelve bin bags of empty Special Brew cans)
2. 'Religious propaganda'? Is she serious?

Last night, in the comments on my blog, the lovely Oliver said he'd left a 'little gift' for me somewhere in the flat. Assuming it wasn't the same kind of gift one of the cats left in Crunchy Nut Mam's handbag, I guessed Oliver may have placed an intricate thistle arrangement somewhere, to help me empathise with the plight he and Gillie endured at Thistledown Lodge.

Unfortunately, I didn't have the happy experience of hunting for said gift and therefore sneakily creating a treasure-hunt-type-activity for Baki which could have taken up a good half an hour, therefore relieving a little mam-guilt. No such luck.

Instead, Cat-Crazy Flatmate beat me to it and placed the gift outside my bedroom door, with her note taped to it (luminous orange paper, so she must mean business), meaning that I, indeed, also nearly tripped on it.

Anyway, in case you're wondering, the 'religious propaganda' is a book. Of course it is. Oliver has a history of ensuring the books I need to read get into my hands.

It was only four years ago that he gifted me a seemingly innocent paperback just before I left with Gillie for our month-long trip to Turkey. It was pre-Mesut, pre-closing-my-business and pre-Jess-getting-her-life-back-after-a-devastating-split-with-highly-inappropriate-fiancé. It was 'pre' a lot of things and I think Oliver had sensed that, even though I'd only known him a short time.

"Just let me know what you think of it," he'd said. I didn't know it then, but that little book was going to change everything.

(*It was 'The Alchemist' by Paulo Coelho, if you're wondering. I do recommend you read it. Like, now. Although I think it should come with a warning. Something along the lines of, 'WARNING! This book has actual life-changing capabilities.'*)

The book that Oliver clearly feels I need in my life right now is a bit different from the last. More factual, more informative, more, well, necessary I guess. The book that almost had me falling to my death as I stepped outside my bedroom, all groggy-eyed and stiff this morning was . . .

The Quran For Dummies.

It's like he typed my name into a Google Gift Finder.

There was a little note scribbled inside the cover.

Hopefully this will pop your Quran cherry.
(Gillie made me write that)
Love, Oliver.

Okay, that made me giggle.

I remember Mesut has told me about Ramadan being a time for extra prayer and religious diligence. It seems I've chosen personal reflection in place of prayer (blogging counts for that, right?). But he also told me that gold star Muslims are supposed to spend their time during Ramadan revising, re-learning and re-reading the holy scripture itself.

This gives me a shiver because so far, the closest I've come to a copy of the Quran is the one that sits on a high, lone shelf directly above the spot where Mesut's mam likes to sit in their living room. In fact, it must have been there that first day we met.

Mesut had told me then, that the Quran will always be placed in the highest location in a Muslim household, not inflicted with the company of any other books nearby and never, ever on the ground. That is why, Dear Reader, I had to pick it up and wipe off a load of muddy paw prints before a religious transgression could occur.

In terms of popping my cherry, well, yes, I am, I suppose, a

Quran virgin. I have had a sneaky look on Amazon at English translations and did consider buying myself a copy so I could swot up. But, when I utilised the 'Look Inside' feature I was put right off. Even though it was in English, the language was so dense, there was no way a malnourished, full-time mam of a Beast-Child could wade through it. I knew it would end up being yet another book that would sit forever by my bedside, gathering dust, and had a sneaky feeling Mesut would not appreciate that. So, I thought it best not to spend the £15.99 at all if it was going to initiate yet more moody silences and death-stares from the pits of hell.

Anyway, I don't need to worry about that now because Oliver has thrown me gloriously into the land of the dummy. What a relief!

Now I'm down and groovy with my new title, I can accept this book wholeheartedly.

Thank you, Oliver!

I expect you'll also want to know how Mesut's mam is getting on.

Okay, so I spent most of today dicking about with Baki at the park and the beach, as it is Cat-Crazy Flatmate's day off and I just didn't fancy being around her for fear of being written at even though we're in the same four walls (it's so *weird*, right?). I've had my mobile close by all day, even when jumping in puddles and sheltering from summer showers under stinky, pissy climbing apparatus.

My phone eventually rang mid wave-jumping on the beach and I was quick to answer it. Mesut made it, after a total of eighteen hours of travelling, to Manevitaş. However, after just ten minutes he was told his mam is being moved to a specialist hospital in Ankara, the very city where his connecting flight had just been. So, by the time I spoke to him, he was on an eight hour coach journey, travelling in the direction he'd just come from.

"How's she doing, sweetheart?"

"Ah, Gulazer, I not even see her yet. I on coach now. But everyone say she open eyes and speaking. She strong enough to move and everyone hoping she get right treatment in Ankara."

"When you do see her, please send her all my love. And Baki's."

"Tabi, Gulazer. Of course. My big brother say she even asking about Baki. And you."

"She did?"

"Yes. She not making lots sense but she say both your names."

"I wish I could be with you. I miss you already."

"Bende. Me too. Everything is okay? Baki is okay? I not like leaving you in Muirdrith when we not know who is saying awful things to Children's Services. I needing you be careful, okay, Gulazer? Maybe stay close to home."

"I will. Although right now I'm at the beach, trying to stop Baki from wearing seaweed. Oh, and guess what? Oliver left me a present. It's to help me understand Ramadan more. It's a book."

"A book?"

I told Mesut about the Quran for Dummies and I think it may have even got a little smile out of him. It's crazy how you can actually hear a smile down the phone sometimes, especially if it's someone you have a connection with that transcends radio waves.

"Is good you reading this, Gulazer. Oliver is good man. I know is not proper Quran, but you must looking after it. My mum would definitely tell you that if she could."

"I know she would."

"Next to your heart, Gulazer. When you pick it up, you

hold it there and never lower. This book part of your heart and your soul now so you needing show respect." I cringed at the thought of the book, back at the flat, carelessly left amongst Baki's Bob The Builder DVD collection. Fingers crossed the spaghetti hoops he chucked around at lunchtime hadn't made it anywhere near.

"Really? But it's only a guide for the Quran, for ignorant waifs like me. It's not the real thing."

"Not matter. Is closest thing we have to Quran so we treating it properly. It needs to be kept somewhere high up and with no fancy stuff. Just pure and plain and safe. I have to go now, Gulazer. Coach is stopping for break. I needing fresh air."

"Are you managing without snacks? Drinks? Your rollies? It must be really hard whilst you're travelling."

"I not thinking like this – it is hard or not hard. I just doing. I love you, Gulazer. Ve seni özleyorum."

"I miss you too. Lots."

When Baki and I got back to the flat, I rescued the Quran For Dummies from the Bob The Builder / spaghetti hoop mash-up and perused the minimal spaces we have. Where on earth to keep it? Especially now that I'd ruled out the stack of books by my bed or the bookshelf we share with Cat-Crazy Flatmate in the hallway. God forbid I put any 'religious propaganda' on there.

We do have a small, wall-mounted cupboard in Baki's bedroom, which is where we keep nappies, wipes and other implements with which to manage a toddler's bum. I thought that, perhaps, the top of the cupboard would be okay so I popped it up there, on its side, meaning it was pretty close to the ceiling. There. That was about as high as I could get it, given the choices available.

I stood back and admired my genius decision. Slowly but surely, even though it is Baki's room and he was currently tugging on my jeans with his snotty fingers, my mind was pleasantly commandeered by images of swirling trails of incense smoke, the gentle twinkle of a tealight or two, the subtle scatter of rose petals . . . surely I could create a shrine-like space for the book? Something special and pretty and sacred?

No, Gulazer.

He wasn't actually with me but you know and I know, Dear Reader, that Mesut would have brought me back down from the dizzy heights of over-the-top interior design.

No, Gulazer. No fancy stuff.

And I knew he'd be right. I knew he'd be right so much, that I even took all of the bum-managing contents out of the tiny cupboard and placed them in a box in the 'coat' cupboard instead. Lord knows what kind of note I'll get about that tomorrow but at least it can't offend any religious sensibilities.

Now the Quran For Dummies sits proud and alone on the highest shelf in the flat, *pure and plain and safe*, just like Mesut instructed. I'll get it down whenever I fancy indulging in a bit of diligent inquiry, probably mostly after sunset when I have at least a little sustenance to fuel my studies.

Right now I'm curled up in bed in this very quiet flat. Baki is deep-sleeping in a position you could accurately call 'arse over tit' after yet another Julia-Donaldson-athon (might patent that phrase); Cat-Crazy Flatmate has chosen to spend her night off actually *in* the pub downing yet more Special Brew; I'm hoping Mesut is at his mam's bedside by now and I'm guessing Goliver arrived home sometime earlier today.

I have a belly full of cheesy beans and Marmite on toast and word on the street is that a family bar of Galaxy is hidden in the patchy sofa of fame. I'm rocking this night of loneliness like it's mine for the taking because I am, Dear Reader, a mother of a toddler and if there's one thing we are known for, it's our hardcore loneliness endurance skills.

'Quran For Dummies' has been removed from its makeshift pedestal and is sitting by my side, waiting for me to stop typing so that I can get on with a bit of self-education. In fact, before starting tonight's post, I flipped to a random page and took a sneaky peak.

You'll never guess the title: 'The Angels: Pure Creations of God'.

Bernie will be happy to know that probably the last thing I think about before drifting off to dreamland is the belief that angels are made of light and are there to inspire and guide devout men and women throughout their earthly life. I'm banking on mine getting his / her groove on, by curing Mesut's mam, bringing him home safely and getting me through the rest of Ramadan without a hitch.

Here's hoping.

Iyi geceler (goodnight).

AngelBernie

Yes! Angels in abundance! Can't wait to hear more about what Islam says about my old pals. Might even borrow the book when you've finished with it if that's okay? Tell Mesut I'll find somewhere appropriate to keep it! And I'm in talks with the angels about his mum. Everything crossed for her.

Jess.AKYOL

Bernie, I just read this line: '*The pure power of angels calls for purity in the human soul and seeks to protect humans from the satanic forces that beckon towards transgressing God.*' How do you like them apples?

AngelBernie

Blimey. My lot are more likely to love you regardless of the satanic forces. Or maybe even because of. Not sure. They're a mercurial old bunch.

ThistleMadMona
Hello Jess! Ailsa finally showed me how to join your blog, m'eudail. I've just read all of your posts so far from start to finish and now I'm addicted! I've had more time for reading now that Oliver and his lady have gone, but I was blessed to have them at Thistledown Lodge. I'm not that bad with my thistles, am I?! My thoughts are with Mesut and his mum. Tell her 'faigh gu math a dh'aithghearr' (Get well soon in Scottish Gaelic).
Jess.AKYOL
Oh Mona, it makes my day that you've started reading my blog!
ThistleMadMona
It's a pleasure. Muirdrith is very lucky to have a writer like you. Did you know I spent a lot of time in Muslim countries when I was on my travels with my late husband? Turkey was one of our favourites but we also spent some time in Egypt, Iran and Jordan back in the day. Stories for a few drams sometime.
Jess.AKYOL
Wow, really? Sounds like your niece should be writing stories about you, Mona. 😉

Angnonymous
The timing of books is so important, don't you think? Sounds like this one has come into your life at just the right time. Mesut has left you in safe hands.
Jess.AKYOL
Yes, I totally agree. Don't know what my life would look like now if I hadn't read The Alchemist. Paulo Coelho is a genius.
Angnonymous
That he is. Maybe you'll get to tell him yourself one day . . . ?
Jess.AKYOL

#goals

Compustable.Apocalips
THIS COMMENT HAS BEEN DELETED

Anonymous
THIS COMMENT HAS BEEN DELETED

Anonymous
THIS COMMENT HAS BEEN DELETED

Not-A-Granny-Flora
Your dad and I are thinking of Mesut's mum. Please keep sending our love. Nice of Oliver to give you the book. I remember when you came home from Turkey having read The Alchemist. Thought you'd never read another book.
Jess.AKYOL
Yes. Oliver is very good at book presents.

Fab4CoolDad
Brilliant present from that there Oliver! He knew that all you needed was a bit of . . . 'Help!'
Jess.AKYOL
Classic! 🎶 🎵 🎶 🎵 I've got no excuse now Dad. 😉

NO_Just_DON'T(1)
THIS COMMENT HAS BEEN DELETED
NO_Just_DON'T(1)
THIS COMMENT HAS BEEN DELETED
NO_Just_DON'T(1)
THIS COMMENT HAS BEEN DELETED

funmum

Have always wondered what the Quran actually says. Islam gets such bad press.
Jess.AKYOL
It really does. It makes me so sad.

Anonymous
THIS COMMENT HAS BEEN DELETED

CrunchyNut_Mummy
What's with all the deleted comments, Jess? Is there a bug in the blog?
Jess.AKYOL
Nope, I'm just deleting all the hateful ones. They're hotting up now. Though I have no idea why.
CrunchyNut_Mummy
Ah, that makes sense. Shame you have to do it though as I guess you're having to read them before deleting them. You've got enough on your plate without having to absorb crap like that. Can't you block them?
Jess.AKYOL
I honestly have no idea. Might have to find out. Thanks for looking out for me.

MaxAttax
I agree with CrunchyNut_Mummy. Try blocking them. This isn't a space for that kind of thing. Peace out.
Jess.AKYOL
Thank you, brother. I didn't know you cared so much.
MaxAttax
Hmph. Don't tell anyone. Must maintain hard man image. Peace out.
Jess.AKYOL
Hard man? Really?

MaxAttax
It's subjective. Peace out.

Night-sun-ella
There must be an aaaangeeeeel . . . playing with my heeaarrrrt, yeeeeaaah! Name that tune.
Jess.AKYOL
Annie Lennox. There Must Be An Angel / Nutter on my blog.
Night-sun-ella
Too easy! Enjoy the book, you fabulous nutcase. Your ongoing endeavours to understand that weird and mystical man of yours are incredible to me. All he needs is a good old-fashioned tongue in the ear. What does the Quran say about that?
Jess.AKYOL
Looked in the index. Ear-tonguing is not there. Must be an anomaly. Will get on to the publisher.

MesutAk1
Ella you dangerous animal. We not missing you. At all.
Night-sun-ell-a
Methinks the long-haired weirdo doth protest too much. P.S. Love to your mum. xxx

OliverChen1!
So glad you got the book even if the discovery of it was bereft of treasure-hunting fun. Can't wait for you to enlighten us all with your new-found learnings. Paulo Coelho better watch his back.
Jess.AKYOL
Massive thanks to you, you big, generous beast, you. Paulo is safe though. Nothing replaces The Alchemist.

FatimaNazar
What a brilliant idea of Oliver's! You'll love learning about the

Quran, Jess. It's the most beautiful book. It'll help you through this tough time.

Jess.AKYOL

Thank you! I'm not sure how much of it I'll be able to take in with my worn-out, food-deprived, crap-mam, husband-missing brain but I will definitely give it a good go.

18

DAY 18 - GLENSÌTH

Muirdrith, Highlands of Scotland, UK
Sat 28th Aug 2010
Sunrise / Suhoor: 6.05am
Sunset / Iftar: 8.27pm

I'm not ashamed to admit that this morning hit me like a tonne of bricks.

But imagine each one of those bricks is tinged with sadness, primed with loneliness and painted with a decent wash of self-doubt – and you might get an idea of how it felt.

This morning, it seemed the heavy, grey veil from the days of postnatal depression was back and had settled itself overnight without asking.

Rude.

It never fails to amaze me how I can be woken by the most beautiful creature on earth (Baki and not one of the cat army) yet still my motivation is lost. Ramadan has, admittedly, got my stomach howling and my body feeling like a lump of lead, but there's more to it than that. The veil holds me back. It brings a sense of disconnect. It provides a constant drag on my soul and a soft, silent threat that everything will be hard. At times like this morning, I can't even be bothered to be sick of it.

It didn't help that Baki woke at an ungodly hour. I dragged him into our bed and his warm, wriggly body filled the space Mesut left behind. Rather than following my genius plan and going back to sleep, he spent about an hour playing the highly amusing game of fake-snoring and fake-waking up approximately one hundred and eighty-two times before literally pushing me out of bed and making sounds I deciphered as demands for breakfast.

I prepared his food on auto pilot, not in the least bit tempted by the banana / Weetabix mush he ravenously chucked down his throat. I did, however, wish to the angels I'd read about last night, that there was a form of shelter other than a café when we got caught in the driving rain at the park later on.

Bloody, buggery Highlands. How dare they be predictably wet whilst I am trying to avoid all eating and drinking establishments?

The café was warm and inviting.

The café smelled of roasted coffee beans.

The café had a special offer on carrot cake.

Fuck, as they say, my life.

A hot water would have to do. And no, thirteen-year-old waitress, I do not even want a slice of lemon in it, thank you very much.

After that decadent indulgence, I was planning the dreary steps it would take to get back home and wondering if it was too early to convince Baki to go down for a nap. However, my plans were scuppered just as Baki was smearing said bargain carrot cake all over his face, because I got a call from Bernie.

"Poppet!" she shrieked down the phone. "Will you come with me and Frida to Glensìth? I fancy a hippy trip and need some new angel cards."

Glensìth. Have you ever been there?

It is, indeed, probably the best place in the world to get angel cards. Or angel anything, for that matter.

Glensìth Community Foundation is the place I was telling you about a few days ago when I was trying to explain Bernie's weird orders from the angels. Remember? She published some seemingly random numbers in the local rag because the angels urged her to do it, and next thing we know, the steering group of Glensìth is on the front page of that same rag, having won the lottery jackpot with those very numbers and they now have all manner of plans to do it up. Apparently one of their members just saw the numbers and knew he had to buy a ticket – the rest is modern, Muirdrith history.

Glensìth is an experimental kind of place. It's nestled in the wildest and most windswept part of Eastern Scotland. It's part commune and eco village for those led by spiritual values, and it's part events base for workshops, courses and talks on everything from eco-living to the power of prayer. Seems an apt place to visit during Ramadan, don't you think?

I met Bernie there within the half hour. Yes, it was still very drizzly and wet but I'd swung home on the way there and Baki and I were now decked out in the kind of waterproofs that were probably invented in Scotland. Beast-Child protested wildly at the way he squeaked and crinkled in his bright blue anorak, but I stood firm. There was no way I was dealing with a sodden wet toddler today.

Despite the weather (and my shitty mood), I enjoyed a little amble around Glensìth. Bernie has actually lived there before, so knows her way around. "How long did you live like a hippy then, Bern?" I asked, as we meandered past a building site that was apparently going to be a brand new 'retreat park'. Baki tried to squeeze himself under a toddler-sized gap in the chicken wire fencing but I managed to grab him before he could be lost to the hippy realm.

"Oh, who knows? I lost track of time while I was here. This place will do that to you. I remember lots of kitchen duties and pulling up weeds left, right and centre. All the talks and workshops were free if you lived in the commune so that was good. Didn't enjoy the fence-building so much so I used to duck out of that all of the time. Actually, the hide-out I used to escape to was somewhere round here. Erm, Yes! Around this corner . . ."

We shuffled across the damp gravel to where Bernie was pointing and found a little shack nestled between two impressive-looking, shiny eco-structures with velvety grass rooves. The shack was more modest but its exterior wooden panels were painted with bright, alternate rainbow colours that blasted through the stubborn grey mist. The door was rounded along the top which reminded me of a hobbit house and there was a soft, yellow glow coming from each of the tiny windows dotted along the top of the walls. Where the shack met the ground, there were great bursts of long grasses reaching out like splashes of water frozen in time. It was a brazen contrast with the organised, uniform allotments we'd walked past so far.

"Aw, I wouldn't mind holing up there myself until all of these Ramadan capers are over. It's so cute!"

"Tis." Bernie agreed. Then Frida and Baki dashed over to the hut, determined to stomp in the puddles and grab the wild grasses around the borders. "Shit. No! Frida, Baki, come back over here. Not your house! You can't play there, dumplings!"

Weird. Usually I'm the one insisting the kids hold back, not Bernie. She always sees our surroundings as a joyful free-for-all and positively encourages Frida to get her toddler kicks doing whatever she damn well pleases. Not today though.

We bundled the kids into their buggies and hurried off away from the shack. "Come on then, Bern, You're going to have to spill. Why didn't you want us anywhere near that cool little hobbit hole?"

"No reason. There were lights on inside, that's all. Just didn't want to disturb the home owner."

"Not buying it. Didn't you say you used to escape there? From all the fence-building?"

"Hmm? Yes. Sometimes. But it was a long time ago. Before I met Logan, even." She did a little shudder and leaned over to peer into Frida's buggy. "You hungry, poppet? Let's go to the Kelpie Café. Mummy needs to rest these swollen ankles."

I sighed audibly at the thought of sitting in yet another café but Bernie didn't catch it. She was already waddling ahead, spitting up damp grit at her heels, on a mission to avoid this conversation. Never mind. If I knew Bernie, once I got a hot chocolate inside her she'd come clean.

The Kelpie Café is definitely somewhere I'll take Mesut when he returns and when Ramadan is over. It's totally my kind of place. Fresh, organic food. Mountains of different, multi-coloured salads offered in a 'pick and mix' kind of affair. More vegetarian and vegan options than you could shake a stick at. Cakes that make you want to say 'fuck it all', drop everything and go live with the hippies.

I'm not going to lie, Dear Reader, even eighteen days into Ramadan and this was pure torture. I have never wanted to lick food off my toddler's face more than I did today. But I didn't. Cos I'm strong (or something).

Bernie was served a sweet, spice-laden hot chocolate, and I watched her relax. Her brow smoothed out a bit and she stopped looking over her shoulder every two seconds. Her dark lashes dipped down towards the steaming chocolate as she raised it to her mouth, dewy twists of copper-coloured hair escaping from her pony tail and almost dunking into the generous swirl of cream. Not for the first time, I thought Bernie might have the friendliest kind of face I've ever seen.

"I know you're waiting," she said, a swish of cream framing her smiling lips.

"I am." I grinned, leaning back in my chair and watching Baki and Frida jump down from the table to explore the Lego stash nearby. "Thought the hot chocolate might do the trick."

There followed a lovely, warm chat about Bernie's days living in the Glensìth community. None of it is secretive, not really. But at the end of the day, this is a blog post on the big, scary internet and I have to respect the precious privacy of my friends. At least, a bit.

I know Bernie won't mind me telling you that she has tinkered with her fair share of natural substances, that she has enjoyed dabbling with the elemental treats offered up by Mother Earth. And, obviously, living in a place such as Glensìth, she wasn't alone. Especially at fence-building time, when a certain group of people might or might not flock to a certain multi-coloured shack to escape such physical toil.

Owner of said shack might have figured heavily in the story Bernie told me. Owner of said shack might have been a big, posh immigration lawyer in a past life but left it all behind to build his own self-sufficient home at Glensìth. Owner of said shack might have been a right one for the delights of Mother Earth especially when he had company. Owner of said shack might have been very, very fond of our lass Bernie.

I'll leave it there.

Sorry not sorry!

When we were just about to get up and drag our toddlers away from spreading the Glensìth Lego stash across the floor of the café, we heard a voice.

"No way, man. Bernie. Is that you?"

Bernie went pale. But a new kind of smile started pinching

at her lips.

"Oh my god. Tis! Bernie, get yourself over here!"

And next thing I knew she was in a tight hug (despite her colossal tummy) with a random man at the back of the café. They oohed and aahed over each other for a while before turning my way in a joyful, tousled bundle. And when they did, I have to admit I got a bit of a jolt.

Because he was handsome.

Like, really handsome.

Not, before you shut down my blog in horrified defiance, Mesut-level handsome. But handsome all the same.

And he had that kind of handsomeness that doesn't stop at a chiselled jaw or sparkling eyes, it carries on, to god knows where (and that's part of the appeal, am I right?) at the edges of his upturned lips, the depth of his unexpected dimples and the impish raise of the sandy-coloured eyebrows.

This, Dear Reader, was Angus.

Angus sat down with us, making a massive fuss of Baki and Frida and I cursed the time-honoured phenomenon that raises the attraction stakes of any man who is good with kids. Then Angus, who still lives at Glensìth, ordered yet more hot chocolates for everyone.

Fucking hell.

"Sorry, Angus. That's really nice of you but I won't have a hot chocolate, thanks. I'm fasting for Ramadan."

"Ah, okay – cool. So you're Muslim then?"

Must. Ignore. Crinkly. Eyes. And. Adorable. Dimples.

"No. Not exactly . . . I'm doing it to support my husband. Baki's dad. He's Muslim in a pretty much non-Muslim country and I thought he could do with the support, even though he's not actually here at the minute. He had to go back to Turkey to see his poorly mam."

He slapped his (rather large) hands down onto his (ample)

thighs and flashed a massive smile at us. "I know who you are! You're the My Little Ramadan lassie. You've got that braw blog. I've been following it! Every day! I've been reading, lassie."

Bernie and I looked at each other first in confusion and then in slow, dawning awareness.

"Angnonymous!" We shrieked.

"Tis I!" He laughed out loud and grabbed both of my hands off the table. "Your blog is brilliant! We're all talking about it here at Glensìth! You're a celebrity, lassie! We've been calling you the Carrie Bradshaw of Muirdrith."

"Sadly lacking her never-ending legs and walk-in wardrobe though. I can't believe this, Angus. You're Angnonyous! Damn it! I wanted to figure out who you were all by myself. I didn't expect to actually walk right into you and land in your lap." May have blushed a touch at this last ridiculously foolish comment, but Angus didn't seem to notice.

"This is just braw, it really is. Bernie here will tell you – I've dipped my toes into most of the big religions. Comes from my days representing people from all over the world in court, I guess. I always figured, I may as well take the best of what each religion has to offer, if you get my meaning? I'm proper interested in Islam though. I've tried fasting myself a few times. Never managed more than a day or two. Maybe after all this building work is over, I'll apply myself a bit better and see where it takes me."

Angus told us about all of the plans for Glensìth, including the almost-finished retreat park, renovations to the events hall and a huge stained glass commission for the main gates to the whole foundation. "I can't even tell you how lucky we were to get those winnings. Ironic, really, because we'd tried for years to get a grant from the Lottery with no success. Looks like the angels were smiling down on us the day I put those numbers on, eh, Bernie?"

"It would seem so. Shall we go now, Jess?" Bernie shot me a wickedly cheeky grin and it all fell into place. No wonder Angus had felt drawn to the numbers, they were put there by his long-lost love! Flipping heck. You couldn't write this stuff.

As we started gathering our things to leave, Angus ducked into the shop adjoining the café and grabbed a deck of angel cards for Bernie. "Here you go, Bern. I think these ones will just about do you." He handed her a small box, marbled and glimmering with deep blues and purples and I might have been imagining it, but the little brush of their fingers made him light up a little. Then he turned to me in what you might call a fluster, and helped me strap Beast-Child into his buggy, who was doing the archy-back thing with an intense perseverance, possibly for some sort of toddler world championship.

"Jess," Angus began, throwing a ridiculously smouldering look my way, whilst he effortlessly calmed Baki with a pat on the belly. "You know, we've a festival of wellbeing happening soon, to officially open the new spaces . . . and I'm wondering if you'd do us the honour of being on the bill?"

"On the bill?" I asked as I not-very-gracefully shoved a dummy in Beast-Child's mouth.

"Yeah. Maybe you could speak about Ramadan? I know Mesut won't want to speak, you said he's a private man an' all, on your blog. But if you'd like to talk about what it's been like, fasting along with him, I'd love to give you a slot on the programme."

And there you have it, folks. I have been asked to SPEAK.

By Bernie's ex-whatever-he-is.

Like, in front of lots of people with my own mouth and my own words.

Shitting hell.

Give me a laptop, a pound of cherry tablet and a quiet night in and I'll give you all the words in the world. But give me an audience and a stage and you might just see Jess in shutdown mode.

What the holy heckfire would I talk about?

Looks like I'll have to think of something because Angus, what with the dimples of romance novel fame and the gap-toothed smile and the hypnotic, drawling Scottish accent may have got a tiny little 'maybe' out of me.

And Bernie followed that up with a very quick, "She'll be there. I'll bring her. She won't let you down. She's got this."

As I said, shitting hell.

The question you might be asking yourself, Dear Reader, as you read this latest development in my, quite frankly, spectacle of a life, is: What will Mesut say?

Well, I couldn't tell you because when he called me tonight, it was all I could do to listen to his worries about his mam.

He says she's been quite lucid, and she knows he's there, by her bedside. All nine of her children are there, and that's a rare thing to have everyone together like that. She's managing to sip water and take some soup but apparently she keeps fighting people off, saying she doesn't want to because it's Ramadan. They've been taking it in turns to read out the bit of the Quran that excuses you if you are ill, but she's not keen. Mesut says she's always been stubborn. At least I know where he gets it from.

Just before the end of our tired and whispery conversation, Mesut did ask me how my day had been. And I took the coward's way out. "Do you know what? It'll all be in my blog. Why don't you log onto it in a couple of hours? That way you can find out what we've been up to."

"You still writing blog then." I think I made out a bit of a sigh. I imagined his lips pressing together and his eyes shoot downwards to the ground.

"Yes, Mesut. I am."

"Okay, Gulazer. I will read."

So, if you are reading this, lovely husband, please know that Baki and I are fine, and we miss you ever so much. We got through our day, and the speaking at Glensìth thing is just a possibility at this time. Nothing's set in stone.

The only thing set in stone is how much we love you and how much we want you back. Maybe meeting Angus today, and making the link with the angels and the lottery numbers and Bernie was a good sign. A sign that everything is connected and everything flows together eventually. Tell your mam I still remember: *We are born out of love. Love is our mother.*

Tatlı ruyalar.

(That's 'sweet dreams' to everyone else.)

Angnonymous
Jess, I can't believe I got to meet you today! Am slightly sad that my comments are now lacking mystery, but feel it will be worth it in the end. Can't wait to get you up there on the stage throwing out your wisdom to the Glensìth massive.

Jess.AKYOL
It was lush to meet you too! Not sure I've got any wisdom to throw out, but thank you so much for asking me. I'll need to have a little think about it.

Angnonymous
Think away. But if Bernie has anything to do with it, you'll be there. She's a little bit magical, remember? I discovered several posts ago that she was behind our supposedly random lottery numbers. #mindblown

Jess.AKYOL
I obviously cannot dispute the magical nature of our mutual friend. #mindequallyblown

AngelBernie
I'm so glad Mesut's mum is strong enough to have a go at everyone about Ramadan – that's a good sign! Today was very exciting, wasn't it? I used my new angel cards to see what they think of you doing the talk and they came up with Indriel. She knows you have a burning desire to change the world for the better and right now you have a mission to spread your word – how freaky is that?! She also says you need to clear yourself regularly if you're going to be able to make a difference.
Jess.AKYOL
Flipping heck, Bernie – 'change the world for the better'? I struggled to even change Baki's post-dinner nappy tonight. And what do you mean, clear myself regularly? Sounds suspiciously like colonic irrigation which I'm most definitely NOT up for.
AngelBernie
Nooooo – it means you're really sensitive to other people's energies so you have to ask the angels to help remove toxins and burdens that come from your efforts to help the world. Think of all the nasty comments you've been deleting. They have an impact. Remember your Mesut sticking up for you at the start of all of this on the comments section (even though he's not actually keen on the blog)? That's because he's your *dark* angel. I've always said that, poppet. But if you need more help just ask your other angels. Or if that feels too weird, get yourself over here and I'll sort you out. I do an awesome cleansing meditation.
Jess.AKYOL
Might just take you up on that. You come near me with a tube I'm running for the hills though.
AngelBernie
We're in the hills. Remember?
Jess.AKYOL
Oh yeah. Beach then. I'm running for the beach.

GILLIE_LASS77
Angus sounds delicious. Can I have some?
Jess.AKYOL
Erm, Oliver?
GILLIE_LASS77
Oh right. Yeah. There was an incident.
Jess.AKYOL
What do you mean an incident?
GILLIE_LASS77
It involved Gretna Green. Can't talk on here. Will call you.
Jess.AKYOL
Gretna flipping Green?
GILLIE_LASS77
I know, right? I'm fuming. Will call.
Jess.AKYOL
Oh, Gillie.

Anonymous
THIS COMMENT HAS BEEN DELETED

LifeIsYoursLindy
Yes! You will totally kill it, Jess! I wish I could come over to see you speak at Glensìth. Do you think it will be recorded?
Jess.AKYOL
I have no idea. Maybe. Gives me the shits just imagining it. Maybe I do need the angel meditation / colonic that Bernie is recommending?
LifeIsYoursLindy
Potentially!
Jess.AKYOL
Will report back. There could be a whole new blog in it.
LifeIsYoursLindy
My Little Colonic Irrigation? Has a nice ring to it.

Jess.AKYOL
I'll pardon that pun. 😉

MaxAttax
Dearest sister, don't you remember the time you had to stand up in assembly and talk about your visit to Beamish Museum? I didn't realise there was such a long drop from the stage edge to the hall floor. Or that 'putting a paper towel on it' was a tried and tested method to treat concussion. Seemed to work though. I'm sure you'll be fine. Peace out.
Jess.AKYOL
Thanks for the reminder, brother.

ThistleMadMona
Oh I know Angus! Such a darling. He'll look after you, Jess – you'll be fine. Glensìth is such a wonderful place.
Jess.AKYOL
Thanks, Mona. Nervous / excited!

ShelleyMadMum
So excited for u Jess! Would love some of those angel cards. I'll have to get myself over there and pick up a pack – might be lucky enough to bump into that Angus too.
Jess.AKYOL
Well, brace yourself. His face is quite disconcerting.

NO_Just_DON'T(1)
THIS COMMENT HAS BEEN DELETED
NO_Just_DON'T(1)
THIS COMMENT HAS BEEN DELETED

Anonymous
THIS COMMENT HAS BEEN DELETED

Glensìth_Comm_Found.
Jess, we're delighted you're coming to do a talk as part of our Festival of Wellbeing. Is Weds 8th Sep okay for you? We'll email you. What's your address? We think we'll just keep your blog title and bill the talk as 'My Little Ramadan – Adventures of a Fasting Non-Muslim in the Highlands'. What do you think?
Jess.AKYOL
Hello! That all sounds great but this is all just provisional, right? You can email me at jessgulazer1978@shotmail.co.uk

Fab4CoolDad
Glensìth has been around for ages, love. Maybe even since the swinging 60s. I believe it all started with impressive gardens featuring huge cabbages that they grew with the divine intervention of angels (look it up – it's true). Could there be anything weirder? The Beatles thought so. Just listen to . . . 'Octopus's Garden'.
Jess.AKYOL
Giant cabbages! Of course – how else would you start a spiritual commune?

MesutAk1
Gulazer, I glad you have good day with Bernie. I knows she look after you. I too tired to thinking about this question from Glensìth – we talk tomorrow? I helping my mum with prayer time now. She asking about you and Baki. And she like that you remember Rumi quote. She saying you knows meaning. 🖤🩶

Jess.AKYOL
Maybe I do. Somewhere deep down. xxx

19

DAY 19 – THE STAY-AT-HOME EXPERIENCE

Muirdrith, Highlands of Scotland, UK
Sun 29th Aug 2010
Sunrise / Suhoor: 6.08am
Sunset / Iftar: 8.24pm

Day nineteen of Ramadan. Be honest, Dear Reader, does that sound like a substantially good effort to you?

Now that I'm closing in on twenty days, it feels substantial to me. Especially as the husband I am meant to be supporting through this whole thing is not even here . . .

Especially as somebody in Muirdrith has it in for me and I don't know how / when they're next likely to strike . . .

Especially as I'm dealing, on a daily basis, with hateful blog comments that question not only my parenting aptitude but also my shoddy representation of Islam . . .

Especially as my tendency to nap, cry and zone out wrapped in a duvet suggests my toddler has distinctly more backbone than me . . .

Now I'm not one to wish my life away but please, for the

love of god (or whoever / whatever is out there), please make the next twelve days easy?

It might help if I actually left the flat.

And I haven't done that today, other than to put the wheelie bin out. It's Sunday though, so not leaving the flat is totally allowed, maybe even necessary. And if one is not going to leave home all day then it is further necessary to stay resolutely in one's grotty pyjamas, is it not?

Baki, bless him, has spent the day decked out in a fleecy little tracksuit number, looking not entirely unrelated to Ali G, but his mammy got down and dirty in her oldest pair of pink flannel pjs. And I don't care about the threadbare knees or the drawstring that has burst into a spray of grubby fibres. They're comfy, okay?

It's hard though, Dear Reader, when there is an integral ingredient missing from the overall stay-at-home experience. No, I'm not talking about privacy, a cat-free environment or even being able to open a door that doesn't have a cantankerous note taped to it . . . I'm talking, of course, about comfort food.

Rolling one's toddler up in the bedroom rug and letting him tumble out time and time again does not quite cut it, if you can't sip Ribena in between takes.

Bob The Builder's incessant quest for a Golden Hammer has the shine taken right off it if you are unable to munch sandwiches and crisps in time to the theme tune.

Scouring the internet for cheap flats and routinely weeping that they are all out of your price range, does not have the same appeal without mugs of tea and piles of custard creams.

The lack of edibles meant I had no other choice than to focus on 'quality time' with the Beast-Child. We discovered some excellent new games such as:

1. The Floor Is Lava (ridiculously easy on account of the miniscule fashion of our only two rooms and the alarming volume of things on the floor waiting to be put away)
2. Seeing how much wet washing we could pile on our heads before it falls off in a big sopping mess
3. Lining all the soft toys up into rows organised by preference and then seeing how far we can kick each one to the other side of the bedroom
4. Seeing how many plastic farm animals we could stuff into the cutlery draw without decapitating the blinkin' highland cow which never seemed to want to get up close and personal with the teaspoons

I might start a You Tube channel.

I did manage to catch a moment to go online whilst Baki was suitably transfixed by Bob and the gang, to find out if I can block the people who are leaving nasty comments on my blog. After a quick Google search, it turns out that I can't block them, as such, but I can choose to approve their comments or not. This is annoying, because it means I still have to read the crap they're saying and let it bore into my soul before I decide whether or not to allow it.

I could report a person if I'm concerned about what they're saying but it's lengthy and complicated. I could disable comments altogether, but, Dear Reader, we both know that sometimes the comments on this blog are more engaging than the post itself. It looks like I'll have to keep on curating the comments and just find a way to let it all slide off me.

I might need your help with that.

I also might need your help coming to terms with two emails I received today. Nothing could have prepared me for what I discovered when I opened up these bad boys. So consider this fair warning before I share them with you . . .

Dear Jess,

We were delighted to hear that you're willing to deliver a talk as part of our Festival of Wellbeing, here at Glensìth Community Foundation.

We've all been following your blog closely since you started fasting for Ramadan and we think what you're doing to support your husband is really lovely!

We have a twenty-minute slot for you on Weds 8th September at 7.30pm. We'd like to bill the talk as 'My Little Ramadan – Adventures of a Fasting Non-Muslim in the Highlands'.

You'll be the penultimate event before we close the festival. Paulo Coelho will follow you with the closing speech.

We have a small fee we can pay you for your time. We hope you will accept it with thanks. Please give me a call to arrange the details.

Sincerely,
Lupa Startforth

Point Number 1:
Paulo Coelho?
Paulo effing Coelho?

The multi-million best-selling author of The Alchemist and a squillion other genius books . . . spiritual leader of, like the *world* and they want *me* to talk before him? Is he going to be in the actual room whilst I bleat on about not being able to eat as much garlic bread as I'd like or my lack of custard creams to accompany my saddo flat-hunting?

How can this be possible?

As I've mentioned before, I've read The Alchemist I don't know how many times. Hell, I could probably credit Paulo Coelho with every single transformative moment I've had over the past four years. This man, Dear Reader, is EPIC.

I can scarcely even describe how this one singular fact adds to the growing sense of dread I have about going ahead with all of this. Is it too much to ask for my Ramadan efforts to suddenly cause some holy beam of enlightenment to shine down on me so that I can breathlessly preach about it on the night?

Paulo effing Coelho.

Point Number 2:

Money? They're going to pay me actual money? Do they know I'm only in this Ramadan game because of some stupid, spur-of-the-moment instant where I felt sorry for my doe-eyed husband? That I also selfishly hoped Ramadan might make me better at life? It's almost laughable that I might be in monetary receipt for such a thing.

Not gonna lie though – it would help with the remote possibility of ever getting out of this flat.

The other email went as follows . . .

Hello Matey!

How's tricks? Just wanted to let you know that all is well back home.

Well, kind of. I'm afraid Gillie and I didn't make it past the border, really, before things started going awry. I don't know why, but it's happened again. That girl really does something to me.

Don't know whether I'm delighted or devastated that I noticed her across the room at that business course all those years ago. Never mind. Time will tell. And I'm obviously glad I met you.

Had a great time up in Muirdrith no matter what came to pass on the road back home.

Have a look at the attached. Some low-res photos of you and Baki from the photo shoot on the beach. There are some absolute beauts, don't you think? Let me know which ones you like and I'll send you the high-res versions.

Love to you and your men.
Oliver.

If the first email from Glensìth didn't cut through the dullness of this day then this one from Oliver certainly did. I totally forgot about Gillie's comments on my blog post last night. Needless to say, I called her, like, asap after reading this message. Baki was still willing Bob to find the Golden Hammer so I had a hot minute to find out what had come to pass.

It might be possible, Dear Reader, that after that phone call, I have never, ever more craved a glass of something alcoholic.

Okay, so yet again I am kind of bound by the laws of not-outing-your-friends'-most-private-and-pending-matters-of-the-heart, but I have been given the go-ahead to give you some skeleton facts. You know, for the purposes of narrative art:

- Goliver stopped for a wee break in Gretna Green
- One half of Goliver got a little excited at 'all the pretty little churches'
- The other half of Goliver took that as a sure sign to rapidly progress the relationship to the next level

- He therefore produced a ring and one of his knees got mucky on somebody's front lawn
- Words were spoken. Rather loudly
- Goliver was asked to leave the area courtesy of Neighbourhood Watch
- One half of Goliver stormed off with car keys and ejected luggage that wasn't hers from car boot onto pavement of one of said 'pretty little churches', screaming words about timing and cliches and downright misogyny
- Other half of Goliver was given no choice but to do the remainder of journey by train on his own
- Goliver is no more

It's sad but it's true.

And it's history repeating itself.

Poor Goliver.

Gillie is okay though. As she always seems to be. It's Oliver I worry about. If you're reading, dear Oliver, Gillie may be my sister from another mister, but you are my angel-life-coach-drifted-down-from-some-random-cloud-four-years-ago and I'm here for whatever you need.

Really I am.

And, Dear Reader, I have to tell you that the photos Oliver took are awesome. I mean, it actually looks like I might be a capable mother and Baki is smiling his little head off in ALL of the pictures. I know Kadafi's dance moves got me all inspired to be me as best I could that afternoon, but Oliver definitely knows what he's doing with composition and light.

And, for once, it doesn't look like I've kidnapped poor Baki from another family – Oliver has captured the likeness in our smiles, the similarity in our eyes and the oneness in our expressions like I've never seen before.

What an honour it is to have these photos. I'll treasure them Oliver, I really will.

And to top this stay-at-home day right off with a big fat cherry, Mesut has just video-called and told me his mam is doing really quite well. Her colour is back and she's smiling. I've even seen her beautiful face for myself and she blew me a kiss down the phone. She has told the doctors she will start fasting again tomorrow whether they like it or not and she intends to go back home to Manevitaş at the earliest opportunity. I suspect she will have a fight on her hands. Not sure even an angel like her can stand up to thirty or so well-meaning family members and a full-on cardiac medical team.

I guess tomorrow will tell.

Phew. This stay-at-home experience has completely exhausted me. What with visions of new flats, speaking engagements, Golden Hammers, churches in Gretna Green, my smiling mother-in-law and Paulo effing Coelho, I think my dreams are sorted for tonight.

May your dreams be as rich and varied as mine, Dear Reader.

İyi geceler. xxx

KadafiDancingKing
I so pleased Mesut's mum getting better. Hospitals good in Ankara so I not surprised. And you! Please follow the goodness to Paulo Coelho at this Glensìth place. You can do it, Mrs Jess! We all know you can.

Jess.AKYOL
Thank you, lovely boy. If I decide to do it, I hope I don't explode with nerves on the day. I really can't believe it. Somebody is smiling down on me. Either that or having a massive laugh.

KadafiDancingKing
Allah has good sense of humour I think.

Angnonymous
Oh, so you got Lupa's email – brilliant! Did I not mention Mr Coelho was coming along? He's a fan of Glensìth. It's his third trip out here. He'll love you, Jess. Besides, Bernie will be there to keep you strong!

AngelBernie
That I will, poppet. I'll be there with bells on! Logan (my HUSBAND) is coming too and maybe even Frida if we can't find a sitter. You taking Baki?
Jess.AKYOL
Oh god, I haven't even agreed to do it yet! But yeah, I expect so. What if he turns into Beast-Child in front of Paulo Coelho? It would be a shame to die of embarrassment just as I reach the end of Ramadan. Glad you're bringing your HUSBAND though.

OliverChen1!
Accurate account of events in Gretna, Jess. And yes, will utilise your excellent listening skills at some point, I'm sure. Glad you liked the photos.
Jess.AKYOL
I really did! Listening skills always available (unless Beast-Child is in mid-meltdown mode which is highly possible, as you well know).

NO_Just_DON'T(1)
THIS COMMENT HAS BEEN DELETED
NO_Just_DON'T(1)
THIS COMMENT HAS BEEN DELETED

NO_Just_DON'T(1)
THIS COMMENT HAS BEEN DELETED
NO_Just_DON'T(1)
THIS COMMENT HAS BEEN DELETED
JESS.AKYOL
I'd appreciate it if you took your comments to somebody else's blog. I'm starting to feel targeted and there's no need for this kind of toxic language. Please don't come back. Thank you.
NO_Just_DON'T(1)
THIS COMMENT HAS BEEN DELETED

ThistleMadMona
Oh Jess, what a to-do you've got going on with those comments there. Take a nice, deep breath, m'eudail and cuddle that lovely boy of yours. It won't be long til your man is back home and you can plan this wee talk at Glensíth together. I know staying at home with a wee'un can be a challenge so if you're looking to get out and about tomorrow, I'll be off shopping in Inverness. You and little Baki are welcome to join if you like? I promise no coffee shops.
Jess.AKYOL
Mona, that's such a nice offer. I'll let you know tomorrow if that's okay?

paulo-coelho-wisdom-shop
Life getting you down? Have all the Paulo Coelho wisdom you need HERE at our online shop of inspiration. We not ever arguing with the wisdom of the universe. Get it now! As good as the real thing!
Jess.AKYOL
Turns out I may be getting the real thing, actually. But thank you anyway.

Not-A-Granny-Flora
Good news on all fronts then (maybe not for Gillie). Make sure you send me those photos of you and Baki. You sure you will be okay speaking in front of all those people at Glensìth? I have been there with your auntie years ago and I think the main hall is pretty big. Do you want help with your speech? I can proof it for you.
Jess.AKYOL
If I decide to do it, then yes please, Mam. But only if you promise not to use a red pen and your journalist's shorthand / indiscernible scrawl? Notes in an email will suffice.
Not-A-Granny-Flora
Rude.
Jess.AKYOL
Accurate.

Fab4CoolDad
I'm with Jess. Accurate. And love? When you've got that Coelho bloke in the room, just remember to listen to the Beatles and . . . 'Act Naturally'.
Jess.AKYOL
I'll do my best! BTW love this song – never heard it before. Is that Ringo singing? He was always my fave.
Fab4CoolDad
Yep – well spotted. It's Ringo singing but it's not a Beatles song. It was supposedly a bit of an in-joke about his shaky acting career at the time. Thought you'd like it. x

Night-sun-ella
No way! I can't believe Goliver didn't make it! I now owe Miles 20 quid!
Jess.AKYOL
Ella, betting on Gillie's love life is in very bad taste. Shame on

you. 
GILLIE_LASS77
What I can't believe is that Miles apparently knows me better than you do, Ella. Extra shame on you.
Night-sun-ella
Okay, okay, all the shame one me. I am now weighed down with shame. Let me know when I can come out. It's heavy.
GILLIE_LASS77
Good. You can come out for Jess's talk on 8th Sep and not until then.
Night-sun-ella
Understood. Do I have to fast like Jess?
GILLIE_LASS77
No. You can have Dotty bring you some small morsels. I will call her on her Fisher Price chatter telephone. Tell her to stand by.

Anonymous
THIS COMMENT HAS BEEN DELETED

Compustable.Apocalips
THIS COMMENT HAS BEEN DELETED
Compustable.Apocalips
THIS COMMENT HAS BEEN DELETED

MesutAk1
I not like idea of this talk at Glensíth, Gulazer, but I am telling you very excite about it. We can talk when I am home? I not want stop you from doing things you love, Islam just part of me and you knows that. My mum is saying I should let you do what is already in your heart. She say I shouldn't mess with your heart.
Jess.AKYOL
You're not messing with it. You're just in it.

20

DAY 20 – BLING ON

Muirdrith, Highlands of Scotland, UK
Mon 30th Aug 2010
Sunrise / Suhoor: 6.10am
Sunset / Iftar: 8.22pm

Last night, after I wrote my daily blog post, I have to admit I did get a little bit dragged down by the hateful shit I had to cut out of the comments. I've Googled this, obviously, and have learned I must not engage with or feed the trolls no matter how tempted I am. It's also not a good idea to disappear into a pit of self-loathing, and go with their general consensus that Baki should, after all, have been taken by the professional child-stealers, in order to be protected from me, an '*incapable, ignorant and Islam-glorifying bitch*'.

So, recognising that going that way would put me firmly in the Shit Mothers Camp, I decided to read through all of your very positive comments FROM THE START. And I just want to start today's post by saying thank you . . .

You really have made this ridiculous challenge not only bearable, but actually *enjoyable* at times, too. I was so happy, in fact, that I made a midnight dash for the kitchen, cheerily ignored a note stuck to the toaster about not allowing foods that are 'foreign' or 'smelly' into the flat, and microwaved myself a platter of hot, lemony, stuffed vine leaves.

Mmmm. They were so good. I sat there in bed, the banquet laid before me where Mesut would usually lie, chomping away on the aromatic, garlicky goodness of my chosen morsels and read all of your gorgeous words from start to finish.

It was a beautiful thing.

This morning though, I suddenly remembered the basic rule of Ramadan which Mesut tried his best to drill into my brain from day one. Do not eat massive amounts of food all in one go simply because the sun has gone down. Yes, you may feel you deserve it, or that you're making up for lost time, but sadly your digestive system will not be able to handle it.

How right he was.

Upon waking, all of my tummy parts were working overtime and my head was thumping. I mean, properly banging. I didn't realise just how bad my head was, until I finally dropped Baki at nursery this morning, and jumped back in the car to go meet Mona in Inverness. I'd decided to take her up on her offer of a shopping trip, but now that I was sitting there behind the wheel, willing my head to chill the fuck out, I wasn't so sure it was a good idea.

I sat and stared at the multi-coloured fence railings of Wee Bairns World, breathing deep and pondering what will happen at the end of Ramadan. I couldn't take any headache tablets, so daydreaming about the end felt like the next best thing.

When the last day of fasting is over, the Muslim population celebrates the festival of 'Eid al-Fitr'. Or, as the Turkish call it, 'Tatlı Bayram'. Bayram is very much like the Christmas celebrations of the West, in that it's a time for families to come together, for children to receive gifts and for people to show kindness and gratitude. It doesn't stop there though, as Eid al-Fitr means, *the feast of breaking the fast*, so there are huge banquets to be had.

During Bayram, shops and restaurants close for about three days, everybody goes to mosque and special prayers are performed in congregation. The housewives slick on some sparkly eye-shadow, the kids stuff their faces with Turkish delight and the elders get even more love and attention. Later on in the year, there is Kurban Bayram (or Eid al-Adha) which is when the whole sheep-sacrificing thing happens. As you might guess, I'm a much bigger fan of Tatlı Bayram, which literally means 'sweet bayram'.

I have no idea what our Bayram will be like. Who knows if Mesut will be back in time for it and, if I'm honest, I couldn't blame him if he wanted to stay in Turkey, keeping an eye on his mam. Even if he does make it back, we won't have millions of family members nearby to make a fuss of Baki and help teach him all about his Islamic heritage. Last night, when I read Mona's comment about shopping, I thought that whatever happens, I should have some small gifts to give Baki for Bayram.

I turned the key in the ignition and my banger of a car roared to life. I reversed out of the parking spot, my sweary-mindfulness skills in full swing in order to cope with that bitch of a headache, because I was still determined to meet up with Mona. However, just as I was about to drive ahead, something stopped me in my tracks.

A cat.

Sat on the road, right in front of me, stubborn as a rock and bathing in a great gush of morning sunlight, was the huge, ginger, brute of a cat from back home. I've never seen this beast away from the flat but I suppose he must venture outside sometimes. He was eyeballing me, I was sure of it. And puffing himself up, acting like some kind of Catzilla.

My headache was giving me no patience whatsoever for this

kind of shit, so I pressed the accelerator, thinking the sound of my car's crappy engine revving and spluttering might be enough to make him move out of the way. No prizes for guessing, it wasn't.

I've no idea how long I sat there for, trying to use some kind of kinetic brute strength to get Catzilla to move the hell out of the way. We were both as stubborn as each other, and it wasn't until the receptionist of Wee Bairns World came outside to investigate the excessive car noises / fumes, that Catzilla gave me the most miniscule nod, picked up his arse like it was a precious jewel, and stalked the hell away.

I swung out of the car park before I could be accused of animal cruelty and sped off to meet Mona in Inverness.

My headache subsided quite quickly after that and my morning of shopping was really nice. However, I did learn that it's way less fun when you can't sashay around with a grandé-mocha-chocca-latté in hand. Never mind. At least those extra pennies went towards prezzies for Beast-Child.

Mona was the perfect shopping companion – far preferable to a furious toddler. I understand now, why Goliver – oops, I mean Gillie and Oliver – could forgive her for the thistle bombardment, and even think it endearing in the end.

She really is the most intriguing person. I feel ashamed of myself for writing her off that day I was waiting in the Co-op queue with my myriad boxes of shortbread, stressed about the Visit From Hell. I wrote her off as elderly and incapable and I couldn't have been further from the truth.

I was right about the slowness though. Mona takes her own sweet time in whatever she's doing. Whether it's choosing some wool for her next crocheted blanket, or picking out a bathing suit for her Bathing Biddies Beach Club (OMG. Where do I sign up?), everything she does is leisurely, steady and deliberate. If you ever get the honour of speaking with her, Dear Reader, you'll notice that her speech is that way inclined too. Not slow because of her elder years – far from it. Slow because she is choosing her words wisely, and she wants you to have the best of her, no matter what the topic of conversation.

"I'm so lucky, m'eudail," she told me, as we sat on a bench in the middle of the High Street, dumping our bags and resting our feet. "I've spent a lot of time in a lot of places and I've been able to collect my favourite philosophies, picking out the ones that shine the brightest to me and putting them into my life. I learned a long time ago that being impeccable with my word was the best way forward."

"What do you mean? Impeccable with your word?"

"Och, it's simple, lassie. No gossip. Only saying the things I actually mean. Not speaking against myself or others. Moving in the direction of truth and love with my words. It's an ancient approach. Sometimes I think younger folk get a wee bit frustrated because I'm choosing my words so carefully. They haven't got time for it."

"Do you mean like a filter? Doesn't that mean you're adapting your words for other people?"

"Not adapting, m'eudail. Choosing. Letting the words come up that are really true to me. Not choosing them for someone else. Choosing them for me."

"Wow. You're a flipping legend, did you know that?"

Mona smiled and took a deep breath, closing her eyes for an instant. She tipped back her curly-haired head and there was a fragrant wave of heathery soap. She breathed out slowly, opening her eyes and looking right at me with a stare as green and pure as a slice of jade. "Och, yes. Of course I do!" And just like that, her legendary status sky-rocketed even more.

Whilst we ducked in and out of various kids' toy shops, which were disconcertingly noisy and garish, Mona told me a little bit more about her life. Her husband, Jimmy, who she'd met at university, had been a book publisher. He travelled all over the world securing deals for translation rights and international publications. She'd never wanted to stay at home, opting instead for a travelling lifestyle together, and she helped him with his accounting along the way.

"Ah, so that's how you've drawn on all sorts of different cultures, then? What an exciting time it must have been."

"Och, it really was. We both adored soaking up new experiences. Everywhere we went, we were creating our own little world of philosophy. Jimmy loved trying new things as much as he loved publishing books. That's why I was so delighted to find out about you and your wee blog. He would have bit your hand off for a publishing contract, were he still here, bless him."

"He sounds amazing."

"Och, he was. We had such adventures." Mona's smile turned soft and sweet, the word 'adventures' still lingering on her lips with an echo of sorts.

"Can I ask you something, Mona?"

"Of course, lassie."

"What about when your adventures were over?"

"What do you mean?"

"I mean, what about when Ailsa came along? How did you go from travelling the world, publishing exciting books, learning about all different cultures, having such a spontaneous and independent lifestyle, to sitting at home with a baby? And please, god, don't give me some crap about that being an adventure in itself."

"Oh I won't give you any crap, m'eudail. I think you know that about me by now."

"I think I do."

"Weesht, it was a good while ago now, that my Ailsa was in nappies. And times were different then, to be sure. But the responsibility was the same, I think. The weight. The doubt. The terror."

"Yup. They sound familiar. How did you stop them from crushing you?"

"What makes you think I wasn't crushed, lassie?"

"Well, you just . . . you speak so fondly of your Ailsa. The two of you obviously have a good bond. And you seem to be very, I don't know, together and resolute in who you are. How did you keep all of that? You know, when Ailsa was a baby?"

"Och, I really don't think I did. I remember every day being a drain – at least for a little while, anyway. My Jimmy used to worry so. He thought I didn't love wee Ailsa the way I should. Because we'd moved around the world so much before we had her, once we settled again in Scotland, we didn't know anybody. Not one soul in Muirdrith. And, as you say, our lifestyle changed so dramatically. Washing nappies and making up bottles was a far cry from signing authors and throwing book parties. I was at the end of myself, I really was."

"How did you find yourself again?" I whispered.

"With time. With love. With acceptance that this was me now. That Ailsa wasn't going anywhere, and I didn't actually want her to, not really."

"How long did it take?"

"I remember it not being that simple, m'eudail. I remember waking up some mornings and seeing Ailsa's little grin and managing to get her ready without a hitch and thinking, '*this is okay. I can do this*'. And then other mornings it would be harder, heavier, more crushing, as you say. So I couldn't tell you how long it took, just that I learned to be in it wholly, completely, but also to take time out of it wholly, completely."

"Meaning . . ?"

"Meaning that when I wasn't with her, after the adrenalin of the birth wore off, I started to relax back into me a bit more. I would go for walks when Jimmy got home from work, or do some gardening when she was asleep. The more I did those things, the more I could be in them completely, and find the parts of myself I'd been missing. Then, the beautiful thing was, that I could give them to Ailsa. She could get her whole mummy instead of a shadow or a flicker of who I'd been."

"So, it just happened over time? That you found your whole self again."

"Yes, I think so. It wasn't linear. It wasn't straight from A to B. Parenthood meanders all over the place, so why wouldn't our identity too? I remember my Jimmy came home from work one day, when our Ailsa was about two, your Baki's age, and he found me crying into a pile of bread dough. I'd had a hard day and I'd thought kneading some bread might help me work out some frustrations. It didn't. Instead, I just couldn't stop crying. This was a time too many for Jimmy, though, and he pulled me away from the kitchen counter and sat me down on a chair."

"What did he say?"

"I remember it so well. He said, 'Mona, this is enough, now. I know you like a good cry, but I need you to remember something. Something I know about you to be true.'"

"What? What did he know, Mona?"

"Well, lassie. He held onto my sticky, doughy hands and he said, 'You are beautiful. Fact. You are strong. Fact. You are tough as old boots. Fact. You are sturdy as hell, you are spiky and you damn well grow wherever you are placed.' And it was at that point my tears kind of splurged into laughter because his face was so serious and he really meant what he was saying, but all I could say was, 'You make me sound like a thistle!'

"I couldn't stop laughing and he got all huffy and puffy because he was trying to make a serious point. He was trying to say that I could get through it because I had all these qualities, qualities that a mum needs, but by that point all I could do was laugh out loud that after all our travels, after everything we'd seen and done together, all he could do was compare me to a flipping Scottish weed!"

Mona was laughing now, as we walked along the aisles of yet another toy shop. She trailed her fingers along a high shelf of wooden toys, and her whole body convulsed in hilarity so that all her shopping bags rustled. "Honestly! A blinking thistle! The cheek of the man."

Have you ever had one of those moments in real life, Dear Reader, where you feel like some overly complex mystery is finally answered and laid out before you, for your slow and bewildered consumption? Well, that's what I felt like today, in that toy shop, standing there and watching Mona have hysterics next to a shelf of hand-painted, wooden parakeets.

"So that's why there are thistles everywhere in your life? That's why you wear them and plant them and why you made that beautiful thistle archway that you brought to the beach for the photo shoot. And that's how you named Thistledown Lodge?"

"Exactly, lassie. Because of my Jimmy. He did me a big favour that day, so he did. Thistles got me through that day and they pretty much have done ever since."

"Cool. So all I need to do then, is pick a robust Scottish weed and suddenly the secrets of motherhood will be bestowed upon me? How about a dandelion? Do you get those in Scotland? I've always liked them."

Mona's laughter ebbed softly to a sigh and she put an arm around me. How I'd come to standing in front of a row of lurid wooden toys, being embraced by an elderly woman who was coming down from a laughing fit, my tummy roaring like an ogre on speed and my head filled with images of Scottish, spiky thistles, I will never know.

Ramadan will do that to you.

After a few moments, Mona released me and picked up one of the wooden parakeets. Its head nodded and the turquoise, glass-beaded eyes flashed at us. “You’re doing a grand job already, lassie. None of this dandelion nonsense. Now, do you think wee Baki would like this for Bayram? It’s a bit different from all that plastic stuff, don’t you think?”

“It is.” I nodded, trying not to feel bad about the Bob The Builder helmet and toolbox I’d already purchased in a frenzy. Baki would bust a gut when he saw them though, so I knew I’d got the right gifts.

“A wooden parakeet it is.” Mona lifted it off the shelf and I stopped myself from doing the British thing, insisting she mustn’t spend her money on my child. The woman had just told me she was constantly impeccable with her word, so who was I to challenge her on something she’d already decided?

“That’s so kind, Mona, thank you.”

“It’s not a worry. And what about you, my dearie? What do we need to get for you on this little shopping trip of ours?”

“Oh, I don’t need anything. Just these gifts for Baki.”

“You’re absolutely sure? You don’t have any exciting social engagements coming up where you might need to look your best? Nothing like that?” That twinkle in her eye was so compelling, the words were out of my mouth before I could even think them through.

“Well I suppose I could do with a new dress or something, for if I do end up doing that talk at Glensíth.”

“My thoughts exactly, lassie. Now let’s get this for Baki and then we can go and get your bling on. I know the perfect place.”

“Get my what on?”

“Get your *bling* on. Isn’t that what you youngsters say these days? Get iced? Glitz up? What I mean, Jess my darling, is let’s buy you something sparkly and fabulous.”

"But I don't even know if I'm doing the talk, Mona. I haven't agreed to anything yet."

Mona dipped her head down and smiled at the ground for a few beats. When she tipped her face back up at mine, it was beaming. Really, truly beaming. "Now you know, and I know, that's complete nonsense, m'eudail." And with that, she threaded her arm through mine and laughed her way out of the shop. "Come on, we'll both get a dress for the big event. And do you know something? You're going to look completely gorgeous."

And there was something about the grip of her arm, the flush of her voice and the aspiration in her step that made me say, "I know."

BLOG POST UPDATE:

It's gone midnight. This is an awful update, but one I have to make. I simply cannot leave today's entry as it is above. Not when I've just had a phone call like that.

Mesut just called me . . . it's all a bit of a blur . . . I couldn't understand him properly because he was crying and there was a lot of noise in the background.

It's his mam . . . she's gone.

Gone.

I'm not sure if I'll be back tomorrow. I'll try. I don't know what happens next. I don't know if I can do any of this anymore. Fasting . . . Glensíth . . . the newspaper . . . blogging . . .

Please bear with me. With us.

She's gone.

GILLIE_LASS77
The thistle mystery is solved! Well done, sweetie. Also glad Mona took you shopping for a dress. You're right, she is a legend. 😁
Jess.AKYOL
The dress I got is SO sparkly, Gillie. You would absolutely love it. It's purple and a tiny bit short. In fact, I'm wishing you left that fabulous long fur-coat you had on when you came up here. The rainbow-coloured one. It would go sooo well.
GILLIE_LASS77
OMG, Jess, I've just read your second entry when my phone pinged that you'd added to the post. This is awful news, sweetie. I'm here for you. Call if you need me tomorrow. Sending all the love.

NO_Just_DON'T(1)
THIS COMMENT HAS BEEN DELETED

Night-sun-ella
Will I be able to see your frock's sparkle all the way down here in Cambridge? Can you angle yourself under the Muirdrith nightsun (!) on Sep 8th so that your ethereal glow bounces approximately 500 miles down the road to me and Dotty? Oh, the glamour! Oh the excitement! Oh the antici . . . . pation. 😂
Jess.AKYOL
Thank you, Frankenfurter. I will try my best.
Night-sun-ella
Have also just seen your second post. Hope you get some sleep tonight, that phone call must have been so hard. 😢😢😢

Angnonymous
Ooooh, things are hotting up now, Jess. Only ten days to go and

you'll be a free woman and you'll have nailed the most incredible talk at Glensìth. And all with your 'bling on' too, thanks to Mona. Rooting for you.

Jess.AKYOL

Thank you Angus. Means a lot. I'll call Lupa tomorrow and we'll chat details about the talk. Can't believe it, but it looks like I'm doing this!

Angnonymous

Just read the last part of the post, Jess. There's nothing anyone can say to help. Don't worry about Glensíth. Just look after yourself.

MaxAttax

I enjoyed the observational drama about the cat. You'd give Beckett a run for his money. Peace out.

Jess.AKYOL

I appreciate the comparison. Because existential absurdity is what I'm going for on this blog.

MaxAttax

Fuck, Jess. So sorry about Mesut's mam. I'm calling you, like, now. I don't care how late it is.

ThistleMadMona

I've read both posts, Jess. My sympathies are with you and Mesut and all of his family right now. Try not to worry about him though, m'eudail. Muslim families have tight rituals around death and they will all be looking after each other. He will have important jobs to do at the funeral as one of her sons and it will all happen quickly, mark my words. I'll check on you tomorrow. Hope you are sleeping now.

Fab4CoolDad

Oh Jess, we're devastated about Mesut's mam. We really hoped we'd meet her one day. I don't know if it's in bad taste, but I feel like a Beatles song might be helpful? So here's 'Free As A Bird', which is what I hope she is now.

Not-A-Granny-Flora
I know you've spoken to your brother. I'll call you in the morning. You'll be okay, and so will Mesut.

AngelBernie
Fuck, poppet. This babe is giving me heartburn in the middle of the night, so I thought I'd have a read of your post as a distraction. I'm ridiculously sorry to hear that Mesut's mum has fled this world. I know it's far too soon to even think about explaining where the angels might take her, but I want you (and him) to know that she's okay. And you'll be okay too. I'm around tomorrow. Call me. Love you all the world.

21

DAY 21 – THE GUEST HOUSE

Muirdrith, Highlands of Scotland, UK
Tues 31st Aug 2010
Sunrise / Suhoor: 6.12am
Sunset / Iftar: 8.19pm

Okay, I'm back.

Writing the second part of my post to you, late last night, feels like a hundred years ago now. I've been on a roller coaster ride of emotions since then, and – to be honest – I'm not sure which way is up.

Despite all that, it seems I am still compelled to write.

So here I am.

I was on a high after my shopping trip yesterday. I had a spangly new dress, a load of new plastic crap to give Baki for Bayram, and a new-found connection with Mona. I didn't even care about the note waiting for me on the front door when I got home, which bleated on about how Mesut's prayer beads should be kept out of reach on account of them being a potential choking hazard to the cats. I just popped those prayer beads away in a safe place and I even stroked a cat or two. It was nice.

I got the phone call shortly after midnight. It was such a shock. I mean, we're never prepared for these things, right? I really thought Mesut's mam was getting better. We all did. How can she have been blowing kisses at me literally hours ago, and now not be in the world? It just doesn't make sense.

Mesut tried his best to stick to the facts in his call. But his voice sounded so broken. As much as he would have wanted to call me, I know how hard it must have been to say the words down the phone.

All he told me was that she suffered a massive heart attack and her body decided it would be the last. It happened whilst everybody except Mesut's dad was out of the hospital room. They'd gone to drink tea at a relative's house nearby and had plans to go back in staggered intervals in the morning so as not to overwhelm her. Her husband, however, could not be tempted from her side.

I guess we only ever respond to these things with the breadth of experience we have of the world so far. For me, that meant I wanted my love and sorrow to flow down the phone to Mesut like a river. I tried to find the words to tell him that I was there for him, that I would hold him, that I wouldn't let him go until he was ready. But I couldn't. Because I wasn't there, was I?

It didn't matter anyway, because he had to get off the phone pretty sharpish. He said the funeral would start today. There is much work to do, apparently.

I think Mona wrote something in the comments last night about Muslim funerals happening very quickly after death. I've checked the Quran for Dummies and it does say something about this. Mesut and his family will be very quick to get his mam back to Manevitaş, where there will be washing and dressing rituals to prepare her body for burial. They will probably hire community prayer rooms near the mosque so that women and children (who wouldn't typically attend the funeral) will be close by and able to pray.

It is believed that social visits can help a family with their grief so Mesut is in for seeing a lot of people over the next few days. As it's Ramadan, however, they won't expect to be fed until after sundown, so they'll probably arrive later in the day, giving the family the mornings to get themselves together. It looks like his sisters will be rolling their sleeves up and cooking like mad as soon as their mam is in the ground.

So sorry for the info dump, but I just don't know what else to do or say. Imagining what is happening for my husband is making me feel closer to him, I guess.

The other thing I found out is that if somebody dies during the holy month of Ramadan, it is actually considered a blessing. Apparently, the gates of Hell are closed during the whole month. Paradise (or Heaven) is the only open door and new souls can pass through them freely. So it looks like Mesut's mam got a free pass. Not that she wouldn't have sailed through anyway.

I sailed through my own doors today. And it was kind of holy, I suppose.

Let me explain.

My phone rang at about 10am, just as I was wrestling my (cooled) hair straighteners out of Baki's fists and trying to replace them with an age appropriate toy.

"Hello, is that Jessica Akyol?"

"Yes."

"Ah, hi there, Jess. It's Sue here. The counsellor from your GP surgery? Do you remember me?" How could I forget her? Sue was the tartan-skirted, shiny-eyed, tissue-offering lady who'd seen me through my worst few weeks of postnatal depression. I'd been expecting a call after the doctor re-referred me but hadn't realised it would be lovely Sue.

"Yes, of course I remember you."

"Fabby. You've been referred for another course of counselling sessions by your doctor and, well, this isn't the norm, but it seems that you weren't actually properly discharged after the last time I saw you. An admin error I expect. So, what that means is that you don't have to start all over again on a waiting list."

"Oh. That's good."

"Exactly. And, I just so happen to have a cancellation this afternoon. I'm wondering if you'd like to come in for your first session? I know it's short notice but I thought I'd call you and offer it anyway."

Today of all days? Would it really be okay to jump into counselling when I'd just had such monstrously devastating news? Could my nerves take it? Could Sue's?

Then I glanced at Baki, who was screaming at a mountain of Cheerios he had poured onto the floor, the hair straighteners not scooping them up and transferring them into his plastic Bob The Builder digger quite as effectively as he would have liked. He looked up at me and screamed even louder, my knackered, grief-ridden face an obvious trigger for his potent vexation.

Fuck it.

"Okay, Sue," I breezed, trying to sound a tiny bit human. "I'll be there. What time?"

"Two o'clock please. Just go to reception and they'll tell you where to go. See you soon."

And that's how it happened that I found myself in a counsellor's office sans enfant for a whole hour today (Bernie's older daughter stepped in as childminder for the bargain sum of a tenner. #becauseimworthit). It's really coming to something when your idea of a break is a box of tissues, a ticking clock and an invitation to bare your soul to a stranger.

Still, a break is a break.

I'll be honest, it's a weird one, writing about today's counselling session here on my blog. It's not that I don't want to share deep and personal things with you, but because this first session came at such an emotionally challenging time, and because I have no idea where this counselling journey will take me. I don't know what, among the things that were said, will be conducive to feeling better and what will be detrimental to healing.

So I want to be careful.

Some of you might be in therapy yourselves. Or contemplating it. Or maybe you have been in the past. I don't want to insinuate that something Sue said, or something I said, is a pivotal or poignant thing. Counselling is personal.

Recovery is personal.

But I can say that Sue is still absolutely lovely. Almost as soon as I walked in there I felt her broad smile wash over me and enjoyed how her hands lifted from her tartan lap so that her open palms welcomed me. It was enough for the tears to start flowing with alarming punctuality, so I told her straight away that my mother-in-law had passed away the night before. I half-expected her to kick me out. You know, tell me that I was too vulnerable or raw or too much of a sopping, snotty mess. She didn't though. She just gestured to the waiting chair and told me to start wherever I wanted.

It wasn't long before the ticking of the clock faded quickly into the background, and off I went into the land of revealing, confiding and recounting, not worrying for one tiny little second that she might have heard most of this before . . .

- The depression that slowly edged into my life after Baki was born – the constant guilt, worry and anxiety

- The immense amount of personal change I've been through over the last couple of years, regardless of how self-inflicted it might be
- The loss of identity since Baki claimed my heart and how I have no idea how to piece it back together with a toddler continually hanging off me
- The miscarriage and how the loss of that baby has left a gaping chasm I don't know how to fill
- The grey veil of depression and although I thought it had lifted, more recently it has been draping itself back over me – especially since my parenting abilities have been questioned and the involvement of Children's Services

I think that was enough to get off the starting blocks, don't you?

Anybody who has had counselling before will know that the first session is really about information-giving and rapport-building. Well, Sue can definitely tick the information box because she now has a wealth of data on my psyche. Hopefully she'll leave that file open though, because doubtless there will be more to come.

As for rapport-building, well we've met before so that flowed pretty easily. It takes a certain type of person to be a good counsellor, doesn't it? It takes the obvious patience, understanding and compassion. But today I sensed a bull-shit filter in Sue that I am definitely going to need in the coming weeks.

Before I left, Sue pressed a square of paper into my hands. "We've got a lot of work to do, Jess, and I can just tell you're committed enough to do it. In the meantime, here's a wee poem you might find helpful. One of my favourites. And kind of fitting because it's by a mystic Muslim poet called Rumi."

Rumi? Wasn't that the same poet that Mesut's mam adored?

Wasn't he the one who said *'We are born out of love. Love is the mother'*? I took the poem from Sue and a quiver of something rippled down my spine. Talk about coincidences.

I left the GP surgery with an inexplicable lightness to my step. I sat down outside on a bench just across the road which was happily sheltered from the sea breeze and also drenched in the mid-afternoon sun. I figured Baki's Cheerio-related screaming would potentially be ongoing and not conducive to contemplating the poetic words of an ancient mystic poet. So I took this moment for me, unfolded the paper and read:

THE GUEST HOUSE

This being human is a guest house.
Every morning a new arrival.

A joy, a depression, a meanness,
Some momentary awareness comes
As an unexpected visitor.

Welcome and entertain them all!
Even if they are a crowd of sorrows,
Who violently sweep your house
Empty of its furniture,
Still, treat each guest honourably.
He may be clearing you out
For some new delight.

The dark thought, the shame, the malice.
Meet them at the door laughing and
Invite them in.

Be grateful for whatever comes.

Because each guest has been sent
As a guide from beyond.

RUMI

Wow.

I love it.

We all know that challenging times can make for valuable life lessons. But what about when you're in the middle of them? What about when they're not over yet?

'*A depression, a meanness*'.

The '*crowd of sorrows*'.

'*The dark thought, the shame, the malice*'.

They're all so difficult to handle and totally (in my case) guilty of breeding yet more negative emotions on top in never-ending, destructive layers.

This poem will, I'm sure, help me sit with all of that shit. Because if it's already there, why put up a fight? Mesut's mam is already gone. He's not here. I can't be there for him. Fighting and refusing and grappling only makes things worse, even though it's completely natural to be sad – devastated, even.

If only I'd allowed myself to *feel* when I lost my baby, maybe I'd be in a different place right now.

Maybe it would have been okay to feel grief over what was essentially a cluster of cells . . . but it was *my* cluster of cells – with promise of a heartbeat and a personality and a soul. The Quran For Dummies tells me that an angel breathes a soul into a foetus at around four months but for me, that soul was there long before that.

This is where I wonder how Muslim women do it. Mesut told me ages ago that his mam was pregnant about fifteen times in total, yet he is one of nine children. That means, and he hasn't given me the specifics, that she miscarried and / or gave birth to babies that didn't make it. Six times.

Six times.

I do hope she's with them now.

When I was in Manevitaş, I observed a sisterhood, a comradery between the women that was really quite beautiful. The startlingly close proximity that they live in, which I actually found stifling whilst I was there, means they can share cooking, cleaning, childcare and shopping but also stories, laughter, worries, fears and dreams. They are each other's guest houses. They stand at the door laughing and invite in each other's crowds of sorrows.

Even through Ramadan.

Or maybe *especially* through Ramadan.

And here's the thing. I am now fasting alone. My efforts to support Mesut with Ramadan have, quite often, been done in quiet solitude but now we are completely separate, two thousand miles apart. Not even our grief can bring us together, as the harsh reality of tradition, culture and religion stride in and claim right of way.

So that's where a sisterhood would usually come in, I guess. If I was in Turkey. But I'm not in Turkey, am I? I'm in the bastarding Scottish Highlands and I'm devoid of other women embarking on the same stupid challenge as me.

So in lieu of an abstaining sisterhood I come back to you, Dear Reader. You are my guest house right now. You are welcoming and entertaining all my shit. And I want to thank you for that.

Again.

Right. It's 8.17pm. I have to eat something. Weirdly, it's the last thing I feel like doing, but I know it has to be done. Do Cheerios count as dinner? I think so. Just need to fish them out of Bob The Builder's digger without waking Beast-Child. Or maybe I'll visit the hole in the patchy sofa of fame. Fuck it, maybe I'll go to the kitchen like an actual normal person and cook myself a meal.

Stranger things have happened.

FatimaNazar

I'm in your sisterhood, Jess! I'm fasting along with you and you're right about women supporting each other in our culture. I don't know what it's like in Turkey, but in Iran we are there for our fellow women without question and treat our friends like sisters. At Ramadan, all kinds of things come out because people are conversing with Allah so closely – it's like a detox for the soul, not just the body. Your mother-in-law really is blessed leaving this world during this beautiful month, but it sounds like you knew she was blessed right from the start. Inna lillahi wa inna ilayhi raji'un.

Jess.AKYOL

Thank you so much! I've had to delete so many horrible comments from other people, mostly bitching about Islam or, at the other end of the scale, how I'm getting everything wrong. But you've been so supportive, Fatima.

LifeIsYoursLindy

Well, after our New Year's Eve on the beach in 2006, I'd definitely include myself in your sisterhood. Keep going, Jess – it's such a difficult time for you and Mesut. I'm guessing it's not a possibility for you to go out to Turkey and join him?

Jess.AKYOL

We chatted about this when his mam was first poorly. A.) we couldn't afford plane tickets for all of us and B.) there's no way he'd be able to support me out there whilst he's busy with all of his family at such a hard time. I'd be left on my own with Baki and wouldn't have a clue what was going on. I had quite enough of that when we've made short visits before, and I know my nerves wouldn't take it again. His family are lovely but I can't understand their language, their culture or their everyday habits. Hopefully next time we go together it will be during a happy time when he can be with us and make the whole experience smoother.

NO_Just_DON'T(1)
THIS COMMENT HAS BEEN DELETED
NO_Just_DON'T(1)
THIS COMMENT HAS BEEN DELETED

GILLIE_LASS77
I can't even tell you how proud I am of you, darling girl.
Jess.AKYOL
Back atcha. Xxx

Night-sun-ella
Flipping heckarama, I am so, unbelievably sad for you and Mesut. So sad, in fact, I feel a song coming on . . .
We are family!
I got all my sisters with me!
We are family!
Get up everybody and sing and dance and show Jess how amazing she is and paint her nails and brush her hair and buy her sparkly things and bring her endless Doritos after sundoooooowwwwwwn!
Jess.AKYOL
Never doubted you for a second, sister.

AngelBernie

So glad you got to your counselling today, poppet. And it's good my teenager could watch little Baki for you – she told me the Cheerio / digger drama went on for quite a while so at least you missed that. Meanwhile, it's character-building for her. I know I'm not fasting – this dumpling of a baby would never allow it – but I'm with you all the way, sister. You know that. You up for toddlers on Friday? That's if my tummy hasn't exploded by then?

Jess.AKYOL

I'm so up for toddlers on Friday. Anything to share Baki's delightful screaming with other people. Maybe he'll eat some crayons for a while and shut the hell up. Only kidding – love his very bones. Sending love to your exploding belly – not long now!!

AngelBernie

Tell me about it. I think the angels want this one out to do some holy business or something.

Jess.AKYOL

With recent happenings, I would not be surprised.

ShelleyMadMum

U r doing so good, Jess! A counselling sesh in the middle of starving yourself and all that you're going through has got to be a challenge. Good idea to come to toddlers on Friday. See you there.

Jess.AKYOL

Indeed you will. Thanks for being lovely.

Compustable.Apocalips

THIS COMMENT HAS BEEN DELETED

Anonymous

THIS COMMENT HAS BEEN DELETED

Anonymous
THIS COMMENT HAS BEEN DELETED

Angnonymous
Counselling saved me several times over. And so did Rumi. Good on you, Jess.
Jess.AKYOL
Really? Yet another coincidence then.
Angonymous
Is it really a coincidence though? Come on, you've read The Alchemist.
Jess.AKYOL
Okay, Mr Everything-is-connected, I get it. And thank you for not pressing me about the talk at Glensíth. Just needed some space before I can figure out what I'm going to do. Do you think the cabbage hippies could do without me?
Angonymous
I think you know the answer to that. 😉

Not-A-Granny-Flora
I can't believe my Baki would scream just because of Cheerios on the floor? And is that really all you're having for dinner? Please get some fish fingers in the oven or something. Do I need to send another food parcel? Have been so worried about you and Mesut. Will the funeral be tomorrow? It's just happening so quickly, isn't it?
Jess.AKYOL
Yeah, it really is. I think the main part of the funeral was actually today. Mesut said they try to do it within 24 hours. Tomorrow there will be more rituals and visits etc. I don't know how they do it when they must still be reeling in grief. It's just awful. I have eaten Cheerios, yes, but I also made a monster of a

sandwich by pinching some cheese from Cat-Crazy Flatmate. So you can calm down, Mother.

Fab4CoolDad
Oh love, I'm glad you got your counselling session sorted and try not to worry about Mesut. He's where he needs to be with his family. I don't know much about Rumi but I do know plenty about the Fab Four and today I want to remind you that I'm sending love From Me To You.
Jess.AKYOL
Oh, Dad. 😢

ThistleMadMona
It's all very strange for us to imagine having a funeral so quickly, lassie, but that's how they do it in some other parts of the world. Use your Guest House wisdom and accept that your part, in caring for Mesut, will be when he comes home to these shores. And he will. Soon.
Jess.AKYOL
Mona The Oracle. That's what they should call you. Can I be in your sisterhood, please? That's if you'll accept such a young and foolish thing.
ThistleMadMona
In fact, there are *only* fools allowed in this sisterhood, m'eudail. And age is irrelevant. Just ask the Bathing Biddies Beach Club.
🤗🏝🤗🏝🤗🏝

22

DAY 22 - PRECIOUS TOGETHER

Muirdrith, Highlands of Scotland, UK
Weds 1st Sep 2010
Sunrise / Suhoor: 6.14am
Sunset / Iftar: 8.16pm

Good news everyone.

Mesut is coming home tomorrow.

I finally got to speak to him tonight, after waiting almost two days since he first told me about the loss of his mam. He sounded absolutely exhausted, bless him. He's been fulfilling all of the duties expected in a situation like this (as one of her sons, there are a lot of duties, apparently) and I suspect the emotion might finally be catching up with him.

"I so tired, Gulazer. I meet with so many aunties, uncles, cousins, I not even know who I am anymore. I needing be with you, so I can remember."

"Are you sure you don't need more time there? It's hard here without you but I can manage a bit longer." (Blatant lie. My mothering skills are shot to shit without him.)

"Please, don't misunderstand me but I not want time with

them like this. There so much sadness here. We all know she now in paradise, that she peaceful and free, but that she not here, with us, is making this trip too strange. I need my Gulazer. And my Baki."

"Well, we do really miss you. What about your dad?"

"He okay. His belief so strong in Allah, he actually happy she finally with him. He saw her too poorly for too long, Gulazer. And he have all my sisters looking after him. He okay."

"How do you feel about it all? I've wanted to hug you so much. I feel awful that I'm not there and that Baki and I couldn't see her before she died."

"Is okay. I so sad, believe me, but I knows as soon as I saw her, she not much longer here. Something about her eyes – I think she knew."

"Well, she did know a lot, didn't she?"

"We have lots of chatting, just two of us, when everybody else out of hospital room. She made me give promises to her."

"What did she make you promise?" Please, please, please don't let it be something along the lines of: *Leave that awful English woman, she'll never be a proper mother*.

"Oh, just things like teach Baki about Islam, give him brothers and sisters, stay true to myself, and – most important one – look after you."

"She really said that?"

"Tabi. Of course. She loving you, Gulazer, as soon as she meeting you. She saying I must support you in everything you do, even if I not understand it, or believe in it myself. She say to me your heart very true. Very pure. But that things not always easy for you because you feel everything, how do you say, bigly? Muchly? She just say, in our chat, *'Aynı madalyonun iki yüzü gibisin. Zıtsınız ama var olmak için birbirinize ihtiyacınız var*."

"Flipping heck. My Turkish just isn't that good. You'll have to help me out."

"Is mean, we two sides of same coin. We opposite, yes, but precious when together. So, you see, Gulazer? I have to come home. And must be soon."

Home. What a strange word for the two of us. Where is our home? Muirdrith? Manevitaş? İpeklikum, where we met? Or somewhere else?

"My home is with you and Baki, Gulazer."

Okay, I'm not gonna lie. There were tears during this phone call. There was also a toddler climbing all over me and pushing baby wipes into my nose and eyes in a not-so-subtle attempt to stop the leakage from my face. But do you know what, Dear Reader? For the first time in a while, those tears felt good. Cleansing, even.

Anyway, the plans are made. The flights are much cheaper if you book them from Turkey, so Mesut's older brother went to the airport today and got the best deal he could. The whole family chipped in because they were so grateful he made it out there in the first place, so there is no need for me to beg the people at Barclaycard to extend my credit limit.

Once I sorted out the leaking face scenario, I popped Baki into his anorak, said goodbye to the cat army and burst out onto the streets of Muirdrith. Even though these last few days have been god-awful, I had a date.

Well, kind of.

Mona, bless her thistle-embroidered socks, set up a little meeting between me and her daughter, Ailsa, the reporter for the Highland News. In her wisdom, she thought I needed a distraction and knew Ailsa had been waiting for the right moment to speak to me. Apparently, today was that moment. And after Mesut's rousing speech about supporting me in whatever I do, I made my way to the coffee shop, where I was to meet Ailsa, with a heart that was actually free of guilt.

It was refreshing.

On arriving, I was highly satisfied to see that Ailsa had a lanyard, a dictaphone, a notebook bursting with scrawl reminiscent of my mam's own journalistic scribble circa 1987 AND she was wearing a grey trench coat with a *matching* hat. This meant she was a Proper Reporter and not just masquerading as such.

I had an overstuffed changing bag, several dummies on my fingers, worn like rings, a pocketful of chocolate raisins AND I had a screaming toddler attached to my leg, who was loudly objecting to his crinkly anorak. This meant I was a Proper Civilian and potentially worthy of real-life story material.

I drip-fed Baki chocolate raisins after wrestling him into one of the insanely small highchairs the café had to offer and tried my best to listen to Ailsa, whilst also not absentmindedly popping a chocolate raisin in my own mouth which, even this late in the game, is still a distinct possibility.

It turns out Ailsa reckons that what I'm doing is unusual and engaging – especially as I am blogging about it each day and creating a bit of a following (did not reveal said following is mostly made up of friends, family and horrible trolls. What she doesn't know won't hurt her, right?).

Ailsa assessed the Beast-Child situation and wisely suggested she attend our toddler session at the community centre on Friday. "Once you're settled there we can do a proper interview and your friends can help out with Baki. I'll bring a photographer and we'll do some pictures with Baki once he's well, a bit more settled." I looked over at Beast-Child, who was by now slapping his chocolatey hands off his forehead and rocking like an extra from One Flew Over the Cuckoo's Nest.

So, by this time next week I will know if I've made the headlines or not. Ailsa has warned me about the fickle process of newspaper publishing and tells me not to get my hopes up. It could be that my double-page spread gets demoted to a line or two in the 'Local News' pages if some other newsworthy incident occurs in the meantime.

All this interest in little old me has got me thinking though. It's a thought I've had lots of times and it feels a bit like welcoming an old friend back into my arms. Here it is:

Aren't people fascinating?

I mean, they really are. No matter what corner of the globe you are from, no matter what you've done or haven't done in your life, there will be at least one engaging story buried in your internal world of experiences and memories. And for that one story, there will be *at least* a handful of people who will be able to find truth and beauty and resonance in it. From your story, they will be able to hear lines and imagine scenes and indulge in scenarios that make them jump and sing with empathy.

How cool is that?

Who knows? Maybe this Ramadan thing will engage people, even if only for a moment. It's certainly taken over my mind and heart for the last twenty-two days AND given me plenty of extra hours of contemplative thinking. Even if I wouldn't call it prayer, exactly, it's been a conversation of sorts. With myself, with you, Dear Reader, with the world, with my will power, with anyone who might be listening.

But am *I* listening?

Have I paid any attention *whatsoever*, to the events of this month so far? Have I listened to my reactions, my instincts, my fears, my truths and my dreams? Have I allowed the emptiness of my belly to facilitate the fullness of my heart?

The jury is out on that one.

Until tomorrow . . . x

<u>Not-A-Granny-Flora</u>

Mesut is coming back? That's good. Reporter sounds worth her salt. Glad she wants photos with Baki in. Ask to see it before it goes to print if you can, but she might not have time. Fingers crossed it makes it to press!

Jess.AKYOL

She seemed really nice Mam. I'll let you know how Friday goes. Any tips?

Not-A-Granny-Flora

Just be yourself. And remember to get key messages in.

Jess.AKYOL

Key messages? Fuck-a-duck. Have not thought about those AT ALL.

Fab4CoolDad

Ah, love. I'm pleased to hear Mesut is starting his journey home. You'll feel so much better once he's back. I'm not surprised your blog is getting noticed. Do you remember your third-year English teacher at parent's evening, begging us to get you to write shorter stories? That was funny. Anyway, The Beatles think you should spread it . . . 'The Word'.

Jess.AKYOL

I do remember that! That English teacher was so brilliant but I do think I ruined many an evening for her with the epic stories I used to hand in. Love the song recommendation today, Dad. Those lyrics have got me going.

Angnonymous

You're getting your fella back – that's braw, Jess, it really is. Can't wait to read your story in the Highland News. Maybe you'll mention your wee talk at Glensìth?

Jess.AKYOL

Fuck-a-duck again! I have totally forgotten to get in touch with that Lupa person because of everything that's been going on.

After my call with Mesut today, I really think the talk might be fine. It scares the shit out of me, but it might be fine. And good idea about mentioning it to Ailsa. I'll totally do that.

MaxAttax
Erm, Jess, I suspect the reporter you describe is, in fact, Inspector Gadget. Next time you meet her please get Baki to pull off her hat. If I'm right, it will be filled with genius mechanisms. Then get him to steal the hat and send it to me.
Peace out.
Jess.AKYOL
On it.

ThistleMadMona
Ailsa told me she met up with you and your wee one today. She's looking forward to Friday. Maybe I'll pop along with her? Would the Toddler group let me in?
Jess.AKYOL
Mona, that would be lovely! I'll put your name on the guest list. Be sure to wear something formal and I'll let the bouncers know to expect you. 😉

Anonymous
THIS COMMENT HAS BEEN DELETED

Anonymous
THIS COMMENT HAS BEEN DELETED

AngelBernie
Mesut is returning? Such good news. I'll look after Baki for you on Friday! Dotty can hide the crayons from him (they still have bite marks in from last time) and we'll ply him with all the chocolate raisins you like. No cherry liqueurs, I promise.

Jess.AKYOL
Knew I could count on you.

NO_Just_DON'T(1)
THIS COMMENT HAS BEEN DELETED
NO_Just_DON'T(1)
THIS COMMENT HAS BEEN DELETED
NO_Just_DON'T(1)
THIS COMMENT HAS BEEN DELETED
NO_Just_DON'T(1)
THIS COMMENT HAS BEEN DELETED

Compustable.Apocalips
THIS COMMENT HAS BEEN DELETED

CrunchyNut_Mummy
Go, Jess! Can't wait to read your article. You're basically our local celebrity. And I'm glad you're doing it all at Toddlers on Friday. I'll be there with bells on!
Jess.AKYOL
Fab! It will be lovely to see you. xxx

23

DAY 23 - SIXTEEN CALLS

Muirdrith, Highlands of Scotland, UK
Thurs 2nd Sep 2010
Sunrise / Suhoor: 6.16am
Sunset / Iftar: 8.13pm

I started today feeling jubilant that in a week's time I will be a free woman. Free from Ramadan.

I am ending today feeling frightened. Just plain frightened.

And not at all free.

But it's not me who isn't free. Not really.

It's Mesut.

Oh god, I really don't know where to start with this. Or how I even managed to open up the laptop and start typing in the first place. All I know is that for the last twenty-three days, writing this blog has seen me through some of the most unfathomable things. I'm hoping today will be no different.

But forgive me, Dear Reader, if I trail off halfway through and don't come back . . .

It's entirely possible.

Baki went to Wee Bairn's World this morning. All was good,

except for a Play-Doh incident which ended up with his play worker having to scoop the stuff out of his nostrils to the rhythms of 'Zoom, Zoom, Zoom, We're Going to the Moon'.

Standard Baki.

I spent that time cleaning and tidying the flat, ready for Mesut's return. I learned from my fateful mistake last time and didn't get rid of any cat litter trays, but I did empty, scrub and re-fill them all, as well as brush cat hair off anything and everything, all under the watchful gaze of that ginger brute, Catzilla.

I plucked away all of the new notes left out for me by Cat-Crazy Flatmate (must review my coat-hanging skills, evaluate my toilet paper usage and apparently my new Turkish flag stickers, recently posted to me from Ella to put on my kitchen cupboards, have no place in a SCOTTISH kitchen). I stuffed the new notes in the bedside drawer where I always shove them. I don't know why I keep them. I guess they might be amusing to look back on one day. You know, one day when I'm living it up in a beachside mansion, in a tropical climate and living off my book royalties. That day.

After all of that cleaning, and the flat finally smelling like lavender-scented air freshener rather than cat pee, I went to pick Baki up from nursery. On the way home, we graced the park with our presence for the umpteenth time this month, and I had a near-fatal lip-licking disaster. The incident involved Beast-Child, his 'generosity' and a rapidly melting Mini-Milk ice lolly being stuffed in my face (is it my fault if I can't get the baby wipes out of the packet quickly enough? We can put people on the *moon* for god's sake, so why can't we design a more effective way to extract a wipe from a goddam hole?).

As I watched my boy play on the frighteningly tall slide and the alarmingly fast roundabout, I mused over how much I have missed actually eating with Baki this month. As long as we've both got something on our plate that doesn't cause an earth-shattering hissy fit from either one of us, then I honestly believe that sharing food with my boy is one of the most blissful things to do.

Maybe it's chemistry.

When I look back on those early days in Turkey when Baki wasn't thriving and my boobs weren't doing what they were supposed to, I realise now that what I was feeling was a profound sense of failure. The one thing my body was supposed to know how to do and it couldn't do it. There was no joy, no satisfaction, no comfort in the simple act of feeding my baby. Instead there was a painful collapse, a folding-in of my soul.

Skip forward a few god-awful weeks and we started on the formula. It changed everything in terms of Baki and his health. Within days he started gaining weight and had more colour in his cheeks. It wasn't long before he became the chubby little thing he was always meant to be and, when we moved to the Highlands, I felt a wicked sense of jubilation whenever Nicky the Health Visitor raised her eyebrows at the upward momentum of his weight centile. I didn't care if he charted off the page, as long as we never went back to that terrifying time of hospital visits, blood tests and whispered fears.

I didn't shake off the sorrow of not being able to feed Baki myself for months though. You could maybe even say years, as he is two now, and it still hurts to think about it. Guilt is an unexpected free gift that comes with motherhood. If I'm offered it next time I hope I remember to turn it down.

But what I'm saying is that maybe it's actually in our chemistry, as mothers, to not only get a kick out of feeding our children, but also that we enjoy eating *with* our children. If this wasn't the case then our survival as a species would be a hell of a lot harder.

I have definitely missed eating with Baki. I know I've joked about the agonies of spilled yoghurt and the drama of ice cream being shoved into my face, but standing there at the park earlier today, I was actually day dreaming about the time when we can share something delicious together. There's nothing better than exchanging cheerily curved, rapturous smiles with a world of flavour behind them.

I want those moments back.

And sitting here now, typing these words on my laptop, it seems so sweet, so innocent, that I had those dreams this morning.

Now my dreams are more heavily loaded.

Blackened, even.

To be honest, I don't even know where I found enough light inside myself with which to recount those innocent happenings from this morning. Oh, to go back to Play Doh up nostrils and the scrubbing of cat litter trays.

Anyway . . .

After we got back, Baki went down for a nap. I ignored Cat-Crazy Flatmate, who was in the kitchen frying slices of haggis (or something) with her cat army swarming and mewing around her, and I retreated to my room for a bit of a lie down. I popped my phone on silent and dozed off quite quickly.

I was only asleep for half an hour but when I woke up, my phone had sixteen missed calls. SIXTEEN.

All from Turkey.

The number sixteen told me that this was shit not to be messed with so I released all worry of what it would cost me and I rang that number straight back.

Mesut picked up. "Gulazer?"

"What is it? What's wrong? Why did you call so many times? I'm so sorry. I was asleep."

A sigh. Or was it a groan?

"I don't know how I say this . . ."

I could hear a lot of activity in the background. A hum of voices, a drone of busy, lagging chatter. "How come you're not on your plane yet? Is the flight delayed? Don't worry. I can come and get you whatever time. I'll just get Bernie's daughter to come over and watch Baki, even if it's in the middle of the night."

"No. Is not that, Gulazer."

"Then what? Did your brother get the wrong tickets or something?"

Right then I heard a gruff, male voice shout something and I imagined Mesut put his hand over the phone because of an instant muffling of sounds. Sounds I couldn't decipher but they seemed anything but good. A cold, slithering fear started to seek rivulets of solace down my spine. The sudden onset of it was startling, like my body knew before I did that I was about to hear something terrifying. Suddenly the line became clear again and I actively shifted my focus from my spine to listening hard. "Gulazer, you not know how sorry I am but I have to be quick because they've taken my mobile. This phone, we all using it."

"All?"

"All of us here. In the room."

"The room? Mesut, you're scaring me now."

"Gulazer, I was going through İstanbul airport to get on plane and they not like my passport. They look me up on computer system and now they knows I not yet doing my national service."

I shuddered and gulped back a huge lump of something forbidding. "The army? But that's okay. You can just tell them you have a job, here in Scotland. They have to let you travel. You have a visa."

"They not seeing it like this."

"But why? What other way is there to see it?"

"They just knowing from records that I thirty years old and I still not doing national service. I tell you before, they not liking that in Turkey. They thinking I not feel proud of country, I not taking on full responsibility. They not want listen to reason."

"But you have your papers, don't you? Something that proves you have the job at the pub? My auntie gave you all that when you started."

"Gulazer, we in such big rush when finding out my mum poorly I think we not pack papers. And if I honest, they not care anyway. They keep telling me I stay here until army come and get me. I staying here in this small, small room with lots of beds and lots of men. Men from all over world trying to get in or out of Turkey. There guards outside. I can't go anywhere, Gulazer. I can't go anywhere."

If I hadn't already been sitting on my bed, I know for sure I would have dropped down onto it because suddenly all of my joints weakened and gravity took on a whole different quality.

"What . . . what can we do?"

"I not know. I ask for a lawyer. I ask for my brother. But nobody knows anything and nobody give me any proper answer. All I knows is guards standing at door and I already see what they do to a person who is trying leave. I can't going anywhere right now. I just hoping they let me see lawyer or my brother before Turkish Gendarmerie take me. There at least five other men in same problem as me so I not top of any list, Gulazer."

"And what happens if the army get there first? Can they really just take you? And if they did, how would I know? When could you come back?" My words were shivering with shock now. Cracked and dripping with fear. I didn't really want to know the answer to any of those questions.

"I not knowing definitely," he said, his voice holding onto mine for dear life. "All I knows is when this happening to my friends in past, was nothing they could doing about it. They go and do full service. Fifteen months."

"Fifteen months."

"Gulazer, I so sorry but I have to go. Someone else needing phone. Please you not worry. I okay. I only in airport now. Like you sometimes saying . . . let's just be in this moment."

It seemed absurd to sign off the phone call like any other, but what was I supposed to do? "I love you, Mesut. I really do."

"Biliyorum. Bende seni çok seviyorum. Kiss Baki for me."

And the line went dead.

And perhaps, Dear Reader, so did I.

Not-A-Granny-Flora
I was always worried something like this might happen, ever since you two got together. I can get your Auntie to re-write Mesut's work papers if that helps? I don't know what else to say.
Jess.AKYOL
There's nothing to say, Mam. I'm in pieces here.
Not-A-Granny-Flora
It might not be as bad as it seems. And please stop fasting now. It's become irrelevant and you're going to need your strength to look after my grandson, as well as get through this.

Fab4CoolDad
Jess, my little darling, Mesut is rock solid and he will be doing everything he can to get back to you and his boy. Don't underestimate him. He'll get his Ticket To Ride, I'm sure of it.
Jess.AKYOL
I don't know if it matters how rock solid he is, Dad. Not this time.

MaxAttax
Shit, sis. What the hell? What a fucked-up system. They can't just hold him there, can they?

Jess.AKYOL
They can and they are.

AngelBernie
Get yourself to my house, Jess. If not now then first thing in the morning. You don't need to go through this alone and the last thing you need is that Cat-Crazy weirdo for company. I'm here and I'm ready.
Jess.AKYOL
Just trying to get through the night, Bern. If my brain cells are unable to make a decision in the morning, my default will be to come to you.

NO_Just_DON'T(1)
THIS COMMENT HAS BEEN DELETED
NO_Just_DON'T(1)
THIS COMMENT HAS BEEN DELETED
NO_Just_DON'T(1)
THIS COMMENT HAS BEEN DELETED
NO_Just_DON'T(1)
THIS COMMENT HAS BEEN DELETED
NO_Just_DON'T(1)
THIS COMMENT HAS BEEN DELETED

ThistleMadMona
Och, Jess. He must be in one of those detaining rooms they have at airports. Somewhere like Turkey, it could well be over-crowded. Remember the thistle? Be spiky and strong, my lovely. You can both get through this.
Jess.AKYOL
Feeling less like a thistle and more like a wilting, lonesome bit of grass. I'm not ready to lose him, Mona.

Angnonymous
Blimey, Jess. This is just awful. You must be beside yourself.
Jess.AKYOL
I am. I really am.

Anonymous
THIS COMMENT HAS BEEN DELETED

Anonymous
THIS COMMENT HAS BEEN DELETED

Anonymous
THIS COMMENT HAS BEEN DELETED

FatimaNazar
Oh no, Jess. This is just awful. Turkey is known for making travelling in and out of its borders very difficult, even if that person is supposed to roam freely by law. They're very taken by official government papers, though. Isn't there any way your husband can pull out something official that shows his status? That he's welcomed in the UK?
Jess.AKYOL
I'm hoping I'll hear more tomorrow and we can come up with a plan to get his papers to him. But Fatima, I don't know if the Gendarmerie will get to him first. It feels like a ticking time bomb.

Compustable.Apocalips
THIS COMMENT HAS BEEN DELETED
Compustable.Apocalips
THIS COMMENT HAS BEEN DELETED

Life Is Yours Lindy

Jess, I could hardly even read the words you wrote today. How on earth could you bring yourself to write them? I'm so rooting for you, and hoping the Turkish Army will see sense and do the right thing.
Jess.AKYOL
Not things they're known for, but thanks, Lindy.

Night-sun-ella
Fuckarama Jess, this post has me floored. What can I do?
Jess.AKYOL
I'm thinking, probably nothing.

Anonymous
THIS COMMENT HAS BEEN DELETED

OliverChen1!
I'm with everybody above (apart from those deleted posts – what is WRONG with people?). I don't know what the answers are. But if anybody can get through it, it is you, matey.
Jess.AKYOL
I'm not sure about this time, Oliver.

GILLIE_LASS77
WTAF? I'm seething for you. Poor Mesut trapped in that awful room! I had no idea something like this could happen. Are you going to be okay looking after Baki whilst going through this? Maybe the nursery could have him for a few more hours whilst you have time to figure this out?
Jess.AKYOL
No Mesut = no income, and I doubt Wee Bairns World will take him for free. This could get a whole lot messier yet. Children's Services could be back on my case in the blink of an eye. Trying not to blink.

24

DAY 24 - MOTHER LION

Muirdrith, Highlands of Scotland, UK
Fri 3rd Sep 2010
Sunrise / Suhoor: 6.18am
Sunset / Iftar: 8.11pm

My day started with this text from Ailsa.

Mum says you had some bad news yesterday. What do you want to do about the interview at the Community Centre. Reschedule?

Nothing from Mesut. Nothing at all.

One of the paradoxical hell-holes of parenting, which absolutely nobody tells you about, is the fact that no matter what shit is going down in your life, you still have to be a parent.

I have never felt this more than today.

Honestly, how am I supposed to change a shitty nappy when it is marginally less shitty than my actual life? How am I supposed to force Weetabix into a toddler's mouth when all I can feel is bile rising in mine? How am I supposed to deal with a 7am tantrum when my own head is spinning out of control?

There is no how.

There is only through.

And that's why I texted Ailsa back: *I'm still going to toddlers. I'll see you there.*

I don't know what part of doing a newspaper interview felt like a good idea, exactly, all I knew was that I had to get through the hours until I next got a call from Mesut. Okay, so maybe I couldn't be Parent of the Year without my husband around, but I could get through it mechanically, methodically, and at least tire Baki out. If there was any logic in my thinking, that was it.

For fuck's sake though, will I ever learn? It would have been distinctly easier to stay at home and pretend the real world didn't exist. In the space of the first half hour, Baki had no less than FIVE tantrums:

1. There was an altercation over inflatable building blocks and Baki's death grip on a pair of crinkle-cut scissors
2. All hell broke loose when he stamped across another child's painting
3. Trike politics once again possessed my child with a staggering hostility to everyone around him
4. A trip to the sensory garden (to calm him down) quickly gave him the excuse to hack at the lavender bush with the crinkle-cut scissors that had somehow found their way back into his hands
5. An unpleasant brawl over a breadstick that he dropped in a random cat poo (I suspect Catzilla – he's just the type to shit on in a sensory garden designed for children)

To top it all off, Baki filled his nappy just as Ailsa arrived with a photographer in tow. Gone were my daydreams of having him sit bobbing on my knee, smiling sweetly whilst I answered the questions. Instead, everybody stared at us for the sixth time that morning, mouths agape, as Baki rolled wildly on the floor in an unrivalled fit of rage, arms and legs spiking out reminiscent of a scene from The Exorcist and his livid motions doing god knows what to the contents of his nappy.

And there I was, crouched over him on all-fours, breathing heavily like a cow in labour, in my own attempts to breathe deep and remember the Guest House poem about accepting all your feelings and allowing them in and being grateful for whatever comes.

Fuck it. I was not grateful for any of this.

Then a soft voice traced a path to my ears. "It's okay, m'eudail. Why don't you take the wee soul for a bum change and we'll get a cup of tea – oops, hot water – ready for you, eh? There's a pet."

No, I could not do it. I could not cry every time Mona opened her mouth.

I looked up and found her in all her silver, curly-haired glory, looking every bit the most perfect Scottish old lady ever. Pink cheeks. Smiling eyes. Nothing but kindness.

"Take your time, lassie. Ailsa could do with slowing down for once. I can't even believe you're here, if I'm honest. I'm guessing you're just powering through until you know more?"

I nodded and turned away, scooping Baki up and dragging him off to the baby change unit. I needed to get it together.

After a bum-changing session that has to top the charts in terms of the absolute volume of shit produced (I blame the Mini-Milk from yesterday), the number of crevices I had to wipe on Baki's chubby body (all of them) and the items of clothing I had to change (and not just his), I re-joined the group. My dignity may not have been in tact but my child was finally quiet and clean.

Bernie took over Baki-watch and Ailsa started up with her

questions about Ramadan, as if the most problematic thing in my life was when I was next going to be able to fill my face. I tried talking about my motivations for doing Ramadan, my decision to drink water and what I've learned throughout the month, but hell, it was just impossible.

"Do you know what happened yesterday, Ailsa?"

"What? Oh yes, Mum told me. Your husband has been detained at İstanbul airport?"

"That's right. I don't know how or when I'm going to see him again, so Ramadan has become a bit of a trivial thing. I'm sorry you've had a wasted journey. I don't know if I can answer your questions how I would have done just a few days ago."

She nodded and the corners of her mouth turned up in an effort to comfort me. She lacked the natural compassion of her mother, but she was trying her best. "Yes. This must be such a worrying time for you. How come they won't let him out of Turkey then? Is it something to do with national service? I believe it's still mandatory over there."

I filled her in on what I knew, how much work it had been to get Mesut into this country in the first place, and how this new life in the Highlands had been in order to avoid this very scenario. "I didn't have a baby with him, only to have him taken away to god knows where for fifteen months. I need him. I'm struggling enough with motherhood as it is, without my soulmate being snatched away from me. How am I supposed to do this without him? Oh god . . . Children's Services are going to be knocking on my door in no time. They'll never trust me with Baki on my own. What if they both get taken off me? What then?"

At this point Mona flew in on her good-witch broomstick and folded me up in a heather-scented hug. "Oh, m'eudail. It's going to be okay. I think that's enough for today, our Ailsa. This lassie needs a break, so she does."

"I'm guessing a few pictures are out of the question?"

"Wheesht, our Ailsa. Come on now. The story can wait."

Ailsa mumbled something incomprehensible as she packed up her briefcase, donned her Inspector Gadget hat and coat and shook her head at the photographer bloke. The story was no more.

And that's probably a good thing.

Now I'd said the words out loud about the fact that Mesut might not come back at all, about my fears of being an even shittier mam without him and of Baki being taken by the professional child-stealers, I was depleted. Properly depleted. Bernie begged me to go home with her but I honestly couldn't fathom the thought of being in somebody else's space.

Mona, despite being more than twice my age, not only pushed Baki's buggy, but also let me lean on her all the way back to the flat. She came inside and didn't leave until Baki and I were sat on the beanbag in his room, equipped with snacks, a duvet and yet another rendition of Bob The Builder and the Legend of the Golden Hammer. I didn't care. The familiarity of it was comforting.

I wasn't tempted by the snacks. Not at all. Baki scoffed the lot and I didn't even try to stop him. I'm sure it would be okay, by Ramadan standards, to nourish myself during this awful, awful time. But I had no interest in food. My tummy could go on growling. Along with my soul.

It's hard to admit this, but not long after Bob and the gang found a map on which to pin their Golden Hammer hopes, my eyes drooped closed. The beanbag was so soft and encased my crumpled body perfectly. That, along with the fact that I'd hardly slept a wink last night, meant sleep was inevitable. I think this was the first time since Baki was a babe in arms that I have gone to sleep whilst he's still been awake.

When I woke I heard shouting. Opening my crusty, swollen

eyes and one quick glance around the room told me Baki wasn't in it. Shit. Should never have gone to sleep.

I hauled myself up and stepped out into the corridor. "Baki?" I could swear that was him whimpering, beneath somebody shouting profanities. But I was so sleepy, it was hard to tell if it was real or where it was coming from. The kitchen, maybe?

I stumbled along the corridor and the words got louder. "Fucking hell. Where is your mother? Fuck off child. That's not your cupboard. Take your dirty Muslim hands off my stuff."

If it hadn't been my child in there I might have been knocked several steps backwards in shock. But it *was* my child. And nothing was going to stop me getting him out of there.

As soon as he saw me, he crashed into my legs and reached upwards with his little hands. He obviously didn't have a clue what had just been said to him, but he understood the tone. And so did I.

I opened my mouth to give Cat-Crazy Flatmate absolute hell.

"Jess, could you please consider *not* leaving your kid to run free through the flat? I'm having a hard enough time as it is, covering all of your husband's shifts. I'm totally knackered. And babysitting for you is something I just haven't got time for."

"What? I just fell asleep . . . he only went wandering for a few seconds. You swore at him . . . you said . . ."

"I needed to get him out of my cupboards. They're mine. They're not for people like him. Like you, even."

"What the . . ? But you can't just go and mention his religion like that . . ."

She bent forwards to stroke the fifty-seven cats that were now swarming at her feet, purring so loud the kitchen floor seemed like a tropical swamp. That's when I'm sure I heard her whisper under her breath, "But it's fine to write a blog about it though." Then she straightened up and looked me right in the eye. "I am too tired to have this discussion. Just please keep your kid out of my hair. Now if you'll excuse me, I'm off to work *your* husband's shift. I'm doing him a favour keeping his job open, okay? You want him to have a job to come back to, don't you?"

"Well, yes, but . . ." Before I could formulate my thoughts, let alone my words, she swept out of the kitchen, the cat army following her. Shit. How the fuck did I manage to get hardly a word in? I'm supposed to protect my child and have his back no matter what. Why couldn't I deal with this like a proper mother?

Fuck. Could this day get any harder?

I carried Baki back through to his bedroom, burrowing my head into his ample belly and murmuring apologies into it as if my words could be absorbed by his skin. I wanted to delete the last few moments, help him forget what a shoddy job I'd just done of protecting him. Why hadn't I given her merry hell like she deserved?

The only good thing to come out of this absolute shit-show of motherhood, was that it finally gave me the motivation I needed to send a pleading text to Bernie. I hadn't gone over there until now because it felt like I would be admitting to the absolute hopelessness of things.

But here I was. Admitting it.

Help. Had run-in with flatmate and couldn't even come over all mother-lion. What is wrong with me?

Oh, poppet. Please come round. There is a Jess-shaped divot on my sofa ready and waiting.

Hold that divot. On way.

So now I am at Bernie's, Dear Reader. I packed up a few bits for me and Baki and we're here for the foreseeable. I can't go back to the flat and face that woman. Not without Mesut there. I'm just not equipped to be the mam Baki needs me to be right now.

Thank god for Bernie. She may be about to pop a sprog, but she's got more courage, compassion and mothering instinct than I'll ever have. That's why I know I'm in the right place. Baki is safe here.

Now I just need to know Mesut is safe too.

Fab4CoolDad
I'm glad Bernie stepped in to help, love. She reminds me of 'Lady Madonna'. But you have far more 'mothering instinct' than you're giving yourself credit for. I've seen you with my grandson.
Jess.AKYOL
Not feeling it today, Dad. Love that song though. And that's exactly who Bernie is like.

AngelBernie
I only help the absolute best people, poppet. You and Baki can stay for as long as you want. No need to go back to that flat with that excuse of a woman. You can help me with the new baby when he arrives, because you are far better at all that jazz than you know. In fact, he's just kicked me to confirm. You can't argue with an unborn baby.
Jess.AKYOL
I don't have the energy to argue. So tell Baby Bernie thank you. And that goes for Momma Bernie too.

OliverChen1!
Oh, still nothing from Mesut then? Matey, I know it's probably the last thing on your mind, but if you still want your story to run then I could send some of my pics from the beach photo

shoot to Ailsa at the Highland News? No wonder you didn't get as far as having photos taken today.

Jess.AKYOL

You can if you like, Oliver. But I doubt they have enough of an interview from me to publish anything. And no, I haven't heard from Mesut all day. I just hope he's safe.

NO_Just_DON'T(1)

THIS COMMENT HAS BEEN DELETED

NO_Just_DON'T(1)

THIS COMMENT HAS BEEN DELETED

KadafiDancingKing

I knows you not want to hear it, Mrs Jess, but you need to keep following the goodness. I long way from İstanbul but I can get there if Mesut is needing it. Shall I go? Just tell me and I will go.

Jess.AKYOL

I don't understand, Kadafi. What could you do if you went there?

KadafiDancingKing

I not know but I definitely can't do anything from here. Let me I go. I will try and see him. Remember my dad mayor in my city? He might help me.

NO_Just_DON'T(1)

THIS COMMENT HAS BEEN DELETED

Angnonymous

I would take Kadafi up on his offer, Jess. The Turkish government are renowned for being corrupt in places. If he can talk the talk he might be able to do something. You said Kadafi was charming, right?

Jess.AKYOL

He certainly is. But in the context of bars and holiday tours. I'm not sure about the big, scary government.
Angnonymous
Where there's a will . . .

NO_Just_DON'T(1)
THIS COMMENT HAS BEEN DELETED

CrunchyNut_Mummy
Jess, I'm sorry you're going through all of this. No wonder Baki was kicking off at Toddlers this morning. His mum's in total turmoil! And I can't believe your flatmate said that to him. It's totally disgusting. One of the reasons I've never been in that pub is because of the atmosphere she gives it. It's kept my friends and I away for years.
Jess.AKYOL
Thanks for the confirmation that it's not just me. Wish I could have protected Baki better than that today, though. Feeling like a massive failure.
CrunchyNut_Mummy
Bull crap. You got him out of there. Best thing you could have done.

NO_Just_DON'T(1)
THIS COMMENT HAS BEEN DELETED

ThistleMadMona
You needed that sleep today, m'eudail, and don't you feel bad about it for one second. The poor wee soul was only looking in a kitchen cupboard. She wants bringing down a peg or two, that flatmate of yours. Fancy talking to a bairn like that. I've a good mind to go over there myself. Being impeccable with my word takes more than one form, you know, lassie!

Jess.AKYOL
Now that I would like to see. Only joking. Please don't, Mona. I had my chance and I lost it.

NO_Just_DON'T(1)
THIS COMMENT HAS BEEN DELETED

Night-sun-ella
Kadafi could save the day! Let him, Jess. Let him swoop in like a superhero and sort this shit out. As for that cat-gathering maniac, how very DARE she speak to my sort-of nephew like that? I'm proper fuming. I'm torn between ripping up the A9 to come and sort her out, and ripping up the A9 to squeeze some love into you. But you've got Bernie so I'm thinking the first option might be doable . . .
Jess.AKYOL
I do love you. But enough now. I need to sleep.

NO_Just_DON'T(1)
THIS COMMENT HAS BEEN DELETED

Glensìth_Comm_Found.
Jess, it's Lupa Startforth here. We've tried emailing you but we recognise that you're going through an exceptionally hard time. If you have a moment, could you please just let us know if you still plan to come and speak at Glensíth on 8th Sep as planned? We understand if it's no longer possible, but just need to fill your slot with something else. Even if you can't speak, you and Baki are welcome to come along to the whole festival for free. You might appreciate the distraction. These are trying times, we know.
Jess. AKYOL
I'm sorry, Lupa. I don't see how I can inspire other people at the

moment. I think you'd better fill the slot with something else. Thanks for the offer of the tickets. I'll see how things are at the time.
Glensìth_Comm_Found.
We understand. x

Anonymous
THIS COMMENT HAS BEEN DELETED

Anonymous
THIS COMMENT HAS BEEN DELETED

NO_Just_DON'T(1)
THIS COMMENT HAS BEEN DELETED

25

DAY 25 - REWARDS

Muirdrith, Highlands of Scotland, UK
Sat 4th Sep 2010
Sunrise / Suhoor: 6.20am
Sunset / Iftar: 8.08pm

The first thing I'm going to tell you, before I even get off the starting blocks about this day, is that there is no news from Mesut.

I've tried calling his mobile and the weird prison-phone he called me from before. I always get the same recorded message in Turkish that I have now decided says something along the lines of: '*This person is not available and this person may never be available again so thank you kindly, stop calling and go back to your sad little life.*'

I do have a sad little life, to be fair.

Poor Bernie has done her best to embody an actual angel all day today. She's the one who got Baki out of bed this morning. She's the one who changed him, dressed him, fed him and gave him toys to play with. I'm the one who stayed in bed, hidden under the duvet, not even coming out to the playful invitation bouncing up the stairs, "Come on, poppet! You can kick Ramadan in the butt and get some of these Muirdrith oatcakes down you!"

But I just couldn't. I was glued to the bed. Glued to Bernie's eighteen-year-old son's bed because he has very kindly gone to stay at his girlfriend's for a few days so Baki and I can have his room.

The room is very grey and black and smells of Paco Rabanne XS aftershave. It made me want to cry. It's the very same scent that my first boyfriend used and it brought back huge, rolling swathes of memories that were shockingly intense. Behind the heat of my closed, swollen eyelids, I could remember so much about being with him. Kissing by the river in the park. Drinking lager on the swings. Reading poetry at the back of the bus and whispered promises of loving each other forever.

Why think of him right now?

For fuck's sake, my husband is more or less imprisoned in a Turkish airport and there I was ignoring our child, having a lie-in and day-dreaming about an ex.

Could I *be* a worse person?

I finally dragged myself out of the sharp-edged, gunmetal pit of a room and shook off those memories with a shudder at the top of the stairs. Bernie must have heard a floorboard creak or something because she was at the bottom of the stairs faster than a fly to shit.

"Oh good, you're up. Come and see what your son's been doing."

When I shuffled into Bernie's living room, Baki hurled himself at my legs and bit down hard into my left calf. He hates me so much for what happened yesterday and I guess this is his way of showing it. I couldn't even be bothered to feel the pain. I just sat down on the sofa whilst Bernie shooed him away, my skin vaguely pulsing in objection.

"We've been working hard all morning and we've made these." Bernie threw some cardboard shapes into my hands that were soft and tacky to the touch. And gritty too. "Oops. Watch out for the glitter. It's not quite dried yet."

I looked down at two cardboard cut-outs of characters, one with Baki's face stuck onto it and one with Frida's. Baki's character wore dungarees, a bright yellow helmet, a tool belt and was holding a large golden hammer in one hand. No prizes for guessing who that was.

Baki screeched at me from the other side of the room, then came thundering over to grab it out of my hands. His mouth popped open and closed a few times as he tried to find the word, 'Bob', but it just didn't come.

"He's rather proud of it." Bernie glowed. "Look at Frida's. Isn't it just precious?"

I looked down at the remaining shape and had to work hard to figure out what I was seeing, exactly. That was Frida's face, for sure, but this was one character I have never seen on C-Beebies. There was a head of curly, silver hair; a huge, rounded belly; one hand holding pens and the other balancing a stack of notebooks; a huge fuzzy coat in rainbow colours hanging off the shoulders; and little sequins stuck all over the ears and face. "Bernie. What the actual . . ."

"Frida couldn't make up her mind so she asked for a bit of all her current favourite people. The belly's mine – of course. The hair is Mona's. She loved Gillie's fur coat so that had to be on there and, whether I like it or not, she was rather taken with Ella's facial piercings."

"Wow. Okay. And the pens and books in the hands?"

"Can't you guess?" Bernie smiled and crouched down to get Frida's attention. "Freedie-pops . . . go and tell Jess about what your character's holding. Go on."

Frida lumbered over to me and pointed with her chubby

little fingers at her character. "Bookz. Bookzes and penzes." Then she pointed at me. "You."

I collapsed back on the sofa and somehow found a smile to throw at Frida. A smile tremoring with tears.

Bernie picked up on it and obviously decided it was best to press forward rather than let me disappear into the depths of the sofa along with my imminent existential crisis. "And look! Look, Jess. This is what the characters are for . . ." She walked over to the far end of the room, followed by our toddlers, where there was a long strip of purple sugar paper attached to the wall with a ladder sketched onto it. It was dotted with globs of glitter and sparkly stars. "It's a reward chart! Each time the kids show us beautiful behaviour, we put their character up a rung on the ladder and when they get to the top they get a nice surprise. What do you think?"

I know it probably wasn't the most tactful answer, but the first word to fall out of my mouth was, "Why?"

"Why?" Bernie threaded a hand through her ponytail and used the other to rub her belly. Well, Logan and I realise that things might get a bit tricky for Frida when the new baby arrives. So we're starting with the positive reinforcement now so there'll be something to fall back on when we're sleep-deprived. And as Baki's here, we thought he could join in too. That's okay with you, isn't it?"

"Erm, yeah. Yeah. Whatever. Do you think it will work?"

"Work? Baki's got a Bob The Builder and Frida's got a fur-coated, feminine voodoo thing going on. There's no way on earth this shit can fail."

So that is how I came to spend a lot of today watching Bernie praise the kids for virtually *anything* just so she could demonstrate what happens when they get to the top of the ladder.

"Oooh, look Baki – you opened a book to read a story."

"Wow, Frida – nice job of smoothing the book pages back out."

"Oooh, look Baki – you got the jigsaws out so enthusiastically."

"Wow, Frida – you cleared up the jigsaw pieces from all over the room."

"Oooh, look Baki – you know how to build really high tower blocks."

"Wow, Frida – you did a great job of saving the telly from being smashed by the falling blocks."

After every bit of praise, Bernie visited the ladder and moved the characters up. I busied myself with tidying the kitchen because I couldn't bear to watch how deep Bernie had to dig to praise Baki. As if his book-demolishing skills weren't enough, when the tower of blocks fell onto Frida's little body, narrowly missing the very expensive widescreen TV, I just wanted a hole to crawl into.

After everybody filled themselves up with beans and cheese on toast for lunch (not me – my tummy is still howling but I fear filling it will somehow cement the sad facts of my desperate situation), Bernie chucked all the dishes in the sink and let out a god-almighty yawn.

"I'm bushed. I feel an afternoon nap coming on." Frida followed suit with a yawn identical to her mother's and lifted her weary arms to be taken out of her highchair. I looked at Baki, and took in his wide-eyed glare, his whole body jiggling, and I knew a nap was the last thing on his mind.

I sighed and picked him up. Bernie was on her way out of the kitchen door with a sleepy Frida clasped around her neck, but still found the energy to suggest I take Baki out. "A bit of fresh air will do you both good. And look at that sky out there. It's almost too blue to be true."

And she was right. One of Muirdrith's famous skies was

beaming across the kitchen floor, flutters of white sunlight skipped over our feet and sapphire streaks cut through the quiet. "Okay. You're probably right."

Getting Baki sorted and ready was surprisingly easy. He was practically hanging off the door, desperate to go out, and Bernie (angel that she is) had already packed a changing bag for him. I tried to tell myself that she was just being helpful and didn't actually want rid of me, but it was a tough ask, considering my mood.

I didn't have a plan. I just got in the car and drove. This has been a thing of mine over the years. Driving to avoid hard feelings. I used to do it all the time with my ex-fiancé, Jack. He was the most stubborn person I've ever met in my life and would never listen to my side of an argument. Hence, arguments didn't even happen after a while. Just lonesome driving. Lots and lots of lonesome driving.

Fuck it. Why am I thinking about my exes so much today?

Anyway, this driving wasn't so lonesome because Baki was in the back, bashing a plastic spade against my seat and making a weird, stuttering sound that only I could possibly know means he wants ice cream.

I hadn't been driving for too long when I spotted a wooden board at the side of the road promising local dairy ice cream and chilled drinks. I took the next turn-off and followed the little wooden signs all the way along a road that got more and more narrow. I realised we were driving towards the sea and that this road would take me to a beach I'd never been to. And it did. It took me to Glensíth beach.

After parking, Baki and I stumbled out onto a great, sweeping landscape of soft sands as pink and rosy as peaches. The wind whipped our hair into peaks but was gentle enough to tease a smile. Even from me. I took a deep breath and realised Bernie was so right. I had needed to get out.

Baki spotted the weather-beaten ice-cream shack before I did. He shook off the grip of my hand and blasted his way through the sands, making little chugging noises and wiping his streaming nose on his sleeves. I felt almost overcome by a surge of fondness for his absolutely delectable little soul, before realising I'd better make it over there before he pushed his way to the front of the queue.

A few minutes later and we were sitting together on a towel from Baki's bag (thank you, Bernie), Baki slobbering all over a double-caramel-choc-choc-explosion in a sugar crystal coated waffle cone (don't) and me poised with the inevitable stack of wipes necessary. It was a tiny moment of calm in the shit-show that currently substitutes my life and I was grateful for it.

I can't believe we have lived here for a year and a half and have not sampled the delights of Glensíth beach before now. It really is stunning. Sorry, Angus and all your cabbage hippy friends. Muirdrith beach stole me for a while but now I may well be converted.

The wind was up, which was a good encourager. Warm enough to enjoy, but cool enough to remind me of the splendour of the Scottish elements. I cast my eyes over the vast fusion of peachy-rose and yellow-gold, noticed the embellishments of mottled pebbles and round, pink sea shells. The sea was a rich, turquoise wash of sapphire, lacerated with incessant, ever-rolling strips of foamy white.

Although the beach was pretty deserted, I saw that there were quite a lot of people in the water. In fact, as I squinted my eyes to make them out, I could see it wasn't just people, it was women. Lots and lots of women.

And there was so much noise coming from where they were swimming. Whoops of joy, cheers of delight. Call-outs across the waves, jokes shouted like lengths of glittering ribbon across the water. Peals of jangling laughter raised the hairs on my arms.

I could see limbs dancing and heads bobbing. Bathing costumes, wetsuits, bikinis and swimming caps dotted with flowers, flashed with stripes, emblazoned in spots in every colour that you could hope for. The overall vision was wild and uplifting, vivid and glowing. I had no clue what I was looking at. All I could think was if you were to pick up a particularly eccentric festival crowd and place it in the ocean – this is what you would get.

I wiped the last of Baki's ice cream off his cheeks and there was barely a milli-second before he sprang to his feet and raced off towards the water. I was suddenly lost in that single-mam conundrum of whether to leave the buggy and the bags alone or leave the child alone. But the wind shook me up and I came to my senses. Buggy and bags. Always.

I ran after Beast-Child. "Baki! Come back! At least let me get your shoes off you if you want to go in the water." I knew Bernie had packed a change of clothes for him so getting his outfit wet wasn't the worst thing that could happen. But did Baki even put the teensiest break in his stride? I think we all know the answer to that.

I looked out to the point in the sea he seemed to be aiming for. There was a figure, standing thigh-high in the waves, waving her arms about like a windmill, smiling and shouting. I thought she was shouting Baki's name, but I couldn't be sure. This woman was quite clearly mental and wearing the most outrageously luminous purple and frilly swimsuit I'd ever seen in my life, as well as a having an inflatable ring wrapped around her waist in the shape of a gigantic Scottish thistle.

Oh.

Of course.

It was Mona.

"Luvvies! You're here! What brings you to Glensíth beach, the pair of you?" Mona waded through the water towards us, her soft, snow-white thighs squeaking against her questionable floatation device and a smile on her lips broader than the beach itself. Baki threw himself into the water before I could yank his shoes off, lunging towards Mona and matching her smile in warmth and size.

"Oh, it's nice to see you, Mona. We just went for a drive and found ourselves here. Killing time, I suppose."

"Och aye. Of course." Baki was splashing around with purpose, gleefully bonking his head against Mona's inflatable thistle, though she didn't seem to mind. "No news then, lassie?"

"No news." I hung my head and stared hard at a pebble on the sand. It had a rope of black seaweed wrapped so tight around it, I wondered if it would crack.

"Well it's a good idea to get yourself to the beach. You coming in?" Mona held out her hand towards me. Baki grabbed her forearm and hung his full weight off it, delighting every time he slipped and fell in the welcoming waves. I briefly wondered how Mona, at her age, could keep her arm held out so strong and steady.

"No, no. Not today, Mona. I'll stay on the beach."

"Alright. Do you want me and the lassies to play with Baki? It's nay a problem, if you want a wee rest."

"The lassies?"

"Yes! Did I not mention? I'm here with the Bathing Biddies Beach Club. We do this every Saturday afternoon, so we do. A wee bit of cold water swimming, an ice cream and a meditation. But we can look after Baki until the meditation bit, if you like?"

"Meditation?"

"Och, it's nothing fancy. It's just a nice lie-down really. It's my turn to lead it this week. See where all the towels are set out over there? We all just lie down – after our ice creams, of course – and listen to whoever's turn it is to lead it."

"This whiffs of Glensíth, Mona. Are they involved?" I

suddenly felt cold. I've let them down big-style by dropping out of my talk at the festival. I know I have.

"No, not really. Other than they put up our poster in the Kelpie Café. Angus might have given us the idea though. He's into all that stuff, isn't he? Now that he's not a big, fancy lawyer anymore."

"I guess he is." By now, Mona had squirmed out of her inflatable thistle ring and handed it over to Baki. He was right in the centre of it, spinning it around his belly and laughing every time one of the rubber spikes whacked him in the face. "Yeah. That's a kind offer, Mona. I'm just over there if he starts playing up."

"Right you are, lassie. Here, take his shoes." She chucked the sopping wet trainers over to me. "You go and relax now." And off she went, pulling Baki along by the floating thistle, back to her fold of Bathing Biddies, who were already making yelps of joy that an actual toddler was in their midst. I turned my back and made my way up the beach, trying with all my might to refrain from comparing their complete captivation with Baki to my own sad and lacking skills as his mother.

I stretched out on the towel and watched the sun-tinged clouds drift by. My eyes were heavy and sore, from all the crying last night, and it seemed like a real effort to close them. I did it anyway, and allowed the clenching sting that tore along the line where my eyelashes met. Shards of blood-red light sliced through the stinging line and I willed my lids to meet properly. *Come on. I just want the dark. I just want the black.*

God, if you've asked me a month ago if I'd like a child-free lie down on the beach, I'd have taken your arm off. Now though, having been given the chance more or less wrapped up in a bow, it seemed I was incapable of it. I sat back up and rubbed my aching eyes hard, punishing them for their ineptitude.

I couldn't get Cat-Crazy Flatmate's words out of my head

from yesterday . . . *"Take your dirty Muslim hands off my stuff."* What the hell? The swearing had been bad but that comment was infinitely worse. Have there been other times she's said stuff like that to him? Times when I've been busy or distracted? How could I have ever let my baby – or even my husband for that matter – anywhere near a woman like that? Sitting there on that beach today, I felt a fury not unlike the one I've felt towards myself since Baki was born. *Who the fuck does she think she is?* I wanted to scream it out at the ocean, out at the sky. But I knew I'd had my chance in the kitchen yesterday and now my voice was lost, broken. The fury curled and writhing inside of me instead.

I came to my senses when I heard Mona shouting. "Jess! I think this wee one's for dreamland, so he is. Look at his darling little face." Yet again, Mona was defying the laws of ageing by slowly plodding over to me, Baki tired and hefty in her arms.

"It's okay, Mona. We can put him in the buggy."

"First he needs out of these wet clothes and into a towel or something. I've got a spare blanket too. I'll go and get it." Mona laid him down on the towel next to where I was sitting and I stripped the sopping wet clothes off his body. He fussed and punched the air a little bit, but sleep was claiming his spirit quicker than his stubbornness could. The ocean-drenched nappy was quite a thing to behold but was nothing I hadn't dealt with before. So, I whipped that off too, and it wasn't long before his talc-dusted bits were safely tucked away in a fresh, dry nappy and a pair of fleecy jogging bottoms.

By the time I'd got him strapped into the buggy, Mona – now clad in a ground-length wearable towel with a hood, arm-holes and a million thistles printed all over it – was back with a blanket. We both did a bit of shushing and cooing and it didn't take much for Baki's eyes to close in exactly the way I wished mine had earlier.

"Thanks so much, Mona. I'm glad we bumped into you. I needed that rest."

"Och it was a joy. He's a joy! Now, why don't you come and join in with our little meditation?"

"What? Oh no. I don't think so. I'm not part of the club, am I? And Bernie will be expecting me back."

"Beautiful lassie." Mona was speaking slowly now. And she fixed me with one of her classic, glassy-green stares. "Come on, now. Be impeccable with your word. Tell me why you really don't want to join us."

"Really?"

"Really."

"Okay, well . . . erm. I can't lie down. I'm too anxious. I can't even close my eyes. It kind of hurts. And . . ."

"Yes?"

"And . . . I'm a bit scared of being alone with my thoughts. I just don't know what to do with them."

"You won't be alone, my darling. You'll be with us. Me."

"Okay."

Before I knew what was happening, Mona was moving my things over to the area of the beach where the rest of the Bathing Biddies were. I followed and dragged Baki's buggy over – he was sleeping soundly by now, wrapped up tight in Mona's blanket, the beach breeze only occasionally causing a flicker of his lips, a twitch of his cheeks.

I smiled at the ladies, who were all finishing off ice creams, and realised I recognised a lot of them from around town: There was the lovely, patient librarian who leads story-time sessions for kids; the lady who's always on reception at the Community Centre when I go to Toddlers; the woman from the GP surgery who showed me through to the counselling room only last week. There were a few more faces I couldn't quite place and all of them were smiling kindly up at me, ready and waiting on their beach towels, for Mona to start the meditation.

I crouched down onto the sand and spread out my towel. I lay down and nestled my back into the warm, spongy surface beneath. I took a huge breath, willing oxygen to find all my muscles and make them relax. Even just a bit. I managed to close my eyes and the stinging was still there, but not so unnerving as before. I was vaguely aware that somebody threw a blanket over me, and I knotted the edges of it into my fingers so that it wouldn't blow away.

I listened to Mona's voice, which started up in its soft, meticulous way. Her words were as mellow as the breeze, the intensity of her compassion reassuring. Somehow, her voice carried above the background noises of the beach whilst also weirdly threading through the rush of the waves, the call of the seagulls overhead.

"Okay. Allow yourself to be here, now. Let your body soften, your attention relax, and your senses reside in whatever they find here. This is time for you to just be as you are. Wholly and completely, be as you are . . ."

Miraculously, my eyes stayed closed and my body didn't protest too much about lying still. It helped that Mona had invited us to just be as we were. I knew by now to take her words seriously, and so when I noticed my shoulders were tense as hell or my fingers were gripping the blanket for dear life, I didn't berate myself. I just let it be.

I was visited by huge avalanches of thoughts about Mesut though. How could I be lying here, on a fucking beach, whilst he's either in detainment or being marched off to the Turkish army?

Every muscle in my body twisted at the thought.

And what exactly did I think I was doing, swanning off to the beach when I was pretty much homeless and husbandless?

If I wasn't careful I was going to be childless too. It was only a matter of time before somebody realised I was doing a terrible job. That Baki would be far better off with a family that has a proper home, no cultural challenges, and a mother who actually knows what she's doing.

I kept lying there, on my towel, trying to allow these thoughts in without judging them. It was hard. I imagined the rest of the Bathing Biddies were lying in some kind of post-ice-cream bliss, whilst here I was, going on my own private joy-ride of internal hell.

I kept trying to let the breeze, skimming my skin like soft kisses, lull me back to the present. But the thoughts dragged me under, to a place where I imagined the sand became heavy with moisture, thick with rot, and transformed, stealthily into a stifling, black sludge.

After a while, Mona's voice changed tone slightly. "I'm leaving you to the sounds of the beach now, ladies. And I'm going to come around to each one of you and, with your permission, use my touch to release some pressure points in your hands, feet and upper body. I'll get round to all of you. Just lie calm and still until then. Enjoy the peace."

It felt like I'd been lying there forever. I was worried about Baki waking up and raising holy hell, thereby completely shattering the meditative state of the Bathing Biddies. I was lying on the periphery of the group and might well be the last person Mona got around to, but that also meant I could jump up and whisk Baki off if need be.

Then I felt a warm whisper at my side. Mona.

"Jess. Is it alright if I lay my hands on you, m'eudail?"

I squeaked a yes and felt Mona's thumbs press into the arches of my feet, just firmly enough so it didn't tickle. I usually hate having my feet touched but this didn't really bother me so maybe the meditation had been good for something.

Then she moved up my body. She focused on one hand at a time, gently pulling on my wrists, my fingers and kneading my palms in soft, circular movements. It was nice. Other than Mesut, another adult hadn't held my hand in a very long time and it felt all at once weird and lovely.

Then she brought her open palms to rest on the front of my shoulders. She put down some pressure and the flat of my back sank further into the sand. Her hands were so warm and I enjoyed the way they stayed there, for long, lingering moments. My eyes were still closed but I imagined Mona's face shining right down at mine and wondered what she saw there. Did she see my sorrow? My guilt? My fear? Or did she have her eyes closed, like me?

She released my shoulders and I sensed that she took a very deep and rousing breath. Her intake was so full, so reaching, that I wondered how lungs as old as hers were capable of such a thing. And then, as the breath she'd been holding escaped her lips in quiet, streaming sighs, she pressed her thumb against the spot on my forehead, just above my eyes.

What happened next is still a mystery to me.

I started crying.

Of course. She's always crying, I can imagine you thinking.

But, Dear Reader, this was *instant.*

As soon as Mona pressed down with her thumb, there wasn't even a split second before tears started flowing. My eyes were still closed. Stubbornly closed, in fact. But tears spilled hot and determined, cascading over my cheeks, down my face, and onto the towel beneath me.

I'd had no warning. You know the kind of thing. A lump in the throat. A tightness of the heart. Nothing. Just tears. And so, so many of them.

Mona must have noticed but she said nothing. The tears just kept coming and the thumb just kept pressing. I wasn't sobbing, there was no noise. I've never experienced anything like it.

I soon started to feel the pressure of social expectations around crying. Shouldn't I blow my nose? Apologise to Mona? Wash my face? But somehow I felt pinned to the earth by her thumb and somewhere deep down in the very core of me, deep down in the pit of that black and rotting consciousness I'd been residing in earlier, I knew this was what I needed.

When Mona lifted her thumb, that's when the sobs came. A blaze of scalding air ripped through my throat and I more or less screamed. Mona lifted my torso and bundled me up in a hug so tight the scream barrelled right into her chest. She didn't seem to notice. "Ssssh, sssh now m'eudail. You're alright. You're really alright."

I'm back at Bernie's now. Holed up in her son's bed and trying not to let the stench of Paco Rabanne drag me off to a land of teenage angst.

When I got back, Bernie had dinner ready, a bath run for the kids, and a reward for Baki getting to the top of the ladder chart. It was a spongy, bath book, just like Frida got, and they spent not less than forty-five minutes playing with them in the bath, along with the inflatable thistle which Mona insisted on giving to Baki before we left the beach.

I really don't know what to say about today. The thumb on the forehead thing was so weird but so is everything else in my life right now.

Tonight I silently sipped a veggie stew Bernie put in front of me, not even bothering to notice if it was after sundown or not. It was. Bernie told me. "I've waited to eat with you, poppet. Though I'm not sure you're even still fasting for Ramadan?"

I told her I don't really know. What seemed like the most huge and impossible challenge at first, now pales in comparison to what's going on. I don't care about food. I don't even think about it. I'm not even trying. I only ate the stew because it was rude not to.

So much for Ramadan changing my life.

The only thing that can change my life right now is a phone call. And that's why my phone is literally on my pillow and next to my head. I don't care about toxic radiation or whatever the hell it is people worry about with phones. I'll gladly let my brain fry if it means Mesut calls and tells me he's coming home.

One thing's for sure – I'm all cried out. So at least I won't wake Baki in the night. The ocean air has completely zonked him and I can hear him snoring now, from his travel cot next to my bed. If only he knew what his mother has been through today.

I hope he never does.

Fab4CoolDad
So sorry you haven't heard from Mesut yet, love. Hopefully there will be good news tomorrow. You have actually been to Glensíth beach before, when you were about five. You made a little friend there called Lucy and all the way home we played this in the car . . . 'Lucy In The Sky With Diamonds'. I know you won't remember, but it was a nice day.
Jess.AKYOL
No. I don't remember that at all. But yes. What a beautiful beach.

Not-A-Granny-Flora
Well, I'm not sure about all that hippy stuff but it sounds like

Bernie is being a great help. Make sure to say thank you and maybe let your auntie know about what that awful flatmate said. Maybe she can kick her out and you can have the flat to yourself?
Jess.AKYOL
She manages the whole pub though, Mam. I doubt that will be happening.

NO_Just_DON'T(1)
THIS COMMENT HAS BEEN DELETED
NO_Just_DON'T(1)
THIS COMMENT HAS BEEN DELETED
NO_Just_DON'T(1)
THIS COMMENT HAS BEEN DELETED
NO_Just_DON'T(1)
THIS COMMENT HAS BEEN DELETED

Compustable.Apocalips
THIS COMMENT HAS BEEN DELETED
Compustable.Apocalips
THIS COMMENT HAS BEEN DELETED

Angnonymous
Ah, it's the most perfect beach, isn't it? Us cabbage hippies don't mind that you took so long to discover it. I love that Mona helped you unblock some stuff today. Did Kadafi make it to İstanbul airport?
Jess.AKYOL
I have no idea, Angus. I haven't heard anything. Maybe he'll comment on the blog tonight and we'll find out.
Angnonymous
🤞

ThistleMadMona
Beautiful lassie, I'm so glad we met on the beach today. You must never, ever worry about crying with me. It's as natural as breathing. Hope Baki likes his inflatable thistle. What a wee darling.
Jess.AKYOL
He LOVES it, Mona. He nearly screamed the house down when I wouldn't let him have it in his cot tonight. #badparent

AngelBernie
It might not seem like it (because I'm perpetually tired) but I'm so honoured that I get to support you through this time, poppet. And all that happened on Glensíth beach – why didn't you tell me it all when you got home? We could have talked spiritual shit over bath-time! Man, you did some serious unblocking. You must be vibing up!
Jess.AKYOL
Bernie, I have no idea what that means.
AngelBernie
Yes you do. You just don't know it yet. 😉

Anonymous
THIS COMMENT HAS BEEN DELETED

Anonymous
THIS COMMENT HAS BEEN DELETED

OliverChen1!
Keep hoping for some news about Mesut every time I log on here. So sorry there's none today. I emailed those pictures to Ailsa. She got them and said thanks but didn't say anything about whether or not your article will be published. I'm guessing you don't give a rat's ass anyway?

Jess.AKYOL
You guess right. But thanks, Oliver.

GILLIE_LASS77
It was only a matter of time before you became a hippy on the beach, sweetie. And remember, hippies are allowed to cry too.
Jess.AKYOL
I'll take that.

Glensìth_Comm_Found
Aren't we lucky to have that beach right on our doorstep? We stage lots of gatherings on the beach, Jess. Some of our community even live there in huts behind the ice cream shack you went to. By the way, we've all got our fingers crossed about Mesut.
Jess.AKYOL
Thank you. So sorry I've let you down.

ShelleyMadMum
Love the idea of the ladder reward chart! Will you get Bernie to share a pic?
Jess.AKYOL
I will.

NO_Just_DON'T(1)
THIS COMMENT HAS BEEN DELETED
NO_Just_DON'T(1)
THIS COMMENT HAS BEEN DELETED
NO_Just_DON'T(1)
THIS COMMENT HAS BEEN DELETED

KadafiDancingKing
I am indeed, in İstanbul, Mr Angus and Mrs Jess! I getting here only two hours ago. I try airport and they not let me see Mesut

and they not even telling me he here or not. Tomorrow, Mrs Jess, I try again. You have my promise.

Jess.AKYOL

Oh my god, Kadafi, you wonderful, wonderful boy. You have just given me something other than terror to go to sleep with tonight. You've given me hope.

NO_Just_DON'T(1)

THIS COMMENT HAS BEEN DELETED

26

DAY 26 - THE LIST

Muirdrith, Highlands of Scotland, UK
Sun 5th Sep 2010
Sunrise / Suhoor: 6.22am
Sunset / Iftar: 8.05pm

Still no news. Let's just start with that. Still no news.

At least, there is no news from Mesut, anyway. You might have noticed, Dear Reader, that Kadafi commented on yesterday's post that he has travelled all the way from South Eastern Turkey, where he lives, to İstanbul airport. For those of you who don't get the geography of Turkey, that's no less than nine hundred miles.

What a boy.

This is what friendship is like between Turkish men. I have witnessed what Mesut and his friends will do for each other. I've heard them call each other, 'Gülüm', which means 'my rose'; I've seen the vast amounts of money they give each other without a hint of wanting it back; I've watched them be there for each other in the middle of the night. If the bonds between

Turkish women is something to behold, let me tell you that the connection between the men isn't far behind.

All I can do is hope that Kadafi might be able to do something now that he's there. His dad is mayor of the city he lives in and although that's right on the other side of Turkey, maybe he'll have some political swag. I'm just praying that Mesut is still at the airport and not halfway to a military camp by now.

It felt wrong that the sun was shining in Muirdrith today. It felt wrong that the clouds were practically smiling and the birds were swooping and singing. It felt wrong to sit in Bernie's garden, watching the kids play, sipping water and letting the sun dance across my bare, white legs. I know Bernie thinks she's helping me by creating a retreat-like ambience but honestly, I can't indulge in it knowing that my husband is suffering.

Have you ever been through something so terribly soul-wrenching, Dear Reader, that you just don't know how to get through the hours? I remember feeling a bit like this when I had my miscarriage. Once the sonographer told me there was no heartbeat, I had to walk around as if the baby inside me hadn't died. As if my body was functioning perfectly and there weren't chaotic and horrifying things happening inside it. I had to do this for three days before going to the hospital for surgery and I've since spoken to women who've told me they've done it for even longer. Weeks, even.

I just don't know how we do it.

But we do.

And that's why I went into town on my own today. Bernie managed, somehow, to get both of our children to go down for an afternoon nap. And she, of course, needed one too. She also needed some things from the Co-op for dinner so I volunteered to go and get them, just to get through the hours.

I crossed my fingers that Mona wasn't working. Not because I don't love the very bones of her, but because I really can't keep collapsing in fits of tears on the poor woman. She probably needs a break. Luckily, she was nowhere to be seen and I did my shopping quickly and quietly.

On the way back to the car, I walked past the doctor's surgery. The doors were wide open (weird) and there was a sign taped up saying *'Free, drop-in counselling today'*. I peered further into the reception and there was an A-board propped on the floor with a Nessie-shaped logo and the words, *'Help in the Highlands'* stretching across it. A few people were milling about in the waiting area, drinking coffee and eating biscuits, chatting happily together in low, measured tones.

I guess I must have been standing there for a beat too long, because a man with a clipboard stepped towards me. "Hi. My name's Luke. Are you here for some drop-in counselling today?"

"Erm. I don't . . . I'm not sure . . . what is it, exactly?"

"It's okay. I know it's a bit nerve-racking." He smiled warmly and gestured towards the coffee machine. I shook my head out of habit. He shrugged and kept talking. "We're a charity called Help in the Highlands and we do free, out-of-hours, drop-in counselling with qualified counsellors. Is that something you might be interested in?"

I realised that standing there, with my heavy Co-op bags, knotted hair that hadn't seen a comb for several days and a denim shorts / baggy t-shirt ensemble that had more holes and dodgy stains than is probably socially acceptable, that I most likely did seem like a prime candidate for such help.

"Err, well I was just passing actually and I don't know if this is really the kind of thing that . . ."

"Jess? How lovely seeing you here."

I snapped my head away from Luke the Clipboard Man and saw Sue, the tartan-skirted counsellor, smiling right at me. Of course. It would make sense that she would be there.

"Oh, hi, Sue. Don't you ever get any time off?"

"Och, it's just something I do once every few weekends. Very worthy cause." She flicked her eyes up and down the length of my sorry-looking body and seemed to make a quick decision. "Do you want a session while you're here? We're quiet today. It's no trouble. You can leave your bags here."

"Hang on!" Luke flicked to a specific page on his clipboard and clicked a biro at the ready. "She'll need to fill in a form or two . . ."

"It's fine, Luke." Sue waved him off and gestured at me to walk ahead. "I've got all of Jess's paperwork. We'll sort out the admin after."

And that's how I came to be sitting, yet again, in Sue's counselling room. It felt a bit like an embarrassment of riches, having had a session only a few days ago. People usually wait for months for this kind of thing. Who was I just to walk in and claim Sue's precious time to myself?

"How've you been, Jess?"

"You wouldn't believe me if I told you."

"Try me." She leaned forward, resting her elbows on her knees and smiled. I noticed a vase of dried thistles to her left and memories of that chat with Mona drifted through my mind.

Strong.

Sturdy as hell.

You grow wherever you are placed.

I took a deep breath. "After Mesut's mam died there was the funeral and then he got detained at İstanbul airport and now they won't let him go and he might have to go and do fifteen months' worth of national service and be away from me and Baki for all that time and my flatmate is a racist and I should never have left Baki alone with her and I was so rubbish at sticking up for him so it looks like I am the shit mum I always thought I was and now I can't go back to the flat and I'm just waiting for Children's Services to visit me any day now and Baki will be gone and Mesut will be gone and I really don't know what will happen to me."

Sue blinked and sat back, lifting her elbows from her knees and placing them on the arms of the chair either side of her. She looked at the thistles. She looked at the box of tissues. She looked at me.

"Wow. You're going through a really hard time."

A blast of air escaped my mouth in a ridiculous, mournful laugh. "Yeah."

"Are you still fasting for Ramadan?"

"Yes. No. I don't know."

"You don't know?"

"Well, I haven't been trying. But I haven't been eating or drinking much anyway. I'm not in the mood."

Sue nodded slowly and tutted quietly. "I can understand why. Where are you staying at the moment, if not at the flat?"

I explained to Sue that I am safe and cared for and she doesn't need to ring the crisis team to come scoop me up. Also stated clearly that Baki is safe and well. Even though she probably would have liked to have seen that fact with her own two eyes.

"So, you're fundamentally okay, because you and Baki are at Bernie's and you've got access to all the basics. But what about you, Jess. How are *you* getting through all of this?"

I told Sue about the strategy of getting through hour by hour. I explained about the reward chart at Bernie's, the strange but cathartic trip to Glensíth beach yesterday and my hopes that Kadafi will be able to help Mesut somehow. "But I have to be honest, Sue, my world feels like it's spinning out of control. I know I can do all the stuff I have to do for Baki. I can change his nappies, I can feed him, bathe him, make sure he's fed. But I know, deep down, that I can't be the mam I need to be now that Mesut is gone. I didn't stick up for him properly when my awful flatmate was blatantly racist towards him. What kind of mother doesn't rip into somebody who does that to her son?"

"The kind who's shocked and appalled?" Sue suggested. "The kind who just wants to get him to a safe place? Exactly like you did."

"I don't know about that." And Sue pushed the box of tissues towards me at exactly the right moment.

"What about the Guest House poem. Has that been a help?"

I blew my nose in an embarrassingly loud fashion and thought about how to answer that. "It was. At first. I really like what it's saying. But . . . well, these feelings that I'm having are so monumentally awful and I can't ask them to come in and stay. I just can't."

"I understand. But they won't stay, Jess. They're just visitors."

"Well, they're not welcome!" I blurted out. "They can fuck right off and stay at somebody else's guest house."

Sue laughed gently and I couldn't help but join in. And there was me thinking that Ramadan had taught me some zen. "Okay. Let's assume these feelings are staying down the road at somebody else's guest house. But they really want to come to yours, because they've heard about the five star accommodation."

"Hah."

"What would it take for you to let them in? What have you relied on in the past to help you move through challenging stuff? Think back to some hard times, if you can."

Dear Reader, I am not one to say I've had it harder than anyone else, but I have to admit that when Sue asked me this question, I could recall plenty of scenarios. There was the devastating split with Jack five years ago; the collapse of my business; marrying in Turkey, away from my family and friends; finding out my dad had cancer; being unable to feed Baki when he was first born; going through postnatal depression and then the miscarriage too. But what had carried me through? What magic formula stopped me from falling apart completely?

"I don't know. Friendships, I guess, have been crucial. Knowing which ones are solid enough to support me."

"Good point. And it sounds like you've already been wise enough to access that through Bernie and your friends on the blog."

"Yeah. I guess. And Mesut. He's been my backbone quite a few times."

"What about before you met Mesut? What did you do before he came along?"

"It's hard to remember. I feel like so much of myself has been lost since Baki was born, I can't remember that far back. Oh god, is that awful to say?"

"No, Jess. It's not. So much of motherhood is transformative and it often happens that our identity can get rocky. Lost for a while, even."

"It does feel like that. I don't know. I used to write in my journal a lot. I used to write lists."

"What kind of lists?"

"Things that inspired me or made me feel grateful. I used to write about my values and my beliefs. That was quite revealing. But I'm not sure I need 'revealing' right now. I just need to know what to actually *do*."

Sue followed my words with quick, velvety assurance. It was almost like this conversation we were having, was a smooth, long ribbon of words where it didn't really matter who was speaking, just that the words were coming. "Yes. I can see that. And I can see that you're already doing a lot but it's what you're doing for yourself that interests me. Could you write one of your lists, do you think? Could you write a list of things that you feel compelled to do, for your own sake and not anybody else's?"

"God, it's been a while. I guess I could. But I don't know where to start. I just wish I had a connection of some sort with Mesut. I think then I could feel settled enough in myself to write something."

"You've told me before that you have a very strong connection with Mesut. That you had that before you even knew you were going to be together. Remember? You told me about your trip to Turkey."

"I remember."

"So where is that connection now?"

"It's still there." My hands flew to my heart and pressed there, without my brain telling them to.

"It's still there but it might feel a bit difficult to grasp, a bit difficult to hold. Is that right?"

"Yes. That's so right. But I know it's still there."

"Okay, so how can we make that connection stronger? So that you can really *feel* that it's still there and be able to get on with making that list. With thinking about you."

"I don't know. I don't know how to reach him without getting through to him on the phone. He won't be able to check his emails or anything like that. I wish there was more I could do for him."

"But you *are* doing something for him. You started this whole month doing something immense for him – something that you told me he was so very touched by . . ."

"Ramadan?"

"Yes. Ramadan."

"I'm still kind of doing it, I just haven't been focused on it."

"Of course. You've had huge distractions. What does Ramadan mean to Mesut?"

"Oh, I know it means a hell of a lot. He's been doing it since he was a young boy and it meant the world to his mam too. She showed him the way. When I offered to join him in fasting this year, he was so intent on doing it right, on making sure I got the things out of it he wanted me to. Like clarity, gratitude, connection . . ."

"Connection?"

"Yes."

"So there we have it."

"So you think that continuing with Ramadan will give me the connection I need to Mesut?"

"And maybe more besides, Jess. You started this for a reason. Maybe you could finish it. How much longer is there to go?"

"Just another few days. Four days including today, I think?"

"Could you hang on for another four days?"

"I could."

"Okay. So how do you feel now that you've made that decision?"

"Oddly better."

"Okay. Can I make a little suggestion?"

"Of course."

"I suggest that when Baki's in bed tonight, and after you've had a nutritious supper at sundown, you tell Bernie you're having an early night. Then, you pick up a notebook and pen. You start writing your list. What can we call it? This list?"

I sat straight in my chair, the first time my spine had properly unfurled for days and breathed in deeply. As the breath expelled from my body I had the name of the list. "Things I Will Do When Ramadan is Over."

"Perfect. Things you will do when Ramadan is over. How does that feel? Knowing that's the title of your list?"

"It feels . . . right."

"Great. Do you have a notebook and pen – nice ones – that you can use to make your list?"

"Don't worry, Sue. I know exactly where I'm going to write my list."

"I don't doubt you for a second. And maybe next time we meet, we can go through that list together."

"Definitely." I smiled (yes, *smiled*) and thanked Sue for her time. I got up and walked out of the doctor's surgery, past Luke the Clipboard Man and out into the bright and sunny streets of Muirdrith. For the first time in a long time, it actually felt okay that the sun was shining and I used its soft, silken rays to coax me all the way back to Bernie's and get through til bedtime.

———

So here I am . . . I've eaten a half-decent meal of cheesy pasta, filled up on Bernie's cherry tablet and am sitting in bed, laptop at the ready. Mesut isn't by my side, but he is in my heart, the fullness of my belly is telling me so. Baki is sleeping soundly in his cot next to me, and I am tapping away at my keyboard as quietly as I can.

I love a notebook and pen, as you well know . . . but it feels right to compose my list here, right here, with you.

I hope you don't mind.

THINGS I WILL DO WHEN RAMADAN IS OVER

- Get Mesut back
- Eat and enjoy 3 meals a day (at least)
- Get somewhere new to live
- Prioritise my writing
- Drop the fear of motherhood

That's enough to get me off the starting blocks, don't you think?

I'm not going to lie, there are some foundations I need to lay over the next few days that are left of Ramadan, if I'm going to have a hope in hell of achieving any of the things on my list. But I'm pretty sure I know where to start . . . And I'm pretty sure you're with me . . .

Am I right?

I know I am. x

Anonymous
THIS COMMENT HAS BEEN DELETED

Anonymous
THIS COMMENT HAS BEEN DELETED

Not-A-Granny-Flora
Good. A nice, practical list to get your thoughts in order. And I'm relieved there are only a few days left of Ramadan. Once you start eating properly again you'll be able to think straight. Let me know as soon as you hear anything from Mesut.
Jess.AKYOL
Will do, Mam, aka champion-list-maker. #ILearnedFrom-TheBest

Anonymous
THIS COMMENT HAS BEEN DELETED

AngelBernie
I'm with you! Obviously. And thank god, finally you're making lists again. I did worry that I hadn't seen one in quite a while.
Jess.AKYOL
I think it was Cat-Crazy Flatmate and all her bloody notes that

have put me off writing my famous lists. That's why I've used the blog instead. The departure from paper and pens has made me feel less of a psycho.

AngelBernie

Glad to hear it, poppet. Can you please add to the list: 'Get out of my own bloody way and grow the fucking angel wings I so deserve'?

Jess.AKYOL

'Fucking angel wings' – isn't that like, blasphemous or something?

AngelBernie

As if. Did you know Archangel Michael is a badass who slays demons and cusses while he's at it? He is the almighty of empowered empaths who does not freak out over a swear word or two.

Jess.AKYOL

Now him, I like the sound of.

NO_Just_DON'T(1)

THIS COMMENT HAS BEEN DELETED

NO_Just_DON'T(1)

THIS COMMENT HAS BEEN DELETED

NO_Just_DON'T(1)

THIS COMMENT HAS BEEN DELETED

Anonymous

THIS COMMENT HAS BEEN DELETED

Night-sun-ella

Yeyyyy! I'm with you, oh beautiful one! Can you add one more thing to the list pretty please? *'Allow my amazing puppeteer friend, Ella to devise a new puppet show telling the story of my life'*. Because I have ALL of the ideas . . .

Jess.AKYOL
This list just gets better and better.

NO_Just_DON'T(1)
THIS COMMENT HAS BEEN DELETED

Angnonymous
Help in the Highlands is such a brilliant charity, Jess. I'm glad you found it. And you're only a few days away from completing Ramadan? You've so nearly nailed it.
Jess.AKYOL
Speaking of nailing things . . . Angus, are you around tomorrow? I'm popping to Glensíth and need to see you. There's something I want to ask . . .
Angnonymous
I'm around but I'll be at the beach working on one of our cabins. Did you see them behind the ice cream shack when you were there with Baki yesterday?
Jess.AKYOL
I did. I'll be there.

NO_Just_DON'T(1)
THIS COMMENT HAS BEEN DELETED

Fab4CoolDad
Can't wait to see what you're going to do over the next three days, love. And of course we're there with you. Maybe more than you realise. If you need me to help you in any way with your list, just ask and . . . 'I Will'
Jess.AKYOL
Quite possibly my all-time favourite Beatles song, Dad. So you got the timing of that just right.

NO_Just_DON'T(1)
THIS COMMENT HAS BEEN DELETED

KadafiDancingKing
Okay, Mrs Jess. I need you to send me your UK phone number. I am in detainee area of airport and soon they letting me into the cell where I can see your Mesut. He still here, Mrs Jess. They tell me that. They not taking him anywhere yet. It's good Turkish government is working so slow. Please send me your number and we can talk about what we can do. Email me at kadafidancingking@turkmail.com – we need to sort out right papers and maybe they believing he not running away from army. Allah is watching. Allah is helping.
Jess.AKYOL
I'm emailing you now Kadafi. Thank you so, so much.

NO_Just_DON'T(1)
THIS COMMENT HAS BEEN DELETED
NO_Just_DON'T(1)
THIS COMMENT HAS BEEN DELETED
NO_Just_DON'T(1)
THIS COMMENT HAS BEEN DELETED

27

DAY 27 - RUMBLES

Muirdrith, Highlands of Scotland, UK
Mon 6th Sep 2010
Sunrise / Suhoor: 6.24am
Sunset / Iftar: 8.02pm

Glensíth Beach was just as beautiful today as it was two days ago. The sky may have darkened with heavy clouds, turning the sand as silvery-grey as a knife edge, but it still caught my breath as I stepped out of my car and carried Baki, sleepy and wriggling in his pyjamas, over the dunes.

Yesterday, in his comments, Angus didn't say what time to meet him there at the beach, but I didn't sleep much last night and felt it was better to get an early start on things. Knowing the insanely glowing complexion of the man, he would be a fan of early starts. Whatever he was doing at the beach cabins, he would probably have started it at 5am with a green smoothie in one hand and meditation bells in the other.

I wasn't far wrong.

I spotted him about the same time Baki started whinging for an ice cream from the shack, which was blatantly closed. There he was, sitting on the rickety wooden steps leading up to one of the ramshackle beach cabins, his sandy hair swept back with a multi-coloured headband, wearing something I can only describe as an actual smock. The sleeves of it were rolled up, to reveal completely unfairly toned arms and swathes of Celtic tattoos that seemed as much a part of him as the dimples that broke on his cheeks as soon as he saw me. He might not have been drinking a green smoothie but he was smoking something that smelled equally as green, which he quickly extinguished when he clocked Baki.

"Jess. Baki. Aw, braw little man. Didn't realise you'd be coming over so early."

"Neither did I, Angus. Is this okay? Are you busy?"

"Och, not yet. I'm supposed to be doing some repairs on this here cabin. A bit of time out from the festival. It's been mad, Jess."

Of course. The Festival of Wellbeing. I still felt guilty about pulling out of my talk at pretty much the last minute. "The festival's been mad?"

"Yeah. Well, it's been really well attended. And everyone's loving the new hall and all of the other improvements. We didn't quite get the retreat park finished but I'm told it's just about there now. I've been working so hard, I'm completely scunnered. Just needed a wee rest so Lupa's sent me out here to fix these steps and do a few other jobs because we've got a new family moving in soon. Do you want to see inside? They're such lovely wee homes. There might be a kettle in there. Could make you a brew?"

"No thanks. That sounds nice but I just need to ask you something. Something big."

"Okay, let's sit." Angus gestured at the wonky steps and we both crouched down to sit there, allowing Baki to plod around in the dusty-coloured sand at our feet. "I hope I can help. Is it about the talk? I thought you said you didn't want to do it."

"No, it's not about the talk . . . it's about Mesut. Did you see the comments last night? Did you see what Kadafi wrote?"

"I did. He's there, isn't he? At İstanbul airport?"

"He is. And Mesut is still there, thank god. Hopefully Kadafi will be able to get in and see him and find out what the hell we need to do to prove that Mesut has a perfectly viable visa here in the UK, and that he has a legit job to come back to. I'm hoping it's just a matter of sorting out the right papers."

"I hope so, Jess. I know what these situations can be like."

"Exactly. And that's why I'm here."

"I'm not following."

"You used to be a lawyer. Didn't you? An immigration lawyer?"

"Well, yes, but that was a long time ago and I'm not up to speed with all of the new legislation."

"Okay, but you're literally the only person I know who can help. Is there any way you can put your head together with Kadafi's and help get Mesut back?"

Angus rubbed his chin and then fixed me with an ocean blue stare. "Och, I'm not sure I'm the best person. I left all that behind a long time ago. I mean, look at me now. I'm a far cry from the power-suited, power-hungry man I used to be."

"But even then, you must have had a heart of gold. You helped all kinds of different people, didn't you? You helped them with fleeing dangerous homelands and getting their families to safety and achieving asylum seeking status?"

"Well . . . yes, but . . ."

"So this would be a walk in the park for you, surely. Mesut isn't in danger. He just needs to come home to his family. To be in the place he has every right to be."

"You're right. But I don't know how much I could do from over here. The Turkish Army is quite a beast to go up against."

"Well I reckon that with you over here and Kadafi over there, there'd be no stopping you. Even if you can get them to hold off making a decision, it would be something. You wouldn't even have to put on your power suit – you could keep wearing that . . . that erm . . . Oh god, Angus, what is it that you're wearing?"

"Tunic?" he laughed. "This is my favourite one, lassie. Don't you like it?" He pulled down on the smock-thingie and stared at me in wide-eyed disbelief. I tried to ignore the way the fabric of it stretched over a clearly-defined set of abs and returned my attention to the matter in hand.

"So you'll help Mesut then?"

"Aw man, Jess! Lupa will be pure dead bealing when she finds out I haven't fixed these stairs but . . . yes, yes I'll help you. Come on. Give me the laddie's email address and I'll go to my shack to see what I can do from behind a desk in the far-flung Highlands of Scotland. You can give me a lift back."

"Of course! I need to find Lupa anyway. Do you think she'll be around?"

Angus looked up at the sky and seemed to search for the sun. "With any luck she'll be having her usual granola breakfast smoothie bowl at the Kelpie Café. She always starts her day with that." Angus picked up his toolbox and, mercifully, Baki followed him as we walked back to the car park, every bit enamoured by the likeness to Bob The Builder's very own stash.

"Perfect. I'll get Baki some breakfast while I'm there."

"What about you? Are you still fasting?"

"Yup. I know it's mad, but it's the only way I feel I'm making some kind of beeline to Mesut. Like he might hear the rumbles of my tummy and know I'm still doing something, anything, for him. Does that sound stupid?"

Angus laughed and threw a cheeky look my way. "No way does it sound stupid, lassie. He'll hear the rumbles of something, my friend. He'll hear the rumbles of something."

Lupa's granola breakfast smoothie bowl looked completely delicious. Must add that to my list of things to do after Ramadan is over. Eat granola at the Kelpie Café.

"So, you want to do the talk after all?" Lupa stared at me, her slate-grey eyes narrowed like pins, but the faintest curve of a smile tugging at her thin, flamingo-pink lips. I hadn't expected her – the chair of the Glensíth board – to be so sleek and shiny and professional. I might have my work cut out for me here.

"Yes. I'm so sorry I've messed you about. And I know it's mere days until your final event. I'm just wondering if you can work me back into the schedule, even if it's at a different time?"

"But Jess, I don't understand what's changed your mind. I've been following your blog – along with everyone else – and I know what you've got on your plate at the moment. Are you sure you've got the energy? The headspace?"

How to explain this sudden change of heart to her? I'd had a hard enough time explaining it to myself, as I tossed and turned in bed last night. All I know is that I sat bolt upright at three in the morning, banging my head on the shelf of football trophies Bernie's son has above his bed, and there was a statement streaming through my mind like wildfire: *You need to do the talk.*

"I have the headspace, Lupa. And the energy too. It's hard to explain but these past few days – and this whole month, really – have given me the chance to figure out what really matters. You and Angus were right from the start. This talk is important. It could be interesting to people, and even helpful too. And for me? Well, I have a feeling it will be yet another way I can feel connected to my husband."

"But he wasn't even keen on you doing it, was he?" Lupa scooped up a spoonful of granola and my tummy growled as she chewed happily.

"You're right. He wasn't. Not at first. But after he spent time with his mam just before she died, he found a different way to look at things. That he doesn't always believe in the *things* I'm doing, but he does believe in *me.* And that's an important difference."

"It is." She smiled and set down her spoon. "No offence, Jess, but I have to be sure that you won't pull out again."

"I won't."

She leaned back in her chair and seemed to assess me in the grand total of ten seconds. Then there was a grin. "Well, you're lucky because we didn't actually find anybody to take your place. So the same slot is still open."

"Before Paulo Coelho?"

"Before Paulo Coelho. And are you still happy with the title? *'My Little Ramadan – Adventures of a Fasting Non-Muslim in the Highlands'*?"

A warm, smooth sensation spread inside my belly and that told me everything I needed to know. "I think it's perfect."

"Really? A lot has happened for you aside from the whole Ramadan thing."

"Really. I promise I'll stay on point, Lupa. But you know and I know that everything's connected anyway, so it's not like Ramadan hasn't taught me a thing or two."

She laughed. For the first time since I'd sat down at her table. And I could sense that cabbage hippy warmth this place was famous for. "Okay. I get that. Go on then. Let's do this."

"Yey! Oh, there's one more thing." This was the bit I had to dig deep for. I had to set aside my ridiculously British overpoliteness and just bloody well ask the question. I bit my lip, dragged my eyes up to meet hers and forced the words out: "How much can you pay me?"

"Och, Jess! There's no need to look so embarrassed! We pay all of our speakers, I think I said something along those lines in the first email I sent out to you? We have enough in the budget to pay you five hundred pounds for the talk. That's for the time you'll be here and all of your preparation and planning. Does that sound reasonable?"

Preparation and planning? Oh yeah, there'd have to be some of that. "Five hundred pounds is great. Honestly. Thank you."

"It's fine. Just send us an invoice afterwards."

Come on, Jess. You did the hard bit, you can do the next bit too. "Ah. Well, erm, actually, I was wondering if you might be able to pay me beforehand?"

She blinked, dabbing the edges of her mouth with a napkin. "Well, it's not standard, that's for sure. You need the money now?"

"Yes. I really do."

"Okay. I'd usually consult the board but as we all know you, and the talk is in just a couple of days I'm sure we can make an exception. Give me your bank details and I'll get it sorted."

Dear Reader, this is way short of all my problems being solved, but knowing that five hundred pounds was going to land in my bank account was exactly what my sorry soul needed to hear. It's only about half of what I need to pay a deposit on a new flat, but it's going to get me well on the way with ticking off the things on my all-important list.

And it wasn't only Angus and Lupa who helped me out today. I was also honoured to have the assistance of Crunchy Nut Mam, and a drove of other mams from the Parent & Toddler group volunteer to come and help me get all of my stuff out of that god-awful flat. It only took one phone call from

Bernie (who stayed home to watch the kids) and the Muirdrith Motherhood Massive were there in a flash.

I timed it carefully so I wouldn't have to see Cat-Crazy Flatmate. I knew she was working Mesut's Monday night shift so we nipped in there and nipped back out again with boxes, bin-bags and bedding, everybody chucking my stuff into their cars until they were full. The cats swarmed around our ankles as if they could stop us and in fact nearly sent a couple of mums flying down the steps outside. But we managed to keep our wits about us and the feline army finally backed off just as I'd emptied the last cupboard.

The last room I did was the kitchen and I stood there for a final few seconds, in the mucky brown pallor of it, remembering the way that terrible woman had spoken to Baki. The racist slur that had found its way out of her mouth and into his beautiful, innocent ears. I looked at the Scottish flag stickers on all of her kitchen cupboards, thought about the times she'd moaned about the smells of Turkish food cooking, prayer beads being left lying around or the fact that she called my Quran for Dummies book 'religious propaganda'. How had I not seen it before?

I'm right to have left that place.

I may not have been able to check the decision with my husband or even notify my auntie. Our stuff might now be locked up in Bernie's garage and I might have nowhere to live . . . but I tell you what, Dear Reader, it still feels so right.

Today has been a busy day, and I've tried to share all of it with you, but there's one thing I haven't told you about in this blog post. And it's kind of important. I'm not sure I could have even written the words you see before you today, had I not had this particular thing at my fingertips. Well, not at my fingertips, exactly. More like flung over my shoulders in the height of boho-glam chic.

Let me explain.

When I went to the flat to get all my stuff, there was a pile of post for me in the Everything Cupboard. Thankfully nothing from the professional child stealers, but there was a mysterious parcel.

I am now wearing that parcel.

And it's all down to Gillie.

Gillie, are you an actual mind-reader? Or have you just known me so long that sometimes the ideas I haven't even had yet channel telepathically through to your brain so you know what to do to support and accelerate them?

Because you sent me your glittery, rainbow, floor-length coat.

And yes, I shall be wearing it, along with the sparkly dress I bought with Mona, to do my talk at Glensíth.

Speaking of which . . . I'd better stop writing now and start prepping that bloody talk. It's all very well bleating on about how it'll connect me to Mesut and give me the chance to speak my truth, but I ain't gonna earn my five hundred quid sitting here looking like a sleep-deprived Elizabeth Taylor.

Must. Get. On. With. It.

Tomorrow, Dear Reader . . . tomorrow. x

GILLIE_LASS77

Don't ask me how I know. I just know, you know? Do you know what I mean? I think you know. Cos I know you know. We both know.

Jess.AKYOL

I do not know and I do not care. I am looking fabulous. That is all.

CrunchyNut_Mummy

It was a joy to help you today, Jess! We were all glad to do it. It got me out of cooking dinner AND dealing with bath-time tantrums so it was a win-win. Muirdrith Motherhood Massive at its best.

Jess.AKYOL

Yep. The MMM was amazing. You all lifted my spirits so much AND got me out of that horrendous place. Thank you.

CrunchyNut_Mummy

We were glad to. That woman has a lot to answer for. The pub hasn't been the same since she took over. So many dodgy types hang out there now. It used to be our local but never again. I'm sorry for your auntie, it must have affected business.

Jess.AKYOL

Dodgy types?

CrunchyNut_Mummy

Types like her. That's all I can say here.

NO_Just_DON'T(1)

THIS COMMENT HAS BEEN DELETED

NO_Just_DON'T(1)

THIS COMMENT HAS BEEN DELETED

ShelleyMadMum

Crunchy-Nut is right! We had a blast, Jess. Just shows where us mums get our kicks these days, doesn't it? 😂

Jess.AKYOL

I know, right? Thank you so very much for helping.

OliverChen1!

You're doing the talk! This is awesome, matey. I just know you've got it in you and I'm glad you've realised that too. Bernie's right, you're vibing up.

Jess.AKYOL

Still have no idea what that means and be careful saying things like that, Oliver. You might have to come and join the cabbage hippies in Glensíth.

OliverChen1!

Don't put it past me, matey . . .

Jess.AKYOL

Okay then. I'll ask Angus where he buys his smocks. Sorry, *tunics*.

Angnonymous

TUNICS. Oliver, you're welcome anytime. Jess, we need to talk. Have been in touch with Kadafi (what a character).

Jess.AKYOL

Calling you now.

Fab4CoolDad

There's so much good news in this post, love. Hoping your friend Angus can help out with Mesut's situation. Maybe the talk will take your mind off things while you wait. If you get really stuck on what to say then you could just find the programme for the whole festival and make it into a song. Don't laugh. It's been done before with 'Being For The Benefit of Mr Kite'!

Jess.AKYOL

Now there's an idea. If only I was as musically gifted as my dearest brother, I might actually have a chance of entertaining the cabbage hippy masses.

MaxAttax

The cabbage hippies will probably be wetting themselves to see Mr Coelho that they won't pay much attention to you anyway, sis. Peace out.

Jess.AKYOL

You've such a way with words, brother. Peace out yourself.

Anonymous
THIS COMMENT HAS BEEN DELETED

NO_Just_DON'T(1)
THIS COMMENT HAS BEEN DELETED

Not-A-Granny-Flora
Glad to hear your lawyer friend might be able to help with Mesut. I'm a bit worried about you being homeless but I'm sure you'll figure something out. Re: the talk. Email me what you've prepped so far.
Jess.AKYOL
Can I just email you a photo of me in my pyjamas and the fur coat? That's about as far as I've got.
Not-A-Granny-Flora
Oh, Jess.
Jess.AKYOL
Indeed.

ThistleMadMona
Well, the news that our Angus is on the case is music to my ears! He's got a stunning track record, though he'd never tell you himself, not since Glensíth came into his life. Sorry for the radio silence here on your blog, Jess. I'm also preparing something special for the festival. Well, for Glensíth itself, really. Oh, and Jess, I'm pleased you're out of that flat. It was no good for you and the wee lad. Mesut will be glad when he comes home.
Jess.AKYOL
I hope so, Mona. I really do.

NO_Just_DON'T(1)

THIS COMMENT HAS BEEN DELETED

Anonymous
THIS COMMENT HAS BEEN DELETED

NO_Just_DON'T(1)
THIS COMMENT HAS BEEN DELETED

Anonymous
THIS COMMENT HAS BEEN DELETED

NO_Just_DON'T(1)
THIS COMMENT HAS BEEN DELETED

Anonymous
THIS COMMENT HAS BEEN DELETED

NO_Just_DON'T(1)
THIS COMMENT HAS BEEN DELETED

LifeIsYoursLindy
You can do this, Jess. You ARE doing it. Don't forget, LIFE IS YOURS.
Jess.AKYOL
Thank you, Lindy. I needed to hear that after deleting all of those horrendous comments. It's good to know somebody's rooting for me.

NO_Just_DON'T(1)
THIS COMMENT HAS BEEN DELETED

KadafiDancingKing
Mrs Jess, your friend, Mr Angus very nice man. We talk on

phone and he tell me what to ask the staff here and I do it. I do it all. I see your Mesut and he quite white and quite thin but he still trying smile. He is saying to you 'seni seviyorum' and 'Baki nasıl?'. I say I knows you both fine because I reading blog but he can't do that because they not let anyone access internet. I staying with my cousin in city and he has internet and printer so tomorrow I will take print-outs of your blogging posts so he can read. He in horrible room, in horrible conditions but he only worried about you, Mrs Jess.

Jess.AKYOL

Reading these words from you, Kadafi, has filled my heart to bursting. Thank you so, so much for being there and for trying your best to get him out. I'm glad you're in touch with Angus. I think it's you who is following the goodness now.

KadafiDancingKing

You knows me, Mrs Jess. Always I try to follow the goodness. Because it is everywhere to follow. 😉

NO_Just_DON'T(1)

THIS COMMENT HAS BEEN DELETED

NO_Just_DON'T(1)

THIS COMMENT HAS BEEN DELETED

NO_Just_DON'T(1)

THIS COMMENT HAS BEEN DELETED

Anonymous

THIS COMMENT HAS BEEN DELETED

NO_Just_DON'T(1)

THIS COMMENT HAS BEEN DELETED

28

DAY 28 - A PATTERN

Muirdrith, Highlands of Scotland, UK
Tues 7th Sep 2010
Sunrise / Suhoor: 6.27am
Sunset / Iftar: 7.59pm

I'm writing this post to you, today, from Bernie's conservatory, just after lunch. Baki is napping upstairs in his travel cot (weirdly, he is sleeping much better in this house than he ever did in the flat) and Bernie has fallen asleep on the sofa with Frida nestled against her gargantuan belly. If I look really closely, I can see Frida's head loll gently under the playful motions of her future sibling. Future as in probably within the next few days. That babe wants out.

This morning, Bernie forced me to take a break from a.) scouring the internet for cheap flats and b.) quizzing all the local estate agents over their rigid requirements for immigrants. She insisted that going to Toddlers would be a good idea. "Come on, poppet. It might be the last one I get to without a teeny-tiny sprog in tow." It was also the last Toddler session I would have to endure without caffeine and sugar, which is rather exciting.

As soon as Bernie and I stepped into the room, letting Baki and Frida make a straight run for the My Little Ponies, we could tell there was something up. A kind of buzz in the air. And all heads turned to look at us.

Well, me. They turned to look at me.

Crunchy Nut Mam was the first one to cut through the weird atmosphere. "Jess. Have you seen it? Tell me you've seen it."

"Seen what?"

She shrieked. As did several other mams. "You haven't, have you? Oh lordy, you'd better sit yourself down. Shit, we can't even bring you a coffee, can we?"

I plummeted into a chair by the soft-play corner. A random child threw a spongy cube at my head, but I didn't flinch. "Why would I need a coffee? What's going on?"

"Here." One of the mums stuck a newspaper in my hands. Then she backed away. "Read that."

I looked down at the paper and there, on the actual front cover, was a massive photo of me and Baki, playing in the waves at Muirdrith beach, Mona's thistle archway stretching out behind us and the dipping, syrupy sun lolling in lazy streaks all around us. Oliver's photo was just beautiful.

"Oh, the photo looks great!" I smiled. So they published the article then? I thought Ailsa must have given up on it."

Crunchy Nut Mam looked at me with a sense of trepidation. "Have a read, Jess. It's a bit different to what you thought it would be."

I looked down again and read the headline:

TURKISH AIRPORT JAILS LOCAL FAMILY MAN

"What the . . ? This isn't what they were supposed to write about. What about Ramadan?"

Bernie looked over my shoulder and grinned from ear to ear. "I *knew* the angels were onto something when they got me to organise that photo shoot."

Crunchy Nut Mam urged me on. "Go on, Jess. Read it. Tell us what you think."

I followed the instructions to turn to page seven and started to read. The other mams moved off to tend to dribbly chins, smelly nappies and toy-related altercations, but I knew they all had half an eye on me, waiting for my reaction.

A Muirdith father is being held in his native Turkey, unable to return to his family in the UK or even contact them.

Mesut Akyol, 31, was born in Turkey but now lives in Muirdith with his wife, Jessica Akyol, 33, and their two year-old son, Baki.

He recently returned to his home city of Manevitaş to go to his mother's funeral and is now being detained at the airport because the authorities say he has not completed his military service.

Jessica, told Highland News she has no idea when her husband will be able to return.

"He is being detained in a holding cell along with 30 other detainees at the airport and hasn't even got access to phones or the internet, so I can't speak to him," she said.

"The authorities say he hasn't done his 15 months national service and hasn't got the correct papers to be allowed to leave the country. I don't know when I will see him again."

The couple met four years ago when Jessica visited the holiday resort of İpeklikum where Mesut was working as a barman. After getting married and having their baby boy, they returned to the UK to start a new life together in Muridrith where Mesut works in a local pub.

"It's been so hard, especially as I have been fasting from sunrise to sunset recently to participate in the holy month of Ramadan. I wanted to support my husband and show him my commitment and willingness to learn about Islam.

"But he had to go back to Turkey when his mam was ill and now she's passed away. We just miss him so much and want him back."

Jessica is due to talk about her and her husband's ordeal and her own experiences of Ramadan, at Glensíth Community Foundation as part of the Wellbeing Festival on Wednesday September 8 at 7.30 pm. Tickets are available from the community centre.

Jessica is also writing a blog about her experiences: www.mylittleramadan.blogginglife.com

"Woah," Bernie said, lifting her head from the paper and towards me, brows lifted and eyes wide. "You are officially the talk of the town."

I nodded, still staring at the words on the page, vaguely aware that somebody was trying to extricate a whole packet of crayons from Baki's mouth on the other side of the room. "I was not expecting that." Somebody shoved a mug of hot water in my hand. Crunchy Nut Mam.

"You okay, Jess? We all thought it might actually be a good thing, didn't we, everyone?"

I looked up and saw an awful lot of heads nodding over steaming mugs of tea and coffee. Murmurs of, *'we did'*, *'it will be'* and *'so good'* floated over to where I was sitting.

"Think about it," Crunchy Nut continued. "Anybody who's anybody is going to see this. The Highland News has a really good internet presence. So, maybe somebody with some clout will see it and be able to help get Mesut back. Maybe it'll go *viral*." She enjoyed that last word a little more than was necessary and curled her tongue around it like it was edible gold.

"I don't want anything to go viral. I just want my husband back and to get on with life."

"You will!" Came several voices at once.

"You totally will," echoed Bernie.

"But what about Ramadan?" I whinged. "That's what she was supposed to be focused on. That was the whole point of the article! She didn't talk about why I've really been doing it, the spirituality of it all, the gratitude you're supposed to feel, the commitment, the clarity, the divinity. She didn't even mention the envelope-licking incident!"

"Or the facial injury from Baki's ice cream!" shouted a woman breastfeeding in the corner.

"Or the X-Factor conundrum!" piped a dad jiggling a baby on his knee.

"Or the cystitis!"

"Costa-del-cat-hair!"

"The patchy sofa of fame!"

"The Quran for Dummies!"

"Thistle Dispenser Lady!"

It was very strange to have all these weird little bits of trivia from my own blog thrown back at me across a room filled with people I hardly knew. I had to break their flow to shout, "Hang on a minute, how many of you have been reading my blog?"

Every single person put their hand up.

I honestly didn't know what to say.

"Thank you." Seemed to be it.

Then I had an idea.

"Okay, if you're all so clued up on my life, I need to ask you one more favour." I grabbed Baki's changing bag from the floor and started rifling through it. I knew it was in there somewhere. Aha. My notebook. I held it up high. "I have not one sodding clue what I'm going to say at my Glensíth talk tomorrow, so maybe you lot can help me. Come and tell me something you've enjoyed about my blog and maybe . . . yeah, maybe something you've learned from it too. Whether it's something about Ramadan or Islam, or even just something that's surprised you. Is that okay? Would some of you be up for doing that?"

There was a beat or two of silence before all the voices started at once. The babies and toddlers were left staring in the wake of their parents as people started to flock round me, asking for their favourite bit to be included in the talk. I honestly couldn't write fast enough. I even got Bernie writing some notes too, balancing a spare notebook on her mega-belly which was quite a sight to behold.

I scribbled like I've never scribbled before and now I'm sitting here, in the drifting quiet of Bernie's conservatory, trying to make sense of it all. Who'd have thought that so many people would like the patchy sofa of fame hack of stowing away sneaky snacks? Or that it's not just me who has ice cream cones shoved in her face, and a child who prefers Bob The Builder over his own mother? I was humbled by the amount of mams who have also suffered with their mental health since having children, and felt tragically comforted by the people who whispered sadly that they, too had experienced loss in pregnancy.

All these people, who I see week-in, week-out and always assume are far superior parents to me, who I thought didn't even notice me, have not only enjoyed reading my blog, but they've identified with it too.

Maybe we are connected after all.

So, if you'll excuse me, I'm going to use what's left of this lunchtime nap-fest to write up some ideas for the talk. I can't believe it's tomorrow. I know there is an email waiting for me from my mam, because I saw it this morning whilst I was navigating numerous conversations with Angus and Kadafi. So, I'll somehow work her professional expertise into the humanistic glow of what I've been told this morning.

I can so do this.

BLOG UPDATE:

I thought I was going to be able to leave it there, to leave you with the idea that my talk was more or less written and my spirits were up.

But what a difference half a day makes . . .

Two things have happened.

THING NO. 1

There I was, basking in the glow of shifting my little family (and my soul) out of that fucking awful cattish-hell-hole of a flat. I honestly thought I'd done me, Baki and Mesut a massive favour.

I mostly wanted it for Mesut. I wanted him to come home to something good – if not an actual home then at least the possibility of one . . . the promise of living with independence, privacy and a life free of racist insults and passive aggressive notes. But instead I've fucked everything right up. Let me tell you how . . .

Angus called around 3pm.

"Jess? Are you sitting down?"

"I can be." I was watching the kids whilst Bernie was upstairs soaking her tremendously swollen ankles in some sort of herbal concoction from Glensíth's natural remedies store. I found a clearing in the sea of plastic, buzzing, flashing crap that Frida and Baki were playing with and sat down. "Go ahead."

"I can't get him home if he doesn't have a home."

"What?"

"It's the simplest thing. I know your auntie has sent off the work contract, so that's good. All of the visa papers seem to be in order and Kadafi has photocopied them and got all the necessary stamps from the Consulate. But I don't have a home address for him."

"Can't you just put the flat down? Do they really need to know we've moved out? It literally only happened yesterday."

"Legally, not a good idea. Mainly because I don't know what's going to happen next. They could either accept all Mesut's paperwork and let him go, like literally in an instant and then he'd be able to get the next flight home."

"Or?"

"Or, they could investigate further and it could go through the courts, taking weeks or even months. If we lie about the address, it's not going to wash well once we go down that road. I wouldn't want to risk it."

"What about Bernie's address? I'm sure she wouldn't mind if we . . ."

"I already thought of that and it's not going to work because they not only want an address but also some formal papers with Mesut's name and address printed on. You know the kind of thing, a rental agreement, a bank statement or something."

"Oh."

"I know. Jess, tell me, is there any way in the world you can get a deposit down on a flat and a rental agreement knocked up in the next day or two? Because I think that might swing it. But it would definitely have to have Mesut's name on it."

My stomach churned. Thank god there was nothing in it. "Shit, I just don't know. I've been looking constantly and there's nothing where you don't need to fork out less than a grand. Plus, it seems landlords and estate agents are really strict when it comes to immigrant tenants – they need all kinds of documents that my auntie never even asked us for when we moved above the pub. I've looked into it and I can't get them sorted without him being here in the UK. Shit, Angus. What are we going to do?"

"Try not to panic, lassie. It's just one blip in the road. We'll figure something out. I've got to go now. Lupa needs me for the festival tonight. And there's a delivery for the retreat park arriving any minute. I'm sorry, I've got to call it a day but I'll be back on it in the morning, alright? Let me know if anything changes. Anything at all."

"I will, Angus. Thank you so much."

"Nay worries. Oh, and I saw your article in the Highland News this morning. Maybe check how it's doing online? It might be that somebody sees it and can do something to help. Might be worth a trawl of the comments."

"Anything. I'll try anything."

"He's lucky to have you, lassie. He really is."

Totally didn't agree but there was no time to ponder on that. I checked that the kids weren't killing each other (Frida was folding and smoothing individual tissues as Baki ripped them out of a box one by one – standard) and fired up my laptop. And it was only a few moments before it happened . . .

THING NO. 2

The article has been read a lot of times. And when I say a lot, I *really* mean it. In fact, the number was ticking up, up, up, just as I was sitting there, staring at the screen in shock.

You'd think I'd be happy. Ecstatic, even, that our story is getting so much exposure. That somebody, somewhere, might be able to help us. But I know you'll agree, Dear Reader, that this is not the kind of exposure anybody would want . . .

Servez her rite 4 marrying a Muslim.

Exactly why this country is going to the dogs – couples like that breeding + diluting our population.

We dont need the likes of him in our country.

He's probly a terorist so keep him out, I say.

Why can't he just follow his country's rules and do the national service? Coward.

Letz not spend our taxes on getting Muslims back into a country they shudn't have been in to begin with. Keep.
Him. Out.

My first instinct was to rush over and hug the kids, kissing their talcy little heads whilst my eyes filled with hot, quivering tears. I felt responsible, somehow, for letting them into a world that was so full of hate and prejudice. I mean, aside from Cat-Crazy Flatmate's toxic insult, I don't think I've ever really experienced real, targeted racism whilst we've been in this country. Maybe the odd stare here and there and some nervous chuckles but never anything so blatant as this.

I can tell you that not all of the comments were like that. Far from it, in fact. The majority of people were expressing their sympathies, asking for more information or wishing us luck. I really don't want to give the impression that Highland News readers are a bad lot. They clearly aren't. But the backlash I've seen today is enough to make my heart race for cover.

And that's not all.

I forced myself to look again at the comment stream. As you know, I'm no stranger to horrific comments, as I've been deleting them, on a daily basis, from this very blog. But I have to tell you that what I saw next culminated in a moment of awareness so agonising, I felt I'd never come down from its dangerous heights.

Dear Reader, I wonder if you already know it.

In amongst all of the comments, all of the hateful, venomous shit that people somehow think is okay to post on the actual world-wide web, I spotted a pattern that made my blood run cold.

I spotted these . . .

Could you please consider keeping people like this out of your newspaper? I'd rather hear about proper Scottish news.

Could you please consider listening to the more enlightened comments on here? Muslims are not welcome on these shores and it's not just me who thinks it.

Could you please consider what bringing people like this to Scotland will do to us? They can stay where they came from and stick to their own cultures and lifestyles.

Could you please consider the danger of promoting the entry of this man back into Scotland? Who knows what risks he brings with him?

Could you please consider the kind of mother this woman is? How can she be trusted with the care of a little boy whilst indulging in extreme Islamic behaviours such as starvation?

Could you please consider why the hell this woman has been asked to do a talk at Glensíth? Why are they actively promoting such extremism?

There were more. Many more.

Do you recognise the phrasing?

What if I told you the username for all of these comments was 'NO_Just_DON'T(1)'. What then?

And what if I told you that this was the comment that really got my attention?

Could you please consider that this woman is not a safe mother if she is cavorting with a Muslim? Somebody needs to take that child and make him safe. Why Children's Services didn't take him when they came here last time, I'll never know.

It was her. All along it was her.

She wrote all that shit on my blog.

She wrote all of these awful things about the article.

She reported me to Children's Services.

Cat-Crazy Flatmate.

And now it's because of *her* I don't have a home and Mesut can't come back.

"Bernie! Finish soaking your feet. I'm going out!" I screamed it up the stairs, with a venom not meant for my beautiful friend. Both kids looked up, eyes as wide as saucers and bottom lips trembling. It was a millisecond before shrieks erupted from their lungs, piercing me in a thousand different ways.

"I can finish now," she called back. I heard water sloshing. "What's up? You sound upset."

I snatched my coat off the banister, grabbed my keys out of the dish by the door and hardened my heart against the screams of Baki and Frida. They'd be okay. Bernie would sort them out.

"I'll tell you when I get back." I didn't wait for an answer but fought my coat onto my shoulders and yanked the door open. I was leaving absolute chaos in my wake, but it was nothing compared to what was going on in my heart. This was an emotion so raw, so sharp, I thought I might bleed from it. How could I *not* be bleeding?

I was going to find her and I was going to have my Mother Lion moment all over again. This time, nothing was getting in my way . . .

"Woah! Jess, love. Where's the fire?"

I'd crashed right into something. Or someone. Standing right there on Bernie's doorstep. And they knew my name.

The rage continued to course through me but my breathing faltered with the familiarity of the voice. The body I'd crashed into was broad and firm, the clothing soft and crumpled, the scent reminiscent of pipe tobacco and car air freshener. I was primed to keep going but the electricity that urged me on also created a natural static that pulled me towards this person.

It was my dad.

"Where are you going in such a hurry, love?"

"Wha . . . what on earth are you doing here?" I heard a car door slam and footsteps clipped, rhythmically behind him.

"Lovely welcome, that is. I told your dad we should have warned you we were coming." Mam leaned in for one of her signature one-armed hugs. I gave it, but my body was still ready to run.

"You're . . . you're here? But why?"

"To sort all this mess out, of course!" My mam tutted and tried her winning smile.

"What your mam means . . ." Dad swiftly picked up the conversation, rescuing it before I dumped them both on the doorstep and kept running, "is that we decided to drive up and be here for you. You're going through a tough time, love and we want to help. With Baki, with finding somewhere new to live. With anything, really. And we wouldn't miss your talk at Glen-síth tomorrow night, would we, Flora?"

"No. Of course not. Are you going to let us in or not, Jessica? Bernie knew we were coming. We're staying with your auntie but we wanted to come here first. As a surprise."

"Well, it is. It definitely is." I let out a long, shooting sigh, the adrenalin that had more or less kept me standing for the last few minutes, streaming out of my body like an exorcism. My dad caught me before I could get up close and personal with the doorstep.

"Let's get you inside. You can tell us where you were going and why you look like you're on a man-hunt."

By this time, Bernie was at the door behind me, two toddlers clinging to her ample hips, dried tears tracking down their cheeks and snotty noses burrowing into the long, black Guns and Roses t-shirt she was wearing. She looked at the state I was in, hanging onto my poor dad for dear life and suddenly seemed to think better of asking what the hell was going on. "Welcome mummy and daddy Jess. Shall we go inside? There's a hoolie blowing up out there."

Bernie was right. Because I'm sitting here now, several hours later, and there is a 'hoolie' as she calls it, tearing through the streets of Muirdrith. The windows are positively shaking and we've had to lock all the toddler paraphernalia into the garage. It's probably a good thing I didn't go out to find Cat-Crazy Flat-mate in this weather, who knows what the strength of my fury might have added to the storm.

"Oooh, the angels know something is up. They're stirring the pot, so they are." Bernie is sitting opposite me in her living room, and my mam shifts uncomfortably in her armchair whenever Bernie comes out with anything remotely angel-related. We're all waiting for my dad to finish cooking the curry he promised us, on the condition that I didn't go out to find that excuse of a woman. In true, respectable parent style, he and my mam insisted I should not go and work out my troubles when I am so incensed with rage.

It pains me to admit it, but they're probably right.

I'm supposed to be continuing with Ramadan as a way to connect with Mesut and wasn't it him who told me, right at the start, that it's a time for words to be chosen carefully? No swearing. No gossiping. No arguing, accusing, shouting or screaming. There's no way the light of Allah can shine through if I'm allowing myself to indulge in all of that. Maybe it is better to put off confronting her until I'm well and truly basking in a holy light of divinity. That'll piss her right off.

Okay, it's 7.44pm. The holy light of divinity will have to wait. My dad's samosas are ON.

I really hope I haven't scared you off, Dear Reader. Please come back tomorrow. It'll be my last day of fasting and I've got the cabbage hippies of Glensíth to entertain. I don't think I can do it without you.

We've come this far together, haven't we?

<u>GILLIE_LASS77</u>
Woah. I've just checked out the Highland News website and you're not wrong about those comments. Was it really her all along?
<u>Jess.AKYOL</u>
The more I think about it, the more it seems it was so obvious. How could I not have seen it before?
<u>GILLIE_LASS77</u>
None of us saw it, sweetie.

Compustable.Apocalips
THIS COMMENT HAS BEEN DELETED
Compustable.Apocalips
THIS COMMENT HAS BEEN DELETED

Angonymous
So sorry about the home address thing, Jess. It often is one small clerical thing that can hold things up, even in massive cases. However, don't fret because I think I might have a solution . . . and it means you can live far, far away from that head-banger of a woman at the pub. I just need to confirm a couple of things. Stand by . . .
Jess.AKYOL
Standing by. I'm so standing by.

Compustable.Apocalips
THIS COMMENT HAS BEEN DELETED

Anonymous
THIS COMMENT HAS BEEN DELETED

Anonymous
THIS COMMENT HAS BEEN DELETED

AngelBernie
Hope you liked your surprise of mama and papa turning up? Talk about divine timing. Who says Ramadan isn't working? Your dad's samosas could solve EVERYTHING. Might ask him to make me a few more if I need something spicy to get this babe out.
Jess.AKYOL
I'm sure he'd be delighted. Thank you for being in on the surprise. I have to admit, it was good timing, even if my anger

didn't think so at the time. It will be good to have them here for the talk.

AngelBernie
I've just thought - isn't your talk at 7.30pm? When is sundown tomorrow?

Jess.AKYOL
It's at 7.57pm! So I should finish my waffle just in time to drop off stage and eat something. Actually, mmmmm, waffles.

AngelBernie
That's it. I'm bringing waffles.

CrunchyNut_Mummy
I told you about that woman. Wish I could have told you more, but Muirdrith is a small town and she has her allies. You just concentrate on your talk and getting your hubby back, Jess. She'll get her comeuppance one day.

Jess.AKYOL
I'm not sure how in-keeping with Ramadan it is of me to say it, but I really hope you're right.

Anonymous
THIS COMMENT HAS BEEN DELETED

Anonymous
THIS COMMENT HAS BEEN DELETED

Glensíth_Comm_Found
We're very excited to round off the festival with you and Mr Coelho tomorrow, Jess! After today's article, we've had a flurry of last-minute ticket sales and I'm pleased to tell you that the event is sold out! Looks like the lovers outweigh the haters.

Jess.AKYOL
Oh. Sold out? Arsing hell.

Compustable.Apocalips
THIS COMMENT HAS BEEN DELETED

Anonymous
THIS COMMENT HAS BEEN DELETED

ThistleMadMona
Wheesht, Jess – what a day you've had of it! I'm not long back from Glensíth myself and that festival is going off with a right bang. I had a delivery to make, which wasn't easy in this hoolie, I can tell you. The Bathing Biddies Beach Club have all bought tickets for your wee talk tomorrow and are beside themselves about it. Don't give that woman a second thought. Remember to be impeccable with your word tomorrow and you'll be just fine. Plus I saw Angus and he's got something up his sleeve for you which could be a few prayers answered at once. Like Bernie mentioned, who says Ramadan isn't working?
Jess.AKYOL
They've *all* bought tickets? Arsing hell yet again.

Anonymous
THIS COMMENT HAS BEEN DELETED

Not-A-Granny-Flora
Sold out? Right, you'd better graduate from that scruffy little notebook and get some ideas down on your laptop. We can shape your ideas properly tomorrow.
Jess.AKYOL
I just wish Mesut was here to support me.
Not-A-Granny-Flora
You're supported in more ways than you realise. He'll be there in spirit.
Jess.AKYOL

Moody, huffy, Gandalf-like spirit?
Not-A-Granny-Flora
Of course. Whatever helps you.

Anonymous
THIS COMMENT HAS BEEN DELETED

Anonymous
THIS COMMENT HAS BEEN DELETED

Anonymous
THIS COMMENT HAS BEEN DELETED

Fab4CoolDad
I didn't get to tell you, because you were in such a rage when we arrived at Bernie's, but the drive up the A9 was glorious. I think that storm was chasing our tail but my little Mini outran it. Maybe while we're here I'll let you . . . 'Drive My Car'.
Jess.AKYOL
Your Mini Countryman? You'd let me drive that? I thought you were getting rid of it in preparation for imminent retiring?
Fab4CoolDad
I know, I can't afford to run it for much longer but I'm getting my last few weeks in. Beep beep, beep beep, yeah!

Anonymous
THIS COMMENT HAS BEEN DELETED

MaxAttax
So, the parents have arrived to sort you out, then? I'm sure Mam used to be one of those cabbage hippies herself, though she'd never admit it. Watch out Glensíth doesn't swallow her up tomorrow night. Peace out.

Jess. AKYOL
I can kinda picture her with flowers / cabbage leaves in her hair.

OliverChen1!
Finally! They published the article! I tried my best to encourage Ailsa in my emails but wasn't sure if she'd do it. I looked online and you're right, it's a beauty of a photo. Concentrate on that rather than all of those nasty comments, matey. I think Crunchy-Nut Mummy might be right – karma will sort out that awful flatmate of yours. She's not your concern anymore.
Jess.AKYOL
Thanks, Oliver. I'm glad I have your photo to focus on rather than all of those shitty words. There's still some rage shimmering in my bones, though. I can't be held responsible for what I'll do if she crosses my path . . .

Combustable.Apocalips
THIS COMMENT HAS BEEN DELETED

Anonymous
THIS COMMENT HAS BEEN DELETED

Anonymous
THIS COMMENT HAS BEEN DELETED

Night-sun-ella
Wish, wish WISH we could zip back up there in Keith the Van and surprise you in much the same way Ma and Pa have! I could have found some more heather on the roadside and thrashed Cat-Crazy Flatmate with it until she apologises and takes all those awful comments down. I bloody KNEW there was something not right about her whilst we were there. Who writes

notes when they can just speak? Somebody with a deep, dark secret, that's who!

Jess.AKYOL

I'm sorry we didn't think to do any thrashing with your last 'bouquet'. It could have done some serious damage and perhaps said flatmate would have been put off crossing me and my little family.

Night-sun-ella

I could have ear-tongued her too. Although, to be fair, that is only reserved for the most special people like your husband, who will be home very soon, if that tasty Angus has anything to do with it.

Jess.AKYOL

I hope so, Ella. I really do. #BlogSqueeze

Night-sun-ella

#AllTheSqueezes

GILLIE_LASS77

I'm back! Don't want to be left out of the #BlogSqueezes so I'm sending #BlogSpooning and power from the #BlogSisterhood

Jess.AKYOL

Ah, how I love you both. #BlogSisters

Night-sun-ella

#BlogAllTheLoveInTheWorld #HopeAngusCanSortOutTheHomeAddressThing #FreeMesut

GILLIE_LASS77

#HaveCheckedAngusOutOnGlensíthWebsiteAndAManThatHotMustBeAbleToDoSomething

Jess.AKYOL

#Stalker #Weirdo #IDoHopeYoureRight

GILLIE_LASS77

#YouKnowImRight

Night-sun-ella

#IKnowYoureRight
Jess.AKYOL
Let's never speak in hash tags again. #ItsConfusing

Anonymous
THIS COMMENT HAS BEEN DELETED

Compustable.Apocalips
THIS COMMENT HAS BEEN DELETED

KadafiDancingKing
I keep following the goodness here in İstanbul, Mrs Jess. Me and Mr Angus, we a team and we doing everything we can. Your Mesut is okay. I bring him simit and cheese and olives because food in that place stale. He still fasting in Ramadan and says he do it for you. For his mum too. And for Allah, of course. He read all your blog posts tonight – every single page I bring him. It make him smile. Lots. I think we all trying to follow the goodness here.
Jess.AKYOL
Kadafi, my darling boy, you ARE the goodness. 😘

29

DAY 29 – THE TALK

Muirdrith, Highlands of Scotland, UK
Weds 8th Sep 2010
Sunrise / Suhoor: 6.29am
Sunset / Iftar: 7.57pm

I am here.

I did it.

I scuffed my way along the rocky road of Ramadan and somehow managed to scramble to the very end.

And to celebrate, I've scrambled into bed.

And it's not even a teenager's bed.

It's mine.

Ours.

Oh, fuck-a-duck, where to begin?

Right, Dear Reader, let me tell you the story of today . . .

This morning I woke to the screeches of Beast-Child clashing with the relentless rattle of every window in Bernie's house. Last night's storm was still terrorising Muirdrith and as I opened the curtains, I saw the sky objecting by chasing lightning streaks with shrouds of strong, black cloud and dead-weight blankets of grey.

I went down to the kitchen, and was surprised to see my mother, who had evidently let herself into Bernie's home, sitting at the kitchen table with her head in her hands. "Och, Jessica, what are we going to do about your talk tonight? I've been scan-reading all of your blog posts and I'm coming up with nothing. This storm is stopping me from thinking straight."

"Morning, Mother. I'm fine, thank you, how are you?" I popped Baki on her knee. He needed breakfast and he needed it now. I knew Bernie had some sugar-laden crap somewhere in the cupboards, so started to root around. "Where's Dad? Did he not come with you?"

"He got a phone call early this morning and now he's off in that Mini of his, probably loch-hopping or something. You know how he comes over all touristy whenever we visit up here."

"I do. Will he be back for the talk tonight?"

"Och, he wouldn't miss that for the world. Now come and sit down. Let's get it planned. If they're paying you five hundred pounds then you need to give them their money's worth."

All the reminder of the five hundred quid did was make my heart plummet into my feet. "Pass me your newspaper, will you, Mam? I need to look at flats first."

"I've already looked. There's nothing. And anyway, you haven't got all the papers you need for a landlord to accept Mesut. You know, you could come back to England and live with us. I know it would be a squish but once Mesut's back, we can look at options again."

I plonked Baki in the highchair and, to his total delight, presented him with a bowl of Frosties. "Thanks, Mam. I'll hold onto that offer."

"And you're staying away from that woman today, aren't you? Please don't let her ruin your day. And no checking the comments on the Highland News article either. It'll do you no good." My mam's cheeks were flushing crimson and she was flapping her fingers about like Bernie does when she's conversing with the angels.

"I'm promising nothing." My chest tightened and my hands curled into fists. "I'm still so angry."

"Of course you are. But we have to look at the bigger picture here. And you're out of the flat now, that's all that matters."

If any of you reading this blog are blessed with a mother of the sensible kind, then you will know that there is no arguing with her when she is on a logic rampage. That was my mam this morning and I knew any emotional eruption of mine would fall on deaf ears. I'd need to save that energy and channel it into my talk.

So we did just that. We trawled through my blog posts, and the squillions of notes I made at Toddlers yesterday. This was, of course, interjected with wiping bums, dispersing toddler-sized snacks and repeating eleventy-billion times that "No, you cannot go outside and play on the swings because they are currently wrapped around the up-turned barbecue on account of this inexplicable, never-ending storm."

I did try to listen to Mam's sage words of advice about structure, themes, timing and key messages. I even opened a Word Document at one point and proudly typed some bullet points:

- *I perhaps love garlic bread more than anything else in the world*
- *I hope I never get cystitis again*
- *Waffle cones have sharp edges*

You see? All the best intentions were there. But the storm going on outside wasn't the only one in our proximity. The one in my head was raging too, and constructing something ordered out of it just didn't seem possible.

When Bernie finally surfaced from her bed, and informed us that the angels had told her I'd be using my wit and my intuition to deliver the talk, it didn't exactly reassure my mam. Or me. Furthermore, when Bernie suggested I take a break and try on my outfit for the evening, I thought my mam might jump into the nearest loch.

"Och, Jessica. You're not wearing that, are you?" I was standing in front of Bernie's conservatory doors, the sky breaking into violent, blackened shards behind me. It was the perfect, moody backdrop to the rainbow, sparkle-fest I now was.

"I really am, Mother, and there's nothing you can do to stop me." Truth be known, I did feel a bit ridiculous in the purple, sequined dress I'd bought with Mona, Gillie's furry, floor length, glitter coat and my signature blue Doctor Marten boots. I mean, who did I think I was? Were mothers even *allowed* to dress like this?

"Sorry, Mama Jess," Bernie grinned, "but she does look amazing. And at Glensíth, anything goes. You're going to really feel the power of that outfit once you get there, poppet. Mesut doesn't know what he's missing."

I knew what I was missing though. I was missing the warmth and reassurance of my husband. After going a week without even speaking to him, I missed the reluctant smiles behind smooth, black hair; the familiar touch of his fingertips against the nape of my neck; the whispers of Turkish endearments, incantations meant only for my ears. Oh god, Allah, the angels, whoever – please let him be okay.

At least god, Allah, the angels, whoever got me through until five o'clock when my mam left. "Your dad will be back at your auntie's by now. I'll go and find out what he's been up to. Only a couple of hours now, Jessica. I know you can't eat anything but at least have a glass of water and put your feet up for a bit."

It was arranged that I'd travel to Glensíth with Bernie, Logan and the kids and my parents would meet me there, taking over Baki-watch whilst I did my talk. Hopefully, Beast-Child would have a personality change for just one evening and sit nicely like an actual human child.

I woke Baki from his mega-slumber and changed him into suitable rock-kid attire in an attempt to dilute down my own extreme look. He was so cute in the Beatles T-shirt my dad brought for him. The ripped jeans completed the look, and nobody needed to know the rips were a result of an unsupervised tree-climbing fiasco a few weeks ago and not down to the latest kiddy trend.

When we arrived at Glensìth, the nerves were really kicking in. I hauled Baki out of Logan's car and almost immediately he squirmed to be set free. Bugger. That lengthy afternoon nap, where I was faffing with different types of mascara, may prove to be my undoing. "Okay, you can walk. But you need to hold Mammy's hand tight and go where I go, alright?" I grabbed his chubby little hand and he jerked his head, which I was taking as a nod. I shoved some emergency chocolates in his jeans pockets and popped one in his gob too. That should keep him quiet for a while.

I swallowed back a massive, lumpy tangle of nerves and straightened up, keeping Baki's hand in mine. I scanned the crowds – yes, crowds – for Bernie, Logan and Frida, and spotted them heading for the new stained glass gates that bordered the Glensíth grounds. Through the cabbage hippy masses, I could just about see that the gates were emblazoned with vibrant purple and green stained glass shapes. Thistles. *Perfect,* I thought, realising that the lottery money that inadvertently came from Bernie's angels had been wisely spent.

I found Bernie and made a bee-line for her. "Have you seen the new gates, Bern? Aren't they fab?"

"Never mind the gates, Jess. Something's not right. Can't you hear that chanting? And what's that weird smell? Logan's gone to find out what's wrong."

I sniffed the air and Bernie was right. There was a weird smell. Burning? The cabbage hippies were probably just grilling quinoa or something. As for chanting, yeah, I could hear it too. "Is chanting not just standard practice here? Aren't they just summoning the cabbage gods?"

"No. The tone's not right. Can't you tell? The angels are flipping frantic. They won't leave me alone." She set Frida down on the ground and rubbed her back, wincing hard. "The babe too. He knows something is up." Baki and Frida quickly realised they weren't escaping the sea of people all around them and started playing in the gravel. A torrent of tiny stones crashed against my calves but I didn't care. I wanted to know what Bernie meant.

It wasn't long before Logan showed up. "Right, I found some bird called Lupa and told her I'm with you, Jess. She wants us all to go through now. She told me not to panic."

"So, basically, panic then," I said as we all followed Logan through the waiting crowds. Lupa was inside, dressed in a fuschia power suit, looking anything but powerful, even though her outfit included a microphone headset and a clipboard. She was more like a luminous beacon of terror.

"Jess. I'm glad you're here. We've got to get you to safety."

"Safety? Lupa, what the heck is going on?"

"It's just a precaution, obviously." She took a deep breath, closed her eyes for a nano-second, then opened them again, trying out a glycerine smile. "It's after your article yesterday. There's a bit of a ruckus. Nothing we can't handle."

"Ruckus?" Bernie asked. "Is it that chanting? Just tell us, Lupa."

Lupa's eyes darted towards the main hall, which was just down a corridor from where we were standing. Instinctively, we all bent our bodies in that direction, trying to catch a glimpse of where the sound was coming from. "No, no – please don't go down there. We can't send anybody down there right now. Least of all you. The police have been called. It's all under control."

"The police? Lupa. What the hell is it?"

Lupa gasped and floundered, opening and closing her mouth like a baby bird waiting for worms. Then she suddenly dipped her eyes away from me, gripped her headset and talked into it at an alarming pace. "Yes, I'm here. No, the police aren't here yet. We need to get this contained. NOW!"

That was enough for me. I ripped myself away from the spot I'd been standing in and tore down the corridor, slamming up against the first set of double doors I came to. Bernie wasn't far behind. The ferocity of the chanting stopped me from going through the doors though, and that was probably a good thing.

Right in front of us, in a curved blockade across the entrance to the main hall, was a solid line of people standing resolutely together. They mostly wore blue, black or red t-shirts as well as the angriest expressions I've ever seen. There was a huge Scottish flag with a red cross stamped onto the centre of it, frenzied and shivering in the balled-up hands of the people in the middle.

The chant grew loud and clear now, heavily insistent. "Stop immigration, stop the invasion! Stop immigration, stop the invasion! . . ." It would have been rhythmical, almost musical, if it hadn't been so horrific.

"Am I really seeing this?" Bernie whispered, backing away from the door. "I think some of those people go to your auntie's pub. What the hell? Jess, you need to get out of here, like now."

"I will. I recognise some of those faces too. I'm sure they hang out with Cat-Crazy Flatmate. And what's that smell? Is it smoke?"

By this time, Lupa had caught up with us and was practically tearing her hair out. "We've absolutely, categorically been told to not approach them until the police arrive. Lord knows how they got into Glensíth in the first place. Jess, you need to get to the Kelpie Café. Now. We'll keep you there until all of this has been . . . removed."

"Okay, okay, but Lupa – why aren't you worried about that burning smell?"

"I am!" She threw her hands up in the air and nearly knocked off her headset. She was as pale as a ghost and as flighty too. The tears brimming in her voice as she dragged us, desperately away from the doors. "We think they're setting a fire in the main hall. We think they're going to try and burn the place down. After all the renovation work has just been finished too!"

"Well, have you called the fire brigade?" Bernie yelled. The chant was getting louder now. There was no way the crowds outside wouldn't be able to hear it.

"Stop immigration, stop the invasion!"

"Yes! Of course! They're all bloody coming. Now will you *please* follow me?"

Lupa was running now, sprinting away from the chanting and towards the Kelpie Café. It was logical to follow her, I knew it was, but something didn't feel right. "Baki! Where's Baki?" I hadn't felt his little hand in mine for a while and the last time I really remembered his presence was when he threw gravel at my legs outside. He'd been with us when we'd found Lupa, hadn't he? He'd stayed with Logan when I'd investigated the chanting, hadn't he? My eyes ripped across the floor, the corridor, the reception area and they burned with the effort. He wasn't there. I checked Bernie, Logan, Frida, who were all speeding away from me, their retreating figures sadly bereft of my son.

"Bernie! Where's Baki? Have you seen him?"

She snapped round to face me, one mother recognising another mother's stark, unbridled panic. Without even turning to face her husband, she demanded, "Logan? Was he with you?"

"N-n-no. He was with us outside and then . . ."

Lupa stomped back towards us. "Jess, we really have to go . . ."

"I'm not going anywhere until I've found Baki!"

I didn't even wait for Lupa's response. My body moved before I told it to. I tore back through Glensíth's doors, through the thistle gates, back out into the roaring swell of the storm and through the droves of people who were none the wiser to my fears. I didn't care if I was ramming them out of the way, I had to get back to the last spot I'd had Baki in my sights.

"Stop immigration, stop the invasion! Stop immigration, stop the invasion!"

The words drummed through my head like a curse, getting louder and louder with every fear-streaked beat of my heart.

I stopped dead in my tracks. This had been the place. Just outside of the gates. Right next to the chicken-wire fencing around the retreat park.

He wasn't here.

I crouched down and scanned the ground, looking for something, anything, a sign that my boy had been here. And there it was, pressed down firmly by a conical heap of gravel. It was obviously strategically placed there in recent minutes, otherwise somebody would have stumbled on it, causing it to blow away in the winds.

It was one of his chocolate wrappers.

I leapt up, clutching the wrapper in my white-knuckled hands and looked all around me. There was another. And another. Thank god. Bless my lad's unquenchable hunger for chocolate. And thank you, Bob the Builder, for always inexplicably piling up stones in your general vicinity.

I followed the wrappers but they stopped at the fence. Where could he have gone from here?

"Stop immigration, stop the invasion . . !"

The police still weren't here. And that burning smell was getting stronger. Everybody around me had started wrinkling their noses and wafting the air.

"Baki!" I shouted, my voice lost in the tempestuous cry of the thunderous skies. "Baki!"

I fell against the wire fencing, feeling it scrape and claw at my skin, even through Gillie's thick fur coat. And that's when I realised I'd been here before. This fencing. Baki had tried to squeeze under it last time I was here with Bernie. There was a hole just his size and I'd had to pull him out of it. Could that hole still be there?

I worked my way along the fencing, clinging to it as if I was on a ship that was about to pitch me overboard. And there it was, framed by a sunny cluster of dandelions, unwilling to bend in the gales that whipped through them. I didn't even think, I just grabbed. I grabbed the edges of the hole and yanked them even further apart so I could fit through. It didn't take long, but it did more or less mutilate my hands and snag on Gillie's coat. Blood dripped from my palms as I ripped off the coat, leaving it hanging, and ducked through the hole, the creases of my fingers screaming loudly in pain.

As soon as I was through the hole I spotted another chocolate wrapper. This one wasn't buried under a pile of stones, it was just drifting across the wasteland of the park. But it didn't matter. Because there were more, and they were leading back towards the Glensíth building, back towards the main hall.

If I knew Baki, then he'd have sniffed out the fiery smell by now. What toddler wouldn't want to follow the possibility of fire? Of dancing, yellow flames? I stumbled through the grasses and cursed my son's natural curiosity for destructive forces.

Up ahead there was a fire-door hanging wide open like the mouth of a monster. A thick rope of steel chain swung madly, having been cut with bolt-cutters. I suspected it led to the main hall and my blood ran as cold as ice, shooting frosty shards into my veins. *Please don't let him be in there, please . . .*

I stepped inside and found that the door led to the very back of the main hall, just next to the main stage. It must have had some kind of sound-proofing because almost as soon as I went in, those terrorising chants, as well as the howl of the storm, slipped clean away. This was a cocoon, a cave . . . a sputtering, malicious heat licked at my face, but the ice in my blood remained.

I heard a cry.

"Baki?"

"No, child. Fuck off. Unless you want to go up in flames like the rest of this place."

"Baki!" I skidded round the corner and came to stand right in front of the stage. I cranked my neck and saw him right at the very back of it, his face covered in melted chocolate, his eyes red and watery with the smoke that snaked around him. He had his back pressed against the wall, and his little face tilted upwards, looking at the person stood right in front of him. The person he knew. The person he'd lived with for the last sixteen months.

It was Cat-Crazy Flatmate.

She was feeding a blaze in the centre of the stage, as if it was nothing more than a bonfire in a back garden. She strode in diagonals across the stage, collecting things – anything, it seemed – to add to the fiery heap. So far it looked like it was fuelled by books, chairs, boxes and festival paraphernalia like flyers, posters, banners and programmes. She hadn't seen me yet. The sound of the spasming flames must have drowned out my cries.

I tried to catch Baki's eye without alerting her of my presence. This was next to impossible because he seemed transfixed by her. She stalked around him and muttered wildly under her breath. I thought I made out the words, "fucking immigrants", "leeches on this country" and "Muirdrith won't be lost". I definitely heard, "I won't be lost", and that's when she noticed me.

"Fucking amazing. What are you doing here? Come to collect your filthy, Muslim child from the babysitter, have you?"

I ignored her and focused on Baki across the flames that were growing higher by the second. "Baki, come here, darling boy. Come to Mammy." He took a step forward but a scarlet flame leapt out and almost touched him. He wailed and stayed where he was. Cat-Crazy Flatmate cackled.

"He's a wimpy little shit, just like his mother. What's the matter, Jess? Are you scared they're the flames of eternal damnation or something? That they're coming to take your sinful little sprog away because you didn't starve yourself properly for Ramadan? Chance would be a fine thing."

"Okay. That's enough." I clambered up onto the stage, heading straight for Baki. "You've made your point, your friends outside have made their point, now it's time to put the fire out and go home. You've got the flat all to yourself now, so you can go back and tell it to your fucking cat army." As I strode across the stage I noticed there was a circle of objects placed around the fire. A very strategic circle of bits of different coloured paper. Did she have her own weird cult or something? Had she written spells or curses? Fuck, this woman was weirder than I thought.

I reached Baki and scooped the warm bundle of him up into my arms. He was whimpering and snotty. But otherwise okay. I crooned into his ear and told him Mammy was here.

"Oh, look at you two. You think you're so fucking perfect, don't you?" Her tone instantly changed from calm to chaos. She whipped off her trademark fleece jacket and threw it, violently into the centre of the fire, hurling the flames upwards and outwards. Then she turned to look at me, her jaw set like stone. "With your holiday romance, and your cute little toddler and your blog and your fucking pathetic 'dreams of being a writer'. Did you ever stop to think for a second that I might not have wanted you to move into the flat. That I might not have wanted a couple like you anywhere near me?"

"No, I didn't actually. Because my auntie – your boss – *invited* us to be there. We had just as much right to live above the pub as you did." I was caught at the back of the stage, and calculating how on earth I was going to get past her and onto the floor below. The fire was broadening, swelling with almost as much rage as her, as me. I had to move before it swallowed us.

Suddenly she looked down at the floor and whatever she saw drew out a laugh as long and sinister as her frizzy, matted hair. She stooped down and picked up one of the bits of paper that formed the strange circle. It was a luminous orange slip, with handwriting I recognised instantly.

It was one of her notes to me.

"What the hell is wrong with you?" I demanded. "Where did you get all those notes from and why would you bring them here, to your little bonfire?"

"Hah! I know you kept these in your bedside table, Jess. I know you were gathering them to use as evidence against me. You made that much clear on your blog . . . but I'm one step ahead of you."

"What? On my blog? I wasn't gathering evidence. I was shoving them away so I'd never have to look at them again. You made my life awful with those notes. Ever since I stepped foot in that flat. Why didn't you just speak to me? It's not that hard. And why the hell did you report me to Children's Services? That was such a low blow." The heat of the fire was positively smothering now. I turned my back to it, hoping it would shield Baki, but he wouldn't really be safe until I got him out.

"Because I wanted you OUT! And speak to you? Honestly? You mix with dirty Muslims! You think the whole fucking world revolves around you and people should just drop everything and read about your problems on the internet. No, I never wanted to speak to you. You're not the only one with problems."

"Okay, I get that. But can we please just put the fire out now? Or let me get Baki past? You might have your problems, but you wouldn't put a child at risk, would you?"

"Why not? When you've put everything of mine at risk? My home? My work? My town? My fucking country? It's made me absolutely sick every day I've had to watch you fawn over that kid. That kid with blood as muddy as the banks of Loch fucking Ness. Do you even know what it's like to be a proper mother? Do you? Do you?" On these last words her voice shattered like broken glass but her bare arms shot down strong and deliberate to the steps behind her. I don't know how I hadn't seen it before, but there was a square can there, and as she unscrewed the lid, a twisted smile gnarling her lips, I just knew it was petrol.

"Don't!" I yelled. I had to distract her. "Don't fucking do that! What do you mean do I know what it is to be a proper mother? Do you?"

"How dare you ask me that?!" She screamed and the can jutted savagely in her hands.

"Because, because . . . you're upset. I can see that. Tell me . . ." *Say what you really want to say, Jess. Be impeccable with your word.* "Are you a mother too?"

I might have missed it had it not been for the yellowing glow of the fire against her face, but I swear her stony jaw softened for an instant. "I am. I was . . ."

"What happened? Where is your child?"

"Don't you speak of him! He's nothing to do with you. Or

me. Not anymore." She turned her whole body towards the fire and took a step towards it, as if in a trance. The heat must have been screaming off her skin but she didn't flinch. "Maybe I'll just walk straight into it. Nobody would care."

"I'd care. Baki would care. We don't want to see you do that."

"You wouldn't give a shit. He won't even remember it when he grows up to be a fucking terrorist or something. And you, you don't even know my name."

"Yes I do."

"Like shit, you do. What is it you call me on your blog? Cat-Crazy Flatmate? I'm not just some old crone with only cats for friends, you know. I have a name. I have rights. I have beliefs and passions like you, I just don't expect the whole world to bow down before them. And I don't mix with people who are only making this country a more dangerous place to be."

"You're the one starting a fire, Kristen. Not him. Not me."

"This isn't dangerous. This is necessary."

"Is it?" I chanced a step towards her, and the edge of the stage. "Kristen, what happened to your son?"

"This is hardly the time or the place, is it? If you'd wanted to talk to me, you could have done it fucking months ago – instead you were too busy being an inept mother and spreading your extremist bullshit through our town."

Another step closer. "Kristen, what happened to your son?"

"Don't you come any closer. I'll throw the whole lot on the fire, I fucking swear that I will. I don't care if I burn alive." She raised the petrol can and shook it hard. Fear barrelled through my body and my legs almost gave way, but I took one more tiny step.

"Kristen, what happened to your son?"

Then the doors at the opposite end of the hall burst open

and a barrage of black and blue figures charged at us. "Stop! Police! Put down the can."

It was in that second I made run for it. I sprinted past Kristen, who was wide-eyed and staring, her mouth torn open at the sudden avalanche of attention charging at her, and without even a thought of how I was going to land, I jumped off the edge of the stage.

The police officers moved faster than I could have imagined and broke my fall. Baki was wrapped so tight in my arms he must have hardly felt an impact. I emerged, breathless and shaking from the cluster of bodies that saved me and one of them pulled back a helmet to reveal a warm, magnetic smile. It was Crunchy Nut Mam.

"I didn't know you were a police officer."

"Part-time. But this is a special occasion," she winked. "Let's get you somewhere safe." Crunchy Nut Mam and two of her colleagues rushed Baki and I out of the door, but I swung my head back to see what had happened to Kristen. They'd managed to reach her, and she was currently having her hands cuffed behind her back, her head hung so low, I couldn't see what was going on with her face. I heard an explosive collision behind me and turned even further to see the fire service doing their thing. The power of the water shooting out of the hose told me the whole stage area would be completely ruined, and made me realise just how close Baki and I had come to being ruined too.

"Are you ready, Jess? Are you sure you still want to do this?" Lupa stared at me with an expression bordering on fascination, as we stood at the entrance to the retreat park.

"Yes, Lupa. I still want to do it. I'm fine. Baki's fine. And your people have spent the last half an hour tending to our every need."

I wasn't exaggerating. Since the showdown with Kristen, Baki and I had been whisked off to the Kelpie Café and offered everything under the sun to help us recover from our trauma. Blankets. Smelling salts. Tarot readings. Reiki. Plus the slightly more conventional tea and biscuits. I was adamant that I wouldn't eat or drink a thing (sundown wasn't far off) and Baki – who'd had a bum change and about a million cuddles – had eaten their entire stock of chocolate flapjack.

What I learned during that time of respite, was that getting rid of the protestors had not been straightforward. There had been violent struggles so getting to the fire had taken longer than the emergency services expected. Nobody had known I was in there with Kristen and Baki.

"How this baby has not shot into the world on pure adrenalin, I do not know," Bernie had joked in the café afterwards. "Oh well. At least the ambulance was close by just in case."

Poor Bernie. Poor Logan. Poor everyone who hadn't known where we were. Whilst I'd been trapped in the main hall, my mam and dad had arrived, my auntie, Mona, Ailsa and all the Bathing Biddies. God knows who else. And all they were told was that Jess was being targeted by racist protestors, Baki had gone missing, and there was a fire somewhere in the commune.

I don't know how my mam hadn't spontaneously combusted.

Crunchy Nut Mam spent a few minutes with me afterwards, taking a brief statement. Once she'd learned that Kristen had shown some of her true colours, she said, "I can tell you now, Jess. I can tell you what happened to her son."

I don't want to go into loads of detail about this here, because it's not my story to tell. And yes, I know she threatened my sanity, my safety, my husband and my actual CHILD so you could say she has it coming to her. But do you know what, Dear Reader? Who am I to judge somebody else's trauma?

All I'll say is that her wounds go deeper than the few burns she might have suffered tonight. And as a mother, I kind of get it.

When Lupa finally dredged herself out of the admin horror that was being boss of Glensíth tonight, she'd asked me what I wanted to do about giving the talk. Apparently Paulo Coelho was on standby, because he'd been stowed away in one of the commune's many eco dwellings, completely oblivious to the theatricals going on. Plus there was that crowd of people at the Glensíth gates, still waiting for the entertainment they'd signed up for.

I knew I wanted to do this. Yes, I was shaken, but I didn't come this far, fast for all of these days, get through all of these challenges, to give up now. This felt like the final leap. The proverbial cherry on the cake.

So I said yes to Lupa. Yes, let's get this show back on the road.

The only problem was our lack of venue. The fire had been extinguished, but the stage was completely destroyed and in need of yet more renovations. There's no way we could do it there.

"The only other space big enough, is the retreat park," Lupa had pondered. "I reckon we could get everyone in there."

"I thought it wasn't finished yet," I said, recalling my recent scuffle under the wire fencing.

"Well, it's Angus's project really . . . he said it was just about finished. And as he seems to have dropped off the face of the earth . . . I think it's my call, don't you?"

"Okay. Yeah. That's a point, where *is* Angus?" Everybody shrugged. I checked my phone to see if there was anything from him. Nothing. "But what about the storm? How would anybody hear me over those winds? What if the heavens open on us all?"

"Haven't you noticed?" Bernie laughed gently. "About the time they got you out, the storm died back." She gestured outside, through the glass doors of the café. "There's been an eerie calm ever since. I reckon it's just for you, poppet."

"Really? Maybe this is what Allah planned all along," I laughed.

"Allah. Or God. Or the angels. Who knows?"

"Enough with the divine interventions! I don't want to know," I said. "I'm just glad."

And I meant it. I really, really did.

So there I was, at the gates to the retreat park, waiting to start my talk. I watched the people filing through and sitting on folding seats which had been miraculously placed there by Glensíth volunteers.

Mam and Dad sat in the front row, with Baki in between them. Bernie, Logan and Frida were the next row back and not far from them was the entire group of Bathing Biddies, chatting excitedly. Ailsa had tagged along with her mum and seemed to be alternately checking her watch and the gates as if she was waiting for somebody important. Suddenly, Mona stood up and walked over to me, holding out Gillie's fur coat in one hand and gesturing for a hug with the other.

"I found it outside snagged up on a hole in the fence, m'eudail, and that was my first clue something was going on. I'm sure I'll find out about the whole thing in due course – Muirdrith is terrible for its gossip – but I just wanted to check you're feeling alright before you go up there and do your thing?"

"Mona, I am strangely fine. And . . . thank you."

"What for now, lassie?"

"Remember what you told me about being impeccable with

my word? Well, it really helped tonight. When I was trapped in there with Kristen."

"Well, I'm very glad about that, so I am. Can I show you one more wee thing that might help, lassie?"

"Of course you can. I'll take anything to get me through this talk."

Mona took my elbow and guided me round the rows of seats to the other side of the retreat park. On my way over there, I scanned the crowd and saw so many people that I know.

Nicky and Aja were sat together, smiling and waving at me in the least child-stealing fashion possible. Not far along from them was Sue the Tartan-Skirted Counsellor, deep in conversation with Luke the Clipboard Man from Help in the Highlands. I saw lots of mums and dads from Toddlers and even Crunchy Nut Mam stood at the back, finally relieved of her helmet and protective gear, back in civvy mode. Half the staff of Wee Bairns World were flocked around Baki at the front, my mam and dad looking on proudly. The only person missing was Angus.

"Right, are you ready, m'eudail?"

"What? Oh, er, yeah." I tried to focus back on Mona but I'd just seen someone saunter through the gates with a familiar swagger and a camera slung around his neck. "Is that? No. It can't be. Is that . . . Oliver?"

I heard a little chuckle at my side. "Och, yes. Did I not tell you? He and Ailsa have struck up something of an affair."

"Mona!"

"Wheesht now, lassie. Let's say it like it is. It's an affair, and probably a mighty good one at that. Now your Gillie's off the scene, I saw a wee opportunity. It didn't take much to get him up here again, let me tell you. Even if it was under the guise of offering him a photography job on the paper. Och, look, he's waving at you. Come on, wave back."

I let Mona raise my arm but then had the presence of mind

to wave it myself. And I smiled. I smiled big. Oliver. Back in Muirdrith. With Ailsa. "Mona, you sly fox."

"Never underestimate an old lady."

"Hah! Exactly. Was that what you had to show me?"

"Och, no. Turn around now, lassie."

"What?"

"Just turn around."

I did what she said and at first I didn't see what she meant. But that was only because it merged so beautifully in its setting. Right in front of us, or above us, to be exact, was the thistle archway Mona had brought to the beach just a couple of weeks ago. But it had changed. God, had it changed.

Where it had been bare, it was now full. Where it had been sparse, it was now decorated. Flowers of blue, purple, white and gold dripped down in artful swarms. Vines climbed, stems stretched and thistles were woven proudly throughout the entire thing. It looked like it had been there for centuries, but Mona insisted she'd only delivered it yesterday. All of a sudden somebody somewhere flicked a switch and the whole thing lit up with a sparkling radiance. Leaves twinkled, petals glittered and the whole structure revealed a magical, reverent space in the park.

Lupa joined us under the archway and plonked a mic on a stand in front of me. "Jess, are you ready?"

I gave Mona a kiss on the cheek and she practically danced back to her seat to join Ailsa and Oliver. I threw on that floor-length beauty of a coat, marvelled at the way it shimmered under the light of the thistle archway and winked at Baki whose gaze had landed on me as soon as the lights went on. "Lupa, I am so ready."

I've been typing for a long time now. A really long time. I've tried my best to give you an account of today and I'm not sure I've got it left in me to give you a word-by-word regurgitation of my talk.

You don't mind, do you, Dear Reader?

If you really want to hear what I had to say, you can head over to You Tube in the morning. I've been promised / threatened by quite a few members of the audience that my words will live on forever.

I remember I started by swearing. Something along the lines of, "Fuck, there are a lot of you" got me started. It was okay though, because that gave me a segue into letting everyone know about the lesser-known side of Ramadan. That it's more than just holding off on the Doritos and Chardonnay. It's about pausing before you speak, being wary of gossip, being – as Mona would put it – impeccable with your word.

I felt the white lights from the archway shine over me and, although it was beautiful, I thought the warm glow of the audience might be even better. It wasn't long before I was in full-swing and my story was going somewhere – it was going to these people.

I was about halfway through describing ice cream injuries, headaches, mood swings and my garlic bread fetish, when I heard an ear-splitting shriek.

Beast-Child.

The audience laughed and I prayed to anyone who might be listening to make that shriek a solitary one. But, come on. As if that was going to happen.

Whether it was the drama of the night finally catching up with him, or he suddenly realised his mother was not at his beck and call, it didn't matter. The end result was that Baki wrestled himself away from my mam and dad, to stand on his own and scream, right in the gap between the front row and the thistle archway.

His voice was on a rampage. Underneath it, I heard a low rumble of concern from the audience. My mam looked on in horror and my dad tried, without any luck, to distract him with a packet of dry roasted nuts.

"Can you give me a second please? Motherhood calls." I dipped my head apologetically and stepped out from behind my mic. It only took me a few steps to get to him. I crouched down to his level and his scream died down to a low-level grizzle. "What is it, lovely boy?" I asked, in a whisper that only he could hear. "I know you've been through such a lot tonight. Do you want to be with Mammy?" He nodded and burrowed his head into my shoulder. He was completely knackered.

I positioned myself back under the archway and balanced my boy on my hip. "Say hello to all the nice people, Baki. They're here to see you and me." He did a sweet little wave and I thanked my lucky stars his fingers hadn't just gone straight up his nose. What I realised as soon as I got there, though, was that I was knackered too, and standing there with a Beast-Child on my hip like that, was simply not sustainable.

"Does anybody mind if I sit down? My hip can't keep up this kind of action for very long." As if by cabbage magic, one of the Glensíth teccies appeared at my side and made the necessary adaptations with the mic stand. By now, I was sitting cross-legged on the dry grass beneath the archway, Baki planted in my lap and I tried to pick up my train of thought. "Wow, this actually feels a lot like story-time at home." A chuckle rippled through the crowd. I knew the Muirdrith Motherhood Massive would get what I meant. *Maybe that's how I need to do this,* I thought. *I'm just telling a story.*

I suddenly realised how to sort this out. Gillie's fur coat was good for more than just elevating my glamour levels. I whipped it off and stretched my legs out long against the ground. I ruffled up one end of the coat over my ankles, providing a soft pillow as a barrier against my boots. Baki took one look and knew what to do.

He climbed onto the cradle of my legs and lay his head down on the furry cushion. He grasped upwards for my hands, and I grabbed them, reassuringly. "It's okay now, monkey. You can have a little rest." I looked up and addressed the crowd. "I hope you don't mind, but it might be the only way we get through this thing. This is how Turkish mams get their kids to sleep." I wrapped the outer edges of the coat over Baki's little body and then began slowly rolling my legs from side to side. Almost instantly, he settled. I remembered Mesut's mam doing the exact same thing with her baby grandson when I'd first met her and felt the presence of her wisdom even now.

I raised my head to start speaking again, doing a bit of mental gymnastics to remember where I left off. Then I noticed a small group of people walk in at the back of the park and I nodded to show it was fine to come in. I couldn't be totally sure, but I thought I knew who it was.

Paulo Coelho.

I could just about make him out. The trademark black clothes. The tanned skin. The goatee and the bald head and the tiny little ponytail. His people milling around him.

And then . . . I froze.

There I was, a vision of rock-star glamour weirdly contradicted by the maternal position I found myself in, without a single word to say. I rocked Baki rhythmically, his heavy lids closing under the sparkling stream of white light we were bathed in. I squeezed my eyes shut too, and heard the soft shush-shush of my glossy tights as my legs rubbed together. But it was my heart that was loudest of all. The thump that overwhelmed any story I might have wanted to tell. Ramadan? What even was that?

Suddenly there was a pressure against my leg and I opened my eyes. My journal. Being pushed towards me. Mam's slender fingers on top of it and words whispered under her breath, "You know it's all in here, Jess. Don't you?"

I picked up the journal and flicked through it. Yes, there were doodles and scribbles and words that didn't even make sense when you threw them together, but they were mine, and that was the whole point.

I took a deep breath, continued to rock my legs and adapted my best story-telling voice. Every single word from then on was directed at Baki, whose eyes were now closed and whose mind had already drifted off into dream land. Hopefully, a dream land laced with my words.

I can't remember everything I talked about, but you've already seen it here on the blog. I covered all the things I learned about Ramadan. I threw in honest descriptions of the blockades to my soul, to my heart, and how clearing my day of eating and drinking thew them into a harsh but truthful light.

I talked about friendship, humour, resilience and trust. Mental health, trauma, miscarriage and love. I invited everybody into my deepest fears about motherhood and described that during this month, somehow, and without really meaning to, I have wrangled with the mysteries of it, descended into its depths and scrambled up its slopes.

"I don't know if I've got motherhood nailed now, thanks to Ramadan, but I do know that I've got to have more faith in myself. If I don't have faith in myself, it's like not having faith in the generations of mothers before and after me. It's like telling them they haven't got what it takes to raise strong, beautiful children. And it's not just about our children, is it? It's about the relationships we nurture, the actions we take, the values we live by. It's about the degree to which we thread love through everything we think, say and do." I took this one moment to cast my gaze around the garden. To really take in this sea of faces all tilted my way, the backdrop of smooth, lavender sky and the final sunset of Ramadan miraculously blanketing the whole park in a cherry-pink calm. I took a deep breath and spoke my final words. "We are ALL born out of love. Love is our mother."

The clapping started almost immediately. My mam sprang up and dashed over to me, carefully lifting Baki off my legs. He was still wrapped in Gillie's epic fur coat and sleeping deeply despite the noise of the crowd. I stood up and held my journal to my heart, a dopey smile planted on my face because I really didn't know what else to do.

Next thing I knew, Lupa was by my side and taking the mic. "Thank you to the heavens, Jess – that was really enlightening. Jess Akyol from My Little Ramadan, everyone!" And the applause rose again, this time with some whoops and cheers coming from people I didn't even know. I hugged Lupa and stepped out of the archway, towards the seat my parents had saved for me.

Logan silently swerved over to me before I had a chance to get there and whispered, "We think Bernie's gone into labour. We've got to go. She said to give you these though." And he placed a colourful packet into my hands. Waffles. "She says you need to eat." Then he dashed off before I had a chance to say, *'What do you mean, LABOUR?!'*

I shot my eyes over to Bernie's chair and saw her trying to get out of it. She looked a little drained of colour, but other than that she was good. She mouthed, "You were brilliant, poppet!" and I thought she might have gone insane.

I mouthed back at her, "You're in labour?"

"I'm fine," she noiselessly implored and then winced slightly as she turned to leave with Logan and Frida. Then she flung her head over her shoulder before disappearing and mouthed, "It's like shelling peas!"

I laughed out loud but was then suddenly distracted by a small group of people making their way towards the archway. I needed to shift if they were going to get past me but my legs had gone to sleep on account of having Baki's gargantuan mass loaded onto them for the past half an hour. I honestly couldn't get them to move.

My fists pummelled away really hard at my stubborn, deadened legs when a shadow blocked the light over me. Somebody was standing right in front of me, offering a hand to help me move.

"Deixe-me ajuda-la, cara senhorita. Let me help you."

I looked up. Kind brown eyes framed in friendly crinkles. An amused, half-open mouth behind a silver goatee. An outstretched hand waiting for mine. I gave it over.

It was him.

Paulo Coelho pulled me gently to the side and I shifted with more grace than I might have hoped for. My legs were back in working order. Appropriate facial expressions, were potentially not.

He smiled and patted my shoulders in a very fatherly way. "Nice quote. I love Rumi." He winked and then turned to step under Mona's incredible archway.

My absolute hero had just winked at me.

"I hate to break up the party with your idol . . ." It was my dad, his face twinkling with, what was that? Pride? ". . . but I think you might be even more interested in who's just arrived." He pointed towards the gates and at that moment I saw two new people walk into the park. I momentarily tutted that they were pretty damn late and had missed all my Ramadan pearls of wisdom. But then I realised who it was.

Those legs of mine have never woken up so fast in their

entire existence.

I ran – no, sprinted – to the gates and threw myself, with a velocity a day-long starved person should not be capable of, at one of those people. His strong, skinny arms knotted around me, his long, loose hair whipped the sides of my face and the entire front side of his body pressed against mine with a force that was powered by nothing but love.

He was home.

Thank god, he was home.

"How? When? What? I. Don't. Understand!" Mesut interrupted every word I said with a kiss. Then any sentence I had any hope of saying was inevitably crushed into another, all-consuming hug. I settled for breathing, for smelling, for absorbing him instead. I didn't care how he got here. Just that he was here.

I suddenly remembered there'd been another person next to Mesut at the gates and tore myself away from him for a moment to find out who it was.

Angus.

Of course it was Angus.

"Och, you two. What a sight!"

"Angus, you're finally here! Where the hell have you been?" I looked between the two of them and recognised that their smiles, as full of joy and achievement as they were, were also quivering with fatigue.

"It's a long story, lassie. But the short version is that I managed to sort out your living circumstances – quite simply, as it turns out – and that was all it took to get your man here back home. I went to pick him up from Edinburgh as he couldn't get a flight for today to Inverness."

The effects of the day were starting to prickle at my body now, I sensed a small shiver that started in my toes and wondered how long it would be before it claimed my whole body. "What? How? I don't get it? Have you magicked us up a flat or something?" Then I turned to Mesut. "I'm sorry, but we're kind of homeless."

"Is okay, Gulazer. Angus telling me everything."

I turned back to Angus and folded my arms across my chest. I supposed I must have looked quite stern, but it was really just an effort to stop the shivering from taking over.

"Okay, okay, lassie. Don't look so cross, will you? It's all good. Remember that beach cabin with the wonky steps?"

"The one on Glensíth Beach?"

"The very same. Well, the family in question decided they wanted to be more involved in commune life so they opted for an eco-house inside the foundation instead. So guess what? It's all yours!"

"What? Are we talking about the same place?" I gasped. "The quaint little ramshackle cabin actually on the beach. The cabin that looks out onto one of the most picturesque seascapes in all of Scotland? The cabin that's frighteningly close to an ice-cream shack and vast expanses of natural beauty and daily access to incredible sunsets and sunrises?"

"You're right. It is pretty stunning." My dad had joined the conversation and slung his arms around both me and Mesut. "That's where I've been all day, love. I got up early this morning and moved all your stuff out of Bernie's garage. The cabin is all ready for you. There's no need to go back to Bernie's tonight, which is probably a good thing if she's busy child-bearing."

"But . . . but . . ." As accustomed as I was to misfortune lately, I grappled in my mind for a reason why this couldn't be happening. "We haven't put a deposit down. We can't afford the deposit. What about all the paperwork?"

"We can, Gulazer. Because Glensíth doing things differently." Mesut smiled that heart-melting smile and I thought it might be the end of me. "We will spend the money they give you for talk on repairs to cabin, so they not have to do it. And . . . this is good bit . . . they offering me job in Kelpie Café. I not going back to awful pub or awful flat. None of us are."

And just like that, Dear Reader, we have a home. A HOME!

And that is how I am here now, sitting up in a bed that is all our own, typing away on a laptop that was only today connected to very dodgy beach-hut wifi.

I don't know how, but after the absolute shock revelations of my husband being back on Scottish turf, and knowing we were able to return to our own four walls tonight, I returned to my seat amid whispered compliments and plaudits from the Ramadan massive, and settled down to listen to Paulo's talk (I call him Paulo now. You know, since he WINKED at me). I can only hope he didn't notice me and Mesut devouring an entire packet of waffles through the whole thing.

At the end of the night, there were whispers of everybody heading back to Thistledown Lodge to sample Mona's whiskey collection. But honestly? After a day like today I think whiskey might have tipped me over the edge. We had a new home to get back to, a toddler to put to bed, and there was a blog post to write.

I tried my best tonight, when we opened the doors of this gorgeous little cabin, to really take in the details. But the tour will have to wait until the morning. All I cared about was the fact that there was a bed for Baki and a bed for us, all made up with cosy blankets and duvets. My exhausted brain did clock a cluster of thistle shaped cushions before I threw back the quilt and climbed inside.

No prizes for guessing who supplied those.

Right now, even though Baki has his own room and cute little toddler bed, he and Mesut are both in a deep sleep beside me. The three of us couldn't bear to be parted. Not tonight.

Baki is curled around my torso like a koala. Occasionally his fingers twitch or his cheeks lift into a ghost of a smile but he's mostly just still. Typing on the laptop has been a challenge whilst he's clinging like this but there's no way I'm complaining. He can cling all he likes.

Mesut is sprawled out, with all of his limbs melting fully into the mattress, disturbed only by the soft, rhythmical reassurance of his contented breath. The gentle glow of a bedside lamp bathes him in amber, so that his skin reminds me of warm caramel even more than usual. He has one leg draped over my shins, encasing Baki in a cocoon of both of our bodies. It's a strange tangle, and I'm not sure how any of us will get out of it. But that's okay.

And if you're wondering, yes, I have heard from Bernie. A little boy arrived a couple of hours ago, born in her own bedroom with only the Muirdrith midwife in attendance. He's healthy and he's well and he's positively cherub like. Hardly surprising.

Okay, that's it – I'm signing off. No more Ramadan blog posts. No more whining on about how hungry or thirsty I am. It's been a trip, people. Thank you for being there one and all.

And now . . . sleep

Fab4CoolDad
At last! I've been waiting all night. I thought I was going to have to crack open another bottle of Glenmorangie. Massively proud of you, love. I can't believe what this day has put you through. The Beatles would be so proud too . . . 'All You Need Is Love'.
Jess.AKYOL
Indeed, Dad. Indeed.

Max Attax
I can't believe you've been through the plot of an entire suspense movie IN ONE DAY. Regardless of that, you took bloody ages to write your post, and now I'm so knackered I look like Ewan McGregor in Trainspotting. Peace out.
Jess.AKYOL
Glad you survived, bro. Peace out.

Angnonymous
Iongantach! There's an after-show party at Thistledown Lodge and it is steaming, man! I need to gan back in the throng and show them how proper Highland dancing is done but for now can I just say a MASSIVE thank you, you bonnie wee lass! You are an uirsgeul (legend in the making). P.S. Good news about Bernie, eh? Bloody love that woman.
Jess.AKYOL
Angus, why on earth are you reading my blog when you should be partying? This is an order to get yourself back in there and bask in the success of your awesome festival. Thank YOU so much for bringing my husband home tonight. Come to the cabin soon and I'll buy you ALL the ice creams.

ThistleMadMona
Oh Jess, we've just read your blog aloud here at Thistledown Lodge (we all needed a sit-down after the Highland Flinging). What a wee miracle you are! For once in my life, I'm lost for impeccable words . . . but your dad's right – it's all about the love.
Jess.AKYOL
Mona, I knew you'd be special from that first moment you nearly made me cry in the Co-op. Thank you for everything you've done, from the meditation on the beach to teaching me all about thistles. YOU are the miracle.

OliverChen1!
Jess Akyol – you really are an incredible piece of work. Can't quite believe what happened before I even arrived at Glensíth tonight. I got some awesome photos, though. And I think Ailsa is going to run yet another story. Enjoy the beach cabin!
Jess.AKYOL
Oliver Chen. Thank you for your abundant photography skills and your ability to repeatedly turn up at the right place at the right time and always, always with the right words. Tis quite a skill. I take it you're staying at the famous Thistledown Lodge? I hear the after show party is 'steaming'.
OliverChen1!
It is. I am. For now. Tomorrow, who knows?
Jess.AKYOL
Oh, I do like your style.

CrunchyNut_Mummy
Wow! What a feat . . . writing this whole blog post when you've endured such a scary, dramatic day! I thought you knew I was a police officer. What a shock you must have had to see my face when you jumped off that stage.
Jess.AKYOL
You are literally my hero.

GILLIE_LASS77
Whaaaaaat??!! How can any of this even have happened? Who'd have thought that a wink from Paulo Coelho could be the LEAST exciting thing to happen to you in a day? God, I love you. xxx
Jess.AKYOL
I love you too. And your fur coat. Which you're not getting back.
GILLIE_LASS77

I know. 😘

Night-sun-ella
Wha? How am I supposed to . . ? I can't even . . . When did you . . ? How did you manage . . ? That's it. I'm done.
Jess.AKYOL
I'm done too. Also, I love you.
Night-sun-ella
#loveyoutoo

Not-A-Granny-Flora
Jess, I'm reading this early Thursday morning – couldn't wait any longer for you to post last night and now I can see why. It's so long! We're both very proud of you though.
Jess.AKYOL
Thank you for coming up here, Mam. You know I'm ever-grateful. And you were genius for bringing the journal. I have no idea what I would have done without it.

Glensith_Comm_Found
Jess, I don't think we've ever had a speaker cause us so much drama! Never mind, we hope you're settling into your new home well. I can go through the contract with you whenever you're ready. You're a cabbage hippy now!
Jess.AKYOL
I can think of much worse things to be.

LifeIsYoursLindy
Woo hoo! You only went and bloody well did it! After you've had a few slap-up meals will you PLEASE get on with your novel? You are meant for so much more than a blog (besides, I REALLY want to meet myself in novel format – I am still in it, aren't I?).

Jess.AKYOL

Of course you're still in it! Lovely Lindy, thank you for rekindling our friendship here on my blog. I'm so delighted you're now living it up in Madrid with your woman. Knew you'd be alright.

FatimaNazar

Eid Mubarak to you and your whole family! I hope the next part of your life brings all the blessings and riches you deserve – thank you for bringing your honest account of Ramadan to so many people.

Jess.AKYOL

Fatima, I don't know if you'll ever realise how important your comments have been to me. Eid Mubarak to you too!

KadafiDancingKing

Mrs Jess! We followed the goodness and now you have your Mesut back. I am reading this the next day after your late post and so I am saying Happy Bayram! Or, how we say it in Turkish, 'iyi bayramlar'!!!

Jess.AKYOL

Kadafi, one day I'll come back to Turkey and hug you like you've never been hugged before. Now go home and get on with your teacher training. The world needs you.

paulo-coelho-wisdom-shop

Life getting you down? Have all the Paulo Coelho wisdom you need HERE at our online shop of inspiration. We not ever arguing with the wisdom of the universe. Get it now! As good as the real thing!

Jess.AKYOL

The real thing? Mate, Paulo and I are on WINKING terms. 😉

30

BAYRAM

Muirdrith, Highlands of Scotland, UK
Thurs 9th – Sat 11th Sep 2010

I know I said there would be no more.

No more Ramadan, no more blogging, right?

But a girl's allowed to stage a comeback.

Besides, I couldn't resist recording these three celebratory days of Bayram (or Eid). It feels like the conclusion to an epic novel of motherhood, hunger and divine intervention.

It all started the best way it possibly could: with ice cream.

Yes, our new home is so startlingly close to the ice cream shack, that on the first day of Bayram we were woken by the sounds of a delivery being made. Baki was out of bed and rattling the front door before I could wake up properly and reassure myself that the 'beep-beep-beep' happening outside was merely the sound of a delivery van backing up and not some apocalyptic alarm.

If I tell you that by nine o'clock, the three of us were sitting at the top of a sand dune, eating double-caramel-choc-choc-explosions and watching the early sun trip across the quivering waves, would you hate me?

Yeah. I would hate me too.

"İyi Bayramlar, husband," I smiled at the man who walked back into my life only the night before.

"İyi Bayramlar, wife," he returned, wiping a smear of ice cream off my cheek and kissing the spot where it had been, thereby creating a new smear. "What shall we do today?"

"I don't know. But if my dad really did move everything out of Bernie's garage then there's a bag of presents somewhere here for Baki. Let's go and look."

The fact that Baki had a whole new home was quickly overshadowed when he saw the Bob The Builder goods emerge from the seventeenth bin bag I looked in. His cries of delight blasted a massive crevice in my heart as I handed the items over. Even the fact that the toolbox made loud and jarring *'Can we fix it? Yes we can!'* pledges every time it was opened, didn't dampen the joy.

Baki was happy playing for a few moments so Mesut and I spent some time getting to know our new home. We made mugs of hot coffee and walked around the place to see what was what.

That morning coffee was glorious, as you can imagine, and there were slim and slinking streams of sunlight tripping through the small windows dotted about the place, landing on our arms, our cheeks, the backs of our necks as we moved through the rooms. Sipping my coffee and moving so slowly through the sunlit cabin, it was hard to know where my skin ended and my taste buds began.

After we discovered that we had two bedrooms, a cute little bathroom with a roll-top bath, an open plan kitchen-diner and a small living room with a squishy sofa (even better than the patchy sofa of fame) and a series of gigantic, chunky cushions lining the outskirts of the room in a weirdly Turkish manner, there was a knock on the door.

Mam and Dad.

As if a new home, presents, coffee, ice cream AND my parents being around all on the same morning weren't enough, we were also basking in the miraculous fact that Mesut was back.

I knew he wouldn't want to talk in depth about his ordeal. Part of me was bursting to ask him for details, to really understand what he'd been through. But I needed to remember that I was processing my own ordeal. I needed to remember that it would all come out if and when it was ready. That time and space was key.

Despite any trauma Mesut might have been through, it still seemed utterly mandatory that he spend at least two hours glued to his phone, bellowing 'İyi Bayramlar' into it at millions of family members back in Turkey. For somebody who is so quiet in many areas of his life, he speaks ridiculously loudly on the phone. Do all Turkish people do this? Must Google it.

Of course, those bellows were laced with a sadness that I could only imagine. Mesut's mam was sorely missing from the phone calls and he handled his sorrow by insisting we all get our best clothes on and go out somewhere nice.

I went into our bedroom and started rooting through some bin bags to find something fitting for the occasion. The sparkling dress and rainbow fur coat from last night lay in a solid pile at my feet and I caught the scent of charcoal, the acrid stench of burning fear. A wave of panic surged through me and my knees knew about it first. I dropped down on top of a bin bag, making the plastic pop suddenly, as the air bolted out of the shiny, black wrap.

Mesut was there before I could draw my next breath, his body as rigid and jolting as mine. "Gulazer, you okay?"

"I will be." I looked up into eyes as brown and lovely as silk. "We will be."

"We will," he agreed. "We are." And we both sat there for a while. Holding each other. On a bin bag.

Eventually I shifted and reminded him we were supposed to be getting dressed so we could do something fun. Something celebratory.

He said, "What about this?" and he kissed me. Full and strong and perfect and in a warm rush of sunshine that darted through the bedroom window right into our souls.

Daytime kissing.

That's what I needed all along.

It seemed only fitting that we ended up in the Kelpie Café on that first day of Bayram. I cringed when the café staff gave us a round of applause on arrival. "Look at my lass," Dad said, puffing his chest out with pride. "A local celebrity if ever I saw one."

"She's got a long way to go yet," Mam interjected. "If she wants to be a writer she'd better pull her finger out."

"Pull my finger out? Mother, I've been blogging like a lunatic for the last month." Mam shrugged and pursed her lips a bit. *Never mind,* I thought. *Just sit down and bloody well order something to eat. Because, you know, you can.*

And I really did. Despite withering looks from Mesut who insisted I go easy on my first day back at normal eating. No fun. I was getting those nutrients back in my body and I was getting them now.

Angus sauntered through the café when I was halfway through devouring my feast, looking only slightly less dashing than usual wearing what I can only imagine is his 'hangover smock'. "Och, lassie," he moaned, slumping down into a chair next to our table. "Did I write a comment on your blog last night? I have no idea what I said."

"It's all good," I grinned. "I now know that you dance a mean Highland fling and that you think very highly of Bernie."

"Have you heard from her? How's the baby?"

"He's beautiful." I got out my phone to show everyone the photo Bernie sent me late last night of her little pink cherub. "And this morning she texted me. You'll never guess what she's going to call him."

My Dad was first with the guesses. "John? Paul? George? All stand-up names. What about Ringo?!"

Angus shook his head. "No. it'll be an angel name if I know Bernie. Michael? Gabriel? Raphael?"

"Nope," I laughed. "She's calling him Paulo. Bernie said she was pissed off about having to leave to give birth before Paulo Coelho did his talk that she thought she'd make up for it this way. That way she'll never forget the night."

"None of us will forget it, Jess," Angus said. "Last night is now the stuff of Glensíth legend." I tried to protest but my mouth was full of veggie burger. Angus kept going. "And I'm only sorry I didn't get your man here, back in time to see you do your thing. I hear it was brilliant. You certainly looked braw in your spangles and your furs and I hear you belted out a totally blasta talk, even with wee Baki to rock to sleep. You're one of the cabbage hippies now, whether you like it or not."

"Is okay. She like it," Mesut said, putting an arm around my shoulders.

Angus chuckled. "Well that's good then. And Mesut, let's get together soon to go over your contract and sort a start date. The Kelpie Café is looking forward to the Turkish flair you'll bring to the menu. We like cabbages, true, but we're open to new ideas." Angus smiled then winced all in one insanely handsome expression then shot out of the café before I could give him the credit he was due. One day I will find a way to thank that incredible man for getting my husband back in the country.

After our brunchathon, we drove back to the cabin to chill for a bit. Mam started unloading bin bags and cleaning the kitchen. Dad cuddled up with Baki on the sofa, slumbering in the company of Bob The Builder paraphernalia.

Mesut took time for a smoke, sitting on the edge of the veranda that wraps around our little cabin. I can scarcely believe we have an actual veranda that looks out onto the actual beach. It seems our life has gone from chaotic to idyllic in just a few very strange days.

I moved some of the cushions from the living room outside and balanced my laptop on a tray I'd found in a kitchen cupboard. Now seemed like a good time to make notes for this very blog post and to catch up on comments from last night.

After Mesut finished his smoke, he sat down next to me and told me softly, in a whispered voice, that now Ramadan is over, we must think about charitable giving. "I knows we been through so much, Gulazer, but we must give to the poor in the spirit of Ramadan."

"How do we do that if we don't have anything to give, Mesut?"

"Is good point. We not really have enough Nisab."

"Nisab?"

"Is hard to explain but is important to give certain percentage of your wealth to charity at end of Ramadan, but only if you meet the Nisab. Is like amount you must have to afford the giving."

"How much is Nisab?"

"Is not that simple. Is from ancient Islam and is about how much gold and silver you own. You weigh it and work out with calculations what you owe for Zakat al Fitr. For giving."

"I don't know about gold and silver but we could weigh a hella lotta Bob The Builder bling."

Mesut smiled and went all Gandalf-like as he stroked his chin and looked off into the distance. I almost dashed off to fetch him a clay pipe. "We been so lucky, Gulazer. I feel like we been given a lot. By Angus. By Lupa. By Kadafi. By your parents and your friends. We now have a new home and I have new job and we have . . ."

"Each other."

"Yes. Is best one. So I feeling I need to give something back. Even though we can't make Nisab."

"We do still have five hundred pounds." I said. "Maybe less a few quid from our mammoth brunch today. Could we give some of that away? I know we're supposed to be using it for the repairs on this place, but maybe we could do those over time, when your new salary starts coming in." As if on cue, a length of drainpipe suddenly fell to the ground after a particularly strong breeze from the beach hit it square.

"We a bit late though, Gulazer. Money supposed to be paid before Bayram prayers finish."

"To be fair, you've been locked up in a holding cell in Turkey and I've been going crazy here in Scotland. I'm sure Allah will understand if we're a bit late."

"Yes. He will."

We spent some time working out, realistically, how much money we could afford to give. Who we would give it to, was another matter altogether, but Mesut informed me that if we couldn't think of a suitable recipient here in Scotland, he could send it to his family and they would distribute it accordingly.

Later that night, after a good, old-fashioned pub meal in Inverness, and when Mesut's family would have been linking arms to begin a raucous round of Turkish dancing, we found ourselves walking along the banks of the river Ness. We watched a disc of magenta sun slip down into a horizon streaked with white and grey, mirrored by the rippling river below.

"How does it feel to have a full belly and watch the sun go down, love?" Dad asked.

"A bit weird, actually," I said, truthfully. "I can't believe I've done a whole month of fasting."

Mesut nodded. "Yes. Ramadan show you that you are . . . '*esnek*'. Is showing your strength. You stretchy, like elastic."

I got a shiver through my entire body. I think Mesut meant 'resilient'. That's my best guess, anyway, but as soon as he mentioned elastic, it reminded me of four years ago, when we first met in Turkey. At first I had no idea about how he was going to change my life, but I did notice a strange pulling at my chest whenever he was absent. Like an elastic band pulling and pulling the further apart we got. That was my first sign that we meant something to each other. A sign from my body that my heart needed some attention.

The body always knows best.

Mam, Dad and I kept walking, pushing Baki in his buggy, who was now slipping softly into sleep. Mesut hung back, perhaps needing a bit of time and space to himself. Who could possibly blame him?

I imagined he was just thinking of everyone back home in Turkey. As lovely as this riverside walk was, it wasn't really in the real spirit of the Bayram he knows and loves. And it couldn't substitute having his mam by his side.

One of the hardest things about relationships is that you can't package the whole world up and give it to your partner, no matter how good you are at gift-wrapping.

All you can offer is yourself.

The following two days of Bayram have been more like back-to-reality for us. Except, thankfully, normality now includes three meals a day, a variety of beverages and a beautiful new place to live.

Oh, and a cat.

Our new normal includes a cat.

Not just any cat, but a brute of a thing. A ginger, scraggly, brute of a thing. Yes, that's right. Don't ask me how the holy heckfire Catzilla ended up outside our cabin, stalking the veranda like some kind of mafia boss casing the joint. But he's here now. And he doesn't appear to be leaving. I never thought in a million years that Mesut would let any cat – let alone that thing – near us again, but we all kind of like his company. So he's staying. At least for now.

I'm guessing he's not getting the same attention he once was living above the pub. I hear on the Muirdrith grapevine, that Kristen has been charged with various offences and is in police custody. However, after hearing her story from Crunchy Nut Mam, I really hope justice doesn't come down too hard on her. Whatever she's done, she's a fractured soul, and only human.

After everything that's gone down, my auntie has put the pub on the market. Apparently, it's become the meeting place for Kristen's gang of protestors and rumour has it they were affiliated with the Scottish Defence League. Not something my auntie wants any links with and apparently the pub hadn't been doing too well anyway. We're not exactly missing hearing the Black Eyed Peas every night. These days we prefer the soft shush-shush of the sea.

Mesut starts work at the Kelpie Café tomorrow, and I think he's quite looking forward to it. I am back to balancing motherhood with an aching need to express my art and be a whole human being. I have another counselling session booked with

Sue next week so I'm holding off on perfecting it just yet. There's time.

Speaking of Sue . . . I came up with a way for us to give our small donation to charity for Zakat al fitr. I was telling Mesut about the help Sue has been giving me and it only took one small mention of 'Help In The Highlands' for me to realise that's where the money should go.

"It was amazing." I told Mesut. "The fact that Sue was just waiting there on that particular day when I so desperately needed some guidance, some way back to myself. It was like divine timing."

"Divine, eh?" Mesut smiled. "And you thinking Ramadan not working."

He really is annoyingly right sometimes.

And guess what, Dear Reader? I may have been struck with something else divine too.

Oh go on then, I'll tell you.

I, Jess Akyol, the woman who has avoided acting on her dream of becoming a writer these past years by having a child on foreign shores, navigating a complex, multi-geographical relationship and grappling with postnatal depression, has been asked to . . . WRITE!

Well, more accurately, I have been asked to *revise*.

By big, important people too.

You won't believe it, but a well-known publisher has been in touch about my blog! They heard about it through their Scottish office by someone who picked up the Highland News. Apparently, one of their talent-scouting people read all my blog posts and decided they could be compiled into a book.

Fuck-a-duck I definitely need to go back and edit out some of the swearing.

I've had a few emails and even a phone conversation with a lovely woman named Prudence, so I know it's a thing and not just one of my blog-haters having a perverted laugh. This is actually happening, Dear Reader, and I need to get my silly brain and my soft, loping heart used to the idea.

I have no idea what this means for my writing other than it raises the distinct possibility that more people might read my words. Isn't that what every writer wants, really? I think it was Virginia Woolf who said, *'Without someone warm and breathing on the other side of the page, letters are worthless'*?

Thank you for being the warm and breathing soul on the other side of this blog, Dear Reader. I know I've already been gushing with my gratitude but please allow me to do it once more . . .

You've been my online tribe, my virtual support group, my digital guests in my digital guest house. I honestly could not have done it without you and I give you all my thanks wrapped up in a tartan, thistle-woven bow. Thank you for being warm and breathing with me through it all . . .

Now if you'll excuse me, I'm off to extract every single swear word from this blog.

Onwards. With love.

Jess.

Night-sun-ella
Flippin' heeeeecccccckkkkkkk! Can't believe you didn't ring me and tell me the publisher news properly although I kind of get why you told us all on your blog on account of dramatic effect AND gathering authentic reactions for your NEW BOOK! Is that all we are to you now? Just potential story lines or tropes that might make it past your ever-roving author's eye? Pleeeeeeeease call me so we can scream down the phone at each other in the proper fashion.

Jess.AKYOL
Right, I'm ringing you right now.
Night-sun-ella
Oh thank the lordy, I feel a whole lot better now. Just needed to hear all that news from the real you, not the blogging you. Dotty thought I'd turned into a monster the way I was screeching. Never mind. She will learn. One day she will have the same kind of #BlogSisterhood as us. Here's hoping.
Jess.AKYOL
She will. Only the way things are going, her sisterhood will probably be, like, an implant or something. #ImplantSisterhood
Night-sun-ella
Noooo! Don't say things like that! I already want to shield her from the world as it is. I want her to know what it is to squeeze a friend's hand, to fall asleep in a mate's lap, to share pints of cider and to cry each other's tears.
Jess.AKYOL
Don't worry. She will. She has an excellent role model. 😘

CrunchyNut_Mummy
Congratulations, Jess! Do you know, I think I once read somewhere that cats gravitate towards people that they communicate well with. You and Catzilla obviously have a vibe. Bets on he's the one who shat in my handbag though.
Jess.AKYOL
Hah! I'd go with that bet. He's a stroppy one. But I kind of like him.

Fab4CoolDad
Well, we're off down the A9 tomorrow, love but we're so glad we could be here for your talk, getting you moved AND your big publisher news. Can't say I'm not proud as punch. Keep going, keep using your life for your craft. And have a listen to

my favourite ever Beatles song about just that . . . 'In My Life'.

Jess.AKYOL

Aw, Dad. I'm glad you were both here for all the big stuff too. A Beatles song every day has been just what I needed to get through it all. Love you. x

Not-A-Granny-Flora

You're very lucky to have got a publisher's attention. If you need me to proof read anything, just let me know. But yes, congratulations. I'm #VeryProud (did I do that right? I've never 'hashtagged' before)

Jess.AKYOL

Beautiful hashtagging, Mam. #JustBeautiful

MaxAttax

Wow. Congrats on all fronts. My Trainspotting demeanour has faded somewhat after the other night's ridiculously late blog post. Now I fear I may resemble the startled expression of Edward Scissorhands after all the news in this post. Next time can I have a trigger warning please? Anyway, well done and all that. Peace out.

Jess.AKYOL

I live to serve. Peace out.

Angnonymous

Beautiful. All of it. The mi gu math pròiseil to know you. Very proud.

Jess.AKYOL

Proud too. And thankful. Nothing to do with your handsome face.

GILLIE_LASS77

Darling girl! I can't believe the way life works out sometimes. You deserve all of this and more. That publisher is blooming well lucky to have you so don't sign anything before getting some advice, is all I'm saying. I can't believe I'm going to be able to walk into a bookshop and say 'that's my best friend's book!'

Jess.AKYOL

Please don't say that when you walk into a bookshop. It's quite cringey. Anyway, let's just wait and see what happens, shall we? Jeez, I've come this far and got this much engagement myself, maybe I don't even *need* a publisher.

GILLIE_LASS77

You're right. But they probably need you. Who doesn't need more Jess in their life? #BeMoreJess

ThistleMadMona

I could not be happier at all your news, Jess. I thought Wednesday's blog post was a winner but this one absolutely tops things off. That publisher had better get ready for some truly epic stories. Gabh beannachd dhut.

Jess.AKYOL

Bless you as well, Mona – and actually, you're the epic one. 

AngelBernie

Just popping in between feeds to say . . . I told you so.

Jess.AKYOL

You most definitely did not.

AngelBernie

I did, you just didn't pay attention. Think about all the times I told you the angels had your back. And come on . . . a book deal? The house on the beach? Your man back in your arms?

Jess.AKYOL

Whatevs. Now go snuggle with Paulo. Literally cannot wait to meet him.

LifeIsYoursLindy
What a brilliant conclusion to your epic month, Jess. I really don't know what to say except you deserve it all and thank you for taking the time to write this blog – it's been wonderful.
Jess.AKYOL
Thank you for finding the blog and coming into my life yet again. I knew we weren't finished that night on the beach.

MesutAk1
So the blogging is over? I finally have my wife back?
Jess.AKYOL
You do. You lucky, lucky man.

KadafiDancingKing
I am certain there is all the goodness in the world in your footsteps, Mrs Jess. Inshallah.
Jess.AKYOL
I'd say it's in yours but hey, maybe that's why we get on so well. Thank you all the world, Kadafi. You'll never know how grateful I am.

OliverChen1!
Well, it looks like I'm here to stay for the foreseeable and although I'm not a natural babysitter, I will do it for you, Jessica Akyol. You'll need me for when you go swanning off to London to discuss your new book deal. Honestly though, matey, if anybody deserves all of this good fortune – you do. And it's a self-made fortune if you ask me, anyway. All that open heart and open mind stuff pays off in the end, eh?
Jess.AKYOL
It does, dear Oliver it does. Except this is not the end . . .

EPILOGUE

Muirdrith, Highlands of Scotland, UK
End of September 2010

I finish reading, fold the letter up and slip it underneath the cushion I'm sitting on. I don't want to wake Paulo, who is sleeping soundly in the cradle of my outstretched legs. Bernie left to teach her Angel class at Glensíth half an hour ago and told me he's soothed by the fresh air. So I brought him out here, to our newly-painted veranda, to get him off to sleep.

I'll put the letter away properly later. For now, Mesut is playing with Baki on the beach and I can just sit here, rocking little Paulo, and think about what I've just read.

It's the most words I've ever seen come from her hand. And it didn't even begin with 'Could you please consider . . .'

She's told me her son's story now. *'The car crash was fatal. He didn't stand a chance.'* The car was driven by the woman he'd fallen for; the woman he'd met on his travels in Israel; the woman he brought home to a new life in Scotland. The Muslim woman.

She'd been driving without a proper license. She'd told him she knew how to drive. She'd wanted to go to a mosque she'd heard about in Inverness and he, being curious and wanting to learn about his partner's religion, went with her.

She survived, apparently, and is now living in Edinburgh with a new partner, a new family. Kristen never forgave her. For stealing her son's heart. For getting behind the wheel. For killing him. She couldn't believe how quickly and easily the police just let her go. While she started a new life in a country that *'wasn't even hers'*, Kristen was left to live an endless nightmare of pain.

'And I channelled that nightmare into something bigger and stronger than me, Jess. I poured it into scheming and hating. And when you and Mesut moved into my own home, I felt under attack.'

I sigh deeply and notice Catzilla stalking towards me. He sits, regally at my feet, as if he's guarding baby Paulo. I know I should probably write back to Kristen now. It must have been hard for her to write that letter. And she does say that she wants my forgiveness. But am I there yet? It's only been a few weeks . . . I just don't know.

And right now, there's something more important to do . . . especially as Mesut and Baki have just arrived back from the beach.

Mesut kisses me. He's all salt, sand and whipped-up sea air. Baki leans against my legs and gets up close to Paulo, gently touching the auburn fuzz on his head with more tenderness than I thought he was capable of.

The moment is serene. So I'm taking it.

"Mesut, can I tell you something?"

"Of course, Gulazer. But I already knows you love me. I knows I best husband in world." He winks at Baki who momentarily smiles but goes back to stroking Paulo like a pet.

"Oh good. At least I don't have to go over all that again."

"What is it, my Yellow Rose?"

"Well, you know how I've been really tired these last few days? And that I've been feeling a bit sick and weird?"

"Yes. End of Ramadan not nice. Is taking time for body getting back to normal."

"Yes, that's what I thought too. But somehow, I thought there might be more to it."

"Is okay. You never doing it before, Gulazer." He pulls me in for a warm cuddle but I sit upright again. I need him to see my eyes.

"I know that. And I also know that there was another reason for it. A different reason."

"What's your meaning?" Mesut asks, slowly realising there might be a matter of the heart going on here, that his wife might be about to blow his world apart with a few simple words.

"My meaning . . . is . . . hamileyim."

I've been practicing saying it.

"Efendim?" he asks.

"Hamileyim."

His words come slowly and softly, like a plant unfurling its leaves in the sun . . . "Hamile misin mi?"

"Yes, Mesut. I'm pregnant."

We sit still for a moment, a silken breeze blowing in from the sea, slipping over us like a waterfall. I watch him carefully and see all the muscles in his face tighten into something resembling excitement. Then his eyes meet mine and every one of those muscles releases into softness, releases into now.

We cry a little bit and hug a little bit and I show him the pee-stick with the two blue lines that I've been carrying around in my pocket for the last three days. Then we go all in for those love-you-all-the-world embraces but quickly have to break apart again to shut down the distinct possibility that Baki might eat the pee-stick.

"It all makes sense now," I say. "Not just fancying a bit of water during Ramadan, but feeling like my life *depended* on it. Garlic bread that tasted like it came direct from the gods. Cherry tablet rocking my world more than it should have done. Being lost in an emotional landslide. It's all because I've been building a new life. Building a whole new person."

"A whole new person . . ." Mesut echoes, and cups my cheeks in his hands. "Baki, we're getting a whole new person!"

And Baki, as calm and steady as can be, goes ahead and speaks the first words he's ever said with actual clarity, in an actual sentence and with a meaning absolutely anybody could decipher . . .

"A whole new person."

THE END

MORE BY ABIGAIL YARDIMCI

Life Is Yours (Book 1)

Destiny Is Yours (Book 2)

Everything Is Yours (Book 3)

My Little Ramadan - (Sequel - Book 4)

Lockdown Love Letters - Coming soon

ACKNOWLEDGMENTS

This is my fourth novel and I still find writing the acknowledgements a bit of a challenge. My peri-menopausal brain is more likely than EVER to miss somebody out but, in true Jess-like fashion, I'm jumping in and giving it my best shot . . .

First up, massive, ridiculously heartfelt thanks to my old pal, Louize Cattermole. You've meticulously read and fed-back on this book, chapter by chapter, word by word with so much truth and genuine care. I wonder what our seventeen year-old, English Lit-crazed selves would have thought about My Little Ramadan? Something tells me they'd be quite cutting.

I got some exhaustive advice on translations in this book. They need to be right otherwise Google Translate can play some nasty tricks on readers. The Turkish was checked and corrected by Kamuran Aydın; the Portuguese by Carmen De Silva and Teresa Plana Casado; and Mona's and Angus's dips into Scottish Gaelic were perfect thanks to Margo and Henry, friends of my beautiful pal, Christy Van Der Meer

I also had some help with the Islamic themes and details. Whilst I checked everything with my husband in the first instance, the world of Islam is vast and I knew his own experience of being a Muslim was finite. Huge thanks go to Momotaz Begum who read the entire novel in record time and coached me on getting things just right as well as opened my eyes even further to the beauty of Islam. Sarah Hislam, who found Momotaz for me is equally brilliant.

There are certain people in my life who continue to offer inspiration for the characters and worlds I create. So genuine thanks go to these people for simply being themselves: Emma Boor, Gemma Cumming, Becky Davidson, Muammer Ernez and James Lowell.

As always, I'm ever grateful to the incredible community of authors out there, ready and willing to support, advise and celebrate my work. Thank you so much to Helen Aitchison, Evie Alexander, Margaret Amatt, Anita Falkner, Dave Holwill (for the most generous grammar tips ever!), Jodie Homer, Chrissie Parker and Hazel Prior, who provided the gorgeous cover endorsement. I just know there will be authors I have missed out so thank you to you ALL for being my friends and supporters when you're working so hard on your own books.

Team Yardimci delivered the goods as usual, devouring their ARC copies and getting back to me with reviews and kind words and assurances this book needed to be published. You make this author's life a lot less lonely and a lot more fun. Thank you for that.

Thank you to Sue Baker, my never-tiring friend, reader and supporter who came up with the hashtag #BeMoreJess - sorry I let Gillie nick it at the end.

Bailey McGinn, you have created yet another beautiful book cover and this time you did it with the pressure of a tight deadline. You've made me so proud to show these books off to the world and that means a LOT.

And what about the READERS? Well, you really do make this job worthwhile. I love the community we've grown together over on my socials, it keeps me going with this whole writing lark and makes me want to deliver amazing books for you. Never underestimate the super powers of reading, recommending, reviewing and sharing. You are my heroes!

Dad - Thank you for inspiring me in a squillion different ways when you were alive, but most of all for the unavoidable Beatles influence. I don't think this book would have been the same without it.

Mam - This book is really about motherhood and so thanks really need to go to you for bringing me into this world. I'm sorry I didn't understand what being a mam was like until I became one.

Matty - Thank you for teaching me all the things. No, seriously, you do, you have, and you keep going. Love you.

Baran and Azad - You filled your Saturdays with You Tube, so I could get this book finished, and never once complained. I am forever grateful and will now make it up to you by forcing you out for coastal walks on the regs. Promise.

Mustafa - Writing this book made me realise we've navigated some pretty choppy waters in the time we've been together. And you know how seasick I get. Thank you for always being my calm, my stillness, my anchor. Let's keep going. x

ABOUT THE AUTHOR

ABIGAIL YARDIMCI is an author, painter and mindfulness practitioner. She is a Geordie girl living by the sea in South Devon with her Turkish husband and two terrifying kids. She loves to blog and gets her kicks through mindful parenting styles, creative living and chocolate.

Abigail's writing inspiration comes from scratching the surface of everyday life to find the underlying magic that connects us all. The fire beneath the frustration, the creativity beneath the boredom, the stillness beneath the chaos.

All of Abigail's books are published by Soft Rebel Publishing and there are more books on the way.

Abigail LOVES connecting with her readers so check her out on social media and sign up to her mailing list now to get a FREE digital copy of Life Is Yours.

---

www.abigailyardimci.com

Printed in Great Britain
by Amazon